THE STORY OF

THE STORY OF

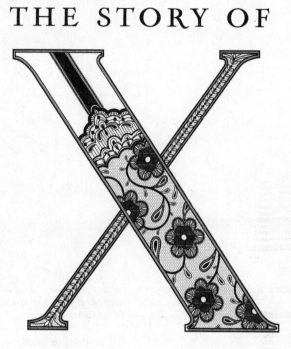

an erotic tale

A.J. MOLLOY

wm
WILLIAM MORROW
An Imprint of HarperCollins*Publishers*

HarperCollins books may be purchased for educational, business, or sales promotional use. For information please write: Special Markets Department, HarperCollins Publishers, 10 East 53rd Street, New York, NY 10022.

Originally published in Great Britain in 2012 by Corgi, an imprint of Random House Group.

FIRST U.S. EDITION

Designed by Diahann Sturge

Library of Congress Cataloging-in-Publication Data has been applied for.

ISBN 978-0-06-226852-5

13 14 15 16 17   OV/RRD   10 9 8 7 6 5 4 3 2

For S

One

So here I am: the Caffè Gambrinus. I'm finally in Italy, having just completed my final exams, sitting at a table on the open terrace of a famous cafe, on a famous street corner in glorious Naples, and the air is warm, and the evening sky is cloudless, and I can smell the garbage, which is piled *that* high across the road.

A cop walks down the street in front of a faded, crumbling, graffitied palazzo. He looks like he is designed by Armani: he has the sunglasses, the gun, the look, the tailored blue shirt and pants, the gleaming leather; the way of slouching as he walks. A cop by Dolce & Gabbana.

He is handsome. There are lots of handsome men here. But the most handsome of them all is sitting about three tables away.

"So who is he, then?"

Jess leans forward; she looks at me.

"Roscarrick."

"Huh?"

My best friend from Dartmouth, Jessica Rushton—funny and sarcastic and pretty, British-born and entirely cynical—raises her very plucked eyebrows and threads back her long dark hair. She tuts.

"You've never heard of Lord Roscarrick?"

"He's a lord?"

Jessica laughs a nicotined laugh.

"Marcus James Anthony Xavier Mastrosso Di Angelo Roscarrick."

"Jesus Christ."

"Close friends call him Marc."

"Well, it saves time."

Jessica grins.

"And he's a billionaire. All of Naples knows *that*."

I look across the tables of the cafe at this man, this apparently rich man. He looks barely thirty, at most. He also looks *amazing*. There is no other word for it. A more complex word would be, well, too complex, too unnecessary. He has dark skin— with distant and very pale blue eyes. A striking contrast. Also a slightly severe and yet compelling profile: hawkish, animal, sad, stubbled, and with a trace of boyishness mixed with pure adult, predatory masculinity. He is sexy; very, very sexy.

This isn't me. I'm not used to this instant reaction. I find myself adjusting my shoulder-length blond hair, wishing I had paid more the last time I got it cut. Wondering if he will look over. He doesn't. He simply sips at his tiny espresso cup, sweetly lifting the china to his lips. Sitting alone. Sipping. Staring at nothing. Impassive. Oh God. That profile.

"You're not falling in love *already*, X?"

Jess always calls me X. It was Jessica who *christened* me X when we first roomed together at Dartmouth. My full name is Alexandra Beckmann. Alex B. X for short. I am Californian, blond, a little bit Jewish, and twenty-one years old. Jess thinks I am naïve. She may be right. I am also reasonably smart and definitely well educated. And I am in Naples. *In Italy.*

Jessica is still talking about this guy. I am just *looking* at him; can't help it. I expected the men in Italy to be clichéd but hot, and maybe a little irritating. This guy is hot, but *not* in a way I expected.

"Meh. Another good-looking bastard . . ."

She talks away. Lighting yet another cigarette, pluming smoke from her mouth into her nose for a professional second. She didn't used to do *that* back in New Hampshire.

"He looks . . . interesting," I say.

It's a helpless lie.

"Steer clear, babes."

"Sorry?"

Jessica laughs smoke.

"Hello, lamb, meet slaughter."

"He's bad news?"

"Ladykiller, with an emphasis on the *killer*. Really, X. Not for the likes of you."

I bridle; I can't help it. I know Jess thinks I am pure white-bread, ingenuous and innocent, just a one-guy girl, and she's not entirely wrong: I am a little prudish and mainstream—compared to her. All through our friendship she's been the drinker, the smoker, the man-eater, the one who has adventures, the one who rolls back to the dorm at three A.M. with another nameless frat boy to spend a few hours snorting lines off the kitchen counter and having sex on the kitchen table. Meanwhile I did the one-boyfriend-at-college thing, convincing myself I was in love, and I definitely did the studying.

But the boyfriend got dull, or I eventually *realized* he was dull, at the same time the studies got more rewarding: I am aiming for grad school. And so I am here in Italy, researching my senior thesis, *Camorra and Cosa Nostra: The Historical Origins of Italian Organized Crime in the Mezzogiorno.*

I want to teach Italian history, but the only reason I chose to do this *precise* thesis was *so I could justify coming to Naples*—to hang out with Jess and have fun. She came out here as soon as she could, six months back; she's taking a year off college. She came to learn the language and teach some English, and in her calls and e-mails she made it sound so exciting: the food, the city, the men; yes, the men. Why not? I yearned to join her.

Because I want to have fun. I am twenty-one and I have had two boyfriends, and one solitary miserable one-night stand. That's it. Jessica openly derides me: an Almost Virgin, the Madonna of New Hampshire.

I turn. The man is looking over. *Gazing my way.* He smiles at me, briefly, sketchily, as if he is puzzled. As if he recognizes but cannot place me.

Then he turns back to his coffee.

"He just looked over!"

Jess laughs again.

"Sometimes he does that, turns his head. It's weird."

"Oh, shut up. This is all new to me." I finish my black stain of coffee; the coffee is seriously good. "I'm not used to all these hot-looking men, Jess. All the boys in Dartmouth are wearing those pastel polos and khakis, like East Coast rich kids."

"Your boyfriend used to wear"—she shudders, visibly—"deck shoes."

"Ugh!" I laugh, too. "Deck shoes with gray socks. Please don't."

"What a total matador *he* was."

Lord Roscarrick is sipping his coffee and not looking at me anymore. I need to defend my ex-boyfriend.

"He was *very* good at math, though."

"Yeah. But he looked like a beach donkey, X. Good thing you chucked him."

"How's it going here, anyway? You still working your way through the male population of Campania?"

"Yes . . . or, at least, I *was* . . ."

Jessica shrugs, moues, and grinds out her cigarette. A supremely chic waiter instantly whisks away the soiled ashtray and, with a charming gesture and a simple "*Signorina,*" replaces it with a clean one, glass and heavy, and engraved with the letters *C G* in belle époque style. The service is impeccable. The Caffè Gambrinus is frescoed and chandeliered and famous. Now I wonder how much this is costing: these excellent macchiatos and delicious little snacks—Napoli salami on the softest cubes of ciabatta. I worked evenings in bars for six months to help pay for this three-month research trip. My budget is limited.

But I don't care, not tonight, not my first night in Naples!

The evening advances. This man Roscarrick is still sitting there; but he is studiously looking the other way, in his fine suit, with his fine profile, and I decide to forget him; there will be plenty more.

The streets beyond the cafe terrace are abuzz with life—couples strolling and flirting, cops smiling and flirting, kids sitting on stationary green Piaggio scooters and flirting. It is all slightly raffish, and superbly alive, and very Neapolitan—though how I can judge this I don't know, as this is my first visit to Naples, indeed to Italy. My only previous visit to *Europe* was a rainy week in London at age eighteen, a present from Mom and Dad, a reward for getting my Dartmouth scholarship.

Mom and Dad. I get a sudden pang of nostalgia, maybe home-sickness. No, it can't be homesickness. I only left home two days ago—the little house in San Jose, the sunny yard, the sprinklers, suburbia, America.

Now I'm in Europe, deepest, darkest, decaying, grandiose old Europe. Already I love it. What's more, I am *determined* to love it.

"You can kinda go off the guys, actually," says Jessica.

I look at her, surprised.

"Sorry? You told me you adored them. Gave me a list of names. Quite a long list."

"Did I?" Her smile is lopsided, almost guilty. Embarrassed. "Sure. Okay. Yeah. There have been a couple." A pause. "Couple of dozen. They're cute—what's a girl to do? But they are so bloody narcissistic, X, it starts to irritate."

"What do you mean?"

"Half of them are mummy's boys. They have a word for it, *mammone*. They live at home till they're, like, *fifty*, and the clothes and the vanity, eeesh." She chuckles some smoke from her ninth cigarette. "Manbags. I mean, who knew? Manbags?"

"Purses for men?"

"Yeah. Leather accessories for men? *Way* too bloody metro-sexual. And the socks, trousers without socks—what is that about?—walking around in a business suit with no socks—put your damn socks on, silly boy—and all the preening and tweak-ing. Christ, there are queues for the gents in the bars longer than there are for the ladies, and after a while it starts to bloody get to you, I mean look—*look* . . ." She gestures rather wildly, her silver bangles jangling on her slender, elegant, suntanned arm, sweeping her hand across the view of Via Toledo and the Opera House and the big square with the Royal Palace that, I think, leads down to the Tyrrhenian Sea. "Look at the damn rubbish, the trash. Why can't they just clean it up? Why not, like, stop fuckin' worrying about your manbag for a while, Signor No Socks, and clean up your damn city. That's what a *real* man would do."

A silence descends.

"I need a drink," she says.

Drinks are ordered. A couple of "Venezianos." I have no idea what a Veneziano is. Jess orders in almost flawless and very enviable Italian; she has gone from halting stutters to apparent bilingualism in half a year. I am jealous. I can barely say *uno*, *due*, *tre*. That's another thing I am going to fix while I'm here: I'm going to learn Italian. That, and maybe, hopefully, please God, fall in love.

Oh God, I would like to fall in love. Really in love. Not pretend-in-love like I did with Paul the Deck-Shoe Mathematician. If I fell in love it would be the first time. And I am twenty-one. I am starting to think I am incapable; barren of love. Poor X. Did you hear about X? Yeah, she can't fall in love; the doctors have tried everything. They say she's going to spinster clinic.

"Signorina. Due aperitivi."

The waiter sets the drinks on the table. Two large, long-stemmed glasses contain three inches, each, of a lurid orange liquid.

I gaze suspiciously.

Jess smiles and laughs. Her dark hair looks very well cut. Different from how it was in Hanover.

"It's fine, X. I know it looks like radioactive effluent, but try it—*delizioso*, and fashionable, promise."

I lift the drink, it smells—and tastes—orangey and sharp and bitter and very alcoholic. It's good.

"White wine, fizzy water, and an orange liqueur called Aperol—*not* with Campari."

"Sorry?"

"That's how you make it, X. A Veneziano. I find three or four *really* set me up for the evening. Or maybe five."

We duly hit on two or three drinks, or five, until the night is squid-ink black and the moon is high and gawping and the operagoers are exiting in their finery across the street, and we are giggling and joking like we are back in the old apartment, the one with the crazy guy downstairs. And while Jessica is flirting with the waiter, speaking Italian, I steal glances across the tables at *him*.

Because all through the evening *he* sits there, in that immaculate suit, and the pristine white shirt, with the silver-and-gemstone cuff links, and the effortlessly silken violet necktie, sometimes taking calls on his slender cell, sometimes standing to greet a friend or an acquaintance.

Every so often, a favored passerby is invited to sit down, and this guy, this amazing-looking guy, with his dark looks and his dark frown and his dark curling locks of hair that fall onto his crisp white collar *just so*, and the soft, pale, slightly sad eyes, and the cheekbones, the almost alien cheekbones, this vision of a man gestures firmly and expressively. He is not quite like the other Italian men; he seems calmer, more centered; distant. Aloof? No, distant. Perhaps a little dangerous.

I realize with a kind of saddening pain in my heart, in my mind, that this man, this tall, rich, untouchable, maybe-thirty-year-old man, is beautiful. Maybe the first truly *beautiful* man I have seen, a darker Byron, a suntanned Bond. I've met plenty of pretty boys before, plenty of funny, plausible, skinny, kick-back-and-play-the-guitar pretty boys; there are lots of them in California; there was at least one at Dartmouth—and Jessica slept

with him. But this man is *beautiful*, in a masculine way. Not remotely gay, not metrosexual, not sockless in a business suit and
toting a manbag, but tall and male and adult and aquiline and
lean and, God, I am drunk.

Jessica tracks my thoughts, as always. She finishes her fourth
Veneziano with a slovenly yet lovable burp and says, "They
say his wife died. Accident. *Or was it?* Then he turned the, like,
family millions into billions. Roscarrick. English dad, Italian
mum. Google is your girlfriend, X. God, I'm hungry. Pizza?"

She is drunk. But so am I. Drunk on all of this. The orange
aperitifs and the acid-yellow Naples moon and the man in the
fine gray English suit. Lord Roscarrick. Lord Marcus Xavier
whatwasit Roscarrick.

"Jesus, X."

"What?"

I have been staring at the sky for two minutes. Now I am staring at Jess—who is, in turn, staring with an expression of shock
at the bill.

"What? What? How much?"

She groans.

"Why did we drink here? We could have gone to my local for
a bevvy. Bollocks."

A cold nausea sweeps over me.

"How much is it?"

"Ninety euro."

"Christ, we only had those Venezianos."

"And the coffees, and the snacks. Bloody hell, what a half-wit
I am, I should have remembered how pricey this place is, sorry."

Jessica has very little money; the teaching job pays a few
bucks. She lives hand to mouth, and she tolerates it well enough.

But a ninety-euro drinks bill could ruin her week. I reach reluctantly in my purse for a card, but the waiter has already glimmered into view, and picked up the check, with a smile.

"But you need my card," I say.

The handsome waiter smiles graciously.

"Is okay! The signor pay. Signor Roscarrick."

"Huh? No—"

I turn, heart jumping, stupidly excited, half embarrassed, to remonstrate in a bogus way—please don't pay—we will be fine. My name is Alex. Alexandra. Alexandra Beckmann. Yes. That's right. With two *n*'s. Here's my phone number. Write it down. Maybe have it tattooed on your hand.

But the table is empty. *He* has gone.

The designer cop leans against the palazzo wall, smoking quietly in the dark.

Two

I want to get *him* out of my mind, so I spend the next day *vigor-ously* unpacking boxes in my new and infinitely tiny one-room apartment near the Castel dell'Ovo.

When Jessica called me in the States a few weeks back, and told me she could secure an apartment next door to hers, she said it was located in a smart new district of the city, Santa Lucia. As I walk out, barefoot, onto the tiny, vine-wreathed iron balcony, I realize what "smart and new" means by Neapolitan standards: it means the neoclassical buildings are no more than two hundred years old, and the piles of uncollected garbage down there on the sidewalk only reach head height.

But who cares? The sky is divinely cloudless, the morning is warm, and if I lean on tiptoe—nearly falling off the balcony—I can definitely see a slice of the Tyrrhenian Sea, heartbreakingly blue, just two blocks away, imprisoned between the buildings of Via Lucilio. On the far horizon is the dark, serrated profile of an island. This must be Capri.

I can see Capri from my balcony.

I've only been here twenty-four hours, and already I love the place. I have to share my happiness. I ring up Jessica, at work, to tell her so. She swears rudely down her cell and tells me to stop being a soppy cow. Very British. Of course, I want to ask her about *him*. But I can't. She would laugh.

"Thanks for getting the apartment, Jess."

"*Prego*. Now get on with your unpacking. And stop thinking about him."

I laugh.

"How did you know?"

"You didn't stop talking about him last night. Can't imagine you've forgotten."

"I'm glad I'm such a woman of mystery."

"Chill out, X. *Relax*. So Viscount Perfect paid for the drinks. So what?"

"Jess, why is there so much garbage everywhere?"

"I told you, it's the Camorra, they rule the rubbish collection, they won't let anyone else collect—it's a racket, a scam. The whole city is a kind of drama—a masked ball, *everyone is in masks, remember that*."

"And?"

"And the garbage guys, when you see them, have armed protection."

"Wow. That's so *nice*."

Jess pauses, and laughs.

"Yeah. 'Course, if you really do want to know more about the Camorra, you could always ask an alleged member."

"What?"

"There's this bloke . . . Lord Roscarrick. Heard of him?"

"No. Tell me more."

"Well . . . I suppose he's quite attractive, if you are into that whole handsome, sexy, charming, billionaire aristocrat thing. I hear some girls like that?"

"And . . . ?"

"Some claim he's high up in the Camorra, or the Mafia; others say he fights them. Gotta be interesting either way. Ring him up and ask for an interview."

"Jessica, now you're suggesting I just call him? Out of the blue? Are you bored? You're bored, aren't you?"

She groans down the phone.

"Thursday bloody morning, every Thursday morning, a class of *principesse.*"

"Okay—"

"They just file their nails and talk about orgasms. Anyway, look, X, I'm not joking. I mean, this guy isn't *unreachable.* If you really want. He definitely gives money to charities that help mafia victims. That could be a way in. Did you *really* like him that much? X? Be honest."

I draw a breath. Did I? Did I? Do I *really* want to respond to that enigmatic overture? Do I truly want to get involved with this mysterious, slightly menacing figure?

YES. Oh God, yes. An almighty YES. No man in my short life has disturbed me, stirred me, roiled the sexual waters in me, the way he did, merely by not really looking at me for several hours, then frowning my way maybe once, then quietly disappearing— after paying for my drinks. That's all he did, but it was plenty more than enough.

YES, I want to get involved. YES YES YES YES YES.

"Maybe," I say.

"Yeah, right. You'd tear his shirt off with your teeth, given half the chance. You tart."

"His bespoke shirt, made with Egyptian cotton, on Jermyn Street?"

She laughs.

"That one. The one hand-stitched by orphans in Antwerp."

"So . . ."

"If you really want to know . . . He lives in a famous palazzo— in the Chiaia."

"The *what*?"

"The Chiaia. It's the, like, really posh neighborhood. And it's about ten minutes' walk from Santa Lucia. Palazzo Roscarrick; google it. He's practically a fucking *neighbor*. You could walk there after lunch, interview him about the Camorra, and be smoking a postcoital fag by teatime. That's if he doesn't have you shot by his gangster pals. Okay, gotta go. Be careful!"

The call is closed. My heart beats on. I stare at the azure Tyrrhenian and the shimmering serration of Capri. So he lives very close. A palazzo. Of course a palazzo. Where else?

I stand on the balcony and willingly tip into a reverie. I imagine him—Marcus Roscarrick, the young Lord Roscarrick, the handsome *signore*—waking up in an enormous room with enormous windows letting in the enormous Campanian light; there are palm trees rustling in a garden outside, the faint noise of Neapolitan traffic rises as a sweet and soothing susurrus. A butler maybe comes in, stooping past portraits of ancestors, carrying fresh breakfast. I see silver pots of coffee, dishes of lime marmalade; I see lemon slices on china and freshly squeezed blood orange juice spilled on endless white bed linen. Blood on pure whiteness.

A naked woman. Is there a naked woman in this imagined scene? Yes, there she is—misted by the Bruges-lace curtains, standing nude and pensive and beautiful at the sunny sash window. Marc Roscarrick rises, also naked, and aroused, and lean—his body like hard, dark, Amazonian wood. He crosses the parquet floor and embraces her slender naked waist; he kisses her pale neck, and she gasps and turns. And it is me, it is me at that window, me naked in his bedroom; I am his mistress, and as I feel his firm hands on my waist I turn and smile and kiss his sweet face, and then I kneel in prayer on the hardness of the parquet floor and I reach for his desire, and, and . . . and. And.

And down there in the Via Santa Lucia a kid on a Vespa is looking up at me. At me, here: barefoot in my shorts, mouth half open, erotically daydreaming. The kid is maybe sixteen; even from this distance I can see him grinning. Then he scoots away, toward the Castel dell'Ovo and the corniche and the dreamy blue Tyrrhenian.

This is absurd. What is happening to me? Erotic daydreams? This isn't like New Hampshire. This *certainly* isn't New Hampshire.

I need to concentrate. I still need to unpack my clothes and my laptop. Clothes first.

But—wow. This is an unexpectedly depressing process. I have brought lots of Zara with me: almost a whole new wardrobe, purchased last month from their store in Union Square in San Fran. At the time I thought I was being clever—in California the clothes looked so European and chic and suitable, if not *perfetto*. They were also pretty cheap.

Now, however, as I unfurl the dresses and pantsuits I cringe. I know Zara is Spanish but somehow it all looks a bit . . . American. Or rather, it looks a bit *suburban* and *shopping mall*. The clothes are nice enough—black cotton pencil skirts, short printed summer dresses, a jacquard miniskirt, a cute lace tube thing—it's all summery and pleasant, cottony and fresh, but here in the actual Italian sunlight it seems to lack real style and sophistication. This will not impress. This is nothing. I've only been here a day but already I know: everyone down there on the Via Toledo is wearing Prada at a *minimum*. Everything is silk and cashmere and fine raw linen. Even the traffic inspectors look like they are patrolling on a catwalk, not a sidewalk.

But I have no choice; these clothes will have to do. I do not have the money to upgrade. So I will have to rely on natural attributes.

Which are?

I walk to the long antique mirror hanging from the wall opposite the old iron bed. The light is slanted. I look at myself. In my shorts. Barefoot. I have a smudge of dust on my round face from the unpacking.

My hair is moderately fine, and swayingly wavy. Most of the time. I am five foot five, and 120 pounds—and some people say I am rather pretty. Once a man told me I was beautiful.

Once.

I step closer to the mirror, examining myself like I am a slave girl in the market—a Roman slave girl in the Piazza del Mercato; I have been doing my research on Neapolitan history.

My nose is cutely upturned, or perhaps it is just a bit crooked? I get far too many freckles. My teeth are near perfect. My ears are stupidly small. Oysters make me sick. And I have only had three lovers.

Three.

The mirror rattles as a truck passes below, over the black cobbles of a side street. Three! I have had three lovers, and I have never had an orgasm from actual sex. And God almighty, I want this to change. I have had enough of being good and dutiful and studying so hard. Just give me one summer, please, one summer of hedonism. And sex. Lots and lots of proper sex.

Maybe I am a slut; maybe Jess is right—maybe my inner slut has just been waiting to emerge, like a garish butterfly from the albino chrysalis of the Good Daughter. A butterfly of the Borgetto, a teetering tart in Prada, an unashamed young mistress of a very rich man. I think I'd rather like to be that, *just for one summer*. Then I could grow old happily, and tell my gratifyingly shocked granddaughters about my one libertine summer in sinful and sensuous Naples.

Oh, Gran, you are such a card!

The clothes are hung in the big old wardrobe; my last task is to unpack the laptop and plug everything in. This is less stressful than unpacking the clothes. There is a rickety wooden trestle table, which will suffice as a desk; I can tuck it against the wall.

The laptop booted up, and keyed into the apartment wireless—shared with Jess—I begin my work. Sourcing the history of the organized crime gangs of southern Italy. This will be the first third of my thesis, and it is already nearly finished. Then comes the field research. Interviews. Expeditions.

Adventures.

I go over my thesis so far.

The Camorra.

> The origins of the Camorra, an organized crime syndicate centered in Naples, are not entirely clear. It may be a direct descendant of a Spanish secret society, the Garduña, founded in 1417—during the Bourbon Kingdom of Naples. Alternatively, it may have emerged out of small, native criminal gangs, already

operating among the poorest elements of Neapolitan society, toward the end of the eighteenth century . . .

The hours pass. I stare, dry-mouthed, at the screen. Palazzo Roscarrick. I could just google it. Palazzo Roscarrick . . .

The 'Ndrangheta . . . The Camorra . . . The Sacra Corona Unita . . .

Dammit. I google it. And it takes just one hundred seconds to source: on a website dedicated to Neapolitan art and architecture. Jessica was right. "Palazzo Roscarrick" is celebrated in art history circles. And it really is about a ten-minute walk away.

I am seized with the desire to go there. Now. But I mustn't. But I must. But I can't. But I can. I can't *not* go there. Why can't I go there? This is my job, this is my thesis. I have an excuse, no, I have a *reason*. I could have stayed at home in boring San Jose researching organized crime on the Net, but I am here in Napoli to see it for real. And Marcus Roscarrick is, apparently, a man who can tell me more: he gives money to mafia victims.

Why does he do that? Out of guilt?

Before my conscience or my common sense is able to contradict, I take off the shorts and pull on some jeans and sandals and a simple white top. Nothing brash. Maybe one bracelet. I like the way Jessica's bangles show off her suntanned wrist. Maybe another spray of perfume? Yes. Definitely. Sunglasses? No.

Okay, yes.

The walk should take ten minutes. But I still walk fast along the hot and crowded streets. Past van drivers and motorcyclists, past trattorias and fashion stores, past red-faced men delivering trays of fresh white creamy mozzarella to the upscale restaurants, where the cooks take a prelunch break down the side lanes, sneaking cigarettes by the potted cypresses.

Then the street opens out and becomes more spacious, and ancient—and confusing. Via Chiaia has turned into a series of marble steps and descending esplanades. I gaze around, bewildered, lost among the hurrying businessmen in exquisite suits and the policemen sharing one enormous pizza outside a cafe. The city rises abruptly from sea level here; do I go up or down? Climbing one flight of polished and venerable steps, I look left, and right, and I start to worry—but no. Wait. That's it. I recognize it from the website.

A large, severe sixteenth- or seventeenth-century building, with Gothic touches and monumental walls. It could almost be a prison, but a beautiful prison, peach and russet and palmed, vast, and shadowy in the sun. And it actually has a plaque: THE PALAZZO ROSCARRICK.

"The" Palazzo Roscarrick? I like the *The*.

Heart somewhere near my mouth, I walk down the narrowing street and approach the enormous doors. My tentative rap of the big iron knocker does nothing. I feel stupid. I feel like an orphan seeking entrance to a workhouse. This is absurd. I should go.

The large door opens. A uniformed man peers out. What is he? A butler? A valet? I don't understand this world.

He looks puzzled. Not expecting visitors. Maybe this is the wrong door.

"*Sì?*"

Oh God. Now I have to use my Italian. My pathetic schoolgirl Italian.

"Uh, *buon* . . . uh . . . *giorno. Parla*—"

"Please. I speak English," the man replies, without a trace of an Italian accent. Maybe he is British. "How can I help you?"

"Uh, I want to see, the . . . um . . . Mr. Roscarrick, I mean the Lord. I mean . . ." This is feeble. I am flushing. I shouldn't have come. "I am an, uh . . . an American student. Well, researcher. I am researching . . . the Camorra . . . No, I mean . . ." What can I say?

The servant, if that's what he is, seems to soften at my panic. The trace of a pitying smile brightens his forty-something face.

"My Lord Roscarrick. You wish to see him?"

"Yes."

"Who shall I say is calling?"

Go on, Alex: go on. *Go for it.*

"Tell him the girl from the Caffè Gambrinus is here."

His eyebrows arch for a delicate moment, and then he beckons me in, through the grandiose door. I am now inside The Palazzo Roscarrick. *The* Palazzo Roscarrick, not any old Palazzo Roscarrick.

I gaze about: it is dark and smells sweet—of beeswax polish, and orchids, or lilies. The ceiling is arched. Beyond is a shady courtyard open to the sky, where the sun slants down, illuminating the sparkling water of a fountain.

The servant reemerges.

"Lord Roscarrick will see you now."

Three

I follow the butler—or valet; I'm still not sure what to call him—as we thread through the halls and corridors of this enormous building.

As we walk, I gawp. *The* Palazzo Roscarrick is just as I imagined it, only more so. Large and sober portraits of eighteenth-century grandees line the long corridor. Huge rooms lead off—I glimpse halls and ballrooms where the windows are high, though many are shuttered. The wallpaper in the corridor is an exquisite, swirling, pale jade green—Chinese, maybe—and surely old.

"This way—please." How big is this house? How rich is the owner?

I want to linger, and look. And admire. The furniture is a mixture of heavy walnut Spanish and lighter Georgian English, with some starkly modern pieces. Likewise, the dark and venerable oil paintings are interspersed with abstractions—swaths of violent, exciting, and very twentieth-century color. A taste has been imposed here, a young and living aesthetic. This is no museum. I notice one wall is decorated with antique guns. At least, I think they are antique.

The servant beckons me around one final corner, through some large wooden doors, and into another open courtyard, and my admiration becomes astonishment. I am staring at a mighty wall of twinned stone stairs, ascending vertically a full five stories, like the ribs from a spine; it is dazzling architecture, and rather disturbing in its theatricality.

"The hawk-wing stairs; typical of the Neapolitan Baroque. Designed by Ferdinando Sanfelice for my ancestor the ninth Lord Roscarrick."

The voice is very English, soft and firm and deep. I know it is *him*, standing behind me. Has he been following me as I walked, leering like a dumb tourist, through his ridiculously beautiful house? Has he been watching me?

He talks on: "The stairs are so grandiose because they are designed for horses. When cavaliers returned to the palazzo, they could ride through the great south doors, directly into the courtyard—then ascend the stairs on horseback, without needing to dismount. The horses were trained to move back down the other staircase and trot into the stables by themselves. Quite insane, isn't it?"

My neck burns at the nape; I can feel myself flushing. I don't want to turn and look at him, this man with his staircase for horses. My sandals are ridiculous and cheap. I should have worn a ball gown. I shouldn't have come.

"So. The girl from the Caffè Gambrinus . . ." His voice softens to an almost-laugh. "It sounds like a novel."

I turn, at last. He is standing there. Half smiling.

"As do you," I say.

"What?"

"*You* sound like a novel."

"Sorry?"

"Marcus Xavier Roscarrick, Lord Roscarrick. I mean— I mean— Ah . . ."

What on earth am I saying? What the hell am I doing? This is virtually an insult. But my mind is torn. He stares at me. I stare back. The servant waits.

He is wearing jeans: soft, worn denim jeans, exquisite brown English shoes, and a faintly Byronic white cotton shirt, half unbuttoned. There is a button missing. The cotton of his dazzling white shirt is visibly frayed. Expensively bespoke and old. The fine leather of the shoes matches his tan, or his natural skin tone. His teeth are white.

The pale blue eyes are not entirely cold. His smile is friendly, if a little detached. At least he's not in black tie and tails, or a vampirish cape. My sandals aren't so stupid, maybe. I wish he were two degrees less handsome. One ounce less handsome. It is too much.

"You want to talk to me about the Camorra?"

"Yes."

"You do realize that is somewhat forthright?" He smiles, glitteringly. "Even a little *dangerous*?"

"Yes . . . I guess it is."

It feels so dumb now. And, of course, very rude. *Somewhat forthright.* But it is also too late. I'm here; I might as well continue.

Lord Roscarrick nods, and turns to his servant, and speaks in rapid, eloquent Italian.

I stare again. Taking him in; no, *drinking* him in.

Roscarrick's effortlessly faded jeans have one rip above the knee, a casually yet expertly positioned flaw. I can see the dark skin of his thigh through the rip. A hint of the animal beneath. My mouth is dry again.

Come on, X, sort it out. Get ahold of yourself. This is just some handsome, enigmatic, thirty-year-old billionaire aristocrat. In Naples. You meet them all the time.

Roscarrick runs a hand through his flowing dark hair as he turns back to me—and that is *the* first faintly false gesture I have seen, the first hint of vanity, maybe. Good! Now I don't have to desire him so much. He is vain. Yes! But the hair is so dark, so curled and coiling, and dark.

"So . . . where were we . . . ? I'm being rude. You must call me Marc. Marc Roscarrick. But what shall I call you . . . Miss . . . ?"

"Beckmann."

His eyes are still wide, still questioning. Naturally he wants my whole name. I give it. Stammering.

"Alexandra. Beckmann. Call me Alex. Or X. People call me X."

"X? Really?"

"Yes. X."

"So not a novel. More a spy thriller."

"Who's the villain, then?"

He pauses. And then he laughs that soft, quickening laugh. Marc's laugh is infectious. Those flashing sharp white teeth, those flashing sharp blue eyes. He is high-spirited, a mettlesome animal, a predator, a hawk that cannot be caged. The chilly blue eyes are slanted, just a fraction. There is a nervous and menacing energy in there, as well; maybe he isn't vain, just animated and taut. I start to yield again. The shirt isn't properly tucked into his jeans, it is lazily buttoned; I glimpse at least an inch of his hard stomach, tan and muscled.

"*Per favore* . . ." He is talking brisk Italian with his servant. I try to look away, to look at the flying stone staircase, the hawk-wing staircase with its lunettes and volutes and Baroque curlicues.

But I cannot concentrate. I am too distracted, and agitated.

"Okay, X." He says the name sarcastically, but not unkindly. "We can have some coffee in the Long Room, and you can interrogate me, and find out if I am a *Camorrista*."

He leads the way, and the servant disappears. The walk is short: we take a left and a right and not for the first time since I arrived here, my eyes widen in admiration.

The Long Room is exactly that: a vast and elongated wood-paneled gallery, with fine, high windows that flood the place with Neapolitan light, and more of those modern abstract paintings rhythmically interrupted by Old Masters. I glimpse a creamy-white naked woman in one painting, coyly covering her loins with scarlet silk; her voluptuous curves are distinctive.

"Yes, it's Titian," he says, following my gaze, and pulling up a chair for me to use. "We also have a couple of Mantegnas. Lots of Watteau. And Boucher. Too much Boucher. The more erotic the better, all that French nudity. My ancestors. Such reprobates." He laughs. "But then, if they hadn't been so sexually rapacious, I wouldn't exist."

"Sorry?"

I sit down, fumbling for a notebook in my bag. I can at least pretend that I am here to do my research, rather than to ogle and stammer.

"Sorry?"

Marc is also sitting, his legs lazily crossed—ankle over knee. I grip my pen. A low marble table divides us. The light slants through the endless windows; lace curtains drift on a warm Campanian breeze. I am a little hot. My top is sticking to my arms.

"My family, on my father's side, are English. We have a seat in

Northumberland, but in the eighteenth century the ninth lord, mad George Roscarrick, did the Grand Tour and fell in love with Italy—and when he tired of all the *drizzle* in England he came to live in Naples, in this palazzo." He gestures freely. "However, as Goethe said: See Naples and die. Just a few years after moving here, the ninth lord caught syphillis, went insane, tried to bite a harpsichord player in the Bourbon court—and expired in a fit."

I am scribbling this down. Roscarrick's speech is quick and articulate.

"But the taste for Neapolitan life, and Neapolitan women, became part of our DNA. The Roscarricks have intermarried with local nobility ever since."

A faint and very different expression crosses his face—a flash of violent anguish. Then it is gone, like a single cloud on a summer's day, and his suave and agreeable smile is restored. He talks some more about his ancestors—the art collection, the palazzo, the duels and the drinking, amusing anecdotes. I tell him a little bit about me—my interest in history, poetry, politics—and he laughs and smiles in the right places.

But even though this is entertaining, I am thinking something else. I saw it. *I saw that pain*, that flash of tragic anger. What is it? Why doesn't someone make it better? Why doesn't he find someone to salve this wound? Perhaps he scares them away, as he slightly scares me.

I can smell the bodywash he is wearing, some delicate cologne maybe, nothing overt; it is darkly alluring, yet subtle. Clean but different. I realize that is what is so intoxicating: he smells deliciously clean, but *different* from me. He is so different from me. Eight inches taller, six foot one to my five foot five. He is stronger. Richer. A little older. Stubbled and proud, and yet there is a pain that needs healing.

I watch as the manservant walks in and places a silver tray of coffees on the little marble table. I drink my delicious, faintly mocha'd dark coffee, trying to clear my head. But I can't. My senses are ordering me about, slapping me. I am dizzy. Quizzed by secret police. I have the lunatic intimation that I could have met my *soul mate.* The way we laugh together; it fits. The bits of me that are missing, is he them? Or is he too forbidding?

X. Calm down.

"Why did you pay for our drinks?"

He nods. As if it is a very fair question.

"I saw your friend, she was appalled by the bill. I wanted to help. I have money, I like to help."

"And . . ."

"And let's be honest. There is another reason . . . Why shouldn't I buy a Veneziano for a beautiful young woman?"

My heart quickens, my defenses rise. This is too fast, too blunt, too cheap. He is trying to seduce me. Okay, I want to be seduced, but I don't want to be *seduced.* Not crudely, not like this. I bridle. I sit back. He looks at me. And smiles.

"Your friend *is* very beautiful."

"What?"

"She is very lovely. I couldn't help myself. Sorry."

"Oh."

"What is her name?"

I am angry now, stupidly angry. Alex, you fool.

"Jessica."

"Ah. Is she American as well?"

"No, British."

"Thought so. She certainly liked to drink." He laughs politely. "I apologize for my candor. I hope I haven't offended. So, do you want to ask me about the Camorra?"

My face is rigid with frustration. I sip the coffee and fume. He didn't desire *me*. He wasn't trying to seduce *me*. He thought I was Jessica. How intensely annoying. I am annoyed with myself, all those stupid, stupid feelings; it was Jessica all along. *The girl from the Caffè Gambrinus*. He agreed to see me because he thought I was Jessica; now he is being polite, and letting me down gently.

Stupid. So stupid. I am such an idiot.

The interview concludes. The coffee is drunk. He tells me that he is involved with import and export—and that is how he has turned the family millions into billions. He adds, with decorous modesty, that he likes to help charities—especially those that help victims of crime. It is obscure, and I don't care. I pretend to take notes. I wonder if he is lying, if he really is just a handsome gangster covering his tracks. Who the hell cares? I am an absurd person. He tells me he loves California, the deserts of the southwest: the true America, the "frontierness." He uses the word *frontierness*. I dislike this.

He obviously senses my discomfort. Abruptly he rises and says good-bye, and he gives me a card, inviting me to call him if I need any more information. I offer a terse thank-you, feeling like I should curtsy, or scream at my own crassness, but instead I say my own good-bye and refuse the offer of assistance and flee down the vast cold marble steps, and make my own way to the door. I can remember the route, left and right, left and right, down this hall, down this corridor—past this suit of stupid overwrought armor. Just get out, get out, *get out*.

The sun is burning when I step into the busy street. I look at my foolish notebook, and hurl it into the big pile of garbage.

Then I notice the policemen, hurriedly taking photos. Of me.

Four

"How many cops?" Jessica asks.

"Maybe three . . . I was, you know . . . *confused*."

We are sitting on the floor in her apartment, next door to mine. The heady scent of nail polish carries in the air: we are doing a restorative DIY pedicure for both of us. This is the first time we have properly talked about What Happened in the Palazzo since I fled, two days ago.

"Well, like I said, there are rumors he is *involved*." She airily gestures at the tall French window and the city beyond. "Half the stuff that comes through the port is contraband. And that's what he does, isn't it, import-export?" She nods, answering herself. "But it's bloody hard to be a successful businessman in Naples without some contact with the Mob. Everybody is involved in some way. Even the pigeons on Via Dante look a bit dodgy sometimes. The way they stare at you, like they are *plotting* something. God, is this ever going to dry?"

She grabs a magazine and uses it as a fan to dry the polish on her toenails. Cotton swabs are scattered everywhere among the magazines and paperbacks. Jessica's apartment is, as usual, something of a mess. When we roomed together in Hanover she used to exasperate me with her untidiness; now that I am living *next door* I find her slovenliness amiable, even lovable. Best of all, it is unchanging. In a confusing world, Jessica is the same, my best friend; my smart, funny, sane, and lovable friend. I really don't mind if *bloody* Marcus Roscarrick desires her, not me.

Her.

Our thoughts are duetting; Jessica looks up from her newly cerise toenails and says, "So he really said I was beautiful, huh?"

I can't stifle the slight pang of jealousy in my heart, even though I love Jessica. She can't hide the flash of sly delight in her cynical eyes.

"Yes. He really said you were beautiful . . ." My smile is brave and maybe less than convincing.

"Jessica Rushton. Apple of a billionaire's eye? Better get my hair cut."

"What are you going to do?"

"Dunno. Shag him?"

"Jess . . ."

She giggles, and then she stops giggling as she looks in the mirror tilted against a bare, painted wall.

"Seriously, I soooooo need a haircut if I am gonna start appearing in celeb magazines." She twists a few split ends between her examining fingers, then says, in a different voice, "The beautiful Jessica Rushton tells us about her lovely fitted kitchen, following her hundred-trillion-dollar divorce from Lord Roscarrick." She glances my way. "We can get a Ferrari. I'll buy you a Ferrari. Babes, I'm sorry, I know you fancied him."

"No, not at all—don't be idiotic—please, Jessica." This is again ridiculous. I am actually holding back tears. How can one stupid man turn me into such a pathetic mess? I hardly know him. He was faintly menacing. Yet I did yearn for him. I did. For that moment. My soul called, and there was a response, or so I thought. Now I feel a bit lonely. Ugh.

Slipping on my sandals, I summon up my common sense.

"No. I'm fine. I am in Naples. I am twenty-one. I have an excellent education. *Avanti!*"

"Attagirl."

"I am going to work. I'm here to work."

And so I do: I work.

For the next fortnight I settle into a satisfactory and rewarding rhythm of hard work and just a little partying. In the mornings I study in my sunlit apartment. I study hard. I am good at studying.

Amid my scattered books, laptop, and takeout cups of weirdly unsatisfactory cappuccino, I drive away thoughts of men with conjugations of the verbs *credere* and *partire*, and the precise structure of the *futuro semplice*.

Tomorrow you will prepare pasta puttanesca.

Domani prepari la pasta alla puttanesca.

This lasts, on average, for about two hours.

After the language learning comes the thesis. Between the hours of eleven A.M. and one P.M., I blot out the memory of *his Tyrrhenian blue eyes* by rehearsing facts about the crime syndicates of south Italy, especially the Camorra, though I am also drawn to the even more sinister and mysterious 'Ndrangheta, the mafia of the toe of Italy.

The 'Ndrangheta is a criminal organization in Italy, centered in Calabria. Though not as famous as the Sicilian Cosa Nostra, or the Neapolitan Camorra, the 'Ndrangheta is probably the most powerful crime syndicate in Italy, as of the early twenty-first century . . .

There is something about the 'Ndrang that intrigues me. Maybe it is just the apostrophe before their name? Like the *The* in The Palazzo Roscarrick.

No. Study. Come on, Alex. Study.

The principal difference from the Mafia is in recruitment methods. The 'Ndrangheta recruits members on the basis of blood relationships. This makes the gangs extremely clannish, and therefore impenetrable to police investigation. Sons of *'Ndranghetisti* are expected to follow in their fathers' footsteps . . .

Gang membership descends by blood. It is hereditary?

Inevitably I think of Roscarrick and his tales of the crazy ninth lord. Marc fits the picture, maybe. But then it is all blood here, the descent of blood, the ties of blood. Everything is related to everyone. I am the pure outsider. I want to know more.

By lunchtime my mind is fried so I change my focus. Every afternoon I put on some little sports socks and my sneakers, and in my innocent summer dresses from Zara I go exploring the intricate and historic suburbs of inner Naples. Whence the Camorra derive their strength, where they recruit their killers and hunt their enemies.

Am I naïve, just wandering around these supposedly dreadful

places? I would never do this in the States: go wandering in the bad neighborhood of a big city alone. And yet I do not feel menaced. Why? Perhaps it is because these slums are so seductive, so charming in their dark and chaotic and sun-dashed poverty—it is hard to feel threatened.

Walking the narrow, vivacious, operetta-singing lanes of Spaccanapoli or the Quartieri Spagnoli is like having a bit part in an Italian movie, made just for God, a movie called *Italy*. It is all so *authentic*: the women sitting outdoors in the narrow alleys washing potatoes over buckets, trimming bearded blue mussels, and gossiping loudly about sex; the old ladies in black, changing flowers and lightbulbs in glazed roadside shrines to Holy Mother Mary; the pretty boys eating drooping triangles of pizza as they sit on their sky blue Lambretta scooters, leaning forward so they don't drip *pomodoro* on their expensive pants; the overtall *feminelli*—the transsexuals—skittering on the black lava-stone cobbles from Vesuvius as they walk down to the ferry port in heels, heading for sexual assignations with the rich on Ischia and Capri.

Less pleasing are the inexplicably silent, garbage-filled piazzas of Materdei, where tubby, half-shaven men in business suits disappear around the corner as soon as I show up—leaving me all alone in the eerie, siesta-quiet sunlight in my Zara dress, staring at a peeling old poster of Diego Maradona.

And then, of course, the unthinkable happens.

It is day fourteen of my work-hard-and-don't-brood-about-him regime. It is all going well. I have a slight hangover. I am in the Quartieri Spagnoli. I spent the previous night drinking cheap Peronis and Raffis with Jessica and a couple of her Italian friends in a bar near the university. We had a nice night. It was fun. We didn't talk about him and we have diligently avoided the Caffè

Gambrinus—and the other fashionable and pricey places where he might be encountered.

But my head is slightly fuzzy this morning. And I am rather lost. I have wandered down an empty and yawning cul-de-sac. I look up at the strip of blue sky, caged between the high slum buildings. It is very hot. Laundry flutters in a desperately weak midday breeze. I am dehydrated. I stare at the lurid panties and erotic lingerie, red and blue and black, swinging in the gasp of breeze, the anarchic and drooping flags of sexuality.

"Hey."

I turn.

"*Soldi.*"

"*Dacci i soldi!*"

Four kids—no, youths—are standing at the end of the alley. Five meters away. They are tall and skinny and walking toward me, and they want money. My Italian is good enough to understand *that*.

Give us money.

I swivel, and then I despair. I forgot. I am in a damn cul-de-sac. Desperate now, I look up—maybe someone is at a window, taking some air. But all I sense is a shutter being closed. People turning away, retreating. Don't watch, don't witness, don't tell. *Omertà.*

"*Dacci i soldi!*"

"But I don't have any money!"

Why am I doing this? Why am I resisting? These kids are surely junkies—four of the thousands of smack addicts of Naples, enslaved by the drugs of the Camorra. Dirty jeans, yellow faces, bloodshot eyes, entirely bad news. They just want some euro to score. Right?

But I have so little money, and I have worked so hard for it. I want to fight them.

"I don't have any money! Leave me alone."

"*Vacca*," one says with a sneer; he is the tallest and skinniest. "*Vacca Americana!*"

American cow.

Fuck them! I get ready to run past them—screaming, screaming for my life—just barge through them. That's what I must do. Just run and thrust my way into the main drag of the Spanish Quarters, where the fishmongers stand in their gumboots, hosing silver scales and fish blood down the dark cobbles, like sequins in red surf.

Then one of the junkies pulls a knife. It is long and evil and it glitters in the hard southern sun that slants down from the strip of slummy sky.

He smiles.

Too late I realize this is much worse than a mugging.

Five

Hell. If I fight back they might kill me, they might not even mean to do it—but that knife. It glitters, malevolent and long.

The first lean guy, with a bad and raw tattoo on his neck like a case of shingles, moves toward me. He is cornering me; like I am just another rat in a Neapolitan alley.

The knife is phallic and stiff. I glance up at the helpless sky, then down the merciless darkness of the alley beyond the boys. No. There is no hope there. Or here. Or anywhere. I am on my own.

Maybe I can beg my way out of this, utilize what pitiful Italian I possess. Staring at the leader of the gang, I implore him.

"*Per l'amore del cielo*"—for the love of God, I beg you—"*ti prego di tutto cuore.*" He laughs and his laugh is like some horrible, diseased cackle.

"Ah, *bellezza, bellezza.*" He turns to his grinning accomplices, then turns back to me, "Fucking sexy. *Sì?* Sexy girl."

It is maybe the only English he knows.

Fucking sexy girl.

My fear rages. And my fury. He is two meters away: two seconds from touching me, and groping me. I am pressed flat to the damp old wall behind. A wall so dark and sheltered and cold it feels like it has never been warmed by the sun. The sun has never reached this deep into the slums—nor into the minds of these men. One of the other youths grins and says, "*Divertiamoci . . .*"

The word is something like *play*. It seems they are going to play with me, and I know what this *really* means.

I feel the first grubby hands on my arms, tugging at my dress, trying to rip it away. The dress is casually and gleefully torn from my shoulder, exposing my bra. A second hand feels for my breasts, lifts at my bra strap, and then the strap is severed with a knife.

I swear at them, crouching and covering myself. Swearing again.

But the boys just laugh. They are all around me; it feels like there are dozens of them, hands everywhere, feeling my hair, touching my arms, trying to pull my fists away.

"Stop!"

I start to kick and to flail; I don't care if I am outnumbered and cornered, *to hell with them.* I am not going to let them touch me. Not going to let them *play* with me.

Now I am writhing in their grasp, wrenching myself free—but they are simply too many—four lanky and grinning Italian youths. I sense I could probably take one of these junkie bastards—knee him in the groin, knock him to the ground—but four? It is too much. I am drowning under their hands as they pull at the fabric, feel for my thighs—

"No, stop! Stop! Please stop! *Please!*"

They just laugh, and their laughter echoes down the empty

lane, down the alley with the shuttered windows and the crumbling walls. A cold hand claps over my mouth, silencing my words. I wonder somehow if I should pray. I haven't prayed in years; maybe now is the time. But then I have an idea. One last chance? Biting the hand that covers my mouth, so it is whipped away, I yell, as loudly as possible: "I know *Marcus Roscarrick*. He is my friend. *Lui è mio amico!*"

The reaction is intense. The boys freeze. The hands pull back. The leader squints at me, looking deep in my eyes, as if to see if I am lying. Another one shakes his head.

"*Guappo.*" The others nod, pale, ugly faces in the dark of the alley. I shout the word again.

"I know him. Roscarrick! *E un buon amico!*"

But it's not working. They are unconvinced. Either they think I am lying or they just don't care. Maybe Roscarrick means nothing. The grins become snarls. Now they come at me again—with renewed intent.

A dirty hand slaps over my mouth once more; another hand is groping, and now I begin to succumb. This is it, I think, this is how it happens, this is how you get raped. My mind is almost detached. I close my eyes as I sink under the ocean of pain and humiliation—

"*Lasciala sola.*"

What?

The voice is new.

Leave her alone.

"*Coniglio!*"

Coward.

Who is this?

I see a strong fist, flying. One of the youths is physically wrenched away—as though he has been plucked up by some deity, by a giant. He is virtually lifted off his feet and thrown to the floor. The leader of the gang swivels and yells, but a fist strikes him hard; his tattooed face rips left and right as he is punched twice, and again, blood squirting everywhere, like scarlet ink.

I can see a dark, handsome face in the gloom of the alley. Who is this? Not Roscarrick, not someone I know. But this man is intervening: he is with friends—young allies—well dressed. They are brawling with the youths; one of the junkies is already on the dirty cobblestones, groaning, but the others are fighting back. I gather my shredded clothes to myself and look for escape. This is horrible. The brawl is intense. Someone is going to get knifed.

And then another voice calls across the cobblestones, masculine, older, arrogant, and everyone is silenced.

"*Cazzo! Porco demonio*—"

This *is* Roscarrick. Unmistakable. His white teeth, his dark face, running toward us. That anger in his blue, blue eyes.

The reaction of the youths is quite astonishing. As soon as they see Marc, their violent defiance drops utterly away. They stare at one another, then at Marc—in desperation. They look like kids, like terrified toddlers. Marc approaches the leader of the gang. And punches him in the face. Just once, but very hard.

And then he smiles.

Marc *smiles*. And the smile is so menacing, so much more frightening than the punch, the youth starts to whimper. He is crying, slumping away, his back to a wall, nose copiously bleeding. He looks terrified. *Terrified of Marc Roscarrick*. It is a look I have never seen on a man before: the look of someone who thinks he is about to die.

Why is he so frightened? Who is Marc Roscarrick, that he could so terrify this boy?

There are too many questions in my mind. I am blinking away my tears of horror, and pulling my clothes back into place, yet still watching. The kids are now being dragged from the scene, hoisted by their collars like schoolboys being led to their punishment. I hear car doors slamming shut; I hear the vivid ripple of expensive tires on old cobbles. Then I hear silence.

Now it is just me and Marc Roscarrick in the alley. He is in a cream linen suit with a blue shirt; I am in a tattered dress. Vulnerable and forlorn, yet rescued.

His gaze is intense: there is anger in the searching blue of his eyes, and compassion.

"Are you all right? X? I am so sorry. So, so sorry."

"But . . . but . . ."

I have already felt myself for injuries. I am all right. Just a few bruises and scratches. But my mind is hurting, furious, bewildered. Who is this man who dismisses me one day, then rescues me the next?

I need to know.

"How did you know where I was? How? How did . . . ? *I don't understand what is happening.*"

Marc is looking me up and down, but not sexually—more like a doctor, assessing. My bare knees are grazed. I look down at my stomach; I realize I have a faint sprinkle of blood on what remains of my blue summer dress. But it isn't *my* blood. It is the blood of the boy who led the assault on me. The boy who was punched so clinically by Marc.

There was savagery there. I look at Roscarrick anew. This man may be an aristocrat, but he is also, what, primitive? No, not primitive. But certainly not entirely refined. I recall the rip in his jeans when I last met him, the dark, hard skin beneath; the glimpse of the animal inside the urban male. His very presence terrified these boys.

I don't know what I think.

"Do you want to see a doctor, Alexandra?"

My wits begin to reassemble.

"No. I am . . . okay, I think. They didn't . . . They didn't get very far . . . You got here in time . . . but I don't—"

"How about the police? Would you like to go to the police?"

I vacillate. Part of me wants to scream my anger from the top of Mount Vesuvius. Part of me wants to totally and immediately forget what just happened, because it was, of course, my own stupidity that got me into the situation in the first place. Wandering around the worst slums of a challenging city, a city known for its crime as well as its swooning beauty—wandering like some damn foolish girl, a naïve and silly Yank abroad.

"Let me think about the police. I don't know."

His smile is grave, even apologetic. I ask the real question: "But how . . . ?" I really need to know now. "*How did you find me?*"

He nods, as if this is a very sensible question. Which it is.

"Sorry, X, you must be confused. Since you came to see me in the palazzo—I have been thinking about you."

Is that a faint blush? No, it is not. But his normal certitude is momentarily flawed. Marc gestures away his own embarrassment.

"Let me get you away from here, let you clean up, buy you lunch? Please. Then I will explain everything."

Who is Marc Roscarrick? What is happening?

I don't care. *I don't care.* A very handsome young man has just

saved me from my own stupidity, and from something worse—
something I don't care to relive right now—and he wants to help
me. I am too weak to resist; I want to surrender.

"Yes," I say. "Please. I'd like to go home."

There is a tingle of silence. He nods, takes my hand and raises
it to his lips, and he kisses it delicately. The silence between us
lingers. I know I want him to kiss my hand again; just *kiss it
again* . . .

Six

No. I pull my hand away as if I have been scalded. What risk am I taking? I don't trust my desire. I am still shaking a little from the assault.

I gesture at the blood on my dress.

"I want to go back to my apartment."

"Of course, of course." He nods attentively. "You must want to change. Come this way, X; my car is parked on Via Speranzella, just a few hundred meters."

I don't know what I am expecting—a Maserati, a Bentley, a horse and carriage with a liveried footman?—but Marc's car is a simple yet very expensive Mercedes sports car: subtle, chic, fast, new, dark silver-blue. A small luxury car for narrow, squalid streets.

I get into the passenger seat. The car smells of him: clean and sophisticated, and also scented with that heavenly yet inscrutable bodywash, that remote cologne. And leather seats. The drive to Santa Lucia takes just a few minutes, from the slums to the boulevards, past the little *bassi*—the cell-like homes of the poor—to the neoclassical apartment blocks of newer Naples.

The drive is almost wordless. I don't know what to say. I am too wary, too upset. And all too attracted to Marc Roscarrick. My feelings are treacherous; I wonder if I am being betrayed by my own sexuality. *Stop this, X. He is just a man.*

But a ruthlessly sexy man.

As he navigates the mad Naples traffic, calmly steering between the Fiat Cinquecentos, Marc glances at the blood on his knuckles. Then he chuckles. Briefly. "Christ, I look like a boxer after six rounds. I didn't mean to hit him *quite* that hard."

His words release my own. A barrage of questions.

"Who was he? Who were they?"

"Well, as the local women say, *Si buca sai, renzo si buca.*"

"Sorry?"

"*Bucarsi.*" He shakes his head. Unsmiling. "It literally means to put holes in oneself."

"You mean junkies?"

"Yes."

At least I got that right. Heroin addicts. Looking for a fix, and then for something more. I don't know what to think about them. Hatred or pity? I feel both.

"What will happen . . . to the junkies? Who were those guys who helped me?"

"Friends and assistants. Giuseppe was the first to reach you. My manservant."

"What will your *assistants* do to them?"

Marc shrugs as he drives.

"Don't worry, my *confreres* won't kill anyone. They will just put the fear of God in them."

"But what then? Will you take them to the police?"

"The carabinieri?" Marc shakes his head. His voice is tinged with contempt. "What is the point? They'd have to build prisons from here to Palermo to house all the addicts, and half of the police are corrupt anyway."

He turns a sharp left, down my street. He talks as he parks. "No. We'll let them go, after giving them a lesson. I don't think they will be assaulting any women for a while." He sighs. "The people I would really like to put in jail are the bastards who get these vermin hooked on heroin. The Camorra. The 'Ndrangheta." His handsome face is tight with anger; it is almost scary, and he turns to me. "I hate them, X. They poison everything. This city should be so beautiful, yet it is so often ugly. Hence what happened to you." He turns the key, and the engine is silent. "Here is your apartment. I will wait in the car?"

"Wait?"

"I'd like to buy you lunch."

"But . . ."

"That is, if you are up to it. Because I *do* want to explain, and I wish to do it in the most civilized way." His stubbled jawline is firm. "And perhaps you shouldn't be alone, Alexandra."

I pause, bewildered. I do feel a need to eat, and an even greater desire to drink some alcohol; to erase the mental images of the assault. And Marc is maybe right: I don't want to be alone.

"Yes . . ." I say. "Okay, yes, but—"

"Take as long as you like."

I climb out of the car, slip upstairs, and quickly shower, washing away the dirt from the grubby hands that groped me, trying to wash away the memory of the entire morning. Then I change into my last new Zara dress: navy blue, trimmed with *broderie anglaise*. I feel the need for softness and prettiness. And then, for ten or fifteen minutes, I simply stand there, silent, contemplative, regretful. Yet trying to move my thoughts from what has happened.

Somehow I succeed. Moments later I am back in Marc's car—but we only drive a few hundred meters, then Marc pulls up and jumps out. We are parked on the seafront that leads to the little bridge. That leads to Castel dell'Ovo.

I've looked at this stone pier, with its castle thrusting formidably into the sea, so many times. I've read about its history: built where a siren of a mermaid was legendarily washed up on the empty Mediterranean shore, thus establishing the city itself, the new city of the sybaritic Greeks—Neo-Polis. New City. Naples.

But this is my first visit to the "island."

Marc opens my door like a chauffeur and we walk across the grand stone bridge to the castle, which is guarded by iron gates. Then we duck left.

To my surprise I see a row of cheery outdoor restaurants, built against the castle walls, sheltered under blue-and-white awnings yet staring out across the Bay of Naples.

We take a table at the very first restaurant. A waitress greets Marc with a wide smile, while another waitress pulls out a chair for me at a table shaded by a parasol. I sit.

"*Signorina, buongiorno—e Signor Roscarrick!*"

Marc is obviously well-known here; his arrival has created a tiny but perceptible hubbub among the other diners, but especially among the staff. I wonder how many other young women he has squired to these tables under this Italian sun, in this same sweet and cooling sea breeze.

I don't care. Nibbling at a breadstick—*grissini*—I gaze and sigh, and feel the sincere horrors of the last hour begin to drop away.

Because if there is any place that might soothe a troubled mind, it is here. The view is so beautiful; the great bay sweeps with cavalier generosity from the ancient glittering center of Naples, past the brooding heights of Vesuvius, down toward the cliffs and beaches of Vico and Sorrento. Italian flags ripple in the mellow wind, yachts ply the prosperous blue waters, smart *polizia* in speedy motorboats unzip the sea into exuberant vees of surf. It is a painting of Mediterranean Happiness.

"It is very lovely," I say, reflexively.

"You like it?" Marc seems genuinely pleased. His white-toothed smile fits perfectly into the scenery. The ocean? Check. The sun? Check. The handsome man? Check. All present and correct. Hmm.

"The waitress knows you, right? I suppose you come here a lot . . . ?" My question is unworthily suspicious. I chide myself for my rudeness. But Marc answers very graciously, nonetheless.

"I know the *owner*, Signora Manfredi. Her husband was a police officer. The Camorra . . . killed him." Shaking his head, Marc glances down at the menu but my guess is that he knows exactly what is written there. He is disguising emotion. He pauses, then his expression lifts and brightens. "I helped her set this place up, with a little loan. In return, she guarantees to serve *all* my favorite dishes. And my very own wines. Here." Marc leans across and points at something on my menu. "You see this one?"

I attempt to read the item. It is impossibly difficult. "*Pesci ang . . . basilic . . .*" I give up. "Um, some kind of fish?"

He nods.

"Yes, some kind of fish. Actually it is angler fish on a basil risotto, with lobster foam. It is quite sensational. You want to try?"

I look at him, and he looks at me.

Kicking off my sandals under the table, I sit back, driving the worries from my mind again and focusing on the moment. Only the moment.

"Why not, Marc. You choose. Choose for me."

He nods, with just a hint of a smile.

"Okay."

I smile in return. I am barefoot in the sun, and now the relaxation is working—it is pervading me like a drug: anesthetizing the pain of the morning. We are surrounded by happy Italian families chattering and eating, where the scents of lemon and good cooking and the glittering sea all waft and refresh.

"And some wine? If you will permit me?"

"You officially have my permission. Not least, Marc Roscarrick, because you're paying."

Where did that come from? Maybe danger has emboldened me, made me flirtatious. He laughs anyway.

"Very good point. Okay, we will have some wines from the Alto Adige—you know it?"

"No."

"It's the far north of Italy, the South Tyrol, where they speak German. One day, maybe . . ." He gazes at me, then shakes his head, as if correcting himself. "The wines are just brilliant, but barely known outside the region. My family has estates there—vineyards and a *schloss*. That is to say, a castle."

"But of course," I say, half smiling. "Who hasn't got their own *schloss*? I used to have a *schloss* but I got bored. *Schlosses* are *so* last year. Now I want a *palacio*."

"Ah. You're teasing me."

"You're a billionaire. The first billionaire I've ever met."

"I'm not sure whether to be gratified, X."

"What's it like having that much money, anyway?" I crunch

a breadstick. He smiles at my audacity. There is a European flag fluttering over his shoulder, bleached pale blue in the seafront sun.

"Not having to worry about money is like not having to worry about the weather," he shrugs. "It is an incalculable advantage; I do know I am very lucky. But I had to work to make a real fortune. And being rich brings its own difficulties."

"Such as? Too many private jets? An annoying choice of beautiful women wanting to sleep with you?"

"No." His sparkling eyes meet mine. "It makes life more . . . ah . . . *complicated.* Say you buy a Tuscan villa. Then you have to pay someone to look after the villa—because you aren't there most of the time. Then you have to pay someone to protect the man who is looking after the villa. Then you have to hire someone to check the man who protects the man who . . . well, it becomes a crashing bore." He pauses. And chuckles, that languid, infective chuckle. "I'm not looking for sympathy."

"You're not getting it."

Our food has arrived. It looks a little odd, and also beautiful: chunks of soft white fish laced with pink "lobster foam," like a kind of translucent froth of pale rose caviar; and all of it lying on the green island of risotto—rice tinged with basil.

And then I taste it.

"Oh my God."

"You like it?"

"It's . . ." I struggle for the words. "It is delicious. Like nothing I have ever eaten."

"Good!"

His smile is wide and dazzling. I can see the dark vee of his bare chest under his open-neck shirt. Dark hairs, a little gilded by sun maybe. His elegant hands reach for a wine bottle that lies tilted in a silver bucket.

"And now the Gewürztraminer. Lightly chilled, from Tremen, in the Etsch valley. That is where Gewürztraminer was *invented*. It matches the slight spiciness of the basil and the angler fish."

My only previous experiences of Gewürztraminer have been cheap German wine, or cheaper Californian remakes. I sip, somewhat reluctantly, but Marc is right. Of course; I bet Marc is *always* right. The wine is delicious. It lacks that icky sweetness I expected; it is rich yet dry, with a ghost of floral perfume. Just perfect, dammit.

We drink and eat, and the conversation warms, and then it positively *flows*: I tell Marc funny stories from my days as a student, stories about me and Jessica. They are not *that* funny, but Marc laughs, and his laughter seems real, and as the lunch proceeds my mind is again suffused with a sense of well-being. The terror of the alleyway seems like it happened to a different person, in a different time.

The wine is crisp and cool and lovely, and the afternoon stretches sunnily ahead, and I can hear people chattering happily away in Italian all around me, and it is like the best sound track ever. I am glad I do not understand the people here, because their talk becomes blissfully meaningless, just a mellifluous burble of foreignness.

At last Marc sits back. And he tilts his handsome head, looking at me with curiosity.

"X. You still haven't asked me about this morning. Are you no longer interested?"

He's right. I haven't asked. Why is this?

It is partly because I don't want to ruin the moment, perhaps. But it is also because my mind is helplessly clouded. And it is clouded by thoughts—not of the morning's events—but of sex. Right now, right this minute, I want to make love with Marc. I want to feel his hands on my skin; his lips on my lips; his hands caressing me, endlessly. I imagine us on a beach, alone and together. The sun above me, Marc above me . . . It feels wholly inappropriate, after what I have just experienced, in the alley; yet it feels wholly natural, too. I want life, and love, even more.

Moreover, I can see by the way Marc looks at me that maybe he wants me *as well*. A moment ago I stood and shifted to another chair to keep out of the beating sun, and I saw him staring at my legs, at my bare feet. With pure and devouring lust. Trying not to look but looking. And now he gazes at me.

The erotic tension between us, the almost-touching-ness, is delicious yet unbearable. Gloriously intolerable. It cannot go on. It must go on. The drought must break, the wet season must return. Yet still the sun beats down.

He raises a hand.

"Perhaps we need a little more wine."

"Do we?"

He nods.

"Something different this time. Something rather special."

Glancing along the table, I notice that the dishes and the plates have all been spirited away, without my really being aware. I am not surprised; Marc Roscarrick is surrounded by a halo of things that just *happen*, appropriately yet invisibly.

The plates have, in turn, been replaced with a new silver bucket and a fresh bottle of wine. Marc extracts this small, slender half bottle; turning it in his hand, he shows me the label.

"It is Moscato Rosa, from St. Laurenz, again in the Alto Adige." Marc pours a couple of inches into a tiny glass, which he then pushes my way.

The wine looks like liquefied amber mixed with the blood of a saint. The aroma is already divine. He gestures at my glass of rosy gold wine. "We only make a few hundred bottles a year; most years we can't make it at all. The climatic conditions have to be absolutely *perfetto*. There are only ten hectares of vineyards *in the world* that are dedicated to this grape."

I pause before I taste. The time has come; before this goes too far, before I drink too much, I really *must* have the answers.

"Marc. How did you know where I was in the Quartieri? How did you know I needed rescuing?"

The breeze ripples the parasol above us. Marc carefully replaces the bottle in the silver bucket, then looks my way.

"The first time I glimpsed you, Alexandra, in the Gambrinus . . ." He gestures helplessly, like someone confessing a dark secret. "I thought you were the loveliest woman I had ever seen."

I stare at him. My mind resists the words, but my heart soars. It soars. It does. I am a fool. But it does. *The loveliest woman I had ever seen.*

Me.

"I am sorry if this sounds glib or facile, X, but it is also the truth. I wanted to come over and talk to you. Immediately."

I manage to speak.

"So?"

"I restrained myself. Instead, I listened in to your conversation. I am sorry. Then I paid for your drinks. I couldn't help doing that at least. And then I left, before I did anything more foolish."

"Why didn't you talk to me?"

He ignores my question.

"But then you came to the palazzo. You were audacious. You were not quite the innocent I imagined. You were also funny and smart and . . . Well, it was very difficult to resist *again*. I am not a man to restrict myself to sentimentality."

What is he saying? I am melting in the words. Melting. But I mustn't. I need to know about Jessica. Why did he tell me he was interested in Jess? Before I can ask, he goes on.

"After you left the palazzo I asked friends of mine—friends, colleagues, servants—to look out for you. Again, I am sorry. I was interfering in your affairs, without your permission, it is unforgivable. But you seemed . . . a little naïve, maybe *too* audacious."

"You had me followed?"

"Not exactly. Watched over? Yes. Watched over is better. But then I heard you were exploring the slums, Materdei, Scampia—dangerous, dangerous places—and I asked my people to be more proactive. Yes, in the last couple of days, you were followed."

I don't know what to think about this. Should I be appalled, disgusted, violated? I am not. I feel *protected. Marc Roscarrick was protecting me.* It is impossible to feel anger. He continues.

"I was in the Via Toledo when my man Giuseppe called and said you were in deep trouble—he got to you first, but I came as fast as possible."

"And saved me. Thank you."

He waves away the compliment.

"It was pure selfishness on my part. I do not deserve your gratitude."

"Sorry? Selfishness?"

The breeze drops. The family at the table behind us has gone. The silence extends. He speaks. "X, I saved you for *myself.* I rescued you because the idea of anything happening to you makes me ill. As you must realize, you are the one I wanted all along."

Now I have to ask.

"But you said Jessica—"

"It was a lie, to save you from me."

His eyes are dark with anger, or sadness, or something else.

"I don't understand. Marc?"

He sighs, and turns away, as if talking to himself. Contemplating the distant blue Sorrentine coast.

"There is danger for you in this, Alexandra. And yet I find myself advancing, nonetheless . . ."

Slowly, he turns back, and stares me straight in the eyes.

"I cannot help it. There is something in you, not just your beauty, something *in* you. I recognized it when you walked in the palazzo. Your bravery, your fearlessness. That bright intelligence. I was drawn to it, irresistibly. Like a kind of gravity." He hesitates, then says, "What is that line in Dante? At the end of the *Comedy*. Like the love that moves the sun and other stars? Yes. *L'amor che move il sole e l'altre stelle.*"

He falls silent. I am silenced. What do I say? That I felt the *same*? Something very similar?

To stifle my words I drink some of the wine, the Moscato Rosa. It is sublime; intensely rich and yet delicately roseate. Sweetness within sweetness. This feels like the most important moment of my life.

"I love Dante, too," I say, slightly faltering. "One of the reasons I came here is to learn Italian, so I can read it in the original."

His eyes flicker over mine.

"Favorite passage?"

"In the *Commedia*?" I consider, then answer. "I think the passage in the 'Paradiso.' When the souls are rising to God—"

He finishes my words for me, not hiding a delighted smile: "Like snowflakes ascending! Yes! It is my favorite passage, too." Our eyes meet again. He speaks the verse in liquid Italian. "*In sù vid' io così l'etera addorno, farsi e fioccar di vapor triunfanti . . .*"

Silence returns. Marc sips at his wine.

Then he sets down the glass. His red lips are now moist with the sweet Moscato Rosa. He gazes into my eyes. His hand reaches across the table and covers mine. He leans nearer. His touch is electrocuting; every other part of me wants to be touching every part of him. The world pivots around us.

"Marc . . ." I say. I am pinioned and choiceless. I want no more delay. Our mouths are inches apart. The world is irrelevant, the universe is nothing, all there is is this moment and this table in this sunny outdoor restaurant with me and Marc Roscarrick as he tilts his handsome face to sink his wet sweet lips onto my waiting mouth.

"I can't," he says. "I cannot kiss you. It is too dangerous. *For you.*" His sigh is tense with grief. "I want you, X, I'm not sure I've ever wanted anything or anyone as much." A slow and horrible pause. "But it is impossible."

Seven

"Still can't figure out *why*."

"So we haven't gotten very far."

"Weird. Really weird. He buys you lunch and says he *adores* you and tells you that you are the most beautiful woman since Helen of Troy, if not slightly prettier . . . and then he says, 'Oh but I can't because of some dark, terrible, brooding mystery . . .' And then he escorts you home and that's *it*?"

"He's offered me a car and driver. So I can go see Naples without getting . . . into trouble."

Jessica nods.

I persist.

"Why would he do that, Jess? Why . . . ?"

"Let me think. I need nicotine to help me think."

She grabs a cigarette and lights it, exhaling blue smoke over the crust of her pizza margherita. Then she says, "Maybe he really is a very important *Camorrista*? And he doesn't want his terrible secret revealed? He does look a bit of a dangerous bastard." She chuckles. "Or maybe it's something *else*. Perhaps he just has *herpes*."

Is that a sourness creeping into her voice? She is my best friend; I don't want her to be jealous or upset at what I've told her. So far her reaction has been good humored, cynical, and laced with amusing sarcasm, typical Jessica, which is perfect. She is what I want to keep me stable. Otherwise I might just lose it.

"Then again"—she blows a smoke ring—"it could be something to do with his wife. Her death."

We have been discussing *him* all night, in this little pizzeria down by the port. Jessica is indulging me with these conversations—and I am grateful. But then, she got to choose the venue.

The pizzeria is open to the sultry night air. We are outside, but I can see inside, where big men with slightly malign haircuts drink shots of rough grappa at the bar. They knock it back in one swaggering toss, then turn around, as if expecting applause. Some of them have scars on their arms—burns and cut marks.

Jessica likes these seedy places; she thinks they are soulful, and true, and authentic. Sometimes I agree; sometimes I don't. Right now I don't care too much. I am not at all far from bewildered, and I am in the vicinity of Very Unhappy. I am still rattled by the assault in the Spanish Quarters, yet that terror has been eclipsed by the clamor of confusion in my heart.

Marc Roscarrick feels the same as me, and yet he cannot allow himself to be with me?

Yet he also offers me a car—and a driver. Giuseppe. Why would he do that if he never wants *this* to go any further?

I gaze across the napkin-littered table at Jessica.

"Am I being stupid, Jess? Do you think I should just forget him?"

She gazes right back at me.

"Yes."

I am bitterly disappointed; I also know she is right.

"However . . . ." Jess adds, stubbing out her cigarette with relish. Her words are smoke in the warm evening air. "I know you won't."

"Sorry?"

"You can't forget about him, can you, hon? It's already gone too far, hasn't it?"

Her voice is uncharacteristically tender. Jessica's expression is accepting and clever. Sometimes I wonder if she sees deeper into me than I can see myself.

"What do you mean?"

"Come on. You're falling in *love* with him, X. I've never seen you like this before, all doomy and mooning . . . Catherine-and-Heathcliffy."

"But—"

"This isn't Deck-Shoe Mathematician, is it? This is the Real Thing. You're practically crying a river 'cause of some *lunch*. I mean, think about it."

Her hands cross the table and she squeezes my hand; it reminds me of the way he touched me at lunch. "Listen, you wanted an adventure, you wanted to take a few risks, you came to Italy to find something new and exciting and, well, this is it. No? He might break your heart, but you might break his."

"But what if he is involved in . . . *something*?"

"So if he is, deal with it. This kind of stuff comes with the territory. When in Rome, sleep with Romans."

"Is that a saying?"

"No." She laughs, lowly. "But it's true. Besides, I'll say one thing for the Mob: they keep all the bloody tourists away.

Naples is the last real Italian city, the last city not overrun with fat foreigners taking photos."

"If he is. I . . . I can't . . . you know."

Helpless. This is helpless. And useless. Marc Roscarrick has made me boring. What can I do?

I glance at the bar again. Half the men in here are probably *Camorristi*. Of course they look like plain dockers and longshoremen, burly and tattooed. But they probably spend their days scamming profits, altering dockets, smuggling contraband, and sending presents to the wives of customs officers. Maybe they get a little violent in a back alley by the Capua gate every so often, beating up on some rival.

Yes, I am sure they do.

And I am also sure that Marc is *not* like these men. He is funny and sharp and dignified and *intelligent*, and he has that lofty graciousness—or is that just his expensive English education and his rarefied European breeding? Maybe it is *all* fake; maybe he is just another dancer at the masked ball of Neapolitan life.

And then there is the way he struck my attacker. I cannot ignore that. The serious punch, the sudden explosion of expert violence—as though he were producing a deadly weapon that he knew exactly how to use.

The blood on his knuckles as he drove. The dark skin, the white teeth, the predatory animal. The way the junkies cowered when they saw him.

"Hello?"

Jessica is waving a hand in front of my face. As if I have gone blind.

"Sorry."

"Let me guess, you were thinking of lottery numbers? The price of polenta?"

"He doesn't want to see me, Jess, so it's all pointless."

"Yeah?"

"He made it clear, he might . . . have feelings . . . but we can't be together."

"Pah." Jessica waves away my plaintive words. She glances up at the waiter, asks for the check. "I don't believe it, babe. He clearly *does* want to see you, there is just some problem. But sexual desire at this level has its own logic. When it happens, a real love attack, then nothing can stop it—trust me." She smiles in the dusk. "He will be back."

I so want this to be true. I am scared that it is true. I need it to be true. I want to fly home at once; retreat from danger and hurt.

Jessica pays the bill and we rise, ignoring the attentive eyes of the burly drinkers, and walk along the Naples waterfront to Santa Lucia. The moon above Capri is pale and loitering; she is a white-faced northern widow in dark southern veils. Mantillas. Suddenly everything seems very sad. The chattering Italians gathered in groups and strolling in families no longer enliven me. It is stupid. I want to cry. What is happening to me? These feelings are entirely overblown and unjustified, and yet they are very real. I am wounded, I am an idiot, I am hurt, I am self-pitying. I am staring at Marc Roscarrick.

Marcus Roscarrick.

He is standing there, in the moonlight and the lamplight, by the door to my apartment. He is leaning against his car, his silver-blue Mercedes, quite alone. He is in jeans and a serene dark shirt. He is gazing down the boulevard at the slice of star-lit sea; he seems oblivious, tall, solitary, shadowy, very pensive. The dark evening light sculpts his cheekboned face. He looks younger and sadder than ever before. Yet more masculine.

"See," says Jessica. "Told you."

Alerted by Jessica's voice, Marc turns, and he stares at me. My mouth is open but unspeaking. I feel like I have been captured in a spotlight on stage, and the whole darkened audience of the city is watching the drama. Everything else yields to silence.

"I'm just going to a bar . . ." Jessica says, and she smiles at me with a significant expression. Then she slips away, into the city—leaving me and him. The only two people in Campania. It's just me and him and the constellation of Orion, which glistens over Sorrento and Capri.

I can tell by his dark, sad, broken half-smile that something has changed, something irrevocable has changed between us; the breach has been made.

He moves toward me. But I am already running toward him.

Eight

It's as if our lips meet before our bodies: it is the first kiss—maybe the first of many, maybe the only kiss, I cannot know, I do not care—and it is hot and brutal. He gathers a fistful of my blond hair and pulls back my head with a jolt of subtle pain—and yet I like it—and his mouth sinks down onto mine, warm and salty and hot and wet. His tongue is in my mouth; it is all instinctive, reflexive, and immediate. I am not thinking about anything. I am just a kiss. I am just this brilliant kiss under Orion.

Our tongues explore, the kiss *thrills* down me; he is kissing me harder and better than I have ever been kissed; I can feel spikes of tingling excitement rippling through me.

Then he pulls back for a moment, and I can see his long-lashed and narrowed blue eyes glittering in the lamplight—so close to mine. I can smell his bodywash and the fine topnote of cologne, and sweet summer sweat, and it is him, him, him.

"I'm sorry, X . . ." he says. "Just can't help it. What you do to me—"

"Again."

This time *I* grab *him* and now we are a drunken couple, holding on to each other on a divine dance floor, on a doomed and pitching cruise ship, stumbling slightly backward, almost laughing, utterly serious, kissing fiercely. His lips are hard on mine again, and this time his firm male hands slip desirously down my back.

I am in a black summer dress and the cotton is thin. Marc is grasping my behind, hard and ardent, clenching me there as his other hand cups my neck, and we kiss, thirstily, again, and again. Then his hand slips around my waist, like a dance partner, swirling me, swinging me on his strength, then coming back and nuzzling my warm neck with his warmer lips. And murmuring . . .

"You smell of strawberries, X, wine and strawberries."

He releases me, still holding my waist, but lacing my white fingers with his darker ones. I sense a surge of something deeper than sex, but also sex, very much sex.

"Upstairs," he says. "*Now.*"

He chooses. I want to be chosen. My hands are trembling, my knees are trembling as I fumble at the door, then at last it swings open and he chases me up the stairs, half laughing, half growling, like some fine animal coming for me, hunting me down, racing up the stairs, and reaching for my giggles. But I disappear into the apartment, and for a second I am alone, but then I shriek with fear—only slightly faked—as he lunges at me desirously once again, chasing me into the kitchen. Then we are standing by the fridge and he is pulling off his shirt.

The kitchen is half dark. The only light is from the street lamps and the Mediterranean moon, slanting silvery whiteness through the window.

His shirt is off, and the moonlight traces, like a black-and-white photographer, the muscles of his chest and his stomach, the hard yet tender rib cage, the taut stomach. His chest is broader than I expected, the musculature a little more defined, even. He is taller and stronger than I am and I experience a tiny, delicate frisson of fear, mixed with abject *want*, wanting of *him*, as he flings his shirt to the floor and stalks closer.

We kiss again, and once more. I am reaching up on tiptoes to kiss his soft lips, once, then twice, delicate and fluttering, entirely sensuous. My tongue is slipping in and out of his lips. What am I doing?

"Enough, X—the bed."

Swiftly and easily, he picks me up, like a groom lifting his bride over a threshold. Then he carries me into the bedroom and throws me onto the bed, and the bed slats creak like they are going to break. *And I really don't give a damn.*

Marc Roscarrick looms over me, bare-chested—a tall, dark shadow high above.

"Stay like that," he says. "Just like that."

I am lying on the bed, arms flung back—but I can't stay like this; I want him too much, so I am fiercely kicking off my sandals, and when I am barefoot he grabs my slender ankle and kisses my white instep, kissing me there with little nibbles of desire. The sensation is divine. It sends the sparks of hot excitement racing through me yet again. But then he drops my ankle, and he pauses for an unbearable moment, an intoxicating moment, and he looks at me in the half-light.

"Do you want me to wear something?"

The moment dances into stillness. Well, do I? Do I want him to wear a condom?

For God's sake, NO. I don't want him to wear *anything*, I want him naked, naked as me, and naked inside me. All my life, all my sensible, dutiful, studious Good Daughter life, I've asked men to *wear* something—the few men I have slept with. But this time I do not care, this time I actively want to be *careless*. I am on the pill, that will do, now hurry up.

"Just fuck me."

Again he *swoops* down on me. Like a predator. Like something not quite human, yet beautifully human. He is hotly kissing my neck and breathing in my scent.

"I want you *naked*."

I stare at him. He is surging with an anger I don't quite understand.

"I want to see all of you—"

For a second he fumbles with the buttons on the back of my dress; I lift myself up on an elbow, so as to help him, but he just laughs—or maybe he snarls—and he rips the dress away, simply rips it off my half-naked body—and flings the shredded garment across the room. I protest in vain in the dark, looking up into his eyes: "But my dress—"

"I will buy you another!" he growls. "I will buy you a *hundred* fucking dresses."

And then he reaches around and unclasps my bra, and he throws that aside, too; and now he looks down at my pale breasts with a tender hunger, and then he kisses them, coldly, yet warmly, the left breast and the right breast, in turn. Carefully and expertly, his fingers toy with my nipples; he bites them playfully, nibbling at one, then the other, and they are hard, and getting harder under his touch.

The desire for him to touch me and take me, *down there*, is becoming irresistible. A space is opening, a wetness, a desperate expectation; my hips move toward his and he knows what I want. His mouth sows kisses down my pale stomach, kissing me to my navel; he is like a dark withdrawing tide, receding down my body, sucking on the sands.

Now I can feel him pulling down my panties along my thighs; my bare foot tingles with the touch of the cotton and then it is gone and his sweet, sweet mouth is on my sex, my desire, my cunt, my vulva.

My wetness is mixed with his wet lips, his hands are on my bare hips, and he is kissing and nibbling, his tongue darts, and then, *yes*. He expertly finds my clitoris with his hard-soft tongue, and he licks me sweet and quick, like a flickering flame, a gentle feathering. And my heartbeat pounds, my entire body tingles, the delicious prickling of this pleasure makes me shiver from head to toe, as he licks and gently bites my clit. And then everything dazzles like a flash of rose lightning, and the words come spilling forth. "Oh God, Marc, oh God."

"*Carissima.*"

He lifts his handsome face.

"Marc, please *don't stop.*"

Who is saying this? Is it me? Someone else? It is me, oh it is me. Once again he tongues at my clitoris, greedy and fierce, and yet tender. And then he turns and licks the soft, trembling skin of my inner thigh, nuzzling at my thigh as I moan just a little, turning left and right in the dark, breathing my excitement. Helpless, shivering, and adored.

Because he is licking me there again. Right between my thighs, where my pleasure meets his desire. I murmur his name into the darkness as I stream my fingers through his soft and curling hair, his dark, sweet, tousled hair; then I greedily press his face closer to my sex, to my climax, my nearing climax—am I actually going to climax?

OhGodyes, OhGodfucking*yes*. Now it *happens*: as he licks and blows and nuzzles on my pulsing clitoris, I finally yield, I tumble, I fall. Blissfully, I trip into the place where I cannot return.

The trembling has become shaking has become hapless juddering, a kind of spasm, delicious and remorseless, and I have to put my knuckles in my mouth to stop screaming with glee—as the explosion of deep and raw and unstoppable pleasure bursts upon me, like scarlet fireworks inside me, deep between my thighs, yet rushing upward.

OhmyGod, oh my almighty God, oh sweet, sweet, sweet, Jesus God. Still the ripples of silver cascade up and down, along my thighs, in my veins. And then come the aftershocks, the helpless quivering, the delicious tremors of my skin. The thudding heartbeat of release.

"That was . . . it was . . ." I can barely speak the words. I look down at him, his dark and beautiful face, his stubbled jaw between my still trembling thighs. "The first . . . the f-f-f-f- . . . the . . . oh Jesus, oh . . . f-f-fuck—"

He is smiling, or something, I cannot tell, but I hear him softly talking, as his face moves to kiss my belly, as his hands push my thighs still farther apart.

"Sei un cervo—un cervo bianco."

He is undoing his jeans.

"Alexandra."

I am helpless and pooled on the bed, half laughing with delight, all wetness and wanting and wildness; I will let him do anything to me now. Anything he likes. He can ravage me and ravish me, and ravel me up. But I also want him *inside me*.

And he knows this.

"Alex."

"Yes?"

"Are you sure? Are you certain, *cara mia*?"

"I am certain, Marc. I am yours, *all of me*."

And I am certain, oh so certain. I am hungry for him.

In the half-light I can see him pulling off his shoes and tearing away his socks until he is a barefoot warrior standing tall, something fine and Greek, something noble and heroic; then he pulls down his jeans and yes—oh my Lord, yes—now I can see his erection, thick and hard and ready. And before I even know it, he is slipping deep inside my wetness, driving inside me—big and powerful. Almost brutal.

The sensation is inexplicable. We fit, we fit together all too well; like he was meant to be inside me, meant to be on top of me all my life, meant to be fucking me. And now my thighs yield to his thighs, my strength succumbs to his greater strength, like this is a kind of fighting, or the most sublime dancing. But this isn't dancing: this is fucking; he is fucking me. Powerful and gentle. And I want to kiss him as we fuck. So I reach my white arms up to bring him down, to kiss his face, so handsome and serious in the moonlight, and he descends, and we kiss, and now our tongues are softly combating, like his maleness inside me.

"I love you inside me."

"I love fucking you."

We kiss again and I gently bite his lips and then he bites my neck a little harder, and I soar upward inside as he thrusts, and thrusts again, and once more.

"No, wait, *I have to fuck you from behind*."

Deftly, he lifts me up—like a ballet dancer, a naked ballerina in his commanding hands—and then he flips me over in a single, skillful movement. I don't know how he does it—how did he do that?—but now I am sprawled facedown on the bed, my cheek pressed into the pillow, and I sense my thighs being hungrily pushed apart, firmly opened to his desire, as he plunges into me again, harder, expert, thrusting, and his weight is on top of me, his chest on my back, and I love it.

I love the sense of his hard body on top, weighing me down, as he thrusts and presses, again, and once again. Oh God. Ohmygod. Moaning and sighing, I twist my face from the pillow to look up at him. He is serious and somber, he is smiling but angry.

"My beautiful girl."

"Fuck me harder."

Breathing deep, he takes me entirely; he thrusts again, deep and slow, and I look up at him once more, as he possesses me; and then his right hand slips under my pelvis and I realize he is reaching for my clitoris as he fucks me from behind.

Oh God no, oh God yes. Helpless and quivering, I turn my face to the pillow and gasp as his fingers find my clitoris, as he presses sweetly with his fingers, pressing and stroking, even as he fucks me. And now the pleasure mounts to a second crescendo, a second cadenza, a brand-new climax, the sensation of his fingers and his driving cock all at once, it is way too much.

Oh yes.

Yesyesyes.

This orgasm is sharper and harder; it is quite different, quite animalistic, and abandoned, and from nowhere I am actually screaming into the pillow, muffling my words, biting the cotton, choking on my own pleasure.

"I never, I never . . ."

And I clutch at the sheets, and I feel my toes curl, and I am yielding. I am taken. And even as this orgasm surges, and shudders, and then subsides into pulsing apparitions, I can feel him approach his own climax.

"Come inside me, Marc, please come inside me."

I did not have to ask; he does not need to be told. Marc presses my face into the pillow; his fingers are fierce on my neck, almost choking. And then his body quivers and shudders, melting into mine. Marc is losing himself, he is shaking like a knife stabbed into hard wood, and then I get the aftershock of my own orgasm as he shudders and gasps, and speaks in dark Italian.

And now at last I hear him sigh, with anguish and release, and then he falls down onto me, and then he slumps to the side of me, the intensity quite gone, his taut muscles slacked. And I am left here whimpering into the pillow. I am actually weeping. I am actually *crying*, that I have had to wait all my life for it to be this good.

Nine

It is still dark when I wake. Marc is asleep in my bed and his dark, masculine beauty appears careless, even more unself-conscious. His sweet and kissable mouth is very slightly open, the white teeth shine in the moonlight, the almost-black hair is curled and mussed. But it is his hands that capture me; male but soft, lying still in the semidark. Somehow perfect and innocent. But how innocent can he be? After last night?

My mouth is parched.

I grab a gown and slip to the kitchen and drink a cold glass of mineral water. I have no idea what is happening to me; probably, surely, Jessica is right, and I am falling in love with him.

For a few minutes I stand alone in the shadowy kitchen, staring through the window at the moon, which stares at its reflection in the Tyrrhenian Sea.

Then I slip back into bed, next to his breathing and silent warmth.

When I wake again it is bright morning, and the Campanian sun already burns through the slats of my rickety shutters, making bar codes of light on the bare walls. He is gone? My soul panics. My heart stutters. No. Not like that, not like this, no—not a one-night stand—not after that. Please.

Be still, X, be still.

He has left a crisp white note on the pillow. An elegant piece of notepaper, carefully folded in two, with *X* written on the front in fountain pen. Where did he get the notepaper? And the pen? How does he do this stuff? Hungrily, I grab the note and read. *You looked so happy to be asleep. I have gone to get breakfast. We will have sfogliata at seven. R. x*

My happiness rebounds. I grab my cell and check the time: six forty. He'll be back in twenty minutes. I shower quickly, then slip into a cool gray cotton dress—and just as I am drying my hair, the doorbell buzzes in my apartment.

"*Buongiorno,*" he says over the frazzly intercom. "*La colazione è servita.*"

A moment later he is standing at the apartment door with a handsome smile and a handful of pastries in a bag—and *due cappuccini* in a cardboard tray.

He is in a new dark-blue shirt, along with the jeans, and those beautiful bespoke shoes. How? He keeps new shirts in the Mercedes? The slightly troubling questions are soothed away by the excellent coffee. And then we eat the pastries; they look a little like croissants—but they aren't.

"Wow, delicious."

"*Sfogliata frolla.* From Scaturchio in Spaccanapoli. They've been making them for a century."

"Fantastic! What the hell is inside?"

"Soft ricotta, with candied fruit and spices. The only problem is not eating ten."

He smiles. I smile. The sun smiles down. There is, remarkably, no awkwardness, no very-first-breakfast-together shyness. We are sitting on plastic chairs on the balcony. Soft white streamers of cloud gently scarf the peak of Vesuvius across the bay; Capri is dreaming in the sea mist.

"So," he says, setting his empty plate to his side. "*About last night.*"

My smile is now a little broken. I'm not sure I want to have this conversation. Last night was *amazing*. But let it be what it was; let us not talk about it, not examine it, not analyze it, ever. Just one perfect night. One perfect night of torrid, primal, and gloriously heedless sex. Never examined, never questioned. Just itself.

"Last night was *perfetto*," he says. "But it was, perhaps, too perfect."

"Sorry?"

He tilts his handsome head, and asks, "You know the phrase . . . *coup de foudre*?"

My feelings flutter inside.

"Yes. *Coup de foudre*. A bolt of lightning—literally."

He nods. I stare at him.

Is that what he thinks this is? Just a flash of madness, and sexual passion? Is that what is happening to us? Something very fleeting? Which will be gone by next week?

He seems to sense my discomfort.

"X, I just want to know something before we go any further."

"Know what?"

"Whether you are . . ." He looks away. "*Prepared*. Because, if you do want to take it further, there are certain things . . ." He lends me his blue gaze once again. "There are certain things you should know."

Things I should know? Enough.

I set down my plate.

"Tell me, Marc, what is this great *mystery*? Just tell me. I can cope. I've got a driver's license. I'm all grown-up now."

He smiles.

"I noticed."

I make like I am going to throw the pastry bag in his face. He smiles apologetically and raises a hand.

"Okay, okay. I am sorry. It is just . . . very difficult. I don't want to frighten you away, the very same moment I have met you. X, you are my *great good news*, like the poet said." He pauses, then: "But there are aspects of my life that are crucial to me, aspects that, if you want to continue seeing me, you deserve to know. And if you cannot accept this part of my life—then it's best we go no further. Indeed, we cannot go any further. For your sake and for my sake."

This sounds unnerving. This sounds pretty bad. I wait, silently, for him to elaborate. But my heart is noisy inside: beating, anxious, perturbed.

He takes a last sip of coffee, then says, "Have you ever heard of the Mystery Religions?"

"No, not really." I rummage through the memories of high school history. "Something pre-Christian, maybe? Uh, I did *modern* history at school, mainly."

"The Mystery Religions are ancient cultic faiths, with enigmatic initiation rituals. They were woven into classical Mediterranean society, Greece and Rome. Some became very popular, like the mystery of Mithras; some remained controversial and orgiastic, like the mysteries of Dionysus."

I stare at Marc. Dionysus. Orgies. *Where is this going?*

"I don't understand."

Marc glances down at the quiet early-morning road. Then he says, "Do you have a couple of hours to spare, right now?"

"Yes. I make my own timetable."

"Do you want to go to Pompeii?" He checks his watch. "We can be there before they open to the tourists; I know the site manager. And there is something in Pompeii that can explain this—explain it better than any words of mine."

It is impetuous and abrupt, but I am getting used to this—because this is how Marc behaves. He is decisive and spontaneous. And I like this; no, I *love* this. The Deck-Shoe Mathematician never whisked me off to Ancient Pompeii. Then again, the Deck-Shoe Mathematician never had anything to do with cults and orgies, either.

Twenty minutes later we are racing through the dreary outer suburbs of Naples. Gray concrete apartment blocks blur past, scarred with graffiti—yet set amid rustling olive groves and scented lemon orchards, stepping down to the glittering sea. They are still lovely despite the squalor. Maybe the squalor is part of it. Love and violence, roses and blight.

Marc talks quickly on his cell phone as we accelerate around little three-wheeled trucks driven by wizened old men ferrying melons.

"Fabio! *Buongiorno . . .*"

I glean that he is talking to the "site manager" at Pompeii.

Soon after, we pull up at some big iron gates. A short, well-dressed man in white jeans and very expensive Armani sunglasses is waiting there. He greets Marc with obsequiousness, and maybe even a hint of fear; and then the man turns and theatrically kisses my hand.

After this little display, the site manager opens the gates and we step into Pompeii.

Pompeii!

Ever since I was a schoolgirl I've yearned to come here—to see the famously preserved Roman city buried under the ashes of the Vesuvian explosion. And I am now seeing it in a position of immense privilege: when it is free of *all other tourists.*

The scholar in me wants to take my time, to drink it all in; but Marc strides ahead, leading the way past the ruins, past the Roman brothels and bathhouses, the shops and *tabernas.*

We stop, at last. It is hot, and I am perspiring.

Marc gestures.

"The Villa of the Mysteries."

We enter, leaving the site manager behind. I glimpse a courtyard, side rooms, and bright floors with mosaics. Turning a corner, we step inside a darker room, elaborately decorated with two-thousand-year-old frescoes, all of them bordered in a dusty and archaic crimson.

A rope blocks a closer view of the frescoes—for keeping back the tourists, I suppose. Marc simply steps over it, then takes my damp hand and helps me over, too.

I am now in the middle of the room. And I can see the poetic and wistful beauty of these images: dancing girls, poignant satyrs, sad, sweet women; here is a delicate aesthetic, bright and alive, rescued from oblivion.

"These frescoes show an initiation rite," Marc explains. "The girl is being inducted into the Mysteries."

With rising curiosity I scan the large and ancient pictures.

On the left, an elegant young woman is being prepared for some elaborate ceremony. Pipes are played. She is sensuously bathed. Something is drunk—is it wine, or a drug, or what? Whatever it is, when she takes it, the woman dances. Dances herself into a frenzy.

My mouth is dry again. I turn to the right. In the last panel the woman has been initiated, and now a slave girl clothes her and coifs her hair. The woman stares at me as her hair is dressed; her expression is pensive, even regretful—but sated.

Sated by what?

I step forward.

In the most important scene, the penultimate scene, paradoxically hidden in the far and shadowy corner of the room, the woman has, finally, stripped herself almost naked. She has her back to us. Her curving body is white and beautiful; she looks divine and highly aroused, responding to some intensely erotic stimulation.

My heart beats. I take in what is happening. The woman is being whipped.

Ten

"What does it mean? I don't understand."

I am backing away from the frescoes.

Marcus studies me in the half-light of the villa, as if he is looking through me, or into me, *far into my past.*

"Clearly, X, it is an initiation." His voice is so calm, almost unnaturally so. My voice is much edgier.

"And this has something to do with . . . *what*?"

He says nothing.

"Marc, talk to me. Explain the frescoes. . . . Why have you brought me here?"

Near-silence prevails. I can hear birdsong outside, and very distant morning traffic. The Villa of the Mysteries seems hushed, as if scandalized and desecrated by our conversation. But how can you desecrate *this*? I stare again at the woman in the farthest, most profound fresco. Then I scan the other images.

Who is the grinning god lying back as if drunk? What is the laureled woman carrying on her silver tray? *And why the hell is the young woman being whipped? Why is she accepting this?*

The frescoes pose too many questions. I don't want to linger to work through them. What's more: very soon the tourists will be streaming in. And our presence here, alone, feels trangressive. Just wrong.

"Marc, can we get out of here?"

"Of course." He gestures at the sunny rectangle of an open doorway. "We can go through here, then—"

I don't wait for him to finish. Stepping urgently over this threshold, I emerge into open air—but it isn't the exterior, it is some kind of interior courtyard with a delicate, green copper statue of Mercury on a pedestal, a lithe and beautiful naked boy, with wings on his ankles. I do not remember the statue.

"But this leads nowhere!"

"X, wait. Just turn left." Left? I hurry on, stumbling on uneven paving stones. My thoughts are a tumult. Did young Roman brides walk this very same passage? Nude and lissome beneath their tunics, in scarlet house sandals laced with gold, did they walk into a darkened room and wait there to be flayed?

And what has this got to do with Marc, or me, or us?

I am lost. Corridors extend on either side. Behind me, Marcus places a gentle and calming hand on my shoulder, guiding me, but I shrink away, and march down another dark passage. I don't want to feel his touch. The press of his hand reminds me, way too distractingly, of last night.

Of him stripping me ruthlessly. Pressing my naked face into the pillow with a tender but dominant strength, faintly tinged with anger.

And yet I loved it. I did. He shucked me, opened me, devoured me. And I loved it. Yielding to his hunger for me, the way he ate me up like I was a freshly caught *ricci*, the sea urchin they serve in the better restaurants of Posillipo. If I think about this—about the sublimity of the sex—I will surrender again. But right now my defenses are up.

"Which way?"

My voice is strained; Marcus soothes, again: "Here, X—just go through here."

I am actually running. Because I desperately need fresh air on my face, not this antique dust. So I hurry along the dark corridor, past more frescoes, and more mosaics. And there, yes—I can see yellow wildflowers dozing in the Campanian sun—the way out of this maze. At last I run into the daylight and the summer breeze and I breathe a deep sigh of relief.

I am actually panting. A tiny bit panicked.

The dapper little man with the white jeans has gone. The ancient Roman road stretches into the distance, lined with Roman graves and Roman houses. It is so very quiet. I gaze about me, reminded of something. But I don't know what of.

Then I recall. It is eerily like Los Angeles. No people on the sunlit streets. *No one walking.* Sometimes Californian cities with their zero pedestrians remind me of cities hit by plague or natural disaster. And here I am again. A city of the dead.

Marcus has followed me into the sun.

"I apologize, X. I didn't mean to upset you."

"You didn't." My voice is petulant. "Didn't upset me. I mean, I mean . . . Oh God."

"Sit?"

Yes. I really need to sit. Casting around, I see a white marble chunk of Roman pillar, carved into a makeshift seat. I go over and sit. And stare down at my painted toenails.

The nails I painted with Jess. How I would like to be with Jessica now, in my apartment, laughing and gossiping and drinking cheap Chianti from the *supermercati*, and talking about old times.

Now it has all changed. My friendly jaunt to Naples has gone dark and different. Better and worse. I have had magnificent sex, maybe life-changing sex, but now it is all deep and mysterious, and troubling. And strange.

Inhaling the scents of sunlit herbs and flowers, flourishing in the wilds of the archaeological site, I turn on my marble throne and say, "Okay, Marc. Tell me."

"Ask whatever you want."

"You're telling me that people used to do . . . whatever is happening in those frescoes."

"Yes. They used to do it." He gazes at me, unblinking. "They still do."

And now the puzzle unfurls.

And I do not like what it reveals. I do not like it at all.

"The Mysteries . . . still exist?"

He smiles. Soberly.

"Yes."

"Where? How? When?"

"Across Italy, sometimes in France, and Britain, and so on. But mainly in Italy."

"Who does it?"

He shakes his head.

"I cannot say."

"You said ask *anything*, Marc."

"You can ask anything of *me*." He opens his arms, accepting and candid. "But I cannot intrude on the privacy of others."

Is this a fair point? I don't know. I don't know what to think at all. The looming truth is too upsetting. I struggle for my next question.

"Okay, what kind of people?"

"They tend to be rich and cultured. Intelligent and educated."

"Why?"

He shrugs, as if this question is beneath him, and maybe beneath *me*. I don't care. I go on.

"When do the Mysteries happen?"

"The Mysteries are enacted every summer. They start in June and end in August or September."

"So they start very soon?"

"Yes."

I have to ask. I don't want to ask. I cannot ask. But I have no choice. Marc is right: this cannot go any further unless I know the truth, and if I know the truth I may not want to see Marc again. My life is maybe changing, again; twice in twelve hours.

I slowly speak the words.

"You are part of it, aren't you?"

He nods.

"And you want me to be part of it, too?"

A terrible pause.

"Yes."

I snap my words.

"And what will happen to me, Marcus? Will I be like that Roman girl in the fresco? Will I get *horsewhipped*?"

He does not reply. I am probably glad he does not reply.

To my left, a bee hovers above a bright scarlet flower, filling the silence with its busy hum. Marc is walking away from me, staring at an old Roman shop. It has a marble counter with circles carefully cut into the level stone.

"These places, these shops . . ." he begins. "Of all the sights in Pompeii, it's *these little shops* that move me the most." He gazes down at the counter, brushes the weary marble with a pitying hand. "They would use these holes for bowls, from which they served hot take-out food. These were cookshops. Fast-food outlets."

He gestures, widely.

"Can't you see her, X? Some flustered Roman housewife, serving at this counter, brushing flies off the mutton, wiping her hands on her apron, wondering about her husband serving in the legion. . . ." A pause. "It always moves me. The living history. The humanity retrieved. The noble tragedy of ordinary life."

Now he turns. And he walks back to me, and for a second there is a menace in his attitude, and his expression. A man used to getting what he wants. Maybe prepared to use violence if he doesn't. Then he pauses, and speaks:

"Flagellation is an element of the Mysteries."

I almost swear.

"You're not even *denying* it, Marc? You admit it? They beat the women?"

"*Beat* is the wrong word. Totally the wrong word."

"Oh. Oh, okay. Silly me. What word? Punch? Smash? What is the *right word*, Marc?"

"Flagellate. It is *consensual*. The whole point is that the initiate agrees to the initiation. He or she must volunteer and submit; there is no coercion. Without the willingness of the initiates, the Mysteries are vitiated, and purposeless. The great secret cannot be attained. The ultimate and transformative mystery, the Fifth Mystery, the *katabasis*, remains unreached."

"So people want to join. So it's like a bunch of kinky freemasons."

He shakes his head sadly—and offers me a handsome and forgiving smile. I suddenly and abruptly want to hit him, and yet I want to kiss him, too. In fact, I maybe want to kiss him even *more*, now that I ever-so-slightly hate him. I'd like to make him angry; I'd like to annoy him a lot, so that he comes after me, like he did last night—chasing me up the stairs, white teeth devouring and carnivorous.

Eating up the sea urchins they sell in Posillipo.

Damn him. *Damn him.*

"Alexandra . . . ?"

Don't look at him, X, don't even look at him.

He sits on his own chunk of Roman pillar and leans forward, talking quietly.

"Alex, the Mysteries are maybe three thousand years old. They stretch back to Ancient Greece, to the groves and myrtles of Attica. It's not a joke; it is not a trivial cult of fools in silly costumes." His voice carries into me, his fine English accent reaching into me; can you be aroused by a voice? How can that be? What do I have to do? Block my ears?

For now I have to listen.

"The *Mysteries* embody sexual and emotional and spiritual truths that take you *closer to the soul.* I was myself initiated as a very young man; what I have learned is now part of me, woven into me. The Mysteries have taken me to places of pleasure and revelation that I cannot describe, but I yearn to share. And I yearn to share the intensity with *you,* X."

"Which is why you want to see me stripped and beaten?"

"I want to see you experience the joys and the truths that I have experienced. So we have a chance to be . . . truly together."

"And being whipped, that's joyful?"

He shakes his head.

"Okay." He sighs. "Okay . . . I am sorry." He runs fingers through his black hair. "Possibly . . . I should have told you this some other time, perhaps I got carried away."

I stand up.

"Y'know, *Lord Roscarrick,* I'm not sure there's ever a right time to be told, *Oh, by the way, I'm really into hitting women while pretending to be a Roman senator—*"

"X, wait."

"But I'm glad you told me, now I can get the train back to Santa Lucia."

"X!"

His voice is stern. I feel, for a second, like a scolded child. This makes me even angrier. But I am duly quiet, as he speaks.

"X, the *reason* I have shown you this is because, once a man is completely initiated into the Fifth Mystery, he is not allowed to have a serious . . . *relationship* . . . with anyone who is not initiated. Those are the rules."

"What? What rules?"

"Ancient rules, serious rules." He shrugs. "Rules that are quite powerfully enforced."

"So you're saying you can't be with me . . . unless I agree to do this? Do all these *rituals*?"

"Yes. That is, I fear, *exactly* what I am saying. I shouldn't really have spent the night with you, but—as I have said—you unman me, X. I am unable to resist. But now I have to resist, unless you agree to this. For the safety of us both."

I snort with contempt.

"So it's a kind of threat?"

"No! Nothing will happen to you if you disagree, of course not. But we can never meet again. Because the desire, at least on my side"—his eyes are glittering and sad—"is simply too much. But the Mysteries are not some horror, Alex; they are divine, they are a gift. You will understand, I promise, if you agree. But it is and must be your choice, and yours alone."

Something in me wants to give him one last chance. He looks so sad and cool and perfect sitting here in the warming sun, showing not a lick of sweat. Just one lock of stray dark hair has fallen forward over his tragically attractive blue eyes, like the angel of male beauty came down and said, *Ahhh, he is too perfect, let this lock fall*. Which of course makes him even more *perfetto*. The firm and faintly unshaven jawline, the glimpse of hard and suntanned chest, the definition of his cheekbones, slanting and aggressive and beautiful.

Enough. To *hell* with his perfection. He may be handsome but I am not going to be whipped for anyone.

"*Ciao!*"

I stand up and start walking, very fast—despite the rising heat. I can hear his voice behind me, calling.

"X. *Per favore, ricordati di me.*"

But I ignore him and stride on. Ahead of me I can see the first tourists at the very end of the Roman road: tourists who are all wearing exactly the same baseball caps and photographing exactly the same chunk of Roman theater.

Pompeii. Ugh. I feel like spitting. I was so excited when I got here. Now it is all wrong. All ruins.

Soon I am deep in the throngs of tourists, then I am exiting through the busy turnstiles as everyone comes pouring in the other way, and I know I have made the right decision.

Yet in my mind I can hear his voice.

"*Per favore, ricordati di me.*"

Why say that?

Forget it, Alexandra. Forget him, and the frescoes, and the Mysteries; forget it all. The dark-haired men in the little cafes with their overpriced Pepsis smile at me as I run down the hill toward the station for Villa dei Misteri and the Circumvesuviana train for Napoli.

Please remember me?

Eleven

"It was actually a pretty clever thing to say."

"Why?"

Jessica pouts at the sun, lies back, and pushes her Ray-Bans up her elegant nose.

"Think about it, babe."

We're lying on the beach at Posillipo, the municipal beach that costs five euros a day and has too many kids screaming and splashing and booting soccer balls, watched over by their big, fat Neapolitan mammas smoking Mild Seven cigarettes, which they stain with vermillion lipstick. Italian women wear more makeup on the beach than I do on the street. I am not sure of my opinion about this.

But it's the first *really* hot Sunday of the summer and everyone is happy and smiling and looking forward to a long Neapolitan lunch of Tufo white wine and big tranches of cassata, except for me. I am brooding and pensive.

Remember me?

Why was that a clever thing to say?

"Okay, I give up, why was that a clever thing to say?"

"Because it's got you wondering, X. And if he wants you to come back to him, which I am sure he does, the best thing is to keep you wondering, unsure, puzzled."

"Sorry?"

"What he said can be interpreted in *so many ways*. Does he mean: 'Remember me because you are never going to see me again'? Or it could be: 'Remember me because I am the sexiest man you will ever meet so you *have* to remember me'?"

"Thanks."

"Or it could be remember him in a wistful, tragic way, like he knows he is gonna be slotted by the 'Ndrangheta next week on the road to La Sanita, so the next time you'll see Lord R is when he's a corpse on the front cover of *Il Mattino*."

She smiles and lifts her sunglasses and winks at me. Then she adjusts her bikini strap. The sun is *hot*. Her bikini is new and chic and emerald green, and maybe Ferragamo? Or at least a very clever rip-off of Ferragamo, made in some Camorra-owned factory in Casal di Principe.

My bikini isn't any of these things, not new, not chic, not a rich emerald green that looks unexpectedly good against a deep Campanian suntan. My bikini is a delicate pink and looked nice in Cali. Not here. *God*. I have a sincere yearning for new clothes. I have no money. I am bored of budgeting.

And then, of course, the deep, sexy voice floats into my head. Him. In bed. With me. Taking me royally, and saying, *I will buy you a hundred fucking dresses.*

No! I sit up suddenly from my beach towel as if I am scalded. What is wrong with me? How could I even begin to think this way? If one of my reasons for desiring Marc is partly, even fractionally, because he's rich, what does that make me? Some mercenary bitch? Virtually a hooker? That is not me!

"Are you okay?"

Jess stretches and puts a hand on my arm.

"Yes. No," I snap. "It's nothing."

"Huh?"

"Okay, I just remembered I dumped a billionaire."

Jess chuckles.

"Well, yes, I guess that's gotta hurt."

She lets go of my arm and reaches for her Marlboro Lights and her lighter with the picture of Balotelli on it. Some soccer player. Black and handsome and Italian.

"Run it past me again, Beckmann: why *did* you dump him?"

I sip my cold mineral water and frown and pout, and answer, "Because he's into that weird cult. The Mystery Religions."

"And what are they, when they're at home?"

"Some creepy ancient religious Greco-Roman *thing*. Where they whip women."

Jess looks up from her beach towel and nods.

"Yeah? What's the problem? Still better than wearing deck shoes."

"Jess."

I chuck a little of my cold water on her hot, suntan-oiled stomach and she shrieks and laughs.

"Beach Nazi."

And now we laugh together like old friends, and it is good. And for a moment the clouds disperse and my brooding and moody thoughts are gone and my mind is as clear as the sky over the Bay of Naples this morning, the sea that stretches to the glimmering sawtooths of Capri. One day soon I am going to Capri.

"Seriously," says Jess. "These Mystery dudes, these blokes in togas, they like to hit women, why and how?"

"Not hit, so much. Flagellate. Ritually *whip*. It is an erotic ritual of submission."

"So it's like a BDSM thing, yes?"

"I guess . . ." I drink the last of the San Pellegrino and screw the cap back on. "Marc emphasized that it was all voluntary, and consensual."

Her face is suddenly serious. She sits up.

"You know, X, there are worse things in the world than a bit of slap and tickle. I had a boyfriend who was into *skateboarding*. He was thirty-bloody-two years old, and I had to watch him jump over three-inch-high barriers and pretend I was impressed. Now *that* was harrowing."

"Flagellation, though? It's perverse."

"Yeah, maybe. Which means Marc is a bit kinky, so what? X, they are *all* kinky, deep down. And if you ask me, all *women* are a bit kinky, too; it's just we've been repressed by the patriarchy." She stubs her cigarette out in the sand, a slovenly, and rather Neapolitan, gesture. I resist the urge to wince. She goes on.

"You know what they say: no woman ever got turned on by a man dressed as a liberal." I chuckle at the line, but she continues, "Aren't you even a little bit intrigued, X? Why not give it a whirl, vanilla girl? It's time you explored your libido. You do have one, don't you?"

"I told you."

"Ah yes, the best fuck of your life. Yes. You told me all about that, babe. He ripped off your clothes and you liked it, didn't you?"

"Yes, a bit . . . Okay, a lot."

"So maybe you'll like some other things. Threesomes. Foursomes. Lesbian costume play. Driving naked in Ferraris with wildly sexy billionaires, poor you."

I put the empty water bottle back in my bag like a tidy and sensible girl. Jess is making sense, maybe. But suburban X is still resisting, very strongly. There were just too many things *wrong* with Marc, quite apart from the Mysteries. The slight but definite menace. The hint of restrained violence. The police interest in his palazzo. The enigma of his departed wife.

Jess is now leaning on an elbow, smoking another cigarette, and openly ogling some Italian guy in his swimwear. I stare beyond her pretty profile at the strange building at the end of the beach. It is an enormous villa, a grand and historic palazzo.

It looks maybe fifteenth century and it is entirely in ruins. The windows are dark and foreboding, the roof is sprouting palm trees. Why? Why is it empty? It has a sublime position, perched above Posillipo beach, gazing out over the Bay of Naples—staring at Vesuvius and the regal sea. If it was done up it might be worth ten million dollars.

Yet it rots?

"It's called the Villa Donn'Anna," Jess says vacantly, following my stare. "They say it's haunted . . . all three hundred rooms. And it was used for orgies."

I gaze at the building. The city still confuses me so much. I need to know more. To learn. To understand. I am not ever going back to Marc Roscarrick, but I want to know why he is the way he is, and why Naples is so broken. And yet so irresistible.

And this is what I do. As soon as I get back to the apartment, a little drunk from too much cut-price midday rosé, I open my laptop, to research. But before I can google "Mystery Religions," I see a notification. I have an e-mail. From Mom. And the subject is: *Coming to see you!!*

What?
Somewhat startled, I open the e-mail.

> Hi, Alex . . .

The e-mail is typical Mom, breathless and loving and badly punctuated. But the meaning is clear: Mom's best friend, Margo—who is much richer—is going to Amalfi for a holiday with friends, and Mom is joining her. My mother is using up some of her precious savings to fly all the way to Italy so she can see her darling daughter and have a nice holiday. She will be here in three days' time.

> I know you don't want your mom cramping your style so don't worry, I won't linger, hon! But we can have a few days together in Naples. I so want to eat the *delizioso* ice cream!

I close the e-mail. My dear, sheltered, suburban American mother. What will she think of Naples? I have a feeling it won't match her gilded and romanticized dream of Italy. But I am glad she is coming. I miss her; I miss all my family. She and I used to be very close. She was a great mom when I was a kid; it wasn't her fault I got bored of San Jose and In-N-Out.

What on earth do I tell her about Marc? Anything?

I decide to file the problem away for another day. Instead, I search "Mystery Religions" and read.

> The Mystery Religions flourished across the Greco-
> Roman world from the fifth century B.C. to the end of

the Roman Empire, in about A.D. 400. The principal
and overriding characteristic of a Mystery Religion is
the secrecy associated with the rituals of initiation,
which lead the celebrant to a spiritual revelation. The
most celebrated mysteries of Greco-Roman antiquity
were the Eleusinian Mysteries, but the Orphic, Dionysian, and Mithraic Mysteries were also famous.

So which Mystery is Marc involved in? Two minutes' research
tells me it is probably the Mysteries of Dionysus, or some vari-
ant, or mixture.

Dionysia, or the Dionysiac Mysteries, were established
throughout the Greek world. Dionysus (Diævvσov)
was the Greek god of wine, but also the god of fertility, and of vegetation.

Male and female initiates into Dionysia followed
different paths. The women followers were known as
the Maenads or "frenzied women" or Bacchants (or
Bacchae), "women of Bacchus." The female initiation
commonly involved drinking and singing and sometimes frenzied dancing (or even howling like wild
animals). It is generally believed that part of the initiation into the cult involved intense sexual activity,
from flagellation to orgies, and beyond . . .

Beyond?

For the next three hours I am immersed in the bizarre world
of Orpheus and the god of ecstasy. Yet my research concludes
with my tired, stupid, and rather wandering mind helplessly

typing in the words *Marc Roscarrick*. Why? Why torment myself? I just want to know. Though I'm not entirely sure *what* I want to know.

A news item tops the page. Yawning from the afternoon alcohol, I click on it. It is a celebrity website. In Italian. Its prose is as breathless as my mother's.

I read on, laboriously translating the words.

The website tells me the *molto bello e scapolo* (the "very handsome and eligible") Lord Roscarrick has been sighted in London, for some festival of Italian films.

There is a small photo accompanying the piece, which I enlarge with a click. It shows him leaving a fashionable restaurant in "*il West End di Londra*," smiling that distant, sad, glittering smile at the paparazzo's camera. I can see there are several young women in his party, caught in the flash of the popping camera; all of them beautiful, of course. Marc stares at the camera; I stare at the women alongside him. Long-legged, like colts, like a millionaire's polo ponies. Gorgeous, expensive women. Fashionable English and Italian girls. Are they initiates, too?

I only know this: that I could have been there. In that photo. If I'd wanted. But I didn't.

I close the website with a fierce pang of jealousy and melancholy, and a sense of deep relief that it is over.

Ciao, bello.

Three days later, my mother arrives from San Francisco.

She is happy and excited and jet-lagged and she almost runs out of the airport as Jessica and I struggle along behind, half laughing, half grimacing, with her bags. In the taxi to Santa Lucia she chatters about nothing and everything. Mom is booked into a cheapish hotel near my apartment. We drop her in the dusty lobby, presuming she'll want a few hours to rest and relax, but ten minutes later, her gray hair still damp from a shower, she is buzzing my bell and in my apartment and grabbing my arm and saying, "Darling! Take me to the Caffè Gambrinus! I hear it's The Place—it's in all the guidebooks!"

I might, ordinarily, be wary of this, for fear of running into Marc. But I know he is out of the country. Mom and I can go anywhere.

Letting my mom take my arm, we step out onto Via Santa Lucia in the early-evening sun. My mom is still chit-chattering about Dad's golf and his retirement and my brothers.

We walk. She talks. We walk and she talks and then I stare. My heart is somewhere near my throat as I gaze ahead. We are crossing the wide empty pavements of Piazza del Plebiscito, with the sun setting pinkly over Anacapri.

And Marc Roscarrick is walking directly toward us.

He hasn't seen me. He is immersed in a phone call and gazing to the left.

"Quick, Mom—this way."

"What?" She is startled. "But I can see the Gambrinus, darling. It's over there."

I tug her.

"Mom, this way!"

"What's wrong?"

My mother is actually a little distressed. Oh God. Too late.

We are three meters apart. He is walking right into us. He looks up and sees me.

We cannot avoid each other.

Twelve

He smiles at me, and at my mother, as if nothing untoward has happened between him and me, ever. It's the same confident, handsome-sad, masculine smile. His manicured hand is extended. His suit is an immaculately dark charcoal-gray, verging on black. The shirt is blinding white; the silk tie aquamarine and primrose. I had forgotten how tall he is.

"*Buona sera*, X."

"Um . . ." I am flustered, stammering like a fool; glancing at both my mom and Marcus. "Um . . . Ah . . . Uh . . ."

My mom. Oh God. She is staring up at Marc as if Jesus had just descended from the heavens to give her a new Bulgari purse. Her expression is somewhere close to adoration, mixed—incontrovertibly—with desire. My mom is experiencing *urges*.

Even worse, I am feeling a slight tinge of embarrassment for my mom; now I see her from Marc's perspective. This overweight American woman in her department-store clothes, her Gap jeans, her mussed gray hair. What will Marc think?

But why should I damn well care what Marc thinks? This is *my mom* and I love her and he can go to hell with his stupid beautiful suits. What right does he have to exude superiority?

And why am I so angry at myself if I don't care about Marc?

"X?"

Marc's voice interrupts my thoughts. Calm but firm.

I come to my senses with a jolt. I've been standing here vexing for twenty seconds. Both Marc and my mom are looking at *me*.

"Sorry. Uh . . . Sorry."

Come on, Alexandra, get a grip.

"Mom, this is . . . Marc. Marc Roscarrick. He's a . . . He's a . . ." *Spit it out.* "He's a friend, um . . . a friend I made here. In Naples, I mean."

Excellent . . . not.

I hurry on.

"And this is my mom, Marc. Angela. From San Jose. She's here on vacation. We're going to the Gambrinus, just for a coffee."

Marc's suntanned hand reaches out and takes my mother's and he lifts it to his mouth and imperceptibly kisses it, graciously and courteously, with that Old World insouciance that is simultaneously amused and amusing.

"I am grateful for the pleasure," he says, staring deep into her bespectacled Californian eyes.

I think my mom is actually going to swoon.

"Well, isn't this nice!" she says, in a kind of falsetto, whooping, I-may-have-recently-inhaled-helium voice; a voice I have literally never heard before. "It's so nice to meet you! So nice!"

Oh lord.

"So, Mom, ah, Marc and I . . ."

I begin to explain our friendship, but then I trail off, embarrassed. What can I say? Oh, Mom, meet Marc, he's a billionaire aristocrat into prehistoric S&M who fucked me into blissful oblivion the other night; shall we have some coffee? A bit of me *wants* to say this, of course. To show off. To tell her that I— yes, me, Alex Beckmann, the studious daughter, Spinster of the Year, two years running—*I snared a gorgeous billionaire. Then I chucked him.*

However, it doesn't really matter what I think because Mom is off, doing her own thing: she is trying to speak *Italian*.

The only problem with this is that my mom cannot speak Italian. As far as I know she has never spoken a foreign language, ever. Trying not to blush, resisting the urge to cover my eyes with my hands in mortification, I stare fixedly at the umbrella pines at the corner of the square beside the dingy royal palace, as Mom says: "Aha! So . . . um . . . *buon gonna, señor.*"

Señor? Does she think he's Spanish?

"Stop now, Mom. Please?

"*Due . . .*" she stumbles on. " . . . *señor* Rascorr . . . *Mie amigo.*"

Please. Stop. Mom.

At last she stops, realizing she is making an idiot of herself, and I can see she is beginning to flush, the color is rising in her cheeks and she is evidently embarrassed. Why should Marc humiliate her like this?

Before I can hit him, or cause a diverting scene, perhaps by assaulting a pigeon, Marc smiles and touches her gently on the shoulder and he laughs that warm, calm laugh and says, "Mrs. Beckmann, *per favore*, the painful truth is, most *Neapolitans* cannot speak Italian, so you really need not trouble yourself on my behalf."

It's a tiny little joke but it's just *exactly* the right little joke to relieve my mother of her embarrassment, and now she giggles girlishly, her humiliation gone. But my confusion is returning in fine style. Marc has said exactly the right thing; my mom is swooning; I think I want to fly to Rome.

"You were going to the Gambrinus?"

Marc is talking to me.

"Yes . . ."

"Will you allow me to buy you and your charming mother an aperitif? It would be my absolute pleasure."

I am in no position to say no. He knows we're going to the Caffè G. My mom now looks like a dog that has just been promised one of those filet steaks from Japan that cost three hundred dollars.

Reluctantly, I surrender. "Sure."

And so we cross the Piazza del Plebiscito and, of course, when we reach the Gambrinus, the waiters make a big fuss of Marc, escorting him, with much feudal bowing and scraping, to his usual table, the best table in the best cafe in Naples. Then the three of us sit down, and we drink Venezianos, and we look out at thronging, lively, triangular Piazza Trieste e Trento. And as the drinks come and go, Marc tells my mom stories about Naples life and she laughs and sips the glowing orange aperitifs, and nibbles the tiny prosciutto rolls, and laughs some more.

Then Marc stands and pays our bill, tipping the waiters lavishly. Finally, he kisses my mom's hand one last time—I suspect she won't wash it for a week—and then he disappears into the Neapolitan dusk.

Mom looks at me. She shakes her head as if amazed.

"Well, my word! What a *lovely* man! Why didn't you tell me you had such lovely friends? Tell me all about him!"

I tell her something about him, and then add some lies. I

tell her I met him at a couple of parties in Marechiaro and the Chiaia. I tell her we are friends and leave it at that. She gazes at me as I speak, sipping her Veneziano. She nods and eats the last delicious miniature pizza. And then she says, "He's not entirely unattractive, is he?"

"Mom."

"What? I'm just *saying*."

"So . . . ?"

"I may be three hundred years old, Alex, but I am not blind. And I am still a woman."

"He's okay."

"I'm guessing he's rich, too. The way he is . . . The way he acts and dresses. A kind of confidence?"

I mumble something about "import export" and "maybe a few million." Mom eyes me. I fidget and squirm, like a petulant child. This is predictable. I don't know why people worry about aging. All you have to do to knock all the years away is hang out with your parents. They can reduce you to a whining teenage brat in a matter of minutes. It's a species of magic.

But I want to move on.

"Shall we get some dinner? We can have pizza—there's a nice place near my apartment, on the Via Partenope."

Mom nods and wipes her mouth with a napkin. And says: "Is he married?"

"Who?"

"Darling."

"No."

"Engaged?"

"Don't know. How would I know? He goes out with models. Actresses. You know. People who appear in *People* magazine. *People* people."

"A rich, handsome man in want of a wife." Her expression is shrewd. Calculating.

"Don't try to marry me off, Mom. Not again. Remember you wanted me to marry Jeff Myerson in San Jose."

"He has Apple shares."

"He's five foot six."

"He could wear heels at the wedding?"

Our laughter is shared. Some kind of sanity is restored between us; the mother-daughter equilibrium has returned. We stand and she takes my arm and together we walk back to the seafront and the restaurants and pizzerias of Via Partenope. And over a margherita and a marinara, Mom tells me all about the family, how my younger brother, Paul (major-league jock, should have studied medicine), is faring at the University of Texas, at Austin, and how my older brother, Jonathan (bit of a stoner, never gonna settle down), has finally sorted himself out and got a nice girlfriend and a well-paying job at Google, and might now settle down.

I listen to all this quite happily, sipping my Montepulciano, literally the cheapest wine on the menu. None of my mom's tattle is news to me—I Skyped both my brothers over the weekend, as I do every week—but there is something comforting in simply hearing her say it, in her warm, loving, heedless chattering way. I am back in San Jose in the big family kitchen that smells of lemon and baking, and the sun is streaming in, and Mom is struggling to make sorbet and laughing as the gunk goes everywhere. And I am eleven years old and happy.

I had a happy childhood; my parents were kind and loving. I loved my brothers. Even the family dog was cute. It feels like a guilty secret, but it is true. Until I was twelve or thirteen I was entirely happy. It was in my teens that the boredom kicked in, or maybe it was something more than boredom: an existential tedium, something deep. Something that has never been satisfied. Going to the East Coast to study was an attempt to quench this thirst, but it wasn't enough. I want to *experience.* I crave something *more.* Life can't just be baking and sorbets and kids and a nice dog, wonderful as they are.

Mom has finished gossiping. I take her back to her hotel and kiss her in the lobby, and tell her how much it means to me, her coming to see me—and it does, it does. And I promise to meet her in the morning at ten to take her sightseeing.

And so I do. And, as I expected, it all goes very seriously downhill.

Mom doesn't like Naples.

I suspected she wouldn't. It's not her kind of place. Too wild, too outrageous, too pungent. Everywhere we go I see her wincing at the piles of garbage, or inwardly tutting at the graffiti, or staring in frank displeasure at the Vietnamese prostitutes inexplicably sitting on sofas in the middle of seedy, smelly, narrow cobblestoned streets by the Stazione Centrale.

Part of me wants to remonstrate with Mom. To tell her to take off her bourgeois suburban spectacles and see the beauty of Naples beneath the dirt and squalor: to see the authenticity, the realness, the incredible history. To see the old women polishing the sacred skulls in the caves of the cemetery of Fontanelle as they have done for centuries; to look in the single windows of the *bassi* and see the aging men in string vests with hairy shoulders eating friarelli greens, in houses built over buried Roman temples; to simply stand on my balcony and gaze down on streets laid out by Ancient Greeks, then look to the west and feel her heart rush at the twilit colors of sunset over Sorrento, a cassata of faded pink, pale violet, Barolo red, and pistachio green—finally melting into the black of night and the diamantine stars.

But my mom sees the grime and the drug addicts, and she doesn't like it. She even dislikes the lack of tourists, one of Naples's main attractions.

We are sitting on a terrace outside a cafe in the Old City, by the archaeological museum, and she frowns and looks tired and says, "Where is everyone?"

We are surrounded by Italians—yammering, gesturing, laughing, arguing Italians. We have barely managed to find a decent place to sit, but my mom is wondering where "everyone" is, by which she means "Where are all the sensible people?"—the tourists, her fellow Americans, English speakers, normal types.

I could tell her that they have all been chased away by the squalor and crime of Naples, and the reputation of the various mafias, but I'm not sure that will assist her mood. Or my mood, for that matter.

Because, if these few days have been a bit of a disappointment for my mom, they have been a total trial for me, too. The encounter with Marc has left me unsettled, agitated, as confused as before, missing him again. Worse still, everywhere we have been in Naples—me and Mom—has somehow served to *remind* me of him.

In the Duomo, the cathedral, we saw the great relic housing the sacred blood of St. Jenuarius—and this reminded me of that blissful roseate wine he served me for lunch, the Moscato Rosa. Every palazzo we explored along Via Toledo has reminded me of the one palazzo above all others: The Palazzo Roscarrick.

And then we went to the museum of Capodimonte, a rigid Bourbon palace, standing stiff and forlorn and unvisited on its sunny little hill, in its dusty little park. This is one of the world's great museums, and this time my mom was actually happy, enjoying her time alone with the Raphaels and Titians, the El Grecos and Bellinis—yet I was transfixed by one particular painting, by Caravaggio.

And the painting was *The Flagellation*.

What can you do? I can be nice to my lovely mom. On the last afternoon we take a taxi to the station; she's getting a train down the coast to meet her friend Margo in Amalfi.

It's four P.M. Mom looks at the waiter and says, proudly, in her improving Italian, "*Un cappuccino, per favore*." I remind myself not to cringe. Was this what I was like when I first arrived? Ordering cappuccino after twelve noon? Now I know it is a total faux pas. Did I eat spaghetti with knife and fork, like Mom? Probably. Oh dear. And now I hate myself for judging my mom. What a mess. Marc, what have you done?

Mom sits and sips at her cappuccino, trying not to look at the beggars across the great station hall. I have to be honest.

"Mom, I'm sorry you didn't like Naples."

"Oh, darling," she says. "It's not that I didn't like it, it's just that it's so . . . *different*."

"I'm sure you will like Amalfi more. It's beautiful. And clean."

Her hand reaches out and touches mine.

"I don't care about Naples. Or Amalfi," she says. "I care about *you*. My darling daughter, my only daughter. I am very proud of you."

"Why?"

"Because," she says, setting down her coffee cup. She stares deep into my eyes. "Because you are bright and beautiful—and because you are doing what I should have done."

I gaze across the table, wondering where this is going.

"You are living, Alexandra. You are alive. Seeing the world. I wish I had done that."

"Mom? What do you mean?"

"X, I love your father and I adore my kids, all three of you, even Jonny most of the time. But . . ."

I have never seen my mom like this—wrestling with some inner truth, something evidently painful. She stares into the deflated foam of her mistimed cappuccino, then looks at me again.

"You know, Alex, *I was never young. Not really.* And that's very sad."

"How—"

"I never realized I was young until it was too late. Please . . . don't do what I did."

And that's that. She stands; her train is waiting. I help her carry her bags to her carriage and she leans out the train window to wave good-bye, and there are something like tears in her eyes as the train takes off, and she mouths the words *I love you*, and I wave at her helplessly. Then I stand, watching the train until it rattles into nothing and, when it is completely gone, I have an enormous urge to cry.

This deep, abiding sadness stays with me for a day. I feel like the wilted dusty palms on Partenope. *I never realized I was young . . . Don't do what I did.*

I want experience. I am young. This is it. I will never be twenty-one in Naples again.

Late the next afternoon, I pick up the phone. Then I put it down. Then I hide it under a cushion. Then I retrieve it, and dial, and count the seconds, and wait.

"*Sì?*"

"*Buona sera.* Uh . . ."

"Yes?"

"Can I speak to Marc? Signor Roscarrick?"

"Who is it, please?"

"Alexandra. I mean X. Tell him it's X."

There is a pause. Marc comes on the line.

"Hello? X?"

Oh God, that voice. That accent. I want to kiss him through the phone. I want to cry on his shoulder. Then kiss him some more.

"Alex?"

"Marc, I . . . God . . . I . . . I want . . . I just, I'm sorry . . . I . . . I wonder . . . what are you doing?"

"You want to see me?"

This is it. I answer: "Yes."

"Come to the Gambrinus."

"Sorry?"

"Meet me there tonight, at seven. We need to talk first."

Click.

Thirteen

The Gambrinus. Of course. This is where it started, this is where it will end—or continue. I sit nervously at the table, trying not to look at my watch. I am ten minutes early. Maybe I should have been mysteriously late? Maybe I should have dressed up? I am in simple jeans and a simple top. I dithered over a minidress, but then I decided that looked too *needy*.

And maybe I am needy. I need him. And his kisses. Sipping my gin and tonic—hard liquor for resolve—I stare across the square. Nervous. And waiting. And looking at my watch again.

And here is Marc. At exactly seven P.M.

I glance pointedly at my watch as he joins me at my table. I need to ease the tension with small talk.

"Are you always this punctual?"

"Blame my mother," he says suavely, sitting down. "She drummed it into me. Punctuality is the politeness of princes."

"Or the virtue of the bored?"

He gazes my way, and he laughs; and our laughter is mutual.

And then I remember that we *get along*. In a very basic and simple way: we get along. And I need to hold on to this, if I am going to do what I have resolved to do.

"So," he says, and he is no longer laughing. "There can only be one reason you have summoned me."

"Yes."

"You have agreed to be initiated."

I swallow some gin and tonic.

"Yes."

His gaze is intense. He reaches out and takes my hand in his. He looks down at my white fingers, laced in his darker hand.

"You are absolutely sure, Alex?"

I hesitate, for a second. I am not absolutely sure. But I am sure *enough*.

"Yes, I am sure."

"Then the next time I see you will be at The Palazzo Roscarrick."

"What?"

He stands, abruptly, and drops a generous offering of euro notes on the table. "The bride and groom must not meet before the wedding; do they have that tradition in California?"

"I don't understand—"

"Come to the palazzo at midnight tomorrow."

"Tomorrow? But, Marc, what do I do? What do I wear?"

He stoops and takes my hand, kisses it. Then he steps away, gestures good-bye, and says, "Come as you are. Take a taxi. I will pay. Midnight tomorrow. *E ciao.*"

My taxi stops right outside the somber russet walls of The Palazzo Roscarrick. In the darkness, the streets of the Chiaia are different, subdued, echoing, and somehow . . . *expectant.* They are also menacingly deserted. I'm glad that Marc offered to pay for a taxi; I wouldn't have wanted to walk even this short distance alone.

Getting out of the car, I look down at myself. Assessingly.

For the last three hours I have been bathing, dressing, and preparing: ruthlessly plucking my eyebrows, glossing my lips just so, drying my hair with great care, and shaving diligently *everywhere.* I am also wearing my best perfume, pretty much my only really good perfume. Marc told me not to worry about my clothes, but I still felt a definite need to feel my best underneath my jeans and top. These careful preparations were also, in part, a way of calming myself before the initiation.

But the ruse hasn't really worked. My mind is alive with anxiety. What's going to happen? Will it happen now? Is this the first of the Mysteries, tonight? Is that why I was ordered here at midnight? But would the Mysteries really be enacted in Marc's very own home? He implied there were special venues, across Italy, Britain, France—that certainly didn't sound very domestic.

"*Grazie, grazie mille.*" Fumbling for the euros in my purse, I pay the cabdriver, who glances first at the money, then at me, and then at the great door of The Palazzo Roscarrick.

Is that a smile of pity or knowingness on his middle-aged face?

The taxi speeds away, scattering a few littered pizza boxes as it disappears around the corner.

The door looms before me. Swallowing away my anxieties as best I can, I hoist and drop the big iron door knocker. The noise clangs and echoes, perturbingly loud and ancient. Everything, in this light, seems older. Antique and historic, and hostile in its strangeness.

The door opens. A face peers out. It is one of Marc's manservants: the same man who opened the door to me the very first time I came here.

"Buona sera."

The familiarity of the face is welcome, but the man barely acknowledges that he recognizes me. Instead, he hands me a fifty-euro note for the cab—which is way too much. I protest, but he will not take change. He is unsmiling, and backs away, inviting me in. His demeanor is stiff and formal.

What is going on?

I step over the low wooden threshold into the hallway with its glinting suit of Oriental armor—samurai? Chinese? Ahead of me, the splashing fountain looks forlorn and silvery in the moonlight. The whole house still smells, quite divinely, of lilies and roses and southern, tropical blooms.

"This way," says the manservant.

We begin another walk through the long, quiet hallways. Everything is so unerringly hushed, and I am flooded with an almighty urge to flee. I hate this silence; it is the silence of a forest where a predator lurks.

Stop it, X.

"Where are we going?"

My question is pointless; I don't really expect an answer. I'm asking just for the sake of breaking the quietness. And indeed the servant does not reply. He walks on.

But then I am alerted by a different noise, and I pause, looking into the scented gloom. Yes. I think I can hear giggles in the distance. Behind a few doors, there are girlish giggles—then nothing.

Is someone watching me from above? The passages and corridors are so dim: lit elegantly yet rather faintly by candles set in beautiful antique chandeliers of gilded wood and crystal.

The historian in me is impressed: the lighting is entirely correct for the period of the palazzo's construction—seventeenth to eighteenth century. Someone with good taste has therefore restored—or fabulously maintained—these light fittings, probably at serious expense.

I have no doubt it is Marc. A man who wears suits that elegant would know how to fix a house with equal flair.

But if the historian in me is approving of Marc's taste, the lone woman is agitated. To hell with the chandeliers; I want neon. I want blazing strip lighting dissolving every shadow. Frightening away the darkness so no one can giggle, unnervingly, in a black and blinded corner.

Finally, the monotone manservant speaks. "This is it."

We've reached a fairly insignificant doorway, painted gray. The servant creaks the ivory door handle and gestures me inside.

"Oh God," I say, quite involuntarily.

The room within is as beautiful as its entrance is humdrum. Lit by soft candles in cages of glass and cast-iron, its walls are decorated entirely in Pompeian style, with frescoes of long-tailed birds and sweet prancing antelope surrounding the kohl-eyed faces of young Roman women, nude or dancing, erotic and demure—with rich scarlet borders of trellised vines and grapes.

"Take off your clothes and wear this," the manservant says. He hands me a soft and folded silk dress, so light in my hands it is barely there.

"But—"

"All your clothes. When you are ready, please exit through that door."

He points to a second door, cut into the Pompeian red decor; it is cleverly made to look like a Roman door, a fake door that is a real door—an elegant trompe l'oeil.

"And remember this," the man adds, ponderously. "If ever you want anything to stop, you must say *Morpheus*."

"Sorry?"

"If ever you are . . . uncomfortable, you must say, out loud, the word *Morpheus*. If you cannot speak, then clap your hands three times."

And that is it. The manservant closes the first door, leaving me quite alone. I can hear the faint strains of music somewhere. And it is beautiful music: soothing choral voices, centuries old, but vivid and tranquil and alive, some kind of Mass.

It is perfectly timed. How could anything bad happen in a world with music like this?

Just take off your clothes, X. That's all. I just have to *take off my clothes*.

In the flickering candlelight I remove my T-shirt, my Converse sneakers, my white socks, and then I unbutton my jeans. I deliberately dressed down as instructed. My only indulgence was underwear: I chose nice panties. Why? Maybe I just knew that most of my clothes were going to be swiftly removed, so it didn't matter.

But now I am naked.

The simple silk dress weighs, in my hands, maybe three ounces. Like something weighed on the moon. I admire its exquisite stitching for a moment, then I slip it over me, and it descends with an aristocratic sigh to my knees. It is sublimely silken, probably the softest thing I have ever worn, and maybe the most expensive.

In the flickering and adoring light of the candles I can see that the dress is a flame-orange hue, verging on red. But it is also see-through. The cleanly waxed delta of my pubic hair is clearly visible.

I can't do it. I just *can't*. Giving in to my shyness, I slip my lacy black panties back on and then I close my eyes and count to seven.

Be calm, X, be calm.

My mouth is dusty dry; my hands are damp with nerves. My white feet are bare on the polished parquet floor. I open the second, "fake" door in the red-painted wall.

And step through.

Beyond, the light is so broken and scintillating, and glittering and strange, I do not quite understand; it takes me several seconds. Then I realize: *the room is made of porcelain*.

During my research into Neapolitan history, I have read about rooms like this—porcelain rooms—built by the richest of the nobility at the very height of the city's power and affluence. Deliriously impractical, almost impossible to keep clean, yet intoxicatingly lovely. The white porcelain of the walls and ceiling is decorated with wild narcissi and curveting blue sea serpents, all fashioned from more porcelain. And the chamber is illuminated by silver and wooden candelabras, which are being held aloft by four servants, who are very much alive.

I do a double take. In each of the four corners is a handsome young man, in uniform—presumably the livery of the Roscarrick family. The servants are staring fixedly ahead, certainly not at me, and they are holding candelabras, which afford the only light.

And in the center of the room is a large, simple wooden chair, with its back to me. The chair looks medieval, like a throne for a Dark Age king. The choral music drifts across the room from some unseen speaker: holy, spectral, sensuous.

"Come here, X."

It is Marc's voice. He is sitting in the chair.

I am glad I wore my panties. I am otherwise naked under this see-through dress: barefoot and nude and bashful, like the women in the frescoes at the Villa of Mysteries. My nipples are tingling in the fresh air of the porcelain room. I am aroused already. I wish I wasn't. But I am.

I step around the chair and look at Marc, who is deep in shadow. I can barely see his face, only his noble profile.

"Don't look at me."

"But what do you want me to do?"

"Bend over, X."

"What?"

"Bend over my knee. The first of the Mysteries is simple submission, in public. I am going to spank you in front of my servants."

I want to laugh; yet the ambience is entirely serious. And a little objectionable. He's going to *spank* me? In front of his servants?

No.

"You can leave. Or you can submit."

"Marc—"

"And you must call me *Celenza*. During the Mysteries, you may only call me Celenza."

"Marc—"

"It means *Excellency*. But in Italian the *c* is pronounced as in cello. So you call me Celenza, or sir—or you can leave. With all that this entails."

My entire upbringing is telling me to go. My feminist soul is instructing me to leave. And yet—and yet—something in me wants him to spank me. Is this me? Is this the effect of the music and the candlelight, and the fabulous room of porcelain? Or maybe I just want *him*, so I will agree to anything?

My mind is swimming. I feel a need to let someone else decide. I feel a need to submit, just to get it over with.

"Celenza," I say, and I cannot believe I am saying it, "spank me."

My whole body is tensed. I walk close, and lay myself over his lap, facedown. My bare feet are in the air, I have one hand pressed to the floor to steady myself. I can sense the servants looking. I don't care so much. This is seriously arousing, and simultaneously disturbing. I am outraged, and yet I am wet *between*.

He gently lifts up my new silk dress and says, "Tut tut, X."

"Celenza?"

"Panties?"

"I just . . . I didn't—"

He doesn't wait for an explanation. He is starting to peel down my best Victoria's Secret panties. With the dark lacy frill. My hand reaches instinctively to stop him—these men are looking at me; surely, they mustn't see me—but then I feel Marc's firm hand on my wrist.

"You have to let me, X."

I want him to stop. I want him to carry on. I want *him*.

Closing my eyes in shame, yet tingling with arousal— why?—I drop my hand.

"Celenza."

He has my permission. Slowly and carefully he pulls down the panties, peeling them down my calves, over my bare ankles, then he drops them into some kind of basket—I can't quite see because I am sprawled. I can feel the cold air on my bottom. This is it. He is going to spank me. In front of these men I have never met. His servants. The intensity of my confusion is baroque. But inside me is desire. Go on and do it. Do it.

He does it. With a smarting and shameful pain, I sense the slap of his hand. My buttocks quiver.

"Count."

What? What does he mean? I manage to speak: "Celenza?"

"You must count, as I spank. In Italian."

A pause. He is leaning to his left and doing something. Then I realize he is drinking red wine. The casual, offhand nature of this is no doubt part of my submission, my initiation. And it too is bizarrely stirring. I can feel the sweet, urgent irritation of a very serious pleasure, like gorgeous pins and needles down there, down there. Oh more. More please. Scratch this gorgeous little itch. Stop this, don't stop. Stop this, but *don't stop*.

He spanks me again, harder this time. My bare ass is in the air and he is spanking me. And men are watching. And I am counting, aloud.

"*Uno.*"

Spank.

"*Due.*"

Spank.

"Open your legs."

I resist this, as best I can, but his firm hand is between my naked thighs, prising me open. And maybe I actually want him to do this. Because I can feel myself dissolving, where my legs meet.

He spanks me.

"*Tre.*"

Again and again he spanks me, and I start to breathe deeper, and then I gasp, with a mixture of shame and shameful delight. I don't know where this gasp comes from; I don't know where this embarrassing *desire* comes from, but it is brilliant and glittering, it is candlelight on glorious porcelain, it is rose and red and fabulous. I want him to spank me *harder*. The humiliation is delicious.

"Celenza."

"X?"

"Spank me harder. Please, sir."

He obliges. This one stings, very beautifully. I am nearly full up, I am almost topping out. Nine, ten, eleven.

Spank.

It is like someone applauding my nakedness. I feel wild; I want to be totally naked. I am tremblingly close to some kind of outrageous and unexpected climax.

"You ran away in Pompeii."

Spank.

"You didn't do what I said."

Spank.

I am half moaning. And wholly desirous.

"I am sorry, Celenza, spank me harder."

Spank.

Oh, his hand on my bare ass. I want it forever. I don't care if men are watching. I want them to watch. The pain is so sweet, so delicate, so erotically naughty and delightfully embarrassing. How can you feel all these things at once? Now I can sense his hand delicately fluttering on my clitoris—then spanking me again—then trembling and soft on my clit—then spank, and spank, and once again spank.

That one was the hardest. I bite my lips. But it doesn't work. I am gasping.

Yes yes YES.

SPANK ME.

As his fingers press with sweet firmness on my clitoris and his hand hits my bare ass, I think of these servants watching *me*, Alex Beckmann, being spanked so hard and so firmly by *him*, Marc Roscarrick. And as he spanks me hard and then hard and then harder, three or four or five more times, this triggers some inner release, some strange, different climax, like a waterfall of silver roses, a cataract of platinum dollars, a glorious uprush of scintillating relief.

"Oh God, oh God . . . ohhh . . ."

"X?"

"*Grazie*, Celenza . . ." I am mumbling, and panting. "*Grazie*."

Fourteen

I lie draped over Marc's lap, half naked and quite replete. He snaps an order in Italian—this time in dense Neapolitan dialect—and his manservants set down their candelabras on side tables and disappear. It is just him and me and the room of prancing porcelain antelopes, eternally jaunting in the guttering light.

I rise unsteadily to my feet, reaching for Marc's shoulder by way of support—my knees are actually wobbling—but he picks me up and carries me to the end of the room. Brusquely, he kicks open a door and transports me into what appears to be a dimly lit bedroom.

I am woozy, made incapable by my strange climax. I nestle my head on his shoulder and kiss the crook of his neck, inhaling his bodywash, inhaling *him*, as he carries me across the room and gently lays me down onto a vast bed. And so I lie there happy, strange, dreamy, and half asleep, yet still significantly aroused.

Then he takes off the dress, strips himself, and begins to make love to me.

First he pushes my thighs apart, slowly and firmly. It is all somehow the opposite of what has gone before: caressing, very tender, and gentle. And I am lost in smooth and bewildered delight. I clutch at the sheets as he descends my body and licks me there, again, where it counts. Celenza, Celenza.

Excellency.

For several minutes he pleasures me, licking my clit with unnerving expertise, biting softly on my thighs, then licking again. Just as I tire of one, he does the other; he senses my sexual moods telepathically—bite, lick, then bite and lick. And as he does this, I lie back in my swooning state and I stare into the darkness, and I gasp and I sigh and I think of the spanking.

It was so erotic, but why? What has he done to me? How could I enjoy that? My feminist self is incensed, but my sexual self is abandoned and gleeful. Positively *gleeful*.

"Marc—"

I am close to coming, oh so close to coming, but I want to kiss him. My handsome man, the man who spanked me.

"Marc?"

He lifts his face from between my legs, he ascends my naked body—and he kisses me deeply, and again. And then he stops kissing me and he slips a thumb into my mouth. For a moment I suck on his thumb—but then I suddenly bite down, pretty hard, to punish him for spanking me. I don't know why I do this.

"Ow," he says. And he smiles.

And I open my mouth, and I say, "You bastard, Roscarrick."

"But you were so beautiful, darling, your beautiful white ass."

"Marc."

"Though, truth be told, it is a little pinker now."

"But they all *saw*."

He smiles again. His breath is scented with wine. We are entwined. He kisses my nose and says, "And you enjoyed it, didn't you?" His pale blue eyes are inches from mine; we are staring into each other's eyes, maybe into each other's souls. "Didn't you? You enjoyed it a lot. *Bad* little girl."

I cannot lie. I cannot even shake my head. I just want him inside me. I just want another delicious orgasm. Like the prosciutto rolls at the Gambrinus. These orgasms are so more-ish.

"Make me come."

"Sì sì, bella donna."

He descends once more and pushes my thighs apart; his expert tongue touches me *there* for about seventeen seconds and then I simply orgasm. Just like that. *Seventeen seconds.* I am grasping the air, my toes tighten, I remember the spanking, and the climax is intense. And oh so easy, so easy.

What is happening to me? It used to be so hard for me to come, so difficult with my boyfriends; now it is like the best kind of childish trick, this is all you do, you see, this is the knack, the way you ride a bike, the way to juggle, just this, just this, just here, just like that, there, you see? Ahhhhh.

Silly, X, silly. It could have been like this all along. All you needed was a handsome, expert, Anglo-Italian billionaire aristocrat; you could have gotten one at the drugstore.

And now I am exquisitely tired.

"Good night . . . Good night."

He kisses the tip of my nose.

"Piccolina."

I am slipping into sleep on Marc's vast white bed. That

music is still playing. Choral and sublime. It is now a lullaby. Sleep comes, quick and demanding. I have final thoughts. Sweet, final thoughts. For the first time in my life, I am going to spend the night in Marc Roscarrick's bed. The sensation is of infinite luxury; cool, clean sheets, and a distant yet profound satiation.

I wake to bright but filtered sun. Marc is sleeping next to me, tanned and handsome with his tousled hair. A stripe of sun illuminates his dark shoulder. I see he has a small scar there: a curious, subtle, curving scar, like a minor knife wound.

Now the memories return, surging and urgent. I try to calm the renewing fight between guilt and happiness inside me. Did I really let Marc spank me in front of his servants? How on earth did that happen?

And yet it was a turn-on. It just *was*.

Public submission. Is that really the first of the Mysteries?

If it was, the Mystery is: I feel *liberated*. Something has unknotted inside me, a psychic tension has been released, a complex knot has been unraveled. So I was naked, and very sexual, and submissive in front of others? So what, who cares, what gives?

Marc sleeps on. I rub my eyes, yawn hungrily, and gaze around the bedroom, seeing it for the first time in real daylight.

It is *not* what I expected. I'm not quite sure *what* I anticipated: four-poster beds, Louis XIV chairs, gilding and paneling and lion paws? But Marc's bedroom is decidedly modern.

The bed is huge and low, dark and wooden. The walls are pale, painted a northern creamy-gray, inset with acres of windows, partly shuttered. Marc must have had these new big windows knocked through. The main table is an entire cross-section of a tree—exquisitely polished—and decorated with an abstract, hand-blown glass sculpture. Minimalist yet expressive.

A few neckties lie discarded on the parquet floor; just the right amount of disorder. The rugs might be from London, modern blocks of color.

My eyes eat it all up greedily. Two Barcelona chairs stare at me from the distant corner. I may not know my Baroque and Renaissance so well, but I know modern art and design. These are surely original Barcelona chairs by Mies van der Rohe.

A large bookcase stands against the opposite wall—full of reassuringly well-read, spine-cracked books. Two sizable and carefully framed photos decorate the wall above me. Are these Gursky? Andreas Gursky? It is all subdued and personal and modern—yet supremely comfortable. You could sleep here for a year, only to be woken by *Vogue Interiors* come to have a look.

The sole touch of historicity—the only sign you are in a Bourbon-era palazzo—is an eighteenth-century portrait of a beautiful woman in a billowing and sumptuous blue dress on the final wall. It looks English. It could be Gainsborough; hell, it probably *is* Gainsborough.

I wonder if that is Marc's great-great-great-whatever grandmother. Probably it is. She's beautiful and slightly sad, framed by her dark room, with a human skull on the table next to her. Symbolizing mortality? Her cleavage is very visible and her lips are very red. Symbolizing sex? There is a riding crop on the floor, too. Symbolizing flagellation? Was she the first Roscarrick initiated into the Mysteries?

Intimations of anxiety begin to needle me. I rise, embarrassed by my nakedness, and cross the room. I'm looking for the bathroom. Here? Or here?

There are two bathrooms. One is darker and masculine, full of aftershaves and razors and shaving mirrors and badger-hair shaving brushes by "Geo Trumper of Curzon Street Mayfair." I see fencing masks and two swords stacked in a dark wooden cupboard. So that's how he keeps fit. Fencing. Dueling. *Swordplay*.

Then I step back out and walk into a second, much more feminine bathroom, which is almost as big as my apartment. Grabbing a bathrobe from the hook on the door, I investigate—feeling a little guilty as I go. And wondering just who else has been in here.

The bathtub is maybe a yard deep; you could wash sheep in it. The fittings are bright and sparkling, the enormous mirrors glitter with decorous lighting. I open a few cupboard doors. The soaps are new and from Firenze, the towels are possibly laundered in heaven. It is like a five-star-hotel bathroom, only nicer.

Maybe Marc could let me live here—just let me live in the bathroom. That would be fine. I could have sandwiches brought in.

I shower under the half-meter-wide showerhead, grab one of the many spare toothbrushes, clean my teeth, dry my hair, then slip into the robe again—still feeling slightly awkward, like this is a hotel but I haven't paid. I step back into the bedroom.

Marc is standing there, also in a bathrobe. He smiles and crosses to my side, then runs his fingers through my shower-wet hair and kisses me deeply. He draws back.

"Good morning, X."

I hesitate. I speak.

"*Buongiorno*, Marc."

We kiss. We kiss again. Three times. He smells of soap and shampoo and himself. The disturbing desire for him returns. The warm sorbet inside, melting sweetly. Wanting to be licked.

Be careful, X. Be careful.

Then I notice that breakfast has appeared, and sits on the bed on two shining trays. This *is* just as I imagined it. Silver carafes of pink grapefruit juice, silver jugs of dark, rich coffee, two tiny silver juglets of gorgeous cream. And plates of brioche, sfogliata, pain au raisin, and various fruits—mango, white peach, and tiny wild strawberries.

"God, I'm hungry," I say reflexively. We are both sitting on the bed now, divided by the breakfast tray.

"You are?"

"Yes. Sorry. Is that wrong?"

"But . . ." He sighs. "All you had to do was lie there, over my lap." He is gazing at me, his face expressionless. "It's not like you burned a lot of calories."

I look at him. What is he saying? I realize—belatedly—that he is joking. I throw a chunk of brioche in his direction. He laughs, and tuts.

"I had to do *all* the work, X."

"Marc!"

"My right arm might never recover. Do you think I should see an osteopath?"

He laughs again. And his laughter is genuine and contagious—and somehow a very serious relief. The tension in me instantly subsides. Now I laugh with him, and I crawl across the bed and push him back onto the pillows, and then I climb up and straddle him. I am pinning him down, his chest under my thighs, and I laugh as I lean down and kiss him, and he laughs as he leans up and kisses me. And then I say, "You were pathetic, anyway, Lord Roscarrick."

"What?"

"Call that a spanking? I barely noticed."

"Oh really?"

"Really," I say. "I think I actually fell *asleep* at one point."

He smiles and sits up higher, but I am still straddled over his groin. I can sense his arousal, hard under me, as he looks at me. His eyes are blue, yet dark with desire, as he says, "Show me your breasts, Miss Beckmann."

"No."

"*Per favore, signorina.* Take pity on a humble billionaire."

"Sorry. I need my breakfast. Then I have to go do some work."

"Really?"

"Really," I say. "We can't all sit around in our *Barcelona chairs*, wearing Gieves and Hawkes suits."

He looks up at me, shrewdly.

"I am gratified."

"Why?"

"No one ever noticed the chairs before."

"They're original, aren't they?"

"Yes," he says. "Purchased them at auction four years ago. I've never . . . well . . . since my wife died. There's never been anyone who really understood . . . *anything*. Not my life, not my interests, not anything." His smile is sweet, almost boyish. And tinged with sadness.

"Well, I'm hungry," I say—though I am glowing a little inside. Climbing off him, I return to my breakfast. He drinks juice and coffee and checks his phone for messages. I eat, happily, and drink coffee, and taste those wild strawberries and sweet brioche. Because I really am famished. Who knew that spanking could be so appetizing? As well as arousing?

"So," I say, swallowing a mouthful of buttered brioche, "Marc. *Tell me.* Was that the First Mystery?"

"Yes." He drops the phone on the bed. "The First and the simplest."

"But what's it meant to prove? I don't get it. I mean . . ." A faint blush rises to my face. "It was erotic, Marc, don't get me wrong. Surprising, but, yes, erotic. Very erotic."

"I gathered."

"But I don't see how they fit . . ."

"The Mysteries are public and often sexual, and to complete them you must show an ability to submit. You passed."

"I did?"

"Oh yes. Top marks. Alpha plus."

"But, God. My bare ass!"

"Is divine. You are Venus Callipygia."

I squint his way.

"Sorry? Venus callywhat?"

"Venus Callipygia. Venus of the beautiful buttocks. Venus of the gorgeous bottom."

"She's a Greek goddess?"

"Yes. And you are her avatar."

He is reaching for me. I giggle and rise, skipping away from his grasp.

"I have to get dressed, Marc. I really do have work to do—studying. Where are my clothes?"

He sighs, semi-seriously. "They're in that wardrobe. Cleaned and pressed."

Of course. Why wouldn't they be cleaned and pressed? He has about six hundred staff, he probably has a whole team of valets, ready to sew new buttons on old shirts overnight.

Opening the closet door I find my jeans and my sneakers and my white socks—and my Victoria's Secret panties. All wrapped in delicate tissue paper. I had thought these black lacy panties were a touch of luxury, of subtle eroticism—now they feel rather stupid and gauche. But I don't care. I am feeling good, verging on gleeful. Emancipated.

Alexandra Beckmann, the Virgin of New Hampshire, has been exceptionally naughty. And I like it.

When I am jeaned and shirted, I turn; Marc is half-dressed in jeans and another immaculate white shirt, with another aristocratically frayed collar. I have questions.

"Marc . . . what happens next?"

He buttons his white double cuffs with silver links and looks me straight in the eye.

"The Second Mystery takes place in two weeks."

I chirp. "What happens this time? Do you spank me in a soccer stadium? Do we dance naked on TV?"

He is not smiling.

"X, you should know . . . The Second Mystery is. . . ." His expression darkens. "More challenging. This is where it *really* begins."

And then that flash of sad anger appears on his handsome face, just briefly. That tragic but menacing anger. And my heartbeat flutters with anxiety and confusion. And my soul is full of helpless and stupid desire. Because I am scared, and I am also falling in love.

Fifteen

It's becoming a cycle, I see it now. Or perhaps a kind of courtly eighteenth-century dance, a cotillion, or a stately minuet, where the dancers—the man and the woman—advance toward each other, then retreat, advance, then retreat, but *each time they advance they get a little closer*, until at last they are united. Forever?

Right now, lying here in my room, clothed but barefoot, staring at the shadows of the sun on the ceiling of my apartment, and otherwise reading a scatter of books, I am pretty sure I am in retreat. Because I am reading more about the origins of the Camorra and the 'Ndrangheta.

I am determined to keep reading because I am determined not to forget the reason I came to Naples, however bewitching my affair—my liaison—my passion—my swooning foolishness— what is it?—with Marc. If I gave up my academic vocation and my projected thesis, I would be abandoning myself entirely to him, somehow.

Besides, I am *interested* in this history, because I am interested in all history.

But the more I read, the more I wonder about Marc, in a bad way. Opening one bookmarked page I frown, and reread an underlined passage for the third time this morning.

> The Garduña was a secret criminal society in Spain, which originated in the late Middle Ages. Initially little more than a prison gang, it grew into a more organized entity, involved with robbery, kidnapping, arson, and commissioned assassinations. The notorious statutes of the Garduña are said to have been approved in Toledo in 1420; according to some historians, the secret criminal clan later evolved into the Neapolitan Camorra during the Spanish dominion over southern Italy.

My eye alights on this paragraph in particular:

> A Calabrian folk song provides evidence for this Italian legacy. It tells the story of three Garduña "brothers," or three Spanish knights, who flee Spain in the seventeenth century after brutally murdering the seducer of their beloved sister. The three men are shipwrecked on the island of Favignana, near Sicily. The first man, Carcagnosso, protected by St. Michael, makes his way to Calabria and founds the 'Ndrangheta. The second, Osso, devoted to St. George, makes his way to Sicily and founds the Mafia. The third knight, Mastrosso, a devotee of the Virgin Mary, makes his way to Naples and founds the Camorra. . . .

I pause and listen to my own heart, softly beating.

Marcus Roscarrick.

Lord Marcus Roscarrick.

Lord Marcus James Anthony Xavier Mastrosso Di Angelo Roscarrick.

Inside I shudder, just a little. Is that mere coincidence? Why would Marc have a name that links him to the Spanish Garduña, the alleged precursors of the Camorra? If his family intermarried with the Bourbon nobility in the eighteenth and nineteenth centuries, then that meant intermarrying with the Spanish as well as the Italians, because the Bourbons were originally from Spain. Just like the Camorra were from Spain—or so it is surmised.

I put down the book and listen to the noises of Naples outside. The ferry for Ischia is hooting in the sun, the taxis are honking furiously on Via Nazario.

I pick up a different book: the etymology of Neapolitan life. Here is a passage I have already scored and underlined, twice.

> *Guappo* (plural: *guappi*) is a word in Neapolitan dialect, meaning thug, bully, or braggart. While today the word is often used to indicate a member of the Camorra, the *guapperia* (or *guapparia*; i.e., the *guappo* culture) predates Camorra and was originally very different.

I bite a fingernail and think.

The street kids who assaulted me in the Quartieri Spagnoli called Marc "*guappo*." I dismissed it at the time, as just some dialect insult. Indeed, I would dismiss it now, if it wasn't for the following passage:

The word derives from the Spanish *guapo*, meaning a bold, elegant, and ostentatious man, and it probably and ultimately derives from the Latin *vappa*. The word might, alternatively, be derived from the Garduña, à criminal organization in Spain. The Garduña was composed of *guapos*, generally good swordsmen, daring assassins, and committed bandits.

Swordsmen. They were fighters and *swordsmen*. Moreover:

The figure of the *guappo* is not necessarily synonymous with the *Camorrista*. He is also and uniquely a historical figure in the Neapolitan area, distinguishable by his dandylike appearance and his ostentatious poise. The *guappo* could be subdivided in turn, into the "simple" or "upper-class" *guappo*, according to the clothes he wore: the former preferred extravagant attire, while the latter preferred to dress in clothes from the best tailors in Naples.

Does this fit Marcus? Yes, maybe; no, surely not? Yes? Marcus Roscarrick is not some aspiring dandy, some silly, swaggering, suited-and-booted hero of the barrios; he is a true aristocrat. He dresses with exquisite taste but it is subtle, unostentatious, discreet, apparently effortless—like an English duke, as I imagine it. Indeed, he dresses like the Anglo-Italian lord that he *is*.

Yet the kids used the word *guappo*, quite definitely.

It's way too much to take in.

I drop the books and sigh. There is more—the Mafia, the 'Ndrangheta, the oaths, the secret meetings, *the initiations*—but it is all so confusing.

And it will have to wait for another day, because Jessica is banging on the door.

"X! Are you up?"

"Uh-huh . . ."

"You got a visitor."

Briskly slipping on my sandals, I open the door. Jessica points excitedly to the balcony and we both step outside into the warm, sunny air.

"See."

We look down. There is a small silver Mercedes sports car parked directly outside our apartment block. A man leans against it, young, handsome, smoking, in a tight and well-fitting black suit and sunglasses. Black shoes. Almost a uniform, but not quite.

"He buzzed my bell by mistake," says Jess, who is wearing a white minidress that manages to be demure and come-hither at the same time. "He's hot, isn't he? Looks like he should be in *The Godfather*. The one with De Niro." She laughs. "Says he's called Giuseppe, and works for Lord Perfect." I gaze down as Jessica babbles away. "I may have to get a tiny tiny tiny tiny *tiny* bit *amorevole* with him."

"Giuseppe? I think I've met him before . . ."

"That's nice. Anyway, he says he wants to see you."

"But—"

"Guess he's your designated driver, sweetie."

"But—"

"Stop butting. The Jesus of Hot is down there. With a Mercedes."

I look down at the car and the driver. I call his name— "Giuseppe?"—and he looks up and smiles. And yes, I definitely recognize him. Because he was the first of the men who rescued me in the Spanish Quarters.

Giuseppe smiles again, very engagingly, and does an amusing and gracious bow, gesturing at the car like a bewigged and powdered servant inviting me to step into a horse-drawn carriage somewhere in the Austro-Hungarian empire in about 1765.

"Yo! Say hello to Cinderella!" says Jessica in a singing voice, doing a special dance move that seems to involve pointing my way, then at the ceiling. "Watch you don't turn into a pumpkin."

"I shall avoid crystal slippers."

Jessica pouts. And sings some more. Then I say, "Why don't you come down with me, Jess? Let's see what it all means."

Two minutes later we are on the sidewalk and Giuseppe is bowing again, and smiling, and saying, in unexpectedly good English, "Hello, Miss Beckmann."

"Hi."

Another sly and winning smile. I hear Jess mutter "Gorgeousaurus Rex!" under her breath, and Giuseppe announces, "I am available to drive you wherever you like. On the orders of Lord Roscarrick."

Confusion returns.

"But why?"

"Because that is my order. Alternatively, you may wish to drive yourself, Miss Beckmann."

Giuseppe is dangling car keys in his hand.

"But . . ." I gaze at Marc's beautiful car, apparently being loaned to me. It is the sister car to his dark, silver-blue Mercedes sports, though perhaps a little smaller. "I can't, Giuseppe. I might scratch it, Neapolitan traffic, you know."

Giuseppe steps closer and folds the car keys into my hand.

"Miss Beckmann, you do not understand. This is *your* car."

"What?"

"It is yours. All yours. A present from Lord Roscarrick." He steps back, does another polite bow, and says, "It is yours to keep. You can drive it to Rome, or maybe Moscow, or maybe not. As you wish." Then he turns smartly on his heels and walks down Via Santa Lucia toward the seafront.

I am opening and closing my mouth in apparent mimicry of a dying fish. Staring at this beautiful car.

My car?

Jessica is gazing at the gorgeous little car in similar style. Finally she says, "A Mercedes sports? He's given you a Mercedes *sports*?"

"I know. I know."

She frowns.

"It's a bloody insult, is what it is. Only a Mercedes?"

She is giggling. Now I am giggling, likewise.

Putting on my best thoughtful expression, I say, "I might have to get a bit *snippy* with him. Tell him I won't accept anything less than a Bentley."

"Or a Lamborghini. With leopard-skin seats."

We laugh. Then I say, "I can't take it, obviously."

Jessica pouts. Again.

"*What?* Why not?"

"Look at it, Jess. It's a Mercedes. It's just *wrong*."

"But wait, X, *wait*. Don't be too hasty. Let's give this a good long think." Jess pauses for a third of a second, then says, "Okay, finished thinking: I say you keep the car, and we go for a ride."

I ponder for a moment. I am very sure I am going to refuse this gift; it is too much, too outrageous. But maybe we *could* have just one ride. One single day of fun. Then return it.

"I'm not going to keep it."

"Really?"

"Yes. Really."

"Okay . . ." Jess nods. "Okay, yes, that's probably best. Tell you what: shall I look after it? I'll give it to a nunnery. Honest."

"But we can go for a ride, for just one day."

Jess punches the air.

"Yay! But where?" Jess moues pensively. "Where shall we go? Amalfi? Positano?"

"Can't. Might run into Mom. How am I going to explain a Mercedes sports car?"

Jessica nods.

"I know," she says. "Let's go to Caserta, that big palace . . ."

"Biggest garden in the world, isn't it?"

"I've always wanted to go there. Come on, Cinderella. Drive like a pirate."

We climb in. I insert the key gingerly. Jessica starts playing with the GPS, eagerly tapping in our destination. I just sit there, staring at the dash in amazement, and with a little trepidation.

I've never driven a sports car before. I've never driven a Mercedes before. And I have very definitely never driven a brand-new Mercedes sports car through the chaotic, chariot-racing streets of Naples, with its battered Fiats and almost-as-battered Alfa Romeos, jostling with garbage trucks that never collect garbage and sinister limousines with very tinted rear windows.

But I turn the key, pull out, and drive anyway. And despite my nearly running over an old lady near Scampia, and despite my nearly driving straight into the plateglass storefront of a Supero Supermercati just outside Marcianise, after a giggly lunch, we make it to the Palace of Caserta.

Yet strangely enough, this famous eighteenth-century place somehow *disappoints* us.

It is said to be the Versailles of Bourbon Italy, and yet—

perhaps like Versailles—it is simply too *big*. The grandiose marble staircases rise like the endless staircases in dreams and they lead into huge echoing rooms filled with melancholy and nothingness, with gigantic windows that gaze at the rather slummy streets of Caserta town. And the gardens are just *numbingly* enormous, stretching miles into the sunlit haze. They intimidate rather than inspire.

Dwarfed and inert, we stand here as Jessica reads from her guidebook: "The palace has some twelve hundred rooms, including two dozen state apartments, a large library, and a theater modeled after the Teatro di San Carlo of Naples."

"Twelve hundred rooms?"

"Twelve hundred rooms," Jessica repeats. "The population of Caserta Vecchia was moved ten kilometers to provide a workforce closer to the palace. A silk factory, San Leucio, was disguised as a pavilion in the immense parkland."

"You could hide New York in this garden."

Jessica nods, and sighs, and we both look up the long, long path that stretches to some faraway fountains. The fountains could be as big as the pyramids; it is impossible to tell at this distance. She goes on. "The Caserta Palace has been used as a location in a number of movie productions. In 1999 it appeared in *Star Wars Episode I: The Phantom Menace*, as the setting for Queen Amidala's Royal Palace on Naboo."

"Naboo? Who knew? We're in Naboo!" I am laughing, but I am also tired. "Come on, Jess. Let's go home."

And so we do. But my mood is darkening swiftly with the day. By the time we are halfway back to Naples the sky is dusky, with threatening rain clouds skidding across the rising moon, and the traffic is slow and painful. Which gives me time to stare out the window in amazement at all the fires dotted across the half-urban countryside; fires on the outskirts of scruffy townships, fires next to tatty old factories.

"What the hell? What's going on?"

I gesture at the fires, crackling in the chilly night breeze. Jessica nods, and yawns.

"You've never seen this before?"

"No."

She rubs her tired face and says, "It's the Camorra—they burn garbage, illegally. Toxic waste, factory trash, anything. They burn it at night. In a zone, like an arc, all around the bloody outskirts of Naples. Some people also call it the Triangle of Death."

"Great. Because?"

"Poisonous waste enters the water system from illegal dumping and burning; the incidence of cancer here is one of the highest in Italy—there's a triangular zone where the Camorra are particularly active."

The traffic speeds up and we drive past more fires. I gaze across the satanic scenery of flames and wind and darkness.

The most paradoxical thing, the most disturbing thing, is that the scenery is kind of beautiful—a glittering nightscape of fires and moonlit palms and desolate concrete suburbs, white as bones. Here is beauty and evil in one. Like a handsome man with a tendency toward violence.

Next week Marc Roscarrick takes me to Capri.

Sixteen

"I can't accept it, Marc."

"Why not?"

"Because it's too much. It makes me feel like a kept woman. Like a kind of pet."

"Would you prefer a plane?"

I gaze at him across the gear well. He is joking. I am not smiling. We are sitting in *my* car, which is now *his* car; we are parked in Vomero, one of the hills overlooking Naples, with its green squares of garden and high walls with security cameras, and garbage that actually gets collected.

"Marc, I'm yours to keep already, you know that. I just don't want—*this*." I grimace and gesture at the dashboard of the car like it is something repugnant, though Alex the Harlot inside me is saying: *Keep it, keep it. Keep the damn car!*

"How about a flat? Can I buy you a flat?" he says. "I could buy you . . . Diego Maradona's apartment. He used to live around here, wouldn't that be nice? Santa Lucia is so . . . *sea level*."

He is laughing. And joking. I think.

"I don't want an apartment!"

"Okay, diamonds. Rubies. All the emeralds of Kashgar?"

"Stop teasing, Marc."

"But I like teasing you, *piccolina*. When I tease you, you wrinkle your nose like a naughty girl and you look . . . ah . . ."

"Spankable?"

"Tut tut, *dolcezza*, don't tempt me."

He squeezes my knee.

"Marc . . ."

He frowns and smiles at the same time. Then he looks at my bare legs under my humble blue dress. He pats my left knee again. And laughs quietly, showing his white teeth.

Marc is in a pale gray suit with a pale blue shirt and a pale yellow necktie, everything is exquisitely pale except his sun-tanned face and his stubbled jaw, and his coiling dark hair that roils me so. It is Saturday. I am trying to return the car, but he insists we go for one last drive before I make a final decision.

I am still absolutely determined not to keep the car. My misgivings about Marc's present were only reinforced by that dreary drive to Caserta, with its slums dominated by the Camorra—then the return journey past the fires that ring the city, through the Triangle of Death, the mafia-infested badlands, the circles of mafia hell.

I guess I need to tell Marc some of this, or he may think I am being petulant.

So I do. As he sits there in the passenger seat, I describe my day trip to Caserta with Jess. His frown deepens until his impossibly handsome face is, once again, quite ugly with anger. He spits the word *cornuti*—insulting the gangsters. I tell him it was like Dante's hell. Like driving through the circles of hell.

" . . . in the Inferno—the cold and the flames."

He nods, and turns away from me, staring through the wind-shield as he speaks the words, immaculately: *"Non isperate mai veder lo cielo: i' vegno per menarvi a l'altra riva, ne le tenebre etterne, in caldo e 'n gelo."* Then he shrugs. "I love that canto: Forget your hope of ever seeing Heaven: I come to lead you to the other shore, to the eternal dark, to fire and frost." A second shrug. "Chilling. Very chilling. It is a good description of Campania under the Camorra."

Now he bows his head—ashamedly? But then he turns and gives me the full 100 percent cold metal blue of his eyes and says, "You really do think I am *Camorrista*, don't you?"

I am flustered.

"No, of course not, but . . ."

"But what, X? What? That's part of the reason you want to return the car, right? You think it has been bought with blood, bought with violence, paid for by all the dead junkies in Scampia."

"No, Marc, I just . . ."

"Do you want to see how I make money? Do you?"

"Well—"

"Do you?"

I look deep into his eyes, and I do not blink as I say, "Yes."

"Give me the keys. To my car." His voice is stiff and tense—with anger.

I climb from the driver seat and we swap sides. He ignites the engine and then roars down the hill of Vomero at approximately 150 kilometers per hour. He may or may not be *Camorristi*, but he certainly doesn't mind breaking a few highway laws.

Maybe six seconds later we pull into the rear of The Palazzo Roscarrick. Marc yanks the keys from the dashboard and hands them to a servant. Then, as the Mercedes is valet-parked, he strides imperiously into his palazzo with me scurrying along behind.

I haven't seen him this *alpha* before. His face is grim; his pace fast and determined. We cross through several hallways of the lovely, grave, and beautiful palazzo like we are walking through a depressing shopping mall as quickly as possible, and then he abruptly faces a door, slaps it open, and ushers me inside.

The room is semidark; it smells of cedarwood and leather. There are computers on a very large steel desk. The walls are painted gray, and almost entirely unadorned, apart from a couple of, I think, Guy Bourdin photos—faintly erotic, surreal, unsettling, abstract. Just distracting enough to let the mind wander before getting back to the task at hand.

"Here," he says, very curtly. "*This* is what I do."

He is pointing at two of the luxuriously slender laptops on the desk. I step closer. Their bright screens are showing cascades of figures in rows and columns, blinking and changing, flashing red and black and gray, like a drizzle of integers. Symbols wink at either side of the columns.

"I don't understand."

He steps close, and points to one of the laptops.

"I am speculating. To be exact, right now, this morning, I have been exploiting a tiny discrepancy in Canadian dollar futures in respect to the interest rate yield on ten-year T bonds."

"What?"

"Canada equals commodities. People emotionally genuflect to commodities in times of instability: they turn to oil, coal, iron, shale, gold. If it gets even worse they will return to Treasuries."

"You're day trading?"

"Exactly. You want to watch me do it? It is nothing special. It's like playing the harpsichord."

He pulls out a very modern leather office chair, sits down, and then clicks on the laptop. He begins typing numbers and keys, then he studies the rows of integers, some of which are now flashing very red and very black, like they have been disturbed, like tiny creatures in suspension, alarmed by a predator, emanating distress signals. His fingers flicker over the keys skillfully. It is indeed a bit like someone playing the harpsichord—it is even more like watching J. S. Bach play his own cantata on a church organ, mastering several keyboards at once.

And it is quite erotic. I always find the sight of a man doing his job, with expertise and accomplishment, rather arousing. That job could be farming, it could be archaeology, it could be cutting trees. All that matters is that it is done well. I suppose this is evolutionary. The only time I ever really desired the Deck-Shoe Mathematician was when he was working equations, swiftly and cleverly. On his own. Then I wanted to kiss him. Right now I want Marc to fuck me.

I resist the urge to confess this.

"So," I say, staring at the whirl of digits blinking red and pink. "What happened there?"

He pushes the chair back and shrugs.

"I think I just made about sixteen thousand dollars. And some trader in London might be going home in a bad mood."

"Does that make you feel good?"

"Yes," he says. "But not as much as it used to. It's . . . capitalism. It is the world. It is the way things are. What can we do? And it is a little safer than what I used to do."

This is the nub.

I stand here in my forlorn blue dress, staring at the billionaire who wants to give me a car.

"What *did* you *used* to do, Marc?"

"I imported Chinese goods into Campania and Calabria. I paid the locals decent money and I also made sure there was no skimming, no bribes, no sweeteners, nothing. And I hired very hard guys to protect my business. So I undercut all the cheap Camorra factories in north and east Naples. I made a huge amount of money and I made a lot of *Camorristi* and *'Ndranghetisti* quite . . . angry. They were going to kill me. But I didn't care. I was so angry myself."

He stands and looks at me, arms folded—defiant, but not superior. Just himself.

"Why?" I ask.

"When I grew up, X, we were genteel yet very poor, we were aristocratic but impoverished, everything was in decline, just as it had been in decline for decades, centuries even, and this house"—he gestures—"was falling apart, almost a ruin. Likewise the estate in Tyrol, the manor in England. The Roscarricks were doomed. Everything was going to be sold, the palazzo was on the market, my history was about to be auctioned. This made me furious, as only an eighteen-year-old can be furious—*incandescent*. I truly wanted to be a painter, an artist, an architect, but I didn't have the luxury. So I went into business as soon as I could, because I was determined to restore our fortunes, whatever it took, to save this great old name, *Roscarrick*. So I did. That is what I have done. I've made enemies, but I've made many millions."

His voice is slightly raised. "And as soon as I was able—before the Camorra and the 'Ndrangheta took revenge—I got out of the import stuff and put everything into a few computers." He points at his laptops and his expression is dismissive, even contemptuous. "Now it is easy. It is like I have built a virtually perfect machine. I merely have to tweak it, to oil the humming engine, and every day the machine churns out money."

The silence in the room is profound. The integers glimmer in scarlet and black on the laptops.

"I'm still not taking the car, Marc. Give it to the poor?"

He laughs unexpectedly.

"Maybe one day you will take it."

"Maybe, but probably not. I want you. Not your money."

He advances toward me, puts a hand around my waist and kisses my neck. The trills of pleasure cascade down me like the numbers on his market screen, flashing red and pink. Oh, Marc, kiss me again.

But he pulls back and says, "Fair enough. But we really *do* have to buy you some clothes. Enough Zara. This time you are not allowed to refuse."

I try to stop myself from blushing. I didn't even realize he'd noticed what dresses I wore.

Yet my yearning for new clothes is sincere and urgent. A smart car I can do without, but if Marc wants me to go to upscale places—like Capri—then I need clothes, I do; I really need them. And that means Marc will have to provide them. Because I simply can't afford to trawl the designer stores.

And provide these clothes is just what he does next.

For the following six hours he takes me on a tour of the most scented, gorgeous, glittering, minimalist retail spaces in Campania, the shops with the huge windows and the tiny stacks of exquisite silk and cashmere, the shops with the acres of unused space and the assistants who look like bored supermodels, the shops that I barely dare to step inside, the shops where you wincingly check a sticker to just look at the price and you think the decimal point is in the wrong place.

And the words! Oh these *words*: they flow around me like honey on this honeyed afternoon: Prada, Blahnik, Ferragamo, Burberry, Armani, Chanel, Galliano, Versace, Dior, YSL, Mc-Queen, Balenciaga, Dolce e Gabbana. Words and words and words.

Gossamer ruffled 100 percent mulberry silk, delicate bias-cut mink on suede, hand-beaded new season mini-jackets, endless dresses of violet and cerise and cream and Neapolitan midnight blue, skirts and pants and miniskirts and entire armloads of diaphanous silk lingerie, high-necked velvet peplum, Sicilian orange print frocks, Lolita pink Mary Jane pumps, Jimmy Choo Jimmy Choo Jimmy Choo.

There are boxes in the back and bags in the front; at one point, Marc switches credit cards and orders a second car; there are so many new clothes and shoes to transport it is embarrassing. And now the snooty girls in the lofty shops are looking at me with envious admiration, like I am the Queen-of-England-to-be; and I am horribly, hatefully, blissfully happy.

"I want you to look like you," Marc says. "But also like you *should* be. The way you *deserve* to look."

And then he takes my hand and he kisses my fingers, as we walk out of the final store and jump into his Mercedes. I put on my new four-hundred-dollar sunglasses and I feel essentially like a younger, happier Jackie Kennedy, as we drive in the sunshine to my apartment.

We both know what is going to happen just as soon as the car is parked. The electricity between us is like an oncoming storm, Marc has seen me in and out of clothes all day, he has seen me nude in dressing rooms, topless in front of mirrors, he has admired my ass and my breasts and the way I bend over in lingerie by La Perla, and he has lusted, he has *lusted*—but he has kept his hands off me. Just.

I know he can't keep his hands off me anymore.

We open the door to my apartment and he tears into me. He flings his jacket away and grabs me, embracing me, jailing me in his arms. Our mouths meet—no, they collide. We kiss as if we haven't kissed since the eighteenth century. His tongue fights mine; I bite his lip, quite hard. He kisses me more: his tongue inside my mouth. But I want all of him inside me.

I have brought up some of the clothes, so there are bags and dresses and tissue paper everywhere—but it doesn't matter. Marc is lifting up my dress, revealing me. He has ripped away my bra, and now he squeezes my nipples, hard, then soft, then softer, until I want him to do it harder.

"Harder."

He sucks on my nipple, my left nipple, as his hand goes down to my panties and tucks inside. He finds my cunt and my waiting clitoris and he strokes it deftly with his fingers, three times, no four times, five times, brilliant times, oh so cleverly, softly and soothingly, teasingly and arousingly. And the buzzing in my head is delirious. I am yearning for him. I need him. I need to see his muscles and his body, need to see him barefoot. And so I rip off his shirt until the buttons fly across the room, until he laughs, and I laugh.

And yet this is serious. As always. The sex between Marc and me is playful—and yet deadly serious, too, like something nearer to religion, sometimes. The adoration, and the reverence; with this body, I thee worship.

Leaning close, I lick his hard and sculpted body, the superb and suntanned ripples of his rib cage, tasting the clean, hard scent of his skin. Then I sink to my knees and unzip his pants. His erection is firm and thick and long. I put it in my mouth and I suck.

I suck. I suck on his lovely thickness, and I cup him there, cupping and sucking, wanting him to come, yet not wanting him to come. The floorboards are hard on my knees but I like the pain, mixed with pleasure. I feel penitent and good, kneeling naked on the floor like a novice: sucking him, and looking up at him, as his warm hands flow through my hair, stroking, then grasping, then almost tugging as I suck him too well, too sharply. Lifting my head, he says, whispering and soft, "No, X—*I don't want to come yet.*"

Hoisting me to my feet, he kisses me full on the mouth. I reach my hands around his waist and return the kisses. Then we fall sideways onto the bed and he half pushes me away, then thrusts my naked legs apart. I am wet, I am very wet. And I watch. And I wait.

He is stripping naked now, and the sight is again majestic, heroic. I'm not even sure he knows it, but he really does look like a warrior, a gracious Zulu brave, the young Achilles. He is also the essence of a man aroused. Abruptly, he climbs on top of me and his hand clamps over my mouth as I say his name, as he enters me again, and again. And again.

Marcus Roscarrick is fucking me. He is fucking me like a king. Like a lord. My lord came home from the wars today, and pleasured me twice in his top boots.

Our bodies sway together, violently, passionately, like this is a street fight tinged with love. He thrusts, softly, then harder, then softly, then very hard. And now he gasps, quietly. And I know he is probably close to coming. I can tell by the rigid glee of his body, but I am way too selfish for this. I want to come *first*.

So I grab his lean, dark hips, and I push him deeper inside me, deeper and harder between my naked and trembling thighs, my bare skin tingling.

I can feel his size inside me, filling me up. His fingers are in my mouth so I suck them, tasting salt, and him, and us. He is thrusting harder, repeatedly. And he has a fierce thumb near my throat as his chest presses down on my breasts and I am half choked.

Now he pulls out, then thrusts his cock, and waits. For an agonizing second. Then he rubs his cock on my clitoris and enters me again. This is good, this is very good. He does it again, with his erection and my clitoris. The blood jumps in my heart. I am sheened with delicious sweat; I am closing my eyes as the pleasure spirals around to that place where he fucks me.

"Carissima, carissima—"

I cannot speak. I don't need to speak. I am biting his shoulders. Biting with desire. And again he pulls his cock from my cunt and then he thrusts it back in, and each time he does this, he rubs my trembling and pulsing clit, and then he stoops and fills my mouth with his tongue and wraps me very tight in his arms, caging my slender shoulders, and this time he thrusts so deep, almost too deep, oh so deep; and then he does it once more, three sweet and glorious thrusts, and I am gasping as he embraces me. I am almost breathless, almost crushed, almost fainting, almost laughing, and at last I shout out in a kind of *agonized* orgasm, an orgasm so vivid and ardent and imperious it is virtually *painful*.

Seventeen

Marc Roscarrick has his own boat. Of course he does. It is a deep, dark Italian blue, and it waits glamorously at anchor in the harbor of Pozzuoli, about five miles north of Naples.

Pozzuoli is very beautiful. Many of the Neapolitan rich live here, in the jumbled white houses that crowd around the domed and ocher-tiled church on the rocky promontory. Tonight is especially sweet and pretty: the moon is an archer's bow of silver in the sky, a million stars are hanging from heaven's black and invisible Christmas tree, and families of well-dressed people parade the waterfront, eating gelati and laughing and gossiping and greeting their friends.

Marc smiles, offers a hand, and I climb, a little unsteadily, onto his motorboat.

"Ready, X?"

"Ready. I guess."

I sit in the back and Marc takes the wheel. Standing on the pier, Giuseppe unleashes the ropes and pushes us away from the jetty. The engine coughs and chirrs, and Marc deftly steers, guiding us between the launches and skiffs, the liners and the fishing smacks—and then at last Pozzuoli bids us good-bye and we are out on the open Mediterranean, which, this evening, is as dark and still as an Aztec obsidian mirror.

Calm beneath the silent storm of those glorious stars.

The sweet sea air is a balm. I sit back in my new Armani dress—my velvet color-blocked rosette Armani cocktail dress, to be precise—and admire my Jimmy Choo heels, before taking in the view. The sea, the moon, the stars, and Marc Roscarrick. And me.

"It is so still!" Marc says. "So incredibly still. The perfect night for the Mysteries." He slows the boat until it is stationary, bobbing on the blue dark swell beneath the myriad glitter of stars. He murmurs again, "The sea is calm tonight. The tide is full, the moon lies fair, Upon the straits . . ."

I recognize the poem. I smile and say nothing. The silent wind is warm and sweet. We are afloat in the Bay of Naples. Just him and me. Just two people, a man and a woman. Two instruments in a perfect duet. The Bach adagio for double violins.

Marc starts the boat again. I regard him with some reverence. He looks so good tonight: he is wearing a divine tuxedo, studiously tailored, splendidly correct, black and white and tall and lean; he looks like a Hollywood matinee idol from a 1940s Oscar ceremony, a sober and handsome and monochrome foil to the woman he escorts.

I wonder, for a second, who designed the first tuxedo, the first dinner jacket? Did someone really think—think hard—and come up with that brilliant combination of black and white? Or maybe it just evolved over time into its present perfection: a Darwinian selection. Because a man seldom looks fitter than he does in a black-and-white tux. And Marc in a tuxedo is particularly male, absolutely virile, *molto bello e scapolo.*

Who were those women pictured with him in *il West End di Londra*?

He stares at me, I stare at him.

I say, "I feel like a nun taking the veil. Is that what I am doing, Marc?"

He smiles sadly. But he says nothing, just steers the boat onward, through the whispering waters. The Mysteries abide. The minutes pass. I am fretful and joyful. Seagulls swoop down out of the night sky, like ghosts in the dark, happy-sad phantoms, then gone, flying into darkness. I want to get there now; I want the Mysteries to start.

"How long to Capri?"

Without turning, he says, "Approximately half an hour. I could go a lot faster but you might get a little wet and ruin that dress."

"What's going to happen, Marc?"

"*Piccolina.* Why should I tell you now, if I've never told you before? The Mysteries are meant to be mysterious."

I sigh, and then I shake my head. Quite firmly. "But I need to know things, if I am going to continue."

"Okay . . . what?"

He is steering the boat and talking over his shoulder. I press on.

"You said that once a man is fully initiated, then he cannot have a relationship with a woman who is not completely initiated."

"Yes."

"Why only men? Doesn't it apply to women?"

He turns. His face is somber.

"The code of honor is stricter for men."

"Why?"

"It just is. It always has been."

I gaze back at him.

"And what if I want to *stop*, Marc? What if I decide I have had enough, after the Second Mystery or the Third?"

"Then you stop. Many people do exactly that. They never go on to the Fifth." He smiles at me. A little regretfully. "But if you stop, that affects us. As you know, I am allowed to be with you for this summer, as you go through initiation—but if you stop before the Fifth . . ."

"We can't see each other again."

"Yes."

The moment darkens. Marc has his back to me again as he guides the boat under the stars, toward Capri. But I have more questions.

"So why is this Second Mystery so important?"

"This is when you will take your vows. And officially be inducted, for the summer."

" 'Officially'? Who makes these rules, Marc? Who runs it all?"

"That is, I am afraid—"

"A mystery. Yes, yes." I smile quietly, but my anxieties remain.

I think about what is to come, and I get a tiny shiver of foreboding. Until now I have been fairly sanguine about the Second Mystery; now I suddenly feel the first tingle of serious fear, or at least unpleasant apprehension. But then I remember how much, despite myself, I wholly enjoyed the spanking. Perhaps it will be thrilling? Something beyond thrilling, something boundary-breaking like the First Mystery? Something important and profound? I hope so, and yet I am also scared it will be too profound. And it will change me.

And I don't want anything to change.

The truth is, I want everything to stay as it is: right here, right now, on a fine night in mid-June, maybe six weeks after I first saw him, with me and Marc alone on a boat beneath the shining stars of the Bay of Naples.

Here. Stop it *here*. Freeze frame. *Cut*.

"Nearly there . . ." says Marc, stretching his arm and pointing at the silhouetted island, at Capri all jagged and sprinkled with houselights.

As we near the port of the island I belatedly realize we are not alone. The closer approaches to Capri are busy with craft; I can see other boats now, small and pricey cruisers, bigger yachts, sleek and costly motorboats like ours. All closing in, all heading for Capri. It is like some wartime evacuation in reverse.

"Your fellow Dionysians," Marc says, as he drops a gear and slows the boat. "Gathering for the Second Mystery."

A minute or two later our boat is moored and lashed, and we are on the jetty, being met by young men wearing dark, dark suits and earphones, and sunglasses—at nine P.M. Tourists sit at the harborside seafood restaurants and gawp in amazement at all the Mystery-goers in their finery, disembarking from their skiffs and yachts: at the men in their sharp tuxedos and the women in their fine dresses with high heels and starry jewelry. They ascend into horse-drawn traps, which are ranked and waiting.

I gaze at my fellow Dionysians, or maybe my fellow novices. There are men and women of all ages, from twenty to seventy. It is impossible to tell who is already initiated and who is undergoing initiation. I can hear snatches of several languages—lots of English, some French and Spanish, Russian, too. Chinese as well. Everyone looks rich, very, very, very *rich*.

And for the first time in my life *I feel rich*, walking past these openmouthed tourists, climbing into the little horse-drawn carriage alongside Lord Roscarrick. I actually feel a base and vulgar thrill of ostentation, of absurd superiority: yes, look at me, and just look at my man.

I despise myself for this, even as I think it, but I just can't help enjoying the catwalk moment.

"They must think we are going to some ball," I say, nodding at the tourists in their T-shirts. Marc nods but doesn't answer, making me feel rather stupid.

As the horse trots on, encouraged by the delicate whips of our carriage driver, I try not to think what *kind* of party I am about to experience. My only choice is to live for the moment. What will happen will happen. As the horse pulls our carriage up a steep, rocky hill, I gaze across the bay at glimmering Naples: so beautiful and innocent from this distance. The feeling is mesmeric; I can hear horses behind me, horses in front, dozens of carriages transporting everyone to the site of the Second Mystery.

The carriage halts and Marc assists me down, lifting me like a child to the ground, and now I realize precisely where we are. My ancient history might be shaky, but I have done enough research to know that we are standing at the northeastern tip of Capri, where the emperor Tiberius lived in A.D. 30, and where he conducted his notorious debauches. The emperor was wont to lie naked in his swimming pool, where small boys were trained to dive underwater and lick and nibble at his groin. The emperor adored this aquatic pleasure; he called the boys his "minnows."

This shard of history pains me. Will the Second Mystery be some reenactment of horrible Roman decadence? Something ghastly and perverse? Once more I am weakened by a fear of what is about to happen. Marc obviously senses it. As we go through a big iron gate guarded by at least ten men in dark glasses and dark suits, who check Marc's credentials, he squeezes my hand.

"*Courage*," he says, using the French pronunciation. "*Courage, ma chère.*"

"But I don't understand, Marc—how do they get permission? This is an archaeological site; it's like renting the Parthenon."

We are following the other Mystery-goers down a cicada-rasping path toward a source of light and music.

"This is Campania, X," Marc answers. "You can buy the Temples of Paestum if you want."

"But who pays? Who are those men at the gate? Are they armed?"

He squeezes my hand again.

"Please don't fret, just let it happen, let it roll over you. That's how the Mysteries work; you mustn't resist. And now . . ." He smiles at me, sincerely, and maybe regretfully. "Now you have to go and dress. Follow the handmaidens."

Two Italian women—young and pretty, and dressed simply in white—take me by the hand. They lead me away from Marc, along an inclined path to a parade of very sophisticated tents: luxurious yet antique marquees.

In front of the largest tent—the one nearest the mighty cliffs that topple down to the dark Tyrrhenian Sea—I can see dancing and I can hear people drinking and chattering. Likewise, I can hear music. These are the fairly normal sounds of a rather swish alfresco party. But we are going into a different tent. It is purple, braided, and imperial—and somehow Roman.

Inside there are several other young women, standing by mirrors and side tables. All of them are being dressed and tended by these Italian girls who wear these simple white shifts.

My guess is that these other young women, standing anxious and stiff, must be my fellow initiates. I glance at them: their young and pretty and rather worried faces. They glance at me, and nod.

We all feel the same.

"Please," says one of the handmaidens. Her English is faulty. But her gestures are fluent. "Take off clothes?"

There are no men in this big silk tent, which is softly lit with hanging lanterns, but I am still seriously shy. I remember Marc's words, and I remember that if I want to keep him—even if it is only for this summer—I have to do as I am told. I must steel myself, and submit. Again.

Taking a deep breath, I nod—and the girls step forward. They evidently want to help undress me, yet I wave them away; no one is touching my precious new Armani frock. I remove it myself and fold it with due diligence, and the girls seem to understand—they let me hang the dress very carefully on a rack. My underwear follows, until I am standing nude. I simply can't look at the other initiates; I am too embarrassed to do that—so I concentrate on what the girls are doing to me.

And they are getting to work on my party costume.

"*Per favore, signorina?*"

I gaze, intrigued. Because they are dressing me in a way I have never been dressed before.

First they take some opaque white silk stockings, and slowly roll them onto my legs, over my knees, up to my thighs. A garter is clasped around each white thigh, to keep the stocking in place. The garter is beaded with gold, and miniature creamy pearls; it is beautiful, probably antique. I am given steep little shoes to wear, which fit perfectly. They have minuscule and baroque silk bows, and very high, blocky heels. Eighteenth-century shoes. Dandyish and sexy.

I am being dressed like an eighteenth-century kept woman. Like a high-class mistress of a Sun King.

"Okay," says the Italian girl. "Please stand."

Carefully, but quickly, she fixes a corset around my middle. I have never worn anything like this. It is a rich, deep scarlet, and gorgeously embroidered, but, wow, it hurts as she stiffly laces up the back tightly, then even tighter. The pressure forces my breasts up and together: it gives me a deep cleavage. The corset is on the borders of being bondage gear—but not quite. It is more subtle than that. Painful, but subtle.

"*Signorina*, please sit, we do the hair?"

I rouse from my self-absorption and look around. It seems I am now alone in the tent; the other initiates have already been dressed and dismissed—to experience their Second Mystery.

"Sit?"

Obediently I sit on a little gilded chair and watch in a large wooden-framed mirror, as the girls lift and comb my hair, adorning it with coils, plaits, mother-of-pearl pins, and small but darling silk bows; curlicues of hair are allowed to descend at my ears. My ordinary blond hair looks wonderfully gold in this flattering lantern light.

The girls are gifted. When they have finished, I stand and stare in the mirror, admiring myself. I am indeed Marie Antoinette.

Except for just one thing. I am wearing *nothing* between my stockinged and gartered thighs, and the gold-threaded hem of my whalebone corset. My carefully waxed pubic hair, my ass, everything sexual—is on display. Everything is *framed*. The delicate and antique costuming of the rest of me serves to make my utter nudity *there* all the more emphatic.

"But what about here?" I say, panicking now. "Where's my skirt, my dress? Underwear!"

The handmaidens shrug, smiling but unhelpful.

"Is done. Now you go to the party?"

"What?"

One girl steps back and sweeps her hand.

"Is very beautiful. You very beautiful. Now finish. Now go."

Go?

No. No way. I cannot do this. Not this. I can feel the breeze on my naked thighs, even on this warm Tyrrhenian evening. My ass is reflected in a dozen mirrors, visible to every gaze. The reflex of shame makes me want to grab at something—anything—to conceal myself.

I sway with profound embarrassment. The girls are looking at me, arms crossed. So this really is my costume: I really do have to walk out into the middle of the party dressed like this. Or rather, not dressed in anything between my thighs and my navel. So that everyone can see.

There is nothing to be done about it. I must *submit*. Girding myself, girding my *loins*, I walk to the entrance of the tent, where a girl pulls back a swath of canvas and silk, hands me a glass of champagne, and allows me to exit.

I am in a daze. The world can see my bare ass, my everything. I am following a lantern-lit path to a kind of terrace in front of that bigger tent, where many dozens of properly dressed people are dancing and drinking and talking. I am naked between corset and garter.

Then the music stops. And everyone turns and looks at me.

Eighteen

At first I am so embarrassed, so ashamed, I want to hide in the bushes with the cicadas.

No one is laughing at me, no one is mocking, or even leering, but everything within me is telling me that this is wrong. But I continue walking into the party-going crowds, between these elegant people holding their slender flutes of champagne, and as I proceed they seem to part, in silent respect.

Now I see, as the music renews, that there are several other women, mingled among the crowd, dressed *just like me*: these are my sisters, also being initiated. I recognize one or two faces. These are the women from the tent, and their pudenda are also on display, fabulously framed by historic stockings and lissome silks and complex corsetry, yet displayed nonetheless.

I have an urgent desire to talk with one of them. What are they feeling? What do *they* think about all this? My slight and natural shyness restrains me, but then I remember: *Hell, X, you are walking around a crowd of elegantly dressed rich people with no clothes there, not where it matters. And you are abashed by the idea of striking up a conversation?*

I notice one girl, slightly apart and alone, standing under a lantern strung from a tamarisk tree. She has a glass of golden champagne in her hand. Her head is tilted. She is listening, it seems, to the music, which is a kind of amped-up string quartet, lyrically classical but played with a definite African rhythm. The music makes me want to dance, but I cannot dance dressed like this. Not sober, anyway.

The girl is very beautiful, with long, dark hair, studded with fine pearls and silver pins. She looks like a large-eyed, taller Jessica—she has the same intelligent and shrewd demeanor.

"Hello," I say.

She turns. Her dark eyes narrow, inquiringly.

"Bonsoir."

"Oh, ah, sorry." I blush. Why am I blushing *now*? "Sorry, I did not realize—"

"No, no. It is okay. I am French, but I speak English." Her smile is thoughtful.

I smile in return.

"Hello."

Now she stares down, quite frankly, at my nudity; then she gestures down at her own white thighs, and dark strip of hair.

"So. What do you think of our . . . *historic* costumes?"

I shake my head.

"I don't know . . . Are they really historic?"

"Yes," says the girl. "They really are historic. They used to wear them at the court of Napoleon. Haven't you ever heard of a furbelow?"

I pause, then I laugh, rather anxiously. It's a clever joke. I think a furbelow is a ruffle or flounce, a frill worn by a pretty girl in the eighteenth or nineteenth century, maybe a particularly lacy collar. But furbelows are definitely the best way of describing the appearance of this girl and me tonight.

This girl? I realize I haven't asked her name.

"I am Alexandra, by the way. Or X."

"Hello, X. I'm Françoise."

We shake hands. I inquire:

"If you don't mind me asking—who is initiating you?"

Françoise gestures at the crowds of people, drinking and chattering and gossiping; the crowds are definitely getting louder and more boisterous as the champagne flows.

"Daniel de Kervignac. French like me. But he is a banker in the City, we live in London."

"Your boyfriend?"

"Yes. Though he is forty-two. So maybe not so much a boy. My *amant* is a better word."

"Okay." I sip champagne. I realize we are making casual small talk. Dressed like the most outrageous whores in history. The contrast is odd. But less odd than it was ten minutes ago.

"And you?"

"Marc Roscarrick."

Her eyes widen.

"Lord Roscarrick? *The* Lord Roscarrick?"

"Yes." My mouth gets ahead of me. "Why? You know him? You know of him? Why?"

She smiles decorously.

"X? I will call you X? Yes, X, *everyone* has heard of Marcus Roscarrick. Everyone has heard of the *molto bello*—"

"*E scapolo Lord Roscarrick*," I add, sighing and shaking my head. "Okay, okay, I get it—I read the websites. I suppose he is a celebrity to most people." I look in her brown eyes. "It's just that I'm from *California*, and European aristocrats are like soccer players to me. We've never heard of them. Might as well be moons of Neptune."

She smiles.

"Good for you. Celeb culture is generally trash. Though your Lord Roscarrick is quite certainly a catch—the catch of the season." She steps a little closer and whispers conspiratorially to me. "What is he really like? Is he, ah, a little . . . dangerous? Like they say? Is he *really* that exciting?"

"Sorry?"

"I mean," her mouth flutters, "his beautiful wife, the other rumors . . . Ah, *forgive me*. This is wrong. I am tattling. You are a lucky woman. And besides, we are meant to be mysterious and enigmatic, no? Standing here with the Origin of the World on show."

She gazes down below her waist, once again, and adds, "This better be worth it. The Brazilian was *immoderately* painful."

I laugh brightly once again. But my laughter is brittle and mixed with more misgivings. What does she mean about Marc? I want to inquire further but a loud French voice interrupts.

"Françoise, J'ai cherché pour toi."

This, evidently, is her boyfriend. He is regulation Handsome Older Guy, graying at the temples, broad shouldered, emanating a sense of wealth and privilege, and wearing a very top-drawer tailored tux. He is no Marc Roscarrick, though.

The Frenchman gives me a brief and courtly nod, his eyes only flickering below my waist for a second. He shakes my hand as we are introduced, and then he takes Françoise's fingers in his own and guides her away. As she goes, she turns, and gives me a warm and expressive glance.

"Good-bye, X," she calls over her shoulder. "I am *sure* we will meet again."

I muse on this for a moment. I suppose she is right. If she is enacting the Mysteries through the summer, we probably *will* meet again. I am glad about this, because I felt that inkling of incipient friendship with Françoise, and I definitely feel I need an ally. I also want to know more of what she knows about Marc. Or do I?

Draining my glass of champagne, I watch, quite thoughtfully, as Françoise disappears deeper into the crowds.

Her white ass looks beautiful and sexy as she walks on her stacky eighteenth-century heels, between the dressed and normal partygoers. I had expected to find the sight somewhat comical, but I don't. Françoise looks imperious; she looks a little glorious; she looks, in fact, like one of those beautiful Arab racehorses, a Thoroughbred being led around the paddock of a racecourse—not for the purposes of leering or jeering, but for the purposes of pure and sincere and wholly serious admiration. The glances she is getting are respectful, maybe even a little awed.

That's it. Her nudity, her seminudity, is giving her a kind of *power.* She is the center of attention, the one carrying it off. I've heard it said before: semi-naked men usually look ridiculous, or at least weakened; semi-naked or half-dressed women, by contrast, have an enigmatic but awesome power—especially over men. And in these strange, strange costumes that power is amplified, and magnified, a classical music turned to the hundredth decibel. Deafening. The Origin of the World.

Goddammit. I take another glass of champagne from a handy silver tray borne by one of the handmaidens, and then I plunge into the crowd myself.

And it works. I get the same awed respect. Older women gaze at me, briefly, with a mixture of envy and nodding empathy. The men are all bowing, very slightly, like diplomats and courtiers acknowledging a superior: a princess or a passing queen. If they had hats they would be doffing them.

Yet there is also a decadence here, as I press between the mingled people. A girl lightly touches my hip as she breezes past. It happens again; it is no accident. I sense another hand, a male hand, on my ass—then it is gone. I turn, to see who it was, yet I am not alarmed. Maybe I am somewhat drunk, but the situation is not distressing, it is playful, delicate, and, yes, erotic.

The fizz of the champagne tingles in my nose. I drink more. People brush past me; I feel more hands on my nudity. I do not mind. It is good; I am enjoying this. And then at last I find Marc, with three other men. He turns and introduces me, but I forget their names because I am a little drunk. The men—English and fair-haired—kiss my hand, and they each look, for a few seconds, at my very obvious, particular, and unusual nakedness. And my shame has gone: I feel a power over them. *Look at me. Go on, look at me. I dare you.* I am laughing now, and joking with Marc. I feel *decadent.*

The music steps up. It is a vividly quick waltz: amplified and underlined by that driving pagan beat. A waltz—thank you, Dionysus—is the only formal dance I know. I look at Marc and he takes my hand in his, guiding me to the wide stone terrace that overlooks the sea, and there we dance, among the other dancers. We dance quickly, my head on his chest, my hand clasped in his.

And I am glad that everyone can see everything; let everyone see it all, let everyone do whatever they want. The night is lovely; the champagne is chilled; the moon is amazed and pleased; the stars are cleaned and polished so bright. And Marc has placed his hand on the small of my back where the tight lacing presses the whalebone into my ribs, forcing my breasts up. I feel perfumed and weightless.

"You look utterly lovely," he says.

"Not ridiculous?"

"Not ridiculous, *carissima*. The very opposite of ridiculous. I am very proud."

"Why?"

His hand has strayed below my corset: it is now on my ass, gently squeezing.

I look at him. And smile demurely. And say nothing. We both pretend that nothing is happening.

"I have seen other women shy away at this point. The Second Mystery is difficult."

His hand squeezes my ass once more. The faint blue stubble of his jawline looks very fine in this sculpting light. His lips are half apart, and smiling; there is a glimpse of sharp white teeth. *Squeeze me more*, Marc Roscarrick, *squeeze me more.*

"What happens to the men?" I ask. "What is the male initiation?"

He looks me in the eye; our lips are three inches apart. We step across the terrace, dancing, and dancing, and turning, his hand still firmly on my bottom, and he says, "It is different. Much more violent. It can be—frightening . . ."

"How?"

"Another time," he says. "But now—just look at you, like a Dresden doll. And only a *little* deviant."

He steps back, releasing my ass, and he twirls me on one hand. This is barely a waltz now, this is more like dancing as I know it normally. Young and free-form. Just heathen. Pagan. Nearer to sex. Quite African. *Dionysian?* People in formal clothes dancing informally quite often look stupid, but here it seems normal: dancing with billionaires and *principesse*, dancing above the ruins of the Villa of Tiberius, dancing above the great marble palace of Iovis, where the aged roman emperor filled his scented garden with naked boys and girls, hidden in niches and alcoves, in honor of the Gods of wildness and debauchery, of Pan and Eros and Bacchus.

And so the night unfurls. I drink too much. Marc tells me that this is fine, he tells me everyone drinks too much in the Second Mystery. We dance close again, and he pulls me to his chest, and slips his hand between my thighs, and rubs me very gently just once—just once, but oh, oh—and as he does this he tells me that drinking is the honor due to Dionysus. Then he tells me things I don't understand—because I am drunk. And because I want him to keep touching me, in public. Make me come in public. Why not?

Yet he stops. Abruptly. And I turn.

Everyone has stopped. The music has ceased. What is this? Grasping my hand Marc guides me across the terrace. Now I see that my sisters—five women who are being initiated—are also being led by their escorting men. We are all walking up some wooden steps to five gilded and feminine chairs that are positioned on a marble dais, above the terrace of dancers.

Silence rules. Marc whispers in my ear:

"Sit."

Obediently, I sit in one of the chairs. I can hear the cicadas rasping again. What is happening? Gazing along the chairs, I notice Françoise seated on my left, with Daniel standing at her side. She looks at me, her eyes are unfocused. She tries to smile. But she also seems rather unnerved.

A young man in a dark suit reads from a kind of parchment.

The crowd is hushed, watching and listening. It is all in *Latin*. Then it dawns: this is the moment when I am enrolled—this is the scene on the frescoes in Pompeii—the man reading from a scroll, announcing the induction of five more women into the Mysteries of Dionysus.

"Quaeso, Dionysum, haec accepit mulieres in tibi honesta mysteria . . ."

The man stops speaking. I get ready to rise, but Marc leans down and whispers in my ear, once again: "Sit, Alexandra, be still."

I wait. The handmaidens are back. And this time one of them is holding some kind of tool—complex, silvery and metallic, vaguely gun-shaped. Is it maybe medical? I try to focus through the alcohol and my rising panic. What is this?

Marc is leaning closer.

"Be calm, X, be calm. *Let it happen.*"

The Italian girl speaks to me: "Please, open legs."

"No."

"Please."

"No."

"Please!"

Reluctant, sobering up very fast, I open my legs. I now understand, suddenly and clearly, what the handmaidens are going to do. I can see it is already happening to Françoise in the seat alongside mine. The handmaidens are going to tattoo me. My induction into the Mysteries is going to be marked on me, forever. Even if I stop right after this, I will always have this branding.

But I have to do it. Don't I? I reach and hold Marc's hand. Very tight.

Everyone is watching. I close my eyes. The shame has returned. I feel a sharp stab of pain in my loins.

Oh God.

The handmaidens are working. It is quite painful—but it is the shame and doubt that really hurt. I don't like tattoos—I have never liked them enough to ever remotely consider one. The permanence unsettles me. And now I am being tattooed, on my thigh, by some strange girls, in front of three hundred strange, rich people, who have all been looking at my nakedness for hours. I want to cry. This hurts. This is wrong. I am not drunk anymore. Marc's hand is tight around mine but it is not comforting.

"No . . ." I say. "I didn't . . ."

The handmaidens are wiping away some blood with cotton wool and water. The tattoo is finished, it seems, but the shame abides.

The champagne is wearing off. I feel mortified and humiliated; I feel embarrassed and stupid. This is some ghastly, tacky ceremony, and I have been a fool; and now I am branded forever, like some kind of livestock.

"Morpheus," I shout. "Morpheus!"

And it works. Everyone stops. But it is all too late; the induction is done, the tattoo is finished. And I hate myself for my stupidity. Wrenching my hand from Marc's, I rise from the chair and run away from the crowds and the music. I run into the olive groves, my hands covering my face in disgrace. I stop in a clifftop clearing, illuminated by the moon and stars.

There is a warm, soft rock, I sit down and weep for a few seconds, or more. Then I feel a wetness. I look down in horror: a trickle of red blood is running down my inner thigh.

Nineteen

The moon is large and melancholy, reflected in the still blue seas, and laying its path of silver on the tiny rippled waves. The olive trees whisper in a barely felt breeze, but still I shiver, here on my smooth rock, ashamed like Eve by my nakedness. I need a fig leaf. I need a cushion. The concept doesn't amuse me. Everything is detestable. I can't even bear to look down and see my new tattoo.

"*Carissima.*"

It is Marc.

"X, I have been looking for you." He lifts a canvas bag. "I brought you some clothes, and something hot to drink."

I gaze his way, then the words tumble out.

"But Marc, but Marc—I can't—"

"What?"

"I can't wear the dress, the Armani dress . . ." My voice is still pregnant with sobs, with near-tears. "I'll ruin it. I am . . ." I take a deep, tearful breath. "Marc, I am bleeding."

Marc kneels and opens the bag. He has bandages, swabs, ointment. He speaks into the bag as he sifts through it.

"I spoke to the handmaidens. They gave me all this, darling. I have a simple black dress for you as well. I had Giuseppe bring it."

He looks up, and adds, "Just in case . . ." He hands the dress over. "It's from Zara."

His kind and amused blue eyes—gray in the moonlight—look deep into my own. I can't help blinking back a few more tears, but these are different: tears of relief, tears of—though I hate to admit it—tears of gratitude. Yet he put me through this. I don't know what I truly feel.

Marc turns away as I wipe myself. I apply some ointment, which is antiseptic, and soothing. The bleeding has almost stopped now; only the pain remains, the pain and the humiliation—though the latter is also drifting out to sea. Perhaps I just panicked. I don't know. I was having a good time—feeling that Mysterious, Dionysian liberation—before it went wrong. Maybe the fault is with me?

Take a deep breath, X.

It is time to look at my tattoo. Shifting a little, I open my thighs. And gaze at my white skin in the moonlight.

And now I want to cry again.

Because the little tattoo is utterly pretty; it may even be exquisite. It comprises a dark and slender arrow, laced with a very sinuous S-shape along its length. The coloring, black to dark violet, is subtle. It is striking and lovely, despite being so small.

"It's an alchemical symbol," Marc says. He is kneeling and staring between my thighs. I am naked down there, of course, but I like him looking. We are both looking at my naked vulva and my new tattoo on my inner thigh.

"A symbol of what?"

"Purification," he says.

He kisses my stockinged knee. I have to ask him.

"Do you like it?"

"I adore it, X. It is wholly exquisite. The symbols change every year, I believe. But I know that one. Beautiful." He kisses my knee, and asks: "But what do you think, X?"

"I'm not sure . . ." I contemplate the symbol. Purification. "I can't believe I am saying this, but I think I quite like it. Yet now I am marked forever? Tattooed and branded?" I lift his jaw so he is looking at me, not at my tattoo, or my nakedness. "You have tattooed me."

"I suppose I have."

The moon shines down, and we stare at each other. Then I feel the cold night air.

"Marc, can you help? I want to get changed."

"Of course."

I stand, lean on Marc, and slip the new black panties on; then Marc kneels beside me and reaches to unfasten my garter. Slowly he rolls down my stockings and pulls them from my white feet. He pauses, and kisses my bare thigh. I shiver—from the breeze or from the kiss, I do not know. Now I want to be rid of the corset. I can't do it myself. It is impossible.

"Marc?"

Kissing my neck very gently, he stands at my back and gets to work, unlacing the whalebone. The corset comes loose and my breasts are exposed. I notice my nipples are hardened. I am aroused, but I don't want sex, not now, not tonight. Quickly, I swoop on the dress Marc brought: plain and black and, yes, Zara. I reach for the canvas bag for something to put on my feet—and I see that Marc even thought of socks and sneakers: new white socks and sneakers. I put them on. They fit perfectly. Of course.

"Now drink," says Marc, taking out a thermos as we both sit down.

He pours the drink into a plastic cup.

I sniff the liquid suspiciously.

"What on earth?"

"An old Roscarrick recipe, fine Islay single malt Scotch whisky, whirred with Bajan cane sugar and just a hint of spice. Scaltheen. It is an absolute panacea, *carissima*. And delicious, too."

I drink the scaltheen. And he is right, it glows down my throat, not like normal Scotch at all. It is ambrosial, it is heavenly, it is the liquor of the gods and it is fitting. The therapeutic warming buzz fills me inside.

Marc lays down a thick tartan blanket for us to lie back on. He makes pillows from my old clothes. He is attending me.

"We can go back whenever you like," he says. "Nearly everyone else has gone already. But it might be nice to lie here for a while? We have Capri almost to ourselves. Quite a rarity."

The whisky is working. The scaltheen is a balm. The two of us lie down and I snuggle close to Marc's strength and warmth, enclosed in his embracing arms: this isn't sexual, this is companionable, this is friendship—deep, deep friendship. I feel safe with him, protected and cherished. I also feel, very woozily, like I could talk with him for hours about anything—politics, science, basketball. More than that, I feel like I could fall asleep this second in his comforting arms. I am tired.

As my mind lulls toward sleep we both stare at the stars.

"Look," he says. "There's my favorite constellation."

He points. I stare.

"Orion the Hunter?"

"No, that group over there, *cara mia*. It looks like you sneezing. The Constellation of Alexandra with Hay Fever."

I laugh quietly.

"Okay, that one over there, that really weird constellation

just under Leo. That's the Constellation of Marc in a Bad Mood. It's famous. They use it to frighten children in Sicily."

He chuckles.

"And over there—there—just under the Pleiades—what one's that? The Constellation of Alex Giving Back the Car?"

"Oh no, no, it's not . . ." I smile, and kiss his neck. "That's the Constellation of Us. That's the Constellation of Alex and Marc, together, and alone, on Capri."

A silence. Marc stares upward, into the turbulent and imperious whirl of stars and moon.

"The Constellation of Alex and Marc?" He sighs. "I like it." He turns and faces me. His eyes are serious and sad, loving and happy. "Sweetheart . . ."

"Yes?"

Our voices are almost whispers. We are both close to sleep.

"Darling, whatever happens, even if you leave the Mysteries, and we can never be together, will you promise me, whenever you are angry or sad or alone, you will go out in the night and look up at that constellation? Will you look at the Constellation of Alex and Marc on Capri, the Constellation of Us? Please." He is nearly asleep. "Please do that, for me."

I yawn, close my eyes, and say: "Yes, but come closer, cuddle me."

Sleep is inches away.

As he cuddles me, I say in a bare murmur, "Marc, will all the Mysteries be like that? It was a bit . . . frightening."

"No," he says; his eyes are closed, too. "Different, different, they are more poetic . . . difficult . . . *carissima*."

He is asleep. I take one last look at the glittering sweep of stars, at the Constellation of Us, and then I close my eyes, too.

Twenty

For the first few days after the Second Mystery, I am in a kind of daze. But it is not traumatic: more dreamy, and heady, and wistful. With just a hint of regret. Something in me has changed. I have visibly been altered, within and without. Every time I strip, every time I shower, I see my new tattoo. It transfixes me. I have started to love it, like a secret but glorious present. One evening I show it to Jessica: I lift up my dress and she stares.

She shakes her head and says, "I want one."

We both laugh. And then I change clothes and Marc calls round and we go to dinner, like an ordinary couple. We are settling into a rhythm. Like ordinary lovers.

But it is a glorious rhythm. Usually we make love in the late afternoon, as the heat of the day abates. Then we eat and drink at night. Sometimes I stay in the palazzo and sometimes he stays over in my tiny apartment, usually with Giuseppe parked outside—possibly armed? Possibly not.

During these days I am seriously happy, even though nothing

spectacular happens. Perhaps I am happy *because* nothing spectacular happens. One night, as I lie in Marc's vast bed, with him asleep beside me, I recall a line I heard in an old movie, *Doctor Zhivago*—where the loving couple live in a shack in the wilds and have to fish and farm and fend for themselves. Then a visitor calls on them and says, "When you look back you will see these ordinary days were some of the happiest of your life."

Staring at the glass sculpture in the shadowy and shuttered light of the bedroom, I wonder if these are *our Zhivago* days. The ordinary days of being in love, the days of simple and innocent work and pleasure, which are, paradoxically, the most precious of all: suffused with an inner well-being. The sweetness of life. Regular, simple, everyday life, inflected by love. But also ennobled by work.

Life is sweet, and strange, and compelling. Leaning to my side I kiss the scar on Marc's suntanned shoulder. I wonder again where he got that. But I have had enough of anxieties. Let it go, let it happen. I kiss Marc once more. He murmurs in his sleep. I kiss his scented and muscled back. I want him to wake up. I cannot resist.

L'amor che move il sole e l'altre stelle.

The following afternoon I find myself lying on my bed, in my little apartment, chewing my pen. This is not unusual for me. The bed is where I seem to work best, maybe because it reminds me of him. And what we do here.

Or maybe that is too distracting. Picking up my notebook, I go over the key facts I have learned about the Mysteries. Somehow my thesis has gotten sidetracked onto the Mystery Religions, but I am fine with this, for now. The Mysteries are just so *fascinating*, especially now that I am enacting them.

Firstly, and crucially, I have discovered that this area, around Naples—Napoli, Capua, Cumae—was always known for its "orgiastic nature." This was the pleasure zone of the Roman Empire. Pompeii itself was a place where people retired to lead the good life; Julius Caesar's holiday home was a few miles north up the coast—though it has since been drowned by a rising sea level. People have come here to party since the first century B.C.

Therefore is it not surprising the Mystery Religions, with their emphasis on vivid debauchery, orgiastic sex, and spiritual eroticism, took root here?

Perhaps. Perhaps yes. I underscore this fact.

And here's another *interesting* thing.

Drink and drugs seem to be key to the Mysteries, in all forms. In the Eleusinian Mysteries, a special potion was drunk during the ceremony, apparently called the "kykeon." Historians know that kykeon got people very inebriated: a certain Greek scholar, Erasixenus, is described in an ancient letter as having died after downing just two cups on the trot.

What kind of drink is this? In one place, the Homeric *Hymn to Demeter*, the recipe for kykeon is actually listed: barley water, mint, and "glechon."

And yet, of course, *no one has any idea what the word* glechon *means*.

I tap the notebook with my pen. It is frustrating and stimulating all at once.

Wherever I look, I come up against this blankness, this big question mark. Something missing. Something still unknown. What is the exact recipe? How did they keep it a secret? Moreover, how did they keep it a secret for such a fantastically long time?

According to the history books, two families of Eleusinian

priests, who handed the Mysteries from father to son and from mother to daughter, managed to keep the secret for nearly two millennia. Literally *two thousand years*. An astonishing feat.

It was either something prepared in a special way or something they *didn't even understand themselves*.

I can hear Jessica coming home from her teaching. Her door slams flamboyantly, and she is singing as she heads for the shower. I don't have to check my watch; I know this means it is near five P.M. In an hour or two Marc will be here, waiting to whisk me away. I love the way he *whisks me away*. Whisk me some more, Lord Roscarrick. Tonight he is taking me out to dinner—again—but he says he wants to show me some of Naples first: some things I have not seen. I look back at my notes, chewing my pen until I remember that it stains my mouth with ink.

So I stop chewing and write a paragraph instead:

> Clearly there was a secret drug or liquor, clearly it was very important, clearly it gave some kind of intense revelation, which made the pains of the Mystery initiations—and they were painful as well as pleasurable—perfectly endurable, for men and women. But what was the final Fifth Mystery? What was the revelation? What was the "katabasis"?

I pause, pen poised, and read my last few scraps of notes. They relate to the punishing secrecy surrounding the Mysteries.

> The laws of Athens and Rome made it a severe crime to speak of what went on in the Mysteries at Eleusis. In 415 B.C. there was a spate of indiscretion about the

Mysteries by the Athenian elite, and a brutal crack-down followed: those who had revealed the secret were tortured and killed.

Tortured and killed?

It is all so tempting, so tantalizing. And what makes it especially appetizing is that it seems the Mysteries have survived, in some kind of authentic form; and I—Alexandra Beckmann—a humble student from Dartmouth—may be *about to discover the secret of the Greco-Roman Mystery Religions.*

I ignore the nagging voices in my head even as I flick through the last pages of my notebook: the voices saying the Mysteries are *dangerous.*

Oh please. That was then, this is now. I am just researching. Right?

Right. I lift my legs off the bed; I've got to get ready pretty soon. Jess has stopped singing, which means she has finished showering, which means it might be time for me to have *my* shower. I've learned that the water system in our apartment block can't cope with two showers simultaneously.

But then my phone rings. The screen says *Marc.*

"*Buona sera?*"

"X . . . How are you?"

I pause. His soft and deep and gently amused voice makes me several degrees happier. I still don't know how this works. Just a voice. But it is his voice.

"I'm done. I've learned everything there is to know about the Rites of Eleusis."

"Impressive."

"Did you know I am technically a *mystes*? That's what the Greeks called an initiate who hasn't completed the rituals. And they thought the Mysteries were so sacred, they didn't refer to them by name—they just called them *Ta Hiera*: the holy."

Marc praises my endeavors. Courteously. I stare out of the window at the sun over the Excelsior Hotel, as we talk.

"You really have been working hard, X."

"I have. It's what I do."

He hesitates, then says, "Actually, there's a rather fine quote you might find useful."

"Go on."

" 'Blessed is he who, having seen these rites, undertakes the way beneath the Earth. He knows the end of life, as well as its divinely granted beginning.' "

"Ooh," I say. "That's *gooooood*. Who is it?"

"Pindar, the Greek poet. Talking of the final Mystery."

" 'The way beneath the Earth.' Wow." I am picking up a pen, scribbling the word *Pindar* in my notebook.

"*Carissima . . .*"

I am distracted.

"Mm?"

"Did you get my present?"

Now I pause, and put down the pen.

"Yes, I did get the present."

It is sitting on my desk right now: a smallish flat box, wrapped in costly silver paper. The gift arrived this morning.

"I haven't opened it yet. What is it? Your presents can be a little unnerving, Marcus."

His laugh is polite. And firm.

"Open it."

"Now?"

"*Per favore.*"

"Okay, okay." Reaching for the box, I retreat to the bed and sit back against the pillows. Quickly I untie the bow and rip the lovely silver paper. The box within is plain, subtle, and gray. I open the lid. And stare at the object nestling inside, cosseted in shapely foam. My cell phone is cradled under my chin.

"What the . . . ?"

"You like it?"

"Yes," I say. "It's great. I've always wanted one of these." I pause. "What is it?"

His laughter is quick.

"Baibure-ta."

"Hello?"

"It's a vibrator, *carissima*. The best vibrator in the world, made in Japan."

Even though I am alone, I am blushing. Quite fiercely.

"But it doesn't, um, uh, ah, look like a vibrator. It looks like . . ." I take the shining metal object from its soft box. It is surprisingly heavy, and carefully, even lovingly, shaped. "It looks like a torture device for elves."

"Try it."

"Marc!"

"Try it."

"I have you for that."

"Just try it . . . Once."

Hmm. Shall I try it? I am giggling. But I am still blushing.

With my cell phone tucked under my chin, I turn the sex toy in my hands. The metal is silvery in places, almost transparent; are there pearls in there, or shining steel balls? I've never used a sex toy before—not properly—I know that Jessica has one and I've admired it, and giggled with her, then forgotten about it. This doesn't look the same; it's much smaller and heavier and very differently shaped. And much, much pricier, no doubt. But I am beginning to see how it might work. You'd put that in there . . . ?

"I've got my clothes on, Marc, or most of them."

"Then take them off."

"*Sì*, Celenza!"

"This isn't the Mysteries, X."

"I know. I just like calling you *Celenza*. I like it when you order me around. But only sexually. You ever do it in a restaurant and I will punch you in the face, Marc Roscarrick."

He laughs again. I love making him laugh.

"I'm putting the phone down, my lord. Hold on. "

Quickly I peel down my jeans. I am already barefoot. Then I slip off my panties, get back on the bed, tuck the phone under my chin. And hold the sex toy in my hands.

"Okay, Celenza. Fire away."

"Press the button at the bottom, the black one."

I locate the little button, which is sophisticated and small. A gentle red light glows inside the vibrator, but much more noticeable is the fairly intense *vibrating*. This isn't unexpected, but it is very different from the crude buzz of Jessica's sex toy.

"Oh my goodness. It's actually alive."

"Now use it."

I hesitate. Am I actually going to do this?

"But, Marc, I'm not sure—"

"Press the silver tip to your *sweet* little clitoris."

I stare at the toy. Then, quite slowly, I open my bare legs. My darling tattoo glows dark, scarlet and violet on my white skin. The machine feels like a small animal, something alive, buzzing deep and wildly. Yearning to do its job.

"Press it against your clitoris."

I hesitate, then I answer.

"*Sì*, Celenza."

Now I close my eyes and press the soft, curving metal against my clitoris. My wetness.

The sensation is too much.

"Oh God!"

"Don't press too hard."

"It's good, it's good, but it's weird . . ."

"Try once more. Do it slowly, very slowly."

I use the toy again. Against my clitoris. Much softer this time.

The pleasure surges through me, starting in my groin, but emanating and rippling.

"Now think of me, *carissima*."

"I am already," I say. And I am. My eyes are closed and I am thinking of Marc.

"What are you thinking?"

The machine buzzes.

"You," I say. "You. Deep inside me."

"What am I doing?"

My body is blushing. But not from shame.

"You are fucking me."

"Am I fucking you hard?"

"Very hard. Your . . . your cock is inside me. I love your cock. But . . . ah . . ."

The machine is too much. Too good. I want this to last.

"Careful, wait . . . Talk to me. How am I fucking you, Alexandra?"

"From behind. You're not naked."

"No?"

"No, but I am. You've come to my apartment, Marc, you've ripped all the clothes off me, you throw me on the bed, you open my legs, brutal—I have no choice, oh God—"

The machine buzzes. I see how it works. My eyes are closed very tight; my heart is beating very fast, but I see how this works. This other part goes there, inside me. Not far. But just enough.

"Oh my God."

"I stripped you naked."

"You did, you did, and now you are fucking me, fucking me hard, and you are calling me your little girl."

"My little girl . . ."

"And I am helpless, you are in me . . ."

"In you?"

"Yes, yes. In me, deep inside me. Deep, deep, deep."

"I am inside you . . ."

"You are inside me so deep, so deep. It is the only thing I can feel. Your cock deep inside me. But mmmm—"

"Wait!"

"I can't."

"*Carissima* . . ."

I am barely able to speak. The machine is alive, and it is pleasuring me. Wonderfully.

"You are fucking me, hard, and it hurts, and I love it, love it, I love . . . I love . . . I . . . I love it, I love it."

"But not only this . . ."

"Mmmmmmarc . . ."

"Press the other part down there."

"Where? I . . . I . . . I don't . . . Oh, yes—" I see. Yes, I see. He means my perineum. And below. And even as I think this, the machine slips. It slips inside me. Anally. I didn't even move it.

"*Oh.*"

Twenty minutes later, I dash into the bathroom, turn the tap and sluice myself with hot water.

The toy is washed and cleaned and in its box. I feel like locking the box away. It is a little too exciting. But I am glad Marc gave me this. I'd rather have this than a car.

Turning my face into the shower water I can't help smiling. Good, this is good. Now I rub myself down using this *divine* soap, which was a gift from Marc. He says it comes from a little monastery in deepest Florence, the *Officina Profumo Farmaceutica di Santa Novella*; apparently the soap has been made by monks and nuns since the fourteenth century.

Subtly floral, discreetly sensual, handmade and skin-loving. The foam is scented clouds. *Sapone di Latte*! I use it everywhere; I probably overuse it, even though the bars must cost fifty dollars apiece.

Thank you, Marc. Thank you for *everything*.

Cleansed and refreshed, I step into the bedroom, quite nude, with a towel turbaned on my head, and for a second eye myself critically in my one good, floor-length mirror. I pinch half an inch in front of the mirror: hmmm. Am I putting on weight? Is all this divine Campanian food in all these glorious Neapolitan restaurants making me *fat*?

The bell rings. And as I pull on my dress, I decide I don't especially care if I am getting fat. This is probably because I *am not* getting fat. It is the miracle of Mediterranean life: I eat anything I want but all the swimming in the sea, and most especially the sex, is keeping me reasonably thin.

The bell rings again. Instead of answering the intercom I run downstairs, barefoot in my dress, with my hair still wet, and

I open the door to the warm summer evening air, and Marc is standing there smiling in his jeans and white shirt and I actually *leap* into his strong arms so that he is staggering back onto Via Santa Lucia, holding me as I kiss him, with my ankles locked around the small of his back.

We kiss. I am acting like a seventeen-year-old. I do not care. I feel seventeen. I am in love. The moon is high over Capri.

"Hello, X," he says, as he puts me down on the ground.

"Hello, Marc," I say. "I'm quite pleased to see you."

He smiles.

"You liked the toy, then?"

"Those crazy Japanese. What are they like?"

"I got it so you wouldn't be lonely."

"Marc, I see you every day. You sleep with me *twice* a day."

"But sometimes I have business. Anyway . . ." He gestures at his parked Mercedes. "Tonight I want to show you something special."

"What?" I am imagining a marvelous meal, perhaps the world's greatest *tonno rosso* recipe, served on top of Mount Vesuvius.

Instead, Marc says, "The Cappella Sansevero."

"But . . ." I say, stammering, and flustered—and excited. I've heard of the Sansevero Chapel, of course; every serious visitor to Naples has heard of the notorious and amazing Sansevero Chapel, every serious art historian in the entire *universe* has heard of Sansevero Chapel. "But it's closed for renovation, Marc. It's been closed for years, no one knows when it will reopen; you can't get in. I tried and tried . . ."

His eyes twinkle *in that way*.

"You are right . . ." He smiles. "But I am paying for the renovations."

He is dangling one large key on a ring. Marc can get me into the Cappella Sansevero!

The drive takes all of three hundred seconds, from the ordinariness of my apartment block to the doors of one of the most sacred places in human artistry. We get out of the car and approach.

The chapel is shrouded in scaffolding, and surrounded—protected—by the narrow streets of Old Naples, the grand and battered heart of Naples, where old men with gray stubble play *scala* outside tiny cafes with bright strip lighting, smoking and coughing and exchanging their amiable insults. *A circolo sociale.*

In the light of dusk, the glass wall shrines fluoresce with yellow electric candles and red plastic flowers and leering, eerie statuettes. There are lots of smiling Holy Marys, the patron saint of the Camorra.

As Marc reaches for the keys, a big blue Vespa emerges abruptly and suddenly from a shadowed corner, and veers dangerously past me, carrying two laughing teen girls in shorts and flip-flops, riding the bike without helmets, their sumptuous dark hair rising and falling in the driven breeze.

I watch them disappear: their happiness, their laughter, their fleeting beauty. Now they are gone; the old roads are almost silent. Washing hangs limply above. The bassi are quiet. A man in a tiny room opposite, framed by his open window, sits watching soccer on a stupidly bulky TV under a portrait of Padre Pio. His artificial leg sits on the table in front of him as he chews provola cheese, rinds and all. Chewing with his toothless mouth.

"Okay," says Marc, disturbing my reverie on Neapolitan street life. "OK, *piccolina*, we can go in."

He is opening the door to the Cappella Sansevero.

The first thing I see is a splendid, small, late-Baroque chapel, lit by one bare builder's lightbulb. Mops and brushes litter the scene, and new ocher brick dust is scattered on the floor, but this debris can't detract from the glittering, jewel-box beauty of the ornately marbled chapel.

Marc tells me the history of the place, but I know it already.

"The seventh Prince of Sansevero, Raimondo, was born in 1710, into a noble Neapolitan family which traced its lineage to the time of Charlemagne. He was said to be the greatest intellect in the history of Naples, versed in alchemy, astronomy, sorcery, and mechanics . . ."

I admire the painted ceiling as Marc speaks.

"The prince spoke half a dozen European languages, as well as Arabic and Hebrew. He was head of the Neapolitan masonic lodge until he was excommunicated by the Church—the slanders of heresy were later retracted."

The floor is a dense and monochrome labyrinth of a mosaic; I know this is meant to represent Masonic initiation. Why is Marc bringing me here? Does this place have something to do with the Mysteries?

Marc concludes, with a sweeping and generous gesture, waving at this chapel he is paying to restore. "The last years of Raimondo's life were dedicated to building this place— Sansevero Chapel—endowing it with statuary and images from the greatest artists of the time. He wanted his chapel to be the beating heart of the Neapolitan Baroque, infused with cryptic and allegorical truths."

"It's . . . very impressive."

"Come," says Marc.

I am feeling somewhat nervous. Because I know this room,

sumptuous as it might be, is certainly not *the* famous treasure of the Cappella Sansevero. That lies down a narrow staircase to our right.

The antechamber is dark: Marc turns on the flashlight in his phone and we descend this constricted helix of cool white marble. The stairs twist on themselves, confusingly. I hasten after Marc's light. At last we reach the dark and somber silence of the crypt. And Marc's flashlight shines on the terrible and amazing treasure of Sansevero.

The Veiled Christ—the *Cristo Velato*—of Sammartino.

It is mind-blowing. It is scary. It is indescribable. But I need to find the words in myself, in my soul, to describe it. Otherwise I will have somehow failed; I will have been revealed and rejected, I will be unworthy.

The sculpture shows Jesus in the tomb. But Sammartino, the sculptor, has draped the dead Jesus, the dead-yet-awakening Jesus, with a soft, gentle, silken sheet, a death shroud of linen, clinging to every contour, *yet it is made out of the same block of marble as the body.*

How was it done? How could you do this? Sculpt a perfect body then, at the same time, sculpt a silken sheet in which to clothe it, the two becoming one? To this day I know that art historians argue over the technique involved; some devotees believe it is simply a work of magic.

"What do you think?" Marc asks.

"It's marvelous," I say, stammering a little. "No, it's more than marvelous. It is miraculous."

And it is. The sculpture is *miraculous*. Perhaps the single most astonishing work of art I have ever encountered. Yet this sculpture is also unsettling; there is something otherworldly about it, something beyond human. It possesses an eerie perfection. It is too much.

"Marc, why are you showing it to me now?"

He comes close, takes my hand.

"Because I want you to be inspired, *carissima*, to see the possibilities that lie within us all. And great art makes us more courageous—makes us stronger."

"Courageous?"

"In a few days it will be time for the Third Mystery."

I say nothing. The chapel crypt is silent. The veiled Christ sleeps, as if about to wake. This is definitely too much; I want to get out. I am feeling claustrophobic. I have been trying not to think about the Third Mystery, I've been trying to live for the day, the hour, the moment—but now the Third Mystery is nearly here, and unavoidable.

We ascend the stairs and exit the chapel. Marc locks the door, and I breathe the warm, muggy, garbage-and-lemon-scented air of Old Naples with relief. The Cappella Sansevero was amazing, but perhaps too amazing. I ask if we can take a stroll before getting back in the car; Marc happily agrees.

Hand in hand, Marc and I walk down the cobbled and sloping Naples streets, past late-night food stores with naked lights showing stacks of dark, glossy eggplants, past fish restaurants where noisy *nonnas* eat on rickety tables in the street, guzzling prawns with Falanghina wine, just as the Romans did, in this very same place, two thousand years ago.

As we approach the seafront, I turn to Marc.

"Where is the Third Mystery? Where does it take place?"

He does not look at me as he answers: "The Aspromonte. Calabria."

I shudder as if chilled by a dirty winter breeze. *The Aspromonte?*

From my studies into the brutal Calabrian mafia—the 'Ndrangheta—I know the meaning of the name *Aspromonte* very well.

We are going to the Bitter Mountains.

Twenty-one

"It's at least five hours into the mountains," says Marc, and he leans across the car and squeezes my knee. But not in a sexual way, more a reassuring way. "Though you wouldn't guess it from the map."

"Sorry?"

We are on the fringe of Reggio Calabria airport, in a battered five-year-old four-by-four. An old rented Land Rover. Marc has gone downmarket.

"We need the car for the roads," Marc explains, as he crunches the gears and winces at the noise. "The roads are hellish up there; a few kilometers can take an hour."

As he waits for a gap in the roundabout traffic, he nods in the direction of some dim, distant mountains, not especially high or dramatic, but possessed of a definite grim and brooding quality. Dark, forested, prohibitive, off-putting. These are the Aspromonte, the Bitter Mountains.

He adds, as an aside, nodding down at the battered dashboard, "Plus, Calabria is quite a good place to be inconspicuous. This is *not* Ferrari country."

At last, Marc pulls out into the parade of Fiats and farming trucks, and we begin our long journey north and then east toward the heart of the Aspromonte. Progress is slow, the traffic is heavy, the roads are narrow. I roll down my window and stare out in some astonishment. I have, obviously, never been to Calabria before.

We are at the very toe-cap of Italy, where the great Italian boot punts Sicily toward Spain, back into her Spanish and Bourbon past. And Calabria is not at all what I expected.

But what was I expecting? I guess I was anticipating something like Naples. Something old and chaotic but charming and Italian and ancient, with palm trees and good *gelati*, and maybe just the odd horrid suburb and leery-eyed junkie to remind you of the lurking criminality.

But here, the criminality does not *lurk*: it shines out. It is overt. The whole place exudes an air of desperate, helpless nastiness. Instead of the odd horrid suburb, there is town after town of intense dereliction and dismay—it's the nice historic buildings that are the *exception*. Maybe there isn't quite as much graffiti as Naples—but that's because half the houses have been knocked down. Or only half built. Or simply left to rot.

The ugliness is extraordinary. I have never seen a truly ugly Italy before.

Marc gestures at one particularly dilapidated block of houses to our left, as the traffic forces us to slow.

"It's hideous, isn't it? Hard to believe that you are in Europe; it feels more like Tunisia. Or Egypt. Or worse . . ."

He is right. I stare at the grisly block of buildings as we crawl past: the bottom floor has some cracked and rudimentary tiling, upper floors are unplastered, and the flat open roof is home to seven rusting washing machines. Inexplicably.

The next block is simply rubble: concrete pillars and broken bricks. Then comes a patch of litter-strewn wasteland. Then a tired food store, and another stretch of trashy wilderness. We pause at traffic lights.

"Why is it like this? The 'Ndrangheta?"

"Yes, of course. But also the earthquakes. They get terrible earthquakes here every ten years or so, which destroy entire towns. . . . It's the poorest part of Italy; it is probably the poorest part of Western Europe."

Marc has one arm hanging out of the car, in that limpid heat, another draped over the wheel, steering it—from the top—with the bottom of his wrist. He is in dark jeans and a darkish blue shirt, with the double cuffs undone, exposing his muscled and suntanned forearms.

It is an elegant and masculine pose, a classic pose even; I can imagine a Renaissance painting: *The Lord Roscarrick in His Rented Land Rover*, attributed to the School of Raphael, 1615. Marc would have looked great in seventeenth-century portraiture. But he looks great now. I gaze his way, quite happily. Contentedly. Remembering.

We had remarkable sex last night. He has developed this trick of giving me committed and lavish oral sex, of pleasuring me that way for twenty minutes or so, slowly building up, and then, just for a second, when I am approaching the apex—the peak, the cliff, the sudden fall into oblivious bliss—he senses my near-to-the-moment arousal and rubs the dark sexy stubble of his chin where previously he had been licking me, and the sudden startling contrast between lushing softness and tickling prickliness sends me into an absolute paroxysm of orgasm. Last night, I actually had to grab a pillow and put it over my face as I screamed with joy and sheer glee.

But Jessica still heard me. This morning, as we rose early to catch our flight to Reggio, she said, "Jesus, X. Why the hell have you got a werewolf as a pet? Someone is gonna complain."

Again, I look across the Land Rover at Marc, thinking how he confuses me, deliciously. Because he is not always this same unselfish and attentive lover. Sometimes he just grabs me and fucks me, quite roughly. He did that after we left the Sansevero Chapel. We got back in his car and drove to his palazzo and then we parked by the rear door, in the dark, and we got out—and suddenly he picked me up and turned me around and threw me over the hood of the car and lifted up my dress and yanked down my panties—snapping the elastic—and he fucked me from behind, over his beautiful Mercedes sports. It lasted all of three minutes. Three sudden and what-was-that minutes.

It was a tiny bit shocking and frightening and very, very hot. Perhaps I shouldn't find this sexy but I did and I do. Then he just zipped himself up, whistled a Neapolitan tune, and escorted me into The Palazzo Roscarrick like nothing had happened, like we had just stepped outside for a quick glass of prosecco. He allowed me to go and get some new underwear from a drawer in his bedroom. I used the moment to take myself to that fabulous bathroom and masturbate myself to orgasm, reliving that brief and bloodthirsty fuck over the car. I came in seconds.

How many orgasms can I have? Can you have too many?

Marc can be brutal, he can be loving; and I like the way I do not know what is coming next.

But I don't like the way I know nothing about the Third Mystery. Why is it being held in Calabria? Why here, in this benighted place?

Spinning out of my reverie, I gaze through the window. I can see the ocean now, the Mediterranean, from my passenger window. Even the sea looks decayed and depressing, despite the hot morning sun on this fine day in early July. Ten weeks have passed since I first met Marc. Ten weeks that have changed everything.

"So . . ." I look back at Marc. "Tell me what you know about the 'Ndrangheta. For my thesis. Might as well do some learning if we are going to be driving for, like, *ever*."

He grimaces slightly.

"I know what everyone else knows, *cara mia*. They are the most evil of the organized crime gangs, and these days the richest and most powerful. It's estimated they control three percent of Italy's GDP—that's way more than Italy spends on defense."

"Jesus."

"Yes. And the 'Ndrangheta totally rule Calabria." He waves at yet another crippled little village, and a concrete restaurant inexplicably situated in a field of weeds. "Some say that if Calabria was independent—which in some ways it already *is*—then it would be classed as a failed state by the UN. Rather like Somalia."

"How do the 'Ndrangheta do that? How can a mafia run an entire province?"

"There are clans of them, ancient and impenetrable. They are fiercely hostile to outsiders, and fiercely loyal to each other, and membership in the 'Ndrang descends by blood. Thus they cannot be broken in the same way as the Mafia and the Camorra have been recently hobbled, by *pentiti*, by remorseful gangsters, plea bargaining."

"The houses . . . The towns . . ."

"The 'Ndrang open hotels and shops to launder money. The prices they charge are so low, they drive all other businesses into bankruptcy. So the local economy is ruined and the only businesses left are 'Ndrang businesses. Therefore everyone in Calabria relies on them, is indebted to them, employed by them, enslaved by them. It is almost feudal. They also take EU money to build factories and roads, but all they do is start building, so they ensure they get the grants—then they quit. The roads are half built, the factories are half built, hence the utter sense of anarchy and dereliction." He turns a rough and sharp left; we are now heading away from the sea, deep and direct, into the hills. "There is also a tax on houses in Calabria—*but it only applies to completed houses*. That's why all the homes look half done, unpainted, and ugly, it is to avoid tax."

I feel I should be taking notes. This stuff is fascinating. I take out my pen and my notepad: I really am going to take notes.

Marc laughs as I do this.

"I admire your diligence, Alexandra Beckmann."

"Some of us have to do stuff, *Lord Roscarrick*, we can't sit around punching the odd key on a laptop and making sixty thousand bucks a minute."

"It didn't used to be that easy," he says, and his tone darkens.

But everything is darkening: the clouds are gathering, and the terrain is worsening. From a narrow but usable strip of tarmac, the road has turned into something close to a dirt path. The Land Rover rumbles over ruts. We pass large, gray, unpainted concrete villas, with big parked cars and dogs barking in the heat.

"Here's something you might find interesting." Marc coughs some dust from his mouth. "Every September the *capos* of the

'Ndrangheta gangs—the clan chiefs—gather in a remote monastic shrine not far from here, deep in these mountains. The Sanctuary of Our Lady of Polsi."

I am writing this down as best I can. The juddering of the car makes it difficult.

"Go on."

"The interesting thing about this meeting at Polsi is that it has been going on for *hundreds of years*. And in the past, until a few decades ago, the meeting was"—he pauses, and searches for the words—"quite bizarre and carnal. The heads of the criminal families were known as the "chief cudgels." The cudgels would lead the way from the nearest village, toward the distant Sanctuary of Polsi, followed by large crowds. The procession took at least two days; they had to walk thirty kilometers. The gangsters were followed by young women and old crones, all wailing and howling, and sometimes wearing crowns of thorns, with blood dripping down their faces; many would do the walk barefoot. But they also drank rough wine and feasted on roast goat, and they bellowed ancient hymns, and danced wild tarantellas all night—to the bagpipe and the tambourine. All night long they drank and gorged and fornicated among the oleander and the oregano. Drunk and crazy."

"So it is . . . Dionysian?" I ask.

"Perhaps," he says. "Dionysus the Greek god makes sense. Calabria was, of course, Magna Graecia in ancient times—this is where the Greeks made their greatest colony; Plato lived around here, as did Pythagoras." He turns and smiles, distantly, handsomely, and shrewdly. Like he knows something I don't. But then he always looks like he knows something I don't.

"Is that enough for your thesis? For now?"

I am scribbling manically.

"Yes, Marc. It's fascinating. Amazing."

"Good," he says, "because we need to think. I'm not sure where we are. . . . It's somewhere along here, on the back road to Plati."

He is slowing the car, and squinting at a road sign. I gaze up at the road sign, too. And shrug. I'm not sure why he is bothering: the road sign is so peppered with bullet holes it is useless; all the names have been shot away.

Bullet holes?

Marc looks at the road sign, then at the map on his iPad. He sighs, shakes his head.

I ask, perplexed, "Surely you must know the way? You've been to the Mysteries before."

He answers without looking at me.

"I only know Calabria because I worked here, remember, importing into Reggio and Crotone."

"So . . . ?"

His reply is brisk. "I've told you before—the Mysteries happen across Italy, and often in England, France, Spain. There are several going on every summer *simultaneously*. People weave in and out of them. You'll meet someone at the Second Mystery who was inducted in, say, London; then you'll meet them again at the Fourth Mystery, not knowing where they were for the Third. It all adds to the mystery."

I sit in the stationary car, slightly openmouthed. For the first time I get some sense of the scale of these Mysteries. Who organizes all this?

I turn to Marc.

"You chose to come to this particular Third Mystery? In horrible Calabria? Why?"

"I was curious. And I need to do some business."

"What business?"

"Nothing serious." He glances down at the iPad. "I think our destination is about twenty kilometers beyond this next village. We can ask here, to make sure. We really do not want to get lost in the Aspromonte."

We rattle for a few minutes down the rubbled road, then we pull a series of very tight ascending curves, climbing a steep mountain. Perched on top of this mountain is a village, which, by Calabrian standards, is adorable. A venerable stone church crowns a dome of huddled old houses. The streets are cobbled; the old men sit on their benches in the hints of breaking sun.

Italy as it should be.

Yet, when we climb out, I get the strangest feeling. There are children yelling at soccer balls in the street, and young mothers shouting out of bougainvillea-framed windows, and a fruit-seller leaning over his produce and arguing affably with some old woman.

But they are speaking Greek. Not Italian.

Marc smiles at my astonishment.

"Yes, it is ancient Greek, *Grico*, from the time of the Hellenic settlers. The language never quite died out in these really remote valleys."

I stand here, in the hazy sun: an American utterly dwarfed by the ancientness of Europe. I am listening to the language of Plato and Pythagoras, spoken by the very descendants of Plato and Pythagoras.

Marc is gesturing and chatting with some locals in Italian. So they are also bilingual, which makes sense.

Retreating from the scene, letting Marc do his thing, I walk over and sit on a bench—and yawn. The drive has been very rough. I am tired; my limbs ache. A long day already. The old man next to me turns and smiles. And speaks ancient Greek.

I nod and smile hopefully at this son of Socrates, and his incomprehensible words.

Oh, Italy. Oh, Europe.

"Okay," Marc calls, returning from his task. He opens the car door and jumps in, and gestures for me to do the same. He seems invigorated. "I was right," he says, switching the engine back on. "Just twenty more kilometers. On the back road to Plati." He points into the darkest valley, incised into the most malign mountains. Of course it would be that way: the most sinister direction.

I sit back. And try not to fret.

But this is difficult. It may just be "twenty more klicks" but the last leg of the journey takes us *another two hours*, driving past landslides, sliding through washouts, climbing horrible unpaved hills. At last I see a town around the next vertiginous corner of pine tree and slender beech.

As we enter the "town," the sense of horrible revelation grows apace. All the ancient and modern houses are derelict. All are grisly shells, with dark, cracked windows and doors cruelly twisted on hinges or simply kicked through.

"My God," I say. "It's a ghost town."

Marc nods.

"Rhoguda. It was finally abandoned in the nineteen fifties. Too many earthquakes. And too many witches."

"But . . ."

"The Mystery will happen in the Bourbon castle, up there on the rise."

I shade my eyes to see: an immense, austere building—

somewhat like a nunnery, half a kilometer beyond and above the town.

I turn and look at Marc. I have suddenly realized.

"This is where I am going to be flagellated, isn't it? This is where I will be whipped?"

He says nothing, just steers us toward the lofty castle.

Twenty-two

Rhoguda Castle can't ever have been beautiful, but it must have once been awe-inspiring: it is still enormous, frowning, military—and austere in that Spanish-Italian style. Just like the Palace of Caserta.

As before, there are dozens of young men in dark suits at the gates, and as before they have unsmiling faces, earphones for communications, and black sunglasses despite the clouds. The ominous creases in their smart jackets—I am now pretty sure—indicate where they holster their guns.

Marc shows his credentials—an ID card, and some kind of small ivory plaque, depicting Dionysus the God clutching his staff of fennel, the thyrsus. I have surmised this is a symbol for the final initiation. I wait patiently, if a little anxiously, as the guards do their thing, and then we are escorted through a large door, big enough for a carriage, and up some plain whitewashed steps to two large and almost empty bedrooms. Some of the ruined castle has been revamped, presumably for the Mysteries.

By whom? Who is paying? Is it Marc himself? Marc and a few other billionaires? What business is he doing?

There are questions I want to ask, and then there are many more questions I probably don't want answered. I gaze about me, a little bewildered; then Marc says I have time to rest before the rituals begin. This is good, because I feel so tired. Kicking off my shoes, I fall straight onto the bed and lapse into a deep, exhausted sleep.

But my sleep is fractious. I dream of Marc and me in a sinking cruise boat; the crockery is crashing everywhere and passengers are panicking. Then I am drowning in a wedding dress, scrabbling at the porthole glass as the water rises—water that is polluted with some kind of red oil—and Marc is putting his hand over my mouth so I can't speak, dragging me under the waves and—

I wake with a start. Barefoot in my jeans on the bed. Startled and alone. My mouth is terribly parched and I run into the bathroom—also austere, but clean and newly painted. I run the tap and fill a glass with the water of the Aspromonte, the Bitter Mountains. And I drink the taste of the dream away.

When I fell asleep it was midafternoon. Now it is quite dark.

The bathroom window is open to the warm night air and the whining mosquitoes. Beyond the crumbling exterior walls of the castle, the mountains recede in their savageness, forested and lightless, apart from the odd pinprick of car lights coming our way. Guests for the Mystery?

In the other direction, the abandoned ghost town of Rhoguda lies in a heap beneath the palace: a silhouette of dark, groping shapes.

I squint at all the ruined houses, the ruined shops and cafes. Who lived down there? Who grew up down there? It must have been an amazing place, once: dreamy and lost in its gorgeous little valley. A village with a frowning priest and a grumpy postman on a bicycle, rattling on the cobbles, and girls singing Calabrian songs as they washed clothes in the clear mountain sun.

All gone now, all ruined, all ghosts. Destroyed by earthquakes, and witches, and the 'Ndrangheta.

I hear a noise.

"Marc?"

No answer. Maybe it was someone upstairs; I can sense floorboards creaking. Other guests are arriving, no doubt, other Mystery-goers, other Dionysians and Mithraists and Eleusinians. And some other women, perhaps, being inducted into the Third Mystery.

I look back out the window. The moon is luminous and wise, staring down. Like she is used to this sort of thing.

Voices.

Now I can definitely hear voices. Outside my room. They sound subdued, like people exchanging confidences—almost whispering, possibly conspiring. Shelving my anxieties, I pad to the door, and listen. The door is slightly ajar, and outside I can see Marc and Giuseppe talking with some other men.

Who are these men? And why is Giuseppe here? I suppose Marc would not risk coming here alone; he would want his best manservant for protection. In the land of the 'Ndrang, the mafia that he angered. But why are they talking in this subtle and conspiratorial way? Marc is frowning, and nodding.

I yearn to see the faces of their interlocutors. These voices sound older—speaking in rapid yet reedy Italian. I cannot quite catch what they are saying: though I hear the word *'Ndrangheta*.

Twice.

A floorboard creaks. The conversation is breaking up. And I

catch a glimpse of a third face. It is the face of a very elderly man, maybe eighty years old. I recognize him. I'm not sure from where, but I know that I recognize him. This man is famous in some way. How?

Marc is coming to the door. I step back in urgency and try to look normal, but he catches me in the middle of the room, like an idiot, just standing aimlessly.

"X?"

"Yes?"

He frowns.

"Are you okay?"

"Of course. I . . . I just woke up. God. You shouldn't have let me sleep so long. Sorry. Sorry. I'm all over the place."

The rush of words seems to soothe him. His frown softens.

"Okay, well, you better get ready quick. The preparation for the Mystery begins very soon."

Only now do I notice that Marc is in his tuxedo. Black and white, showered and sleek.

"Oh, but what do I wear?"

"Nothing."

"What?"

"Just have a shower, *carissima*. That's all you need to do. The girls will be in to help."

He turns and leaves. I stifle my fears and make for the shower. It is good and hot. As soon as I am dried, the handmaidens come in, wearing those simple white tunic dresses. Where do they find these girls? How do they employ them?

Just let it roll over you, X.

My anxiety is also tinged with real excitement. I remember, now, how much I enjoyed, at least at first, the sensuality of the

Second Mystery, the feeling of an inner revelation, even empow-
erment.

Come on, then. I am ready.

Ready for *whatever*.

The girls smile, but they speak no English and their accents
are so thickly Calabrian I can barely understand a word. But it
doesn't matter: it is clear what they want me to do.

One girl gestures that I sit on the bed. I do so, a little shyly, as
I am quite naked under my enrobing bath towels. My shyness is
ignored; the handmaidens remove the towels and then I am just
naked. Now a third girl kneels and pushes my thighs apart. She
squints and examines the tattoo, and then she turns to the other
girls and nods.

She gestures. The handmaiden wants me to stand. So I do.
One of the other girls steps forward; she is clutching a small,
white porcelain jar. She opens it and I can see glittering color
inside, a liquid gold. Then I realize what is happening: they are
painting me. Two of the handmaidens have brushes, the others
hold the paint. My bare skin is going to be adorned.

It takes almost an hour. Yet the hour passes quickly. The girls
kneel and swirl me with colors: gold, magenta, and lapis lazuli.
The swirls are abstract yet very sensuous, curving around my
breasts, decorating the swell of my stomach, traced delicately
along my naked thighs, making tender gestures to my pubic
hair; my feet are left unpainted, as is my face—and my behind.
Why?

The sensation of being painted is not unsexual. The whispering tips of the paintbrushes, the soft and gossipy murmur of the
girls. I begin to feel resplendent as I stare down at my gorgeously
decorated naked body. The colors are stealthy yet glittering. I

am gilded and majestic; my skin is narcissus-yellow and glowing red and Byzantine purple.

I am a work of art.

The painting is done. I stand here, depicted. The girls whisper among themselves as they wait for the paint to dry. Then the smallest handmaiden steps close. She is holding something: it is a plush velvet collar, a sort of dog's collar.

The collar is fixed around my painted neck. Then a second girl clips a long silver chain onto the collar.

I wait here naked. Chained. Collared. And painted.

Marc enters the room. He bows graciously to me, then takes the other end of the silver chain, and gestures toward the door.

My Lord Roscarrick is apparently going to lead me naked out of the room, by a chain attached to the collar. The only thing I am allowed to wear is high heels: the girls have brought some elegant black leather stilettos. Sexy shoes. I glimpse the label as I slip them on. Blahnik. Designer Mystery Religions. The Italian touch. But the mood is somber, not amused.

Marc is gesturing again. I take the deepest of breaths.

"*Sì*, Celenza."

I nod my submission. Marc lifts the chain and leads me outside, downstairs and along a corridor, where I glimpse people in dark candlelit side rooms: Kissing? Fucking? I don't know. They are just writhing shapes. Low laughter. That music is filling the air again, sweet choral music but with a low, driving rise, a holy bell, getting louder and louder, ominous and very beautiful.

And at last I recognize it: Arvo Pärt, the *Cantus*. For Benjamin Britten. There was a girl at Dartmouth who loved this music. Sad and yet sensual in the extreme. It fills all the rooms, churchy yet pagan.

I am led on the chain, exactly like a dog, or a slave, by Marc, my slavemaster. But somehow I do not mind: if I am a dog I am a splendid dog, I am a royal hound, the lion-hunting dog of an Assyrian king, a prized and beloved Borzoi.

Marc leads me into a sizable room, which seems to be a chapel. I glimpse the shape of an apse, a nave, an altar. The music rises. There are many people in here—two or three dozen—all dressed mainly in black. And they are masked.

Everyone is masked, apart from Marc and me—the naked woman in the center: me, feeling like a splendid hound, an animal in her glorious coat, wearing my golds and crimsons.

I gaze around at the big candlelit room. It is shadowy, with hints of purple in the darkness. It is warm and scented and lovely. The air is incensed. The candlelight is flickering, and it flickers, particularly, off my painted bare skin. I am glittering. Literally sparkling. Shining in this light. My mind is losing focus. The perfume of the incense is powerful.

"Alexandra," says Marc.

The chain is tugged and I step forward, until I am at the very center, the pivotal point around which the room revolves.

"Celenza."

Two masked men step forward and remove my collar. Then they take my wrists and tie them together with a soft rope. The knot is tight and I wince slightly. But it is not so painful. I watch, with unexpected calm, a strange lack of anxiety, as my cuffed wrists are then lifted as one, and attached to an iron ringlet that hangs from the ceiling by its own black iron chain.

I am being shackled—my arms are handcuffed high above me. And I do not mind. What has happened to me? The elaborate preparations have acted like some drug, spinning me out, taking me into a different zone. Tranquil, and sexual, and not myself.

Marc is standing right in front of me. Watching me being

shackled. I look at him. He looks at me. We stare deep into each other's eyes.

"Drink," says a handmaiden, offering me a cup, like someone offering vinegar to Jesus.

The cup is metal, and the liquid appears thick. The blood is rushing from my cuffed and hoisted arms, making me feel light-headed, but I drink anyway. And this, it seems, is no vinegar. It is a sweet wine, extremely strong—laced with something I can't identify.

"Alexandra of the Third," says Marc.

Something is happening. I close my eyes. I sense what is coming. They are going to whip me.

I wait, utterly tensed. The music swells and ebbs. I wait some more, and then—

Crack.

I feel the first impact of the cane on my backside and it stings, very badly, yet the stinging is sugared with pleasure. I stare at Marc. He stares at me. He is watching me being whipped. We have become the frescoes of the Villa of the Mysteries.

"Drink."

The handmaiden steps forward and I stoop my head and sip; some of the wine slips down my chin. I feel like a shackled wild animal. I understand why they would want to chain and cuff me. I sense a certain dangerousness inside me.

Crack.

I do not know how long the caning lasts. The alcohol, if that is what it is, makes me even dreamier. All I want to do is look at Marc as he looks at me and watches me being beaten. And he does, he watches. Unsmiling. Yet somehow intense. Our eyes seldom leave each other's gaze.

Between each lavish and stunning blow, the handmaidens

give me this gorgeous wine to drink and I guzzle it down thirstily. I am reveling: let them all observe me. Let them regard my beauty being beaten and whipped. My naked and painted skin in this dark, sacred space. The masked faces all around me are dipped and admiring. Reverential.

The music has changed, though it remains choral and quite fitting. The caning is sumptuously erotic: the snap of the rattan on my flesh; the sense of pain and the wine on my tongue. The candlelight is gorgeous and soft on my sparkling skin. I am not cold, and I am not too warm. I am beautiful, I feel more beautiful than I have ever felt. Look at me, Marc.

He looks at me.

Then I speak. "Do it again," I say. To no one, to everyone, to Dionysus. To Marc. "Do it again, Celenza."

Marc nods at someone behind me.

And whoever this person might be, whoever is hitting me: he obliges.

The impact of the cane is so sharp I can feel myself quivering. And trembling with pain and pleasure. And still I hang suspended, swaying from the blow, barely able to touch the floor in my heels. After the next exquisite strike I shudder and moan and know I am close to something—but it is not an orgasm; it is a different kind of climax. Another shivering inner release of psychic pain. What is this?

Marc observes.

I speak. "Do it again."

Crack. I am nearly done now: close to my conclusion. I stare down at the floor and then I realize: a handmaiden is kneeling there *with a mirror.* She is tilting the mirror for my benefit: *so I can see myself*, naked and shackled, being caned. And, yes, I do look beautiful, I do. But why? Why can flagellation be beautiful?

Is that what Caravaggio was asking? The cane hits me one more time and I moan, very quietly, and I look at Marc and he nods.

"Enough," he says.

And the caning stops.

The handmaidens step forward and untie my hands. I rub my raw and aching wrists; then I am deftly collared and Marc leads me away, by my silver chain, to a side room: a luxurious, rather Oriental room.

The collar is detached. Marc says quietly to me, as he kisses my hand, "Rest here, X, for a few minutes."

Then he disappears. I gaze around. This is a haremlike chamber with towels and silk cushions and copper bowls of water, and candlelit mirrors. Thirstily, I drink the water and the wine offered by the attending girls. They have wrapped me in a silken robe, and so I lie here, half dreaming, drinking the wine, my mind oddly empty. Then Marc is standing in the doorway; he gestures to me.

I follow Marc outside. I am in my silken robe but it hangs loosely open, showing my breasts and my small waxed triangle of pubic hair and I don't care. My sexuality is surging inside me. I want Marc. I want him. I want him to take me.

But Marc has other plans; he escorts me to the center of the chapel, which is full of more masked people, more candles, and more choral music, this time deeper and more intense, and then I see another painted and gilded naked woman who is shackled— just as I was shackled. She has her back to me, her nudity is hoisted and she is ready. Marc hands me a rattan cane and says, very quietly, "Beat her."

For a moment, I pause. This is different. I have to do the caning?

The silence is intense. Then I look again. I recognize the body, the shape of the young, ripe buttocks. The white ass, unpainted.

It is Françoise. And now Françoise turns and looks at me. Her arms are hoisted in the air; she is shackled to that hanging iron ring. Smiling softly, she gazes in my eyes, and she says, quite sadly: "It is okay, X. I was the one caning *you*."

Françoise turns her back to me once more; her beautiful head is bowed and waiting.

I look at Marc. He nods. So I lift my arm. And I strike.

Twenty-three

"Ouch."

"Ah, *mi dispiace*."

"You're meant to have a tender touch, Marc. Being an aristocrat."

I am sprawled across Marc's lap, the way I was sprawled when he was spanking me in his palazzo. But this time my dress is lifted and I am exposing my bare ass to his hands, not so that he can *spank* me, but so he can anoint my tender and inflamed skin with antiseptic cream. A cream that is rather cold.

He dabs a little more of the perfumed cream, and rubs it on me, where the rattan cane bit into my flesh. No blood was drawn, but the reddening pain is real enough.

"You really do have a quite ravishing arse," he says, meditatively, as if admiring a Rubens portrait acquired by an ancestor. "This seat of Venus, this throne of majesty . . ." His fingers massage me, soothing me with medicinal cream, and I stare down at the polished wood floor, still a little drunk and woozy, and confused, and ashamed. And aroused. And hungry.

I look over my shoulder where the seventeenth Lord Roscar-rick is kneading lotion into my ass.

"Are we done, Celenza?"

"Yes," he says. "We're done." Gently and approvingly, he pats me twice on the butt, like I am a reliable little sports car, then he puts the cap back on the ointment. I stand up and walk over to look at myself in the mirror, twisting my head to see my body from behind, illuminated by soft lamplight.

The pink welts are dwindling, but the biting memories will not evanesce so easily. The way I enjoyed caning white and curving Françoise; the delicious taste of the heady and curious wine; but most of all the view of my own flagellation in the mirror of Marc's eyes. Him watching me being beaten, naked and caned. Something deeper than sex has been stirred in me this night. But it is sex, too. Oh, sex. My libido is unfurled. I am finding it difficult not to jump on Marc. Yet I also feel shame for what I have done. And the shame itself is part of the pleasure.

How does this work? Is the transgressive quality the key to it all? The key of the Mysteries?

I let my dress fall, and turn toward Marc, who is now sitting languidly in a chair, gazing at me. He is still wearing his very *dashing* tux but his tie is effortlessly undone, and his white shirt is ripped open by a few buttons, revealing a swooping triangle of his dark, sexy chest; somehow he looks like a handsome young gambler who has lost it all on a Mississippi riverboat, and who has now blown the last of his inheritance on champagne. There is a nihilism in his smile, an anarchy in the ruffled curls of his black hair, an insouciance in his pose: one leg stretched out, one elbow resting on the chair back, leaning to the side, assessing.

"What time is it, Marc?"

He glances at his silver watch.

"Three A.M."

"Is it?"

I have totally lost track of time. The wine, the whipping, the music. The Mysteries ended with a kind of cadenza as everyone drank more of the spiced and sugared wine in the candlelit chapel. The music got louder and louder, and then it became more modern and percussive.

And I danced with Marc. But this was a wild dance, wild and romantic at once. We danced out through the floor-length windows onto a vined and lonely terrace, high above the ghost town, beneath the ghostly moon, in the empty valley filled with moonlit summer mist. We danced and held each other tight, as the music ascended and crescendoed, and then somehow we ended up here. At three A.M. I have showered the paint away and put on a dress. With no underwear.

"I'm hungry," I say.

He sits forward, and turns toward the door, and calls, "Giuseppe?"

With military immediacy the door snaps open.

"*Signor?*"

"We'll have our picnic now."

"*Sì, signor.*"

What is this?

I watch with intrigue as Giuseppe and two of the handmaidens—don't they ever sleep? Maybe no one sleeps during the Mysteries—bring in three large wicker baskets and a tartan blanket. I recognize the blanket from Capri. The girls lay out plates, cutlery, and wine bottles, and then such a spread: ciabatta bread, fat salamis, and just unwrapped cheeses—cubes of the best Taleggio, creamy and melty Gorgonzola—and big, fat Neapolitan tomatoes, with little green caper berries, and juicy pink-and-purple cherries, and soft red *soppressata* sausages, my new favorite Mediterranean cured meat, soft and sweet, a kind of transgender *saucisson*.

Giuseppe and the girls disappear. The food awaits us on the rug, like an image of cornucopia in a seventeenth-century still life. A glimpse of the land of Cockaigne. Peasant heaven.

"You think of everything," I say, swooping down on the food, kneeling rather eagerly.

"That is my job," he says, looking at me deeply. "To think of *everything.*"

He gazes at me again as I grab a knife and slice into the long, juicy salami and—rather unfemininely—shove the delicious salty meatiness into my mouth. I do not care. I am a shameful creature, I am a bad and terrible girl; but I am also a hungry bacchante, a starving maenad. Marc slips off the chair and grabs some ciabatta, tearing a big, rough, peasanty fistful, which he slathers in Gorgonzola.

We eat and drink wine, and we smile—and then we laugh. We drink more wine. I feed him a slice of *saucisson*. He feeds me two cherries, letting me bite the sweet, yielding flesh as he plucks the stalk away. I giggle. He kisses the underside of my white wrist. We share the *soppressata*. I put my hand down his shirt just to check if his heart is working. He eats a slice of fine lemon tart and then kisses me with his sweet lemon mouth.

It is a midnight feast; it is a childhood dream of a picnic, made somehow illicit and more delightful by the hour. The moon smiles down over the Aspromonte. Marc pulls down my dress and pours a little Taittinger Comtes de Champagne on my breasts, sucking the champagne from my stiffening nipples, the cold, cold bubbles making me wince with pleasure. I breathe deeply in the half-light. He kisses me again, and sucks and licks the champagne away. There is cherry juice on my white skin. Champagne in my hair, champagne everywhere. Enough time has passed. The cutlery is scattered. The cherries are crushed. The rug is ruffled. Let the moon wash the plates.

In the morning I yawn and rise, smiling at the ceiling and turning over to cuddle up to Marc, but he is gone. Gone? The dent in the pillow is faint, meaning he has been gone awhile. Instead there is one of his elegant notes, written in fountain pen. Folded on the bed next to me.

> *Gone to Plati for a meeting. Have some breakfast downstairs.*
> *I will see you at three. La Serenissima awaits! R. x*

Plati? Meeting?

I lean to the other side and check my watch: my God, it is twelve noon. Leaping from the bed, I run to the bathroom and scald myself with water—it is too hot, especially on my still-tender ass. Then I towel myself down, then go to the big, heavy, Bourbon-style wardrobe and pull it open. Giuseppe, or someone, has carefully hung all of my clothes here; I could very easily get used to this aristocratic lifestyle.

I choose a simple Prada summer dress, light marine blue, and laceless white tennis shoes. I have a yearning for simplicity. Exactly how did I ever reach a stage when a thousand-dollar Prada dress counted as "simplicity"?

Now I am a little agitated. Plati? Meeting? Meeting *who*?

I run to the door. Giuseppe is nowhere but I can hear voices downstairs. The voices of people chatting and eating? It sounds like the voices of breakfast in a big hotel—and I can smell fresh coffee, too. I run down the stairs and turn right—no, this is just the rear courtyard. I am gazing at parked cars—some expensive, some utilitarian. Marc's Land Rover is here. So he must have gone off with someone else. Who? Giuseppe?

Heading back into the castle I step left, and right, following the scent of fresh baking, and the chatter of people, encountering a big wide terrace with large tables and parasols under the sun. And people taking a very late breakfast. The white-dressed girls ferry coffee, juice, croissants, and confitures to the various guests.

This must have been the open terrace, staring out over the valley and the forests and deserted Rhoguda, where Marc and I danced last night. It looks very different by day. More daunting, somehow, with all these sophisticated people; these smiling, rich faces, male and female, young and middle-aged and elegantly old, people I dimly recognize, but from where? From last night? Perhaps, but maybe elsewhere. Celebrity websites. Newspapers. Gossip magazines.

Abruptly, I feel awkward. There is no Marc to guide me through this daunting world of European wealth and upper-class decadence. No Marc to escort me gallantly to my table, his firm hand on the small of my back, gently pressing, guiding, and teaching me without my even realizing.

I gaze around.

"Alexandra?"

A lifeline has been thrown. I crane to see, and I spot Françoise, at the most distant table. She is waving me over.

I nod at one of the white-dressed girls. "Cappuccino, *per favore.*" And I step to the table with its white metal chairs where Françoise is just finishing a croissant.

She smiles at me slyly and says, "Good morning."

"*Bonjour.*"

Her smile widens.

"I bet you are good at tennis. *Quite* the forehand."

"I am known for my dramatic service game."

She laughs politely.

"Did you enjoy it?"

"It was . . . exhilarating," I say. "So, I suppose, yes. I did." I am looking at her, directly, brazenly, as I reach into the basket and take a croissant, smoothing it with apricot jam. Sweet, dark yellow jam; dark, bitter coffee with milky froth. Delicious.

Her eyes glitter. She is in jeans and a simple white T-shirt. Dressed further down than me. But I can remember her undressed entirely: painted and naked, hoisted and at my mercy. I can remember my arm raised, caning her beautiful white ass. It was arousing. Why? I cannot be bisexual, can I? No, I really don't think so. I want men too much—I want Marc Roscarrick *far* too much. But it was exhilarating, and also *arousing*, in its own way.

"What about you?" I say, sipping more coffee. "What do you think about . . . all of this? I mean the Mysteries, as a whole."

"They are changing me," she says simply. And she seems pensive as she gazes over the old crumbling Bourbon balustrade. The somber forests of the Bitter Mountains lie beyond. "Daniel told me the Mysteries would do this—change me. I didn't really believe it, but it is true. I am seduced. I love it all—I adore the Mysteries, I even like the drama, the intrigue: Where are we going next? Who will be there? What will happen to me? But"— she hesitates, and turns to me—"they are also . . . rather frightening. *Un peu dangereux.*"

A white-dressed girl waits patiently at the tableside; I ask her for more coffee. Then I turn back to Françoise, and I ask her about Daniel. She tells me he is doing business this morning; they will be leaving in the evening. *Doing business*, just like Marc.

She duly asks me about Marc, where we met, where he is. I tell her, happily. But then, less happily, I remember the words she used in Capri.

I really need to clear this up. Marc's disappearance this morning is niggling.

"Françoise, on Capri, you said something about Marc."

A soft, warm breeze—rising from the deep valley below— ripples the canvas of the parasol as she listens to my question. Her expression is honest and candid. But also a tiny bit anxious.

"I shouldn't have said anything."

"Françoise?"

"Really, I don't know anything more than that."

"Yes you do."

"But—"

"Tell me. Please. As a friend."

"But—"

"Françoise!"

She looks at me, takes a deep sigh, and says, "Okay. There is gossip. The thing he did. But I shouldn't have said what I said. These are feeble rumors."

"The thing he did? You mean the Camorra? That he is in the Camorra?"

She gazes at me, frowning deeply.

"No."

"Then what? What? His dead wife? His money? What?"

A bird of prey is circling above us. The terrace is now largely deserted, the breakfast tables strewn with tousled napkins, the chairs set back. We are almost alone. Where is Marc? How dare he just leave me here? To go for a meeting in Plati? I surge with sudden but righteous anger.

"Françoise, I want to know everything. Everything, anything, *everything.* Tell me. I've had enough of all the enigmatic bullshit."

Françoise winces, but she also nods.

"All right. The very wildest rumor I heard is this." She breathes in—and breathes out. "I only learned this the other day—because I was talking to a friend, an Italian girl from the Second Mystery, talking to her about you. And then I mentioned Roscarrick and this girlfriend of mine, her name is Clea, well, I mean, she is, you know, connected in Rome . . ."

"Françoise!"

"Okay, okay. They say Marc was involved with the 'Ndrangheta—as a very young man—here in Calabria. . . ."

"What is it? What did he do?"

A pause. Finally she answers.

"He is said to have killed someone. Shot him in cold blood. In broad daylight. In Plati."

The eagle is still circling above us, mewing as it hunts. A forlorn but sinister noise. I am stunned into silence.

Françoise reaches across the table and holds my hand with her two hands.

"X, please remember this. Marc Roscarrick is young and handsome, rich and clever—in a very envious society. This isn't America, where people celebrate success—this is old Europe. Deepest, darkest old Europe. People often resent success, it breeds bitter jealousy. So I suspect the rumors are merely that. Put your mind at rest."

Put my mind at rest? My mind is on fire. Marc is a murderer?

And then a switch is thrown. I turn from Françoise and stare at the circling eagle.

Plati.

I recall the face of the old man at the door last night, talking in that conspiratorial way with Marc. I thought I remembered it; now I realize why I recognized his face. I have seen it often in the newspapers, seen it in the *Corriere della Sera*. Not because that old man is a famous politician or an actor or industrialist, but because he is a notorious gangster: one of the most infamous and powerful 'Ndrangheta gangsters of all. I can even recall his name.

Enzo Paselli.

And that's why I have heard the name Plati. It is the home of the 'Ndrangheta, the heart of their terrible darkness. The home of the Clan Paselli.

I rise, abruptly.

Françoise pales.

"X, where are you going?"

"Plati. It is near here, isn't it? It must be. You carry on down the road, Marc said."

Her shock is vivid.

"You can't. That is crazy. They have . . . they kill people . . . the roads are frightful!"

I am running from the breakfast table. I am running through the castle. I am climbing into the Land Rover. And, as I guessed, the keys are hanging from the dash. Who would dare to steal a car from a party attended by Italy's most brutal gangsters?

I turn the key and rev the engine.

But I hear a voice. It is Françoise. Running out the door, onto the gravel.

"Don't do this, X. You mustn't. Plati is a terrible place—very dangerous—Alexandra!"

I reverse the car, and turn right. Taking the dirt road to Plati.

Twenty-four

The road to Plati seems okay at first, but then it narrows to a slender strip of flattened earth, curving around a steep mountainside. The valley yawns away at my left, filled with rocks and dull gray grit, a river of dust being shunted all the way to the gray-turquoise flatness of the Ionian Sea: at times I can glimpse the water through the beeches.

It is bleak. I imagine in spring there might be wildflowers here, the flash of pink oleander and yellow broom—the glint of water, torrents of snowmelt maybe—but in the hot high summer it is just rocks and dust and nothing. And a road that disappears.

Skidding around another dust-shrouded corner, I see that a landslide has swept this entire section of the "road" clean away. I am going to have to edge the car across a hundred yards of treacherous debris. There is the hulk of a burned-out Fiat maybe a quarter of a mile below, trapped by the trees; the last rusting remains of someone who didn't make it.

And yet I edge the car forward: I change down a gear; I change up a gear; the engine complains. Slowly I inch the car across the stones and mud and rubble; the whining, growling Land Rover engine is the sound of my determination, verging on desperation.

I have to get to Plati. I have to know the truth about Marc. And Enzo Paselli, I am sure, will tell me the truth, if I can find him.

Why I think this, I do not know.

The Land Rover squeals. I force my foot down and the car shoots forward, squirting stones, and the rear wheels begin to slide perilously to the left, and they are actually *lifting*, but the front wheels *bite* and the Land Rover surges on and we are back on the road. The car and me. Alive.

But even as the relief surges, more doubts assail me. Maybe Marc will be there, talking and laughing at a white café table, sipping amaretto, reminiscing about the men they murdered.

I shudder.

A murderer?

Please don't let Marc be a murderer.

I drive on. Just drive. Just get there. Eat up the kilometers. The road is dusty, rubbled, winding, and endless. I glimpse the odd wild horse staring perplexed at me, wondering what a car is doing in the middle of a sunburned forest. Then at last the road improves, and my anxiety tightens.

What if Marc went to Plati for some confrontation? Marc, don't do this to me. Don't be this. Don't be one of them.

Plati.

There it is. I am descending from a narrow, treeless pass into a different valley, and now I can see a town, not as small as I had expected, littering the slopes below. The town looks like trash and debris rudely scattered by someone upending a sack, and then walking away. There are half-built houses everywhere, half-built roads, half-built shops.

"Eh! Eh!"

Two kids are shouting and pointing at the car. I am passing a walled cemetery on the outskirts of Plati, and they are playing some purposeless game among the tombs—but when they see me they shout and jump excitedly.

"*Signorina! Signorina!*" One of them makes an obscene phallic gesture and the two boys laugh and whoop. I cannot work out if they are astonished by the arrival of someone on the absurdly dangerous back road, or acting as some kind of lookout for everyone in the town.

Then I realize they are simply astonished that *anyone* unknown should come to Plati. Because I get the same wide-eyed, mouth-half-open expression from everyone. There are old men outside a grimy bar, sharing a bottle of grappa—and they all turn, as one, and gaze at the strange vehicle passing by. One of them shakes his head, somberly and gravely, as if amazed to the point of being *offended*.

I am properly frightened now. Plati is hideous, and the sense of hostility is intense. For a moment I get the strongest desire to just press on, floor the pedal, keep driving through this ghastly town, get onto a proper road, then head on down to the coast, and Reggio, and the airport.

But I can't. I have to know the truth about Marc. I park the car in what amounts to ugly Plati's closest approximation of a central square, a piazza, though in reality it is just a bunch of slightly taller, unfinished cement buildings, gazing at a flat and empty car lot. It is Islamically austere.

Then I spy a big utilitarian bar, half hidden by a concrete wall. The bar boasts a few plastic tables out front, a few drinkers staring glumly back at me. This is it. Cafes are the center of Italian sociability and this is the biggest cafe in town. If I am going to find Enzo Paselli and the truth about Marc, I will find it here.

I take a seat at one of the plastic tables, ignoring the expressions of everyone else: the guy tapping on the side of the nose to signify the odor of something suspicious, the guy pulling down his eyelid, telling everyone, keep your eyes wide open.

A sad-looking waiter comes over to my table. His reluctance is obvious, his body language is overt. He doesn't want to speak to me; he wants me to go away. But I have stopped blushing; I am already too far in.

"*Signorina . . . ?*"

"Espresso, *per favore.*"

His eyes brighten, he looks intensely relieved at this—the lady just wants a quick coffee, then she will be gone.

But I add, in Italian: "I am looking for Enzo Paselli."

Sto cercando Enzo Paselli.

The waiter's face goes rigid. I have surely violated some terrible code merely by mentioning the name.

He does not reply. Wordless and pale, he turns and disappears into the cafe. Everyone stares at me from the other tables. Two youngish mothers, with babes in arms, are openly grimacing. A trio of middle-aged men, in neat blazers and well-pressed pants, sharing a nice-looking bottle of Nero d'Avola, stare in amazement at this stupid blond American woman.

The waiter returns.

"Espresso" is all he says, as rudely as possible, dropping the tiny white cup and saucer on the unwiped table. He so obviously yearns for me to drink. Just go, *signorina*, just quit.

I look up at him and repeat. "*Sto cercando Enzo Paselli.*"

The waiter stands back and looks around the tables, seeking moral support, some assistance with this crazy American woman who wants to get herself shot.

My heartbeat is accelerated and constant; I have my fears, but I am still determined. The rigmarole is repeated three times in an hour. Each time the waiter comes out, I order coffee, or water, and I ask to see Enzo Paselli; each time he looks at me with his pale, sad face and says nothing, then he brings me the coffee. I can hear the other cafe-goers whispering. One of the middle-aged men rises and leaves his friends. Gone to get a gun? To get some thugs?

A car backfires somewhere and I think for a moment, almost with relief, that this is it. Someone is shooting someone. I want to cry. I want to get away from horrible Plati. But I need the truth about Marc. So I stand and I go right up to the waiter, who is virtually shrinking from me, and I say: "*Sto cercando Enzo Paselli!*"

This time he responds with another classic Italian gesture: hands pressed prayerfully together, then shaken up and down—the gesture that says, please, please, please, do not be unreasonable.

"*Signorina, per favore, non si capisce—*"

"*Sto cercando Enzo Paselli!*"

I am practically shouting. I am quite crazy. They are entirely justified in having me taken to the police, but of course no police ever come to Plati.

And then I feel a hand on my arm. A short young man is touching my elbow. He says, in thick Calabrian, "*Venga con me.*"

Come with me.

He could be taking me to my car, he could be taking me to be killed. He has a large tattoo on his neck. His motorcycle boot heels are stacked. He leads me around a littered corner and I immediately see another cafe, more refined, with proper awnings, and tablecloths on proper tables.

And there is Enzo Paselli. Eating his late Sunday lunch, alone. And looking at me. He has half a bottle of wine. He is eating snails. *Babalucci*, attached to green fronds.

He actually stands as I approach the table. He is in pale blue slacks and a wide-collared shirt, which shows his withered old neck. His chest hair is quite silver. His face is very lined; he is totally bald. Yet still he exudes menace, even a kind of lethal virility. A killer with false teeth.

He extends a liver-spotted hand. I shake it. His shake is weak. Insubstantial, barely there. He must get someone else to do the killing.

Then he sits down and eats a tiny snail. The snail drool runs down his chin and it shines in the sun as he speaks. He talks in perfect American-accented English.

"I understand you are looking for me."

"Yes."

He smiles. The snail drool still glistens.

"You know this is a very stupid thing to do."

"Yes."

"So why?" He eats a second snail: squidging it between his false teeth. "Why come to Plati?"

A silence. What do I say? Enzo interrupts my thoughts.

"You are aware, young lady, that they kidnap people here. There are tunnels under *every* house. Bodies are interred in the forests all around. Many, *many* bodies."

"I am the girlfriend of Marc Roscarrick and I want to know the truth."

A second silence, but much briefer. He nods my way.

"So you are Alexandra Beckmann. I thought as much."

I stare at him, astonished. He does not respond, just picks up a napkin as if he is going to wipe the disgusting slime from his chin, but instead he uses it to flap away a fly. Then he leans forward, and takes a slurp of wine—Greco di Bianco. The fly buzzes. I ask, stuttering, "How do you know who I am?"

He smiles and swallows the wine.

"It is my job to know everything. Otherwise . . ." He eats another snail, popping it in his mouth. "Otherwise I would be one of the bodies in the forests above Gioia Tauro."

A long pause ensues as he munches and drinks and stares at me with his watery eyes, with the snail track on his chin. I wonder if he leaves this drool there deliberately, to freak me out, to repulse me; a piece of mafia theater. If so, it works—I am at the edge of my ability to keep control, to not run away.

This is it. I speak.

"Please. Can you tell me the truth about Marc Roscarrick? I know you know him. I saw you in Rhoguda Castle last night. I want to know the truth about him and what happened in Plati."

Enzo Paselli thoughtfully munches his snails, detaching them carefully from slimy green fronds, then skewering them with a tiny fork and slipping them in his wet old mouth. He swallows, and answers.

"You are a brave woman, Miss Beckmann, coming to Plati on the back road from Rhoguda. Coming to the most dangerous town in Italy. You know this is also the *richest* town in Italy? But the money is buried, like the rotting bodies." He sits back. "So you are brave, very brave. And I admire bravery. It is the greatest human virtue, the virtue of Jesus. Therefore"—he smiles—"I will tell you the truth about Marc Roscarrick."

He lifts his wineglass and tilts it slightly, admiring the straw-gold color of the liquid. Then he goes on. "Roscarrick is a murderer. It is true. He killed a man, here in Plati, in the middle of the day. Next to that cafe where you had your several espressos."

The sun is hot and cold on my neck. I can feel a faintness. It is over. It is done. My love, my lord, my loneliness. All over.

Enzo Paselli is smiling. His false teeth are stained with snail juice. It is a grotesque comedy, and I am not laughing, not laughing at all.

"But he had a reason. You should know the context."

"What?" I try to keep control. "Tell me the context, please."

"Lord Roscarrick went into business here, importing through Reggio—"

"Yes. I know this."

Enzo Paselli nods at me, and eats one of his last little snails. Then he goes on. "He *angered* many people here in Plati. He annoyed several rather *important* people. He did not put any sugar in our coffees. You understand?"

"Yes."

"Certain of these people wanted him gone, they wanted Roscarrick gone. They gave the job to Salvatore Palmi. You will not have heard of him. But everyone in Calabria has heard of him, or at least of his nickname, *Norcino*." A pause. "The pig butcher."

Enzo drinks a large gulp of wine, breathes out, and goes on. "Norcino couldn't get to Roscarrick himself, he was too well guarded, but he could get at Roscarrick's employees, Roscarrick's workmen. So Norcino went to work, he butchered several of Roscarrick's workers. Chopped them up. He slaughtered three in one week. Literally sliced them to pieces, alive. He had special knives."

I stare at the old man; the snail drool has dried to a powder on his chin. The afternoon has stopped. We are totally alone, out here in front of the restaurant, though I can see dark, worried faces inside—staring out at us.

Enzo pushes away his plate and concludes his story.

"Salvatore Palmi was, in truth, a disgusting psychotic. He was loathed, he was feared; even in Plati he was regarded as . . . beyond the pale. But the police were too scared to do anything. Salvatore was working for the clans, the *capos*. Untouchable and unstoppable. But Norcino liked his work a little too much; he just loved making his human prosciutto. The next week Salvatore killed Roscarrick's foreman—he killed him at home, in front of his own children, chopped off his head—and then he killed the wife, immediately after. Simply because he liked killing."

A nausea rises in me. Enzo shakes his old hairless head.

"Everyone was paralyzed with fear. Salvatore was like a family dog, a Rottweiler, that has begun to scare the family. Too big to control. He would sit at that cafe, where you had your espressos, on a Sunday morning, with his acolytes. Salvatore the pig butcher never dreamed that anyone would have the balls to just drive into Plati."

I stare at Enzo. He nods.

"But Marc Roscarrick had the balls. The next Sunday, after the butcher had sliced up that family, your boyfriend just drove into Plati, into that square, and he walked up to Salvatore with a gun in his hand. Salvatore was drinking prosecco. Unprepared, at ease, and totally shocked. Roscarrick lifted Salvatore to his feet, dragged him into the center of the square, made him kneel, and shot the pig butcher in the head. Then Roscarrick got into his car and drove away."

A sip of wine, a wise little smile.

"It was the bravest thing I have ever seen, and, as I say, I admire bravery. It was also very clever: it was so impressive it became legend, it gave Roscarrick a reputation, a reputation he still has. Many people began to believe he had powers, influence—he must be high up in the Camorra, how else would you find the balls to do that?"

"So he isn't in the Camorra?"

Enzo ignores me.

"Normally the *people* in Plati would have taken revenge for such an affront, but this time we decided to be more politic. After all, he had got rid of our problem, the dog that grew too big." Enzo stiffens, as if he is about to rise. "We met with your Lord Roscarrick. We called a truce. We told him to get out of Calabria, and we agreed the 'Ndrangheta would, for once, take no revenge. And there it is. And that is why I met with your boyfriend last night, and again this morning. To ensure the truce remains." Enzo smiles his stained and withered smile. "I like Roscarrick, but he perplexes me. I still do not know if he is saint or sinner. Where did he get his money from, to start that business? His family were impoverished. Then his rich young wife died, so suddenly. That was an evil fortune."

He waves the napkin at the fly once more. "And now, Alexandra Beckmann, we must say good-bye. If you ever come to Plati again you will find me at this restaurant; they do excellent osso bucco in the evening. But for now you must go; I cannot keep the dogs in the kennel all day. Go before you are taken to the forests above Gioia Tauro. Go."

Half stumbling, half dreaming, I rise and walk to the corner, and cross the grubby piazza, and climb into my car. This time I am taking the main road, around the coast of Calabria. I want safety, I want to get out. Please get me out of here. Please please please please God.

The car roars out, and down. My mind whirls: I am escaping. I am leaving Plati. The one good road descends the valley. I race through the olive groves, going too far, racing like my thoughts, and then I turn a corner and I see a car coming toward me. Two men. Two faces. The road is single tracked. We have to stop. I look at the men in the car. One of them gets out. I stop.

It is Marc. Standing there, his face taut and sad and desperate.

I climb out of my car, my knees are shaking. He looks at me with those sad, pale, beautiful eyes. Six yards away.

"X," he says. "X . . . I thought . . ."

I am sobbing so hard I am close to fainting. And I am running into his open arms.

"Marc. Marc. *Marc.*"

Twenty-five

Marc presses me close to his chest as I weep, gulping sobs. Then he lifts up my face and kisses me, twice, on the forehead, then on the mouth. My crying mouth, salty with tears. He speaks.

"I went back to Rhoguda, to the castle."

"But, Marc—"

"The girl, Françoise, she said you'd gone to Plati—on that terrible back road—on your own?"

"I had no choice—"

"I thought the worst." He kisses me. "I thought you might have driven off the road, been killed. Then . . ." He kisses me again, twice, quickly, fiercely. "Then I thought you . . . even if you'd made it to Plati, what then? What would you do? What would you say? You could have been . . . anything . . . anything could have happened. I sent someone down the back road to check, and Giuseppe and I raced here to Plati."

He lifts my face by the chin. And he asks, "What happened?"

The sobs are subsiding. I wipe my face with the back of my

hand, smearing away the salt and wet. Giuseppe steps forward with a tissue, and hands it to me. I murmur, *"Grazie."*

Then I dry the tears, properly. Giuseppe is holding the car door open. Breathing deeply and slowly, calming myself as best I can, I climb in the front; Marc follows me, taking the wheel. Giuseppe goes to the Land Rover. We are escaping, heading south, aiming for the Ionian Sea.

I speak. "Marc, I saw Enzo Paselli. He told me, about . . . the butcher. What you did."

Marc is silent as he drives. His profile is tense, pensive. He does not look my way as he says, "And?"

I touch his arm.

"Take me away from here, Marc. Anywhere. Just anywhere." He turns to me. His hand falls onto my thigh, but it is passive, gentle, calming. I am stifling a sudden surge of more tears. The emotions are too much.

The traffic ebbs and flows on the narrow Calabrian roads; the ugly towns blur past. Eventually I rouse from my strange, dreamlike state.

"Where are we going?"

"The airport, then South Tyrol."

"Tyrol . . . ?"

"Giuseppe can go back to Naples. We can get a direct flight to Verona, and drive from there. I want to get out of the south, just for a while."

"Okay . . . okay. Tyrol. You have a house there, a schloss."

I remember: South Tyrol. Of course. I have never forgotten that dreamy wine. The Moscato Rosa.

"It is peaceful and it is beautiful," he says, staring out at one dilapidated building with half its façade torn away. "It is safe and far away. And then," he turns to me, "then we are going to Venice."

Twenty-six

By the time we land at Verona airport, my nerves are calmed. Somewhat. Outside the little terminal, Marc is greeted by a friend—or acquaintance—or servant—and given the keys to another car: a small and fast BMW. It occurs to me how every transaction in life is made so much smoother by Marc's immense wealth; yet he made that money by fighting the mafias. And in the end he had to kill someone.

I want to run away forever. Yet I also fiercely want to kiss him. Instead, I silently climb into the car and we make the drive to Tyrol.

At first the landscape is desultory; north Italian suburbia. Carrefour supermarkets and concrete canals; lots of commuters looking hot and irritable as the sun begins to set. It is in the eighties here, even at eight P.M. The dusty sunburned plains of Veneto. Parched and brown. Like me. I feel parched and brown. I want sex. I want to resolve the tension in my head with sex. It is the only way I can get over this. The only way I can really get back to Marc.

Sex.

I wonder if I should just lean across and kiss him. But I can't. Somehow. I don't know why. So I shall just sit here, wanting him, but watching the cypress trees whir past. Watching the Alfa Romeo showrooms, and the shallow hills.

But then I see the mountains ahead. My eyes widen. Some of them are snowcapped; immense and mighty, crystalline and glittering. Signs for Trento and Bolzano tell me we must be getting close; we are certainly roaring up the autostrada, driving straight along an enormous river valley as the mountains encroach on either side.

"It's stunning," I say, gazing out the car window. These are practically the first words I have spoken in two hours. They are almost reflexive: an instinctive reaction to the sudden splendor. I still want Marc.

"Just wait, *cara mia*; it gets better," says Marc. And he pushes the pedal and we overtake a long Czech truck as he races us north. And as we accelerate, I see what he means.

The landscape is now perfect, like a fairy tale. Vivid green terraces of vines and apple orchards ascend to cliffs where dreaming castles shine in the shadows and the sun; above and beyond the castles, and the ancient hilltop villages, are the mountains.

"The Dolomites."

I have never seen mountains like this; they look unreal, like a gifted child's idea of mountains: enormous spires of gray and glacial rock loom ten or fifteen thousand feet in the air. Quite vertical. Like stone-and-ice pinnacles. Like cathedrals waiting in the sun. Waiting for what?

"I stayed here a lot when I was a boy," Marc says. "My mother and sister still live here."

He is taking us off the autostrada; now we are threading down a narrow country road, through more vineyards, where old men stoop and examine grapes; through lush emerald farms where horses canter in meadows, past painted old villages with medieval churches. I am trying not to think about Marc and me naked. Perhaps I have become obsessive. Can you have a sexual psychosis? Have the Mysteries made me oversexual?

Abruptly, I realize.

"All the signs are in German."

"We have passed the linguistic watershed," he says. And I try not to look at the way his muscled arms turn the steering wheel, or the way his stubble underlines the certain firmness of his jawline, or the way his cheekbones slant quite dangerously, predatorily, and aggressively. I can imagine that handsome face wrought with anger, killing someone. I can. Yet I still want to kiss him. This is surely wrong.

"Ten miles back they speak mostly Italian, here it is German, yet they are still Italian by nationality. Italians who park sensibly."

Another sudden turn takes us onto a long graveled drive. I gawp. It ends at a very large and handsome old house, covered with vines and bougainvillea, and boasting a large and battlemented tower in the corner.

"Schloss Roscarrick. My mother and sister are away; they will be here tomorrow."

He spins the car, flamboyantly, on the gravel, and parks in front of the big main door. A middle-aged man comes hurrying out. He is in shorts and sandals and a T-shirt, yet I gather from his demeanor that he is a servant.

"*Guten tag*, Klaus," Marc says, climbing out. The servant smiles, takes the key and nods, very politely, my way. Then the servant says something, apologetically, about working in the garden. At least, this is what I surmise, from "*garten*," as my German is pretty poor. Marc nods and happily accepts the apology. He gestures at the luggage in the back. "*Ein uhr? Im Zweiten Schlafzimmer. Danke*, Klaus."

Marc takes my hand. He leads me to the big door. I cannot bear this anymore. As soon as the door shuts behind us, I reach for his face and kiss him.

He does not require encouragement. He actually lifts me off my feet, and we kiss. And kiss again.

"Marc," I say, half crying, half smiling, "I think you have to fuck me. Or I am going to run away."

He drops me to the floor and starts ripping at my clothes. But I am also ripping at his. His shirt, I tear at it. I want to bite his bare and toned chest. Make him bleed. I want to see him aroused by me. I want that power over him.

"This way," he says, pulling me roughly and gorgeously by the hand. "The bedroom is up here."

The stairs are huge and wide and grand. And he is trying to strip me even as we ascend. Pushing him away, I kick off one shoe, then another. Now I am barefoot. And running. He is running after me. Tearing off his own shirt, throwing it over the balustrade. It flutters in the warm, soft air, a pennant of his lust.

"Where is the bedroom?"

"In here," he says. I turn to him. The bedroom door opens to his hand. We step inside and the door slams shut behind. His shirt is off. My dress is pulled away. I am in my underwear, panties and bra. I want to be naked for him, naked with him. But I am hot—sweaty and hot after that long drive, and the flight. I want to be clean.

"I need a shower."

"Then let me wash you."

He picks me up, and carries me, draped facedown over his shoulder, into a big and bright and fabulously modern bathroom. Steel glitters everywhere. I gaze around. Marc paid for this. He paid for all of this.

Now my Lord Roscarrick sets me down on the bathroom floor. He unclasps my bra and peels down my panties; I am naked, impatient and perspiring.

"So wash me."

Once more he picks me up, like an ice skater hoisting his partner, and he takes me and he drops me in the shower. He turns a steel dial and warm water comes gushing out. Shirtless, Marc takes the showerhead, on its bending steel hose, and he begins to bathe me. His hands are soaped and warm. It is the same soap he uses in Naples. The soap from Firenze. The scent is divine, and Marc is cleaning me.

He gushes water over my feet, soaping my toes, carefully, sweetly, elegantly. He lifts my feet and washes them clean, toe by toe. When the washing is done he kisses them. And sucks one, then two. Now he drops my feet and he foams and waters my calves, my knees, my thighs. He is studious, dedicated. Diligently he massages my ass with soap suds and clean hot water, and the pleasure throbs somewhere within me; but I wait, and watch, as he turns me around and directs the hot and lovely water on my pubic hair, and my sex, his hands slip between my wet, soapy thighs. And this is too much.

"Get in the shower with me."

"In a minute, *cara mia*, just a minute."

He is soaping my breasts now. Frowning, massaging, covering me with this scented and angelic foam, his soft hands, his hard hands. Lifting the showerhead above my head he jets the water onto my hair and my face; I close my eyes as the water sluices the very last of the sweat from my face. My eyes are shut tightly. And then I can feel his soft mouth on my lips. Kissing me quite hard.

Marc is in the shower. He has kicked off his jeans. He is naked with me and his erection is there. I can feel it against me. I open my eyes. I reach down and hold his cock, his adorable thickness, in my hands. I take some of the foam and I wash his desire. Reverent and careful. I love his erection. I love him. I love his desire for me. How could I doubt him?

As soon as he has washed himself down, he flicks the water off, and we step onto towels, and we dry each other. Then we look at each other and we actually *run* into the bedroom, naked and clean and young and in love. And ready to fuck. Like normal lovers. But better. But worse. But wait.

We are on the bed. He wants to take me. I stop him, and shake my head. Then I reach out a hand, and I grasp him *there* in my hand. And now I look him in the eye. And I say, "You killed a man."

He nods, his blue eyes glittering.

"I killed a man."

"You had to do it?"

"I had to do it."

"I can forgive you . . ."

"*Can you?*"

I grasp his cock tighter. His eyes narrow. Our faces are inches apart.

"Yes. I can. Because I love you. Roscarrick, I fucking love you. And I wish I didn't. But I do."

It is the first time I have said it. One or two tears are rolling down my face. I let go of Marc. I lie back on the bed.

"Now do it, do it, take me, please, before—before I change my mind—before it falls apart—before I give up and run away."

He nods. Then he stoops down to lick me. But I don't want this. Reaching out again, I take his face in my hands, and I lift him up; I kiss him on the lips, his red, fine lips, and then I kiss him again.

"Marc, I am ready."

Wordless, he pushes me onto my back, he slaps my thighs open. And then he leans forward and looks me hard and commandingly in the eyes and he smiles very faintly—and enters me hard.

The sense of relief is *intense*. I am grinding my teeth together. This is painful. This is brilliant. He drives his cock into me again. And again. I am so very wet. And not from the shower. He thrusts, and I gasp. Out loud. Almost crying again. This is vivid, this is what I want: nothing gentle, not now, not after today. No languid foreplay. Just this. Just him. Hard. Possessing me. All of me.

We fuck each other. That is the only way to describe it. We are fucking each other. Taking what we want from each other. Devouring and appetitive. I kiss him on the shoulder, magnificent and hard. Then I bite him. Hard. And kiss him again.

He gasps.

"You."

I scratch my nails down his back as he enters me again, deep and deeper. He gasps. I know this is painful. I want it to be painful. For him as well as me. I gaze into his eyes as he rises and closes, entering me, once and again. And I say, "I love you, you bastard."

I scratch again. He thrusts again. I caress the cruel and tender beauty of his jawline.

"I hate you but I love you."

"X, X . . ."

He lifts my legs so my feet are pressed on his chest, even as he fucks me. My small and bare white feet. Pressed on his hard, sun-tanned, and dark-haired chest. He fucks me. Then he separates my feet, his hands hard around my ankles, and he moves my legs higher, doubling them back, almost painfully, like he wants to go even farther into me. Deeper, so I am crushed underneath him.

I am submitting. He is dominant. He has my feet pushed so far back I can feel the wall with my toes. I like this, I like the subtle pain; I let him ride me, drive me, control me. Do what he wants with me. He is close to coming, I can tell by the angry beauty in his eyes. Abruptly, he lets my legs fall. And he relaxes for a second, pausing, waiting.

Now I come back at him.

I bite the skin on his shoulder as he enters me again. That heavy, masculine shoulder. These murderous arms. These lethal hands. This duelist. Marc Roscarrick.

"From behind."

Who am I? Giving orders?

Marc obeys. He turns me over. In that balletic way, twirling me in his hands, spinning me round. Like I am a toy, or a favorite tool. Then he opens my thighs again. Oh, oh yes. Now we are nearly done. I sink my face into the pillow. Knowing what comes next. Delighted by what comes next.

But what comes next is different. He thrusts inside me eight or nine times, dominant and hard, and gorgeously deep—but then he withdraws. He reaches under my stomach and picks me up, bodily, and carries me across the room.

To the window. And the big window is wide open. I can see the mountains and the forests, and the darkening blue evening sky. The mountains are red, glowing gorgeous red, in the setting sun. Marc drapes me over the window ledge. It is cushioned with leather. I am facing out, at the mountains. He is behind me.

Then he enters me again. He is fucking me over the window ledge. From behind. I can feel the cooling sweet evening air on my breasts. I can smell the pine forests and the mountains. I can see the glaciers of the Dolomites. I can feel his fingers on my clitoris. I can feel his desire inside me. I can feel the tears on my face. I can feel the shudder of my orgasm approaching. Like horses in the distance. Thundering.

Twenty-seven

"So South Tyrol is nice?"

"Beautiful, really, really stunning. The Dolomites are just amazing. Le Corbusier said they look *designed*—and they do."

"Le Creuset? The guy who makes saucepans? Who gives a toss what he thinks about the Dolomites?"

I suspect Jess is joking.

"Not Le Creuset, Le Corbusier. The Swiss architect."

"Oh."

"They are ravishing, Jess. There are these green, green meadows with wildflowers and sweet, warm lakes, at four thousand feet, and then these enormous rose-gray peaks, like cathedrals—a parade of Gothic cathedrals."

"Yeah?"

"Yes, really."

"Meh. Mountains. Who needs 'em? Overrated."

I smile. Jess laughs on my phone screen. We are Skyping. She is in her room in Naples, with the ironic calendar of Mussolini on the wall. I am in a large room on the second floor of a rented palazzo on the Grand Canal. And I am in Venice. We drove down here from Marc's Tyrolean family home this morning. We parked the car in Mestre and got the boat across the lagoon.

Venice!

"So you went to his famous schloss and stayed there and ate *kartoffelsalat* and everything?"

"*Ja. Es schmeckt gut.*"

"And you are fully, you know, recovered from your wounds?"

"I am perfectly fine, thanks for asking."

"Well, hey. I just worry about your *ass*, X. I'm guessing it's taking a lot of punishment?"

Jess is mildly irritated that I am not telling her more about the Mysteries. She wants details, the more salacious the better. But, naturally, I can't tell her very much.

"Trust me, I am fine. We're all fine."

She rolls her eyes and chuckles. Then she says, "So what was the schloss like?"

"Big and . . . imposing. And I met his mother and sister."

"Really? Lady Perfect. And?"

Her eyes are wide with anticipation.

"They're not quite what I expected, actually. The sister is very sweet, very English, slightly reserved, rather funny. The mother is more, sort of, Teutonic."

"Yeah?"

"Blond and Nordic. Like a Norman queen. Eleanor of Aquitaine. Is Aquitaine in Normandy?"

"Yeah, probably. But I thought the mama was from Naples, X? Blue-blooded Neapolitans and all that?"

"Well, yes. That's what I mean. She is not what I expected. And there is something a little sad about her." I look over my own shoulder. I can actually hear a Venetian vaporetto hooting its way up the canal. I reckon I can hear tourists heading for the Rialto. Or St. Mark's Square.

I am desperate to get out there, to see it all, because I have, of course, never been here before; we have arrived just in time for the Fourth Mystery, which is happening tonight.

Venice!

I turn back to my laptop, and Jess's happy, smiling, pretty, funny, snub-nosed British face. My friend. I miss her. It's been three weeks since I was in Naples. Three weeks since Marc flew me to Calabria, then the Tyrol.

The emotions of those moments still make me shiver. Marc Roscarrick has truly entered my soul. There will be no getting rid of him now.

I rouse again from the memory, and gaze at Jess, who is checking some text on her phone. And smiling. I say, "How's everything in Santa Lucia?"

She looks up and shrugs.

"Pretty cool."

"Teaching?"

She grimaces—but in a contented way. A half-smiling way. *Hmm.* I sense there is some secret there, she has got something to tell me. But Jess has questions of her own.

"So, X . . . I've been meaning to ask. How about . . . *it*?"

"Sorry?"

Her voice drops an octave, and quite a few decibels.

"I mean, you know, it, the *thing*, the thing thing, what happened in Plati. Are you, like, over that?" She squints, close to the camera. "Can you cope with all that?"

I have told her this story in an e-mail: I sent it two weeks ago. I told her everything: all I had learned about Marc killing a man, in cold blood. Maybe I shouldn't have told her; but she *is* my best friend, and I had to share it with someone: it was too much to own by myself. I had to dilute the knowledge, and spread the burden.

Her e-mailed reaction was total shock and surprise. With not a trace of her usual sarcasm, or cynical amusement. Which only served to underline the seriousness of the facts I was relating.

But she also expressed her worries for me, as she is expressing them now.

"I think I am okay," I try to reassure her. "Because when you hear the context, what he did was . . ." What's the word? Acceptable? No. Understandable? Not quite. Justifiable. Yes. It was *justifiable*—rough and personal justice, meted out in a land effectively without the law.

Marc, as I see it, had little choice. Otherwise Norcino, the psychotic killer, would have carried on killing, slaughtering men and women, literally mincing them up. That is how I have rationalized it anyway; that is how I cope with the knowledge.

I tell this, once again, to Jess. She nods, gravely.

"You could argue that what he did was heroic," she muses. "You could also say that Marc is still a killer."

"Jess."

"Hey, don't get me wrong. It's not that I *object*."

"Okay . . . ?"

"I'm actually agreeing with you, X. Because it is a different world. Down here in the south, the Mezzogiorno. This isn't the peaceful towns of New Hampshire, is it? This is their world, their laws." She frowns. "Fact, I was thinking about this the other day. And I decided: who are we to judge Marc? I could have married an RAF pilot who drops bombs on kids in the Middle East in some pointless war. Would that be any different?

Would that be any better? Yet no one would think ill of me then, would they? No one would ask me: Oh, how can you bear it, knowing what he did?"

I nod, and say nothing. It's an interesting point—possibly a good point, a point that makes me feel better. But it's not a point I want to discuss now, because I can hear Marc downstairs, talking to the maid who comes with our hired apartment. We have to get ready soon. Apparently there are handmaidens coming to dress me, here, in preparation for the Fourth Mystery. I am guessing these costumes must, therefore, be quite elaborate.

But before I go, I want to know Jess's news. I know there is something.

"Okay, Jessica, I have to say bye."

She nods and looks at her phone, checking the time. "Yep, six P.M. Better get cracking. I'm going to Vomero this evening—"

"Vomero?"

"Uh-huh."

There it is *again*. That flash of a secretive smile. And now I think I have guessed. There is a *man*. I have seen that fleeting smile before, and it normally indicates there is a new body in Jessica's bed.

"Who are you going to Vomero with?"

She shrugs.

"Just *someone*."

"A new boyfriend?"

She shakes her head. Then she smirks. Then she nods.

"Yes. A new boyfriend."

I squeal.

"Oh my God. So go on then—tell me! You have to tell me!"

"Well . . . It's . . ." She looks away from the camera. "It's tricky. I didn't . . . I don't . . ."

This is odd. It isn't like Jessica Rushton to be bashful or reticent about her love life. Usually she tells me every last detail. Every last *inch* of detail. With relish. Then she demands the same of me. She loves gossiping about men and sex. I'm not averse myself. This shared fascination with the intricacies of love is one reason she and I get on so well.

So why is she being so coy?

"Jessica?"

She looks directly at the camera. She sighs and says, "I'm seeing Giuseppe."

What?

"You're seeing Giuseppe? Marc's Giuseppe?"

"Yes."

I clap my hands. I am genuinely delighted. I knew she had a thing for him. *Gorgeousaurus Rex.* He is also very likable and charming. Excellent!

"But that's great!" I say.

She looks at me, then she breaks into a smile.

"You're sure? You're totally sure? You're sure you're okay? You don't think I'm crowding you or anything?"

"Jessica Rushton, don't be an idiot. Course not. It means I get to see you more."

She nods. "Well, yeah, it does! Giuseppe is flying to Venice tomorrow—Marc's orders. He actually wants me to come with—but—until I'd spoken to you—I didn't know what to tell him."

"So do it! Fly up! Of course you must fly up! We can drink Bellinis at Harry's Bar. This is great!"

"Okay." She beams back at me. "This is cool! Don't worry, I'm not doing the weird Mysteries or anything. Not that I'm invited anyway. But I will see you in Venice. Tomorrow."

"Okay, bye!"

I give her a wave; she waves back and says, "Don't fall in any canals."

And then the screen goes black. I sit back. I am happy. I am truly happy. The world is perfect once again.

Or at least it is *almost* perfect. There is just that last niggling doubt, the tiniest serpent in this otherwise pristine paradise: the doubt about Marc's wife. I cannot forget what Enzo Paselli said over that restaurant table in terrible Plati. His words about Lady Roscarrick's sudden death, which meant her money went to Marc . . .

That was an evil fortune.

But I don't *want* to think about it. I want to be *happy*. So I am happy. And tonight I will be Alexandra of the Fourth.

Twenty-eight

Three hours later, I step out onto the damp, mossy pier of our private rented palazzo, the Palazzo Dario. I am alone. Marc is still inside, finishing some business, attending to those digits that drizzle down his laptop screen, blinking scarlet and black.

I glimpse my reflection in the starlit water of the Grand Canal. And I can't help smiling.

The handmaidens have done their costuming: I am in a high-waisted, narrow-sleeved, purest muslin Regency ball gown, colored a very soft cream. It is adorable. I look like a Jane Austen debutante: the long, silk gloves, the satin dancing pumps, the bracelet high on my arm, and a single strand of fine pearls. The muslin is superbly fine; it is also rather see-through; I am wearing cream stockings underneath but, of course, no underwear.

However, it is dark. So no one can tell. Or so I hope. Stepping forward, I look up and down the canal. The gondola is booked for nine P.M.; I know that I am early—but I wanted to enjoy the view.

My heart flutters as I look up at the house where I am staying. We only arrived here this morning and I barely know the place.

But I love it already.

By day this palazzo—from what I have glimpsed—is very pretty; by night, softly lit by canal lights, Venetian stars, and Gothic lanterns, it is a vision, a mirage of spectral beauty: of deep-violet recesses and doomy black windows and a rich, melancholic stony gray, and all of it made more intangible and alluring by the swaying light reflected from the water all around. The sight of it makes me unsteady; it makes me feel unbalanced, like I am inwardly dancing to the eternal and unheard music of Venice.

Chattering laughter drifts across the canal. The scents of wine and diesel; of perfume and smoke and the distant sea.

The Bridge of Sighs. St. Mark's Square. Santa Maria della Salute! So much of this city is already inside me; I have been here so many times in my imagination, in my yearning daydreams, in my schoolgirl and student fantasies of travel. I don't know what to think of the reality; it is so intoxicating I am not sure this *is* reality: Venice looks like a gorgeous copy of itself, like an incredibly well-realized backdrop in a movie, and I am part of the drama. *Alexandra of the Mysteries*.

Is that the Gritti Palace Hotel? If I stand on tiptoe, in my satin pumps, I can see chic men and women eating on a lamp-lit terrace across the wide, dark waters of the Grand Canal. Their laughter carries, along with the sultry tinkle of cutlery and glass. Then a louder noise intrudes: Venetian *polizia* in a moonlit blue boat are speeding down the canal toward the tower of St. Mark's campanile, red and ghostly on the near horizon.

Right in front of the palazzo, four poles are candy-striped blue and white with golden caps, lit by heavy Gothic glass lanterns hanging from hooks. I turn, and look up again. The Palazzo Dario has strange chimneys: "carpaccio" chimneys they are called, top heavy and archaic, weird shapes framed by the clear and starry night sky. The Gothic tracery of the palazzo's façade is famous. The balcony is exquisite.

And the legends that attach to this place are quite romantically tragic. I have done my research. Famous people have expired in various ways in the Palazzo Dario. An Armenian diamond merchant died here "enigmatically" in the early 1800s. Then the house was bought by some British bigwig, Rawdon Brown, who committed suicide after his fortunes were exhausted by his obsessive restorations. An Irish lieutenant marshal owned it next, but he died "mysteriously" in 1860; then came a colorful series of contessas and counts, the last of whom was knifed to death by his lover. Then a rock band manager: murdered. Then a financier: drowned. Then an exorcism: failed.

And now: me. And I wouldn't have it any other way.

"Ah, Mistress Beckmann. What news on the Rialto?"

It is Marc. In his Regency dress. He looks magnificent: a darker, taller Darcy. He is dressed in narrow black trousers, or maybe breeches, which end in long leather boots. Above the waist he wears a plain-fronted, high-collared white shirt, a sumptuous purple vest, and a long, sweeping, and very dark frock coat, with tails. The costume is finished by a rather dandyish top hat. I myself am hatless, but my hair is gorgeously coiffed: piled in curls that are meant to look natural and even tousled, but aren't. Very clever.

Marc clutches his white silk gloves in one hand as he steps onto our private marble pier and bows.

"Look at you." He gestures at my dress, then he steps forward and takes up my white-gloved left hand, and he kisses it, courteously.

"She walks in beauty like the night," he murmurs, "Of cloudless climes and starry skies, and all that's best of dark and bright, meet in her aspect and her eyes."

Marc takes my muslined waist in his arms and kisses me on the lips.

"Celenza," I say, pressing his chest with a flat hand, as if half resisting. But I am not resisting.

Marc smiles reassuringly.

"Are you ready for the Fourth?"

Am I ready? I am not sure. The nerves flutter within. But there is also a determination. I have told Marc I love him, because I love him; I cannot go back now.

I do a fake curtsy, which somehow turns into a real curtsy.

"*Sì*, Celenza. I think so."

"You really are *very* convincing. An American princess in Venice. Inexplicably dressed like Elizabeth Bennet." He gazes past my shoulder. "And now, the gondola."

I turn on a satin heel. Emerging from the flickering semidarkness is the long, dark shape of a polished black gondola; it silently knocks into our pier. The gondolier is handsome, of course.

"Signor Roscarrick?"

"*Sì*."

The narrow black gondola is upholstered with plump silk cushions of scarlet. Marc assists me into the boat and I lie back on the sumptuous pillows, with Marc beside me, and I stare up at the warm, clear skies.

I can smell his bodywash; he is showered and handsome in his

Regency clothes. I want him. I want Venice. I actually want to have sex here and now. *Tooling in a gondola.*

The gondolier churns the water and we are slowly sailing up the Grand Canal. The gondolier is singing a song, very quietly. It is a cliché, yet it isn't. Why shouldn't you sing when you are a gondolier in Venice? Where else, where else in the entire world, is there a better place to sing as you work?

The whole city is singing, silently, on this warm, stilled, summer evening of perfection. We pass under the Accademia Bridge, where faces stare down at us, looking at the film of Venice, looking at us, the film stars. The movie of X and Marc.

I am dreaming. I am not dreaming. I am really here, we really are passing Palazzo Fortuny and Ca Rezzonico, we are passing under the arching whiteness of the Rialto, we are looking at the houses where Wagner died and Marco Polo lived, the houses where Stravinsky wrote and Henry James sighed, the houses of Browning and Titian and Casanova, the palaces of poets and doges and princes and courtesans. I lie back, holding Marc's hand, enrapt. Still dreaming, never waking. Never wanting to wake. Murmuring the words myself: "She walks in beauty like the night, of cloudless climes and starry skies."

Now I am here, I realize Byron was writing about *Venice*, not a woman. The city *is* the dark, seductive, moody woman, elusive, flashing-eyed, complex, ever sexual—and flooded every month, yet somehow enduring. Venice is a dark, beautiful, and suicidal poetess always trying to drown herself in a lake.

And Marc has slid his hand discreetly up my dress.

I say nothing. I point at one palazzo, fairly austere and gray.

"Isn't that Byron's *house*?"

"It is. The Palazzo Mocenigo."

His hand is still between my thighs. Seeking, seeking.

"He lived there," Marc goes on, "with a fox, a wolf, at least two monkeys, and a sickly crow."

His fingers stroke me, there, finding the source of my pleasure.

"A sickly crow?" I say innocently, trying not to gasp.

"I believe the crow expired. And that's where his mistress threatened to drown herself in the Grand Canal. She survived."

The gondola turns, gently steered by the gondolier. Marc withdraws his hand from under my dress, and I feel a faint pang of regret. I want him. I have a terrible and naughty urge to lean across and unzip those fine black breeches and take him in my mouth.

What are the Mysteries doing to me?

Whatever it is, I like it. And I like being in Venice. We are heading north, up a narrower canal, and as we go it is the *little* sights that intrigue me, the fleeting and tantalizing glimpses of side canals, the couple kissing down a dark tiny *calli* as if they cannot be seen, a tiny church that stares at itself in the black, oily water. Then someone singing in a yellow-lit room, then another gondola carrying a woman crying, then fleeting lights in black alleys—that end in a wall with blinded Gothic windows.

"Marc?"

I hold his hand tighter. The Fourth Mystery is approaching.

"Kiss me."

He leans to his side and kisses me, quite fiercely, on the lips, then he lifts his handsome face away.

"Can you see us?" he says. And I realize he means the Constellation of Us: up there, near Orion.

I nod, with an unexplained urge to cry.

"I can see us, Marc. I can see us."

The silence is maybe the most stunning quality. Venice at night. No cars. No engines. Is this the most silent city on earth?

Just the quiet slap of canal water on medieval marble, and the gentle caroling of a gondolier. And beyond it silence. Dead and beautiful nothingness, like a city on the edge of dissolving.

The gondola is steering us to the very edge of Venice. I sit up; now I can see open water, the wider lagoon. Glittering lights from Murano, maybe, then the low, dark, somber shape of the cemetery island: the island of death.

"We're nearly there," says the gondolier in English.

He needn't. I know we are approaching because we are now, abruptly, in a crush of other boats, more gondolas, some water taxis, *lots* of water taxis. A vaporetto is berthed on the waterside that fronts the wider lagoon. People are stepping off all the boats and gondolas in elaborate clothes, exquisite Regency costumes, just like me and Marc. Again. I can see dresses of mull and gauze, and delicious silk satin, and bodices and chemisettes and gowns from the Empire and the Directoire. And men in fitted tailcoats and high white collars and stiffened silk cravats.

These are my people. Hard as it is for me to believe.

I turn and look above them. And ask, "Is that it? That building?"

I am staring at a modest, square palazzo, evidently historic, situated forlornly at the very end of the canal. Facing the lagoon, the building is somehow isolated and cruelly exposed, like a child sent into a corner of the classroom.

"It is the Casino degli Spiriti," says Marc. "It has a rather baroque history: hauntings and artists, poets and orgies." He lifts my arm and assists me off the gondola. "Please do not worry, X. The Fourth Mystery is one of the sweetest."

Of course I am worrying. But I am stirred and excited too, as I see the now-familiar girls in white coming to greet us and give us glasses of wine, as we wait to step inside.

The gondolier poles his boat away; the other boats disperse.

One of the handmaidens steps forward and squats down in front of me. Then, quite brusquely, she lifts up my translucent muslin dress, revealing my nudity to the world, to all the people around me.

I have been told to wear no panties. That I have obeyed this firm instruction is now obvious to everyone. The girl squints and she examines my tattoo, above my garter, and then drops the dress with a curtsy.

All of this is being done on a canal sidewalk in Venice, watched by dozens of people, dozens of rich, sophisticated people—some of whom I recognize: celebrities, politicians—and yet I suppress my shame and embarrassment. I drink wine and talk with Marc as the girl does her job. The people all around me talk and nod and drink. And then we are led by one of the handmaidens inside the Casino degli Spiriti.

The house is larger than it looks from outside. The bottom floor is shadowy and quite grand. It is also slightly sinister in its darkness. Cryptlike, even. It has a faint odor of damp from the lagoon, lapping outside. Now we are invited upstairs. This floor—the *piano nobile*, the principal floor—is brighter and *much* more impressive. White stone Gothic arches and white marble pillars support a tall and elaborately plastered ceiling; the room is wide and airy, and akin to a ballroom. Mildly erotic frescoes adorn the walls, blush pink and white, with female nudes and cherubim. Tiepolo, perhaps.

The handmaidens are dutifully handing out large metal cups.

"This is kykeon," says Marc. "Drink an entire cup."

Kykeon? I have, of course, heard of this. The drug of the Eleusinian mysteries. The fabulous yet secretive narcotic.

For the first time tonight I seriously pause. Drugs? I do not take drugs; my only experience of drugs has been the odd hit of marijuana, which made me sick and made the room spin. Marc senses my hesitation.

"It is all legal, made from herbs, and wildflowers."

"But what herbs?"

"I've not the faintest idea, X. It is a *mystery*."

He smiles. Regretfully.

The handmaiden is staring at me. I chasten myself for my timidity. I have come this far: I want to know the Fourth Mystery and I cannot lose Marc. Just cannot.

Leaning across, I take a cup and gulp from it. Deeper and deeply. The taste is dark and a little bitter, and maybe spicy. Like cold mulled wine. It is not unpleasant. I lift up the cup, again, and drink the last drop. Marc does the same with his cup, looking me in the eye as he does so.

"Everyone takes the kykeon."

And now the music starts. It is a beating, pulsing African chant. I recognize it, but cannot name it.

"The *Missa Luba*," says Marc.

Of course, that's it. The *Missa Luba*: a mass recorded in Belgian Africa decades ago.

It is the perfect music for the moment, because the kykeon is acting with extraordinary quickness. I am seeing things. I hold on to Marc's hand. I am actually swaying, really swaying this time. Perspiring. Somewhat frightened.

"Do not fight the kykeon," Marc whispers, gently kissing my pale neck. "Think of it as a gondola, *piccolina*, taking you down a canal in the darkness. The warm and sultry darkness."

For a second, I stare at his handsome and distant face, and then a moment later I am turning and looking at a different handsome face that I also know. Who is this: an actor? Am I dreaming? I am not sure, because I can see more famous faces. A very well known politician. Next to him some Internet billionaire. A celebrity model. Then another politician, from America, with his wife. Global moguls and supermodels.

I am losing my grip. Marc holds my hand, in its silken glove, very hard. This is like some gilded sex party for the rich and famous, but most of all, *the very powerful*. Unless I really am dreaming; unless the hallucinations are lucid, and the drug extremely potent. I do not know. I feel faint.

"Can we get some air?"

Marc nods. "Of course."

Walking to the window, I gulp the fresh warm air off the lagoon. When I turn, I realize Marc is standing next to a beautiful young woman of about eighteen in a bright red Regency ball gown. The girl smiles at me and then she steps around me. What is she doing? I turn to see. The girl is kneeling behind me, slowly slipping her fingers up my dress. She begins to stroke my clitoris.

"You are wet," she says.

I look down at her, then I turn back and stare at Marc.

"Yes, I am," I say.

She strokes my clit some more. We are standing beside a group of people dancing. But we are standing still as she strokes me, flicking, touching, and thumbing my clit. And Marc and I gaze at each other.

My senses meld. I give in to the pleasure and the visions. Oh. Oh, yes. The girl is very pretty; I have no idea who she is. I moan a little, I can't help it. She continues to stroke me. I don't want her to stop. This is good, this is good. But she smiles and suddenly removes her hand. Then I hear her skip away, disappearing into the milling crowd, leaving me panting. Close. So close. Where am I?

"Marc, who was that?"

He shakes his head.

I whisper, "A mystery. Yes, I know. A mystery. Marc, I feel strange."

He takes my hand again. And I lean on his shoulder and I feel a surge of sexuality. Of real and powerful abandon. I want to have sex with Marc, here, in front of these people. Rip away that cravat, that starched white shirt; unbutton those Byronic breeches. It is very difficult for me not to do this. The long leather boots are quite ravishing.

The music is so loud, it is verging on painful. I have no idea what time it is, or how much time has passed.

Marc murmurs, his wine-scented words warm in my ear.

"Do you want to lie down? The kykeon is even more effective if you lie down."

I'm not sure I could handle the kykeon being any more *effective*. But he is right: I have to lie down. Colors riot in my mind; the frescoes seem to be moving. Cherubim are toppling off clouds.

I stumble through the people, as Marc leads me by the hand. I see men in military uniforms and women in white gauze dresses, and those little Regency jackets—Spencer jackets?—framed by more wide-open windows. The cemetery island is dark and visible on the black Venetian horizon. There are large wooden stairs to my left, which sway in my vision. Marc points, but I am already heading that way, holding his hand.

I need to go up those stairs.

At the top Marc pauses: a gilt-rose corridor stretches away. I spy a wide bed in a large gold-and-purple room. Letting go of Marc's hand, I walk in at once and lie down, kicking off my satin dancing pumps. Is this the third floor? Now I see there are people in this room. I rise to leave, confused, but then Marc is at my side. Murmuring, murmuring.

"Lie back . . ."

I do as I am told. Because I really do want to lie back. I want Marc to lie on top of me. But instead a young woman comes over to the bedside and gently hoists up my muslin dress above my waist, exposing me, and then she removes my dress completely, pulling it over my arms, and taking off my bracelet. The girl is about nineteen or twenty, dressed in silk and muslin, with her hair beautifully pinned high above her head.

I am lying on my back on the bed, naked apart from my white silk stockings and gloves, and another young woman is on the bed with me. The girl is dressed for a period production of *Pride and Prejudice*, and yet she is also holding a long glass dildo.

Marc is still there. Standing by the bedside.

"Marc?"

"Accept, Alexandra, accept."

I accept, I accept, I accept. I presume the second girl is going to put the dildo inside me, but instead she moves to my side and slips off my gloves; then she takes my right wrist and abruptly snaps it in a handcuff. My wrist is then cuffed to the metal post of the bed frame behind me.

I gaze at the male and female faces looking down at me as my second wrist is also shackled. Then my ankles get the same treatment. Padded cuffs are snapped around my ankles, which are manacled to the bedposts. Now I am completely vulnerable. And the idea that I am handcuffed to the bed, and that the only thing I am wearing is my white silk stockings, and that everyone can see this, and that all these people are looking down at me, admiring me, is unfeasibly arousing and disturbing all at once.

I gaze at Marc for reassurance.

He nods.

I lie back.

Now the girl leans in and licks between my legs for a few moments, then she opens my thighs and pushes the dildo deep inside: she is pushing it in and out of my sex.

I sit up.

"No, Marc, I—"

The girl speaks: "X, *per favore*."

How does she even know my name? How? I do not know. But she is very pretty and her voice is soothing. Marc is standing next to some other men about the same age as him, calmly surveying me. What is this? I am on a bed with people I do not know and this girl is pushing a thick crystal dildo into my vulva, deep inside, deep, deep inside. I kick my shackled heels at the silk sheets beneath me, struck with the pleasurability of this, the troubling, deep, hard pleasure.

The crystal dildo seems to be warm: how do they do that?

"Alexandra . . ."

This pretty girl says my name again, then she pulls out the dildo and her little tongue is licking my clitoris; she is talented. My mind swirls as I look into Marc's eyes, his loving and distant blue eyes. The music, the music. Are there two tongues? Like little cats' tongues, hard and soft, licking my clit. There are three girls now. The third girl stoops and bites, playfully, kittenishly, at my nipples.

Three girls, one of them naked. And Marc. Standing in his long leather boots and that high white collar; he has removed the dandyish top hat and his hair is tousled and I want to run my fingers through his uncombed coils of black hair. But he just looks at me. It is maybe a loving glance, but there is lust there, too. Glittering and powerful lust. He is enjoying looking at me; he is enjoying watching me do this.

So that makes me enjoy it more. I begin to moan as one girl

fills me with warm thrusting strokes of the dildo, even as she whispers and licks at my clit, speaking sweet Italian to my clitoris. The second girl is very quietly biting my nipples, tweaking them; her perfume is delicious. I stretch and kiss her young, soft breasts. The third is putting something inside me, another warm, vibrating way of filling me, anally, beautifully, I never knew, I never knew. And the music is still throbbing and chanting, louder and stirring.

"You look beautiful," says Marc, staring down. "So very beautiful."

The windows are open. I can see the stars up there, and down here. Stars and stars. The music drums. The girl thrusts the warm crystal dildo in and out. I am sprawled and open and naked on this bed, with people all around me. I wish I could be more naked. More filled. More. More.

"*Sanctus . . .*"

In and out and in and out. *Clitoris.* Dildo. Anally. *Kissing.* My sex is licked and teased and licked and I am shivering now, shivering with pleasure, trembling, drowning, the drowning palazzo, the soaking furs and cinnamons.

Hosanna.

Deep inside me. Deep inside me. I see the stars. So many stars. Marc is the stars. I begin to come.

Dominus.

The orgasm is coming. The dildo thrusts. The girl licks my clit. The girl *bites* my nipples. The orgasm is coming, is coming, is coming.

"Marc!"

I feel his hand in my hand. I am still shackled.

"*Tesorina.*"

The orgasm is tremblingly close . . .

The three girls thrust and bite, lick and drum, and then at last I come, with an outright spasm, unleashed energy. I am panting, and yelling, I am writhing, and the girls are *holding* me down. Because I am shaking, trembling, and possessed, the liquid ejects from my sex in a glorious arc, and I lie back in a kind of delirious and picturesque agony, crucified by this plea-suring, ravening climax. Then, even as the colors whirl, I know that all I want is Marc. I want Marc. Marc on top of me. Marc, Marc, Marc, Marc.

"*Marc.*"

"Alexandra, *cara mia.*"

I open my tear-wettened eyes.

It is him. The girls are unlocking the cuffs and shackles and he is lifting me up off the bed. I am naked in his arms, half fainted, like a woman being rescued from a fire, and Marc is lifting and carrying me out of the bedroom.

I whisper my tears of bewilderment and gladness into his chest and he carries me, naked, downstairs, right through the crowds, right out of the door and out of the building into the warm night air. He carries me naked down the path to the jetty. And lifts me naked into the boat.

And now I am naked in a gondola. Lying back on the cush-ions, legs sleepy and open, white-stockinged thighs trembling still, just a little. I am utterly ashamed and yet half of me doesn't care who sees. Who looks. Who sees my fur and my skin. I am a naked woman, in nothing but white silk stockings, in a black boat, on the black, black waters of the Cannaregio Canal, in the velvet black city of dreams and decay. I blush and I feel the cold breeze on my bare skin, yet something in me resists clothes.

The gondola rocks, weaves and sails, and then stops. In a little side canal. A small, ancient church looms above us, ghostly in the moonlight. The gondolier disappears. Marc is half standing in the boat above me. He is unbuttoning himself.

I open my trembling legs. I reach hungrily for his desire. He is unbelievably hard.

I lean to suck him but he pushes me down. He pushes me hard and forces me back. Then he opens my thighs with his hands and he is inside me, filling me.

"You were so beautiful." He kisses me. "So fucking beautiful."

He fucks me, making the gondola rock on the waves of ancient Venice. And my stockinged feet are in the air. And people can see. I am sure they can see. Everyone can see Marc as he fucks me. Again. And again. And once more. Ah.

Twenty-nine

I don't have time to comprehend what has happened to me at the Fourth. Because the following morning, almost as soon as I stir in the big bedroom with its views of the Grand Canal, I am told Jessica and Giuseppe are here. So Marc and I go to breakfast with them, and then Marc takes me on a whirling weeklong tour of Venice: a delicious confection of art and music and Venetian-Gothic architecture and excellent cocktails at Harry's Bar.

Jessica and Giuseppe join us for some of these jaunts, but mostly we go exploring on our own. Marc knows Venice well: he tells me he used to stay here as a very young man, taking weeklong trips from South Tyrol during his long vacations from Cambridge University.

But of course I expected Marc to know Venice very well, because he knows *everywhere* very well. He could probably do a decent guided tour of the moon. Ending at a discreet but fabulous trattoria.

First, we go to the Frari—Santa Maria Gloriosa dei Frari—in

the San Polo district of the city, quite near the Rialto. I have no idea where the San Polo district is, or what it means, but Marc reassures me it is important.

"It doesn't look like much," I say, gazing at the drab, squat, redbrick exterior.

But inside: ah.

Inside there is an awe-inspiring *Assumption*, by Titian, a painting, Marc tells me, that moved Richard Wagner to immediately write *Die Meistersingers*. Then a harrowing statue of a geriatric St. Jerome by Alessandro Vittoria, which Marc says was modeled on an aged Titian. I stare at the old man, at the presaging of death. I know death has something to do with the Mysteries: every one of them is a little death, as the French call an orgasm. *La petite mort.*

Why did I enjoy the Fourth Mystery so much? What was in the kykeon? Why did I like Marc looking at me as I was pleasured by women? I know I am not lesbian, but my sexuality is so much more complex and intricate, and rich, and various, and multiform, than I ever comprehended.

So the Mysteries are teaching me about sex and my sexuality, but they are now teaching me something else. It is something to do with love or God or death. It is there. In my mind. In my senses. Like a delicious and haunting scent I can remember but not name. Not quite yet.

I recall that Pindar quote: *Blessed is he who, having seen these rites, undertakes the way beneath the Earth. He knows the end of life, as well as its divinely granted beginning.*

Marc interrupts my thoughts by steering me, gently, to the other end of the church.

"And this is the Pesaro Altarpiece." He kisses my neck, once, then twice. "Henry James said: 'Nothing in Venice is more perfect than this.' Of course, he hadn't encountered you, right now, standing in the shadows of the Frari."

Now he lifts my hand and kisses my folded fingers. I gaze at him for a moment. His dark hair, my white fingers. And then I reach out and pull his handsome face toward mine. And we are kissing each other. Really quite hard.

And so it goes. The next place is the Scuola Grande di San Rocco, with its Tintorettos, then a swift gondola-hop takes us to Ca' D'Oro, the Golden Palace, where we see the famous view of the Grand Canal, and after that Mantegna's *St. Sebastian*, where Marc points me to the haunting inscription: *Nothing but God endures, the rest is smoke.*

But most of all I am taken by a small, anonymous sculpture of *A Centaur and Achilles* on the ground floor, although it is seemingly ignored by everyone who is rushing to view the Grand Canal. I look for a long while at the sculpture. It reminds me of Marc and me: Marc carrying me from the Casino degli Spiriti. Naked and vulnerable, Alex of the Fourth. I was the small boy, he was the Centaur.

The dreamy days go by. The Doge's Palace. The Titians and Tintorettos of Santa Maria della Salute. Giorgione's *The Tempest*. Walls of Veronese.

Then we visit the beautiful Brancusis and Pollocks of the Guggenheim, a white marble canal-side villa so close to our palazzo we can go back to the Palazzo Dario for hungry sex before lunch, which is precisely what we do.

Running across the little bridges of Dorsoduro, we skip through our private palazzo garden with the citronella trees, and hasten up the sixteenth-century stairs. Then we strip each other naked and fall with laughing abandon onto our large Napoleonic bed with the windows open to the Grand Canal. Rising above me, Marc throws me on my back, he is glorious above me, and then he takes me. He possesses me; he owns me; he encompasses me; then he imperiously turns me over and he is hard and then harder *inside* me, taking me from behind, roughly, pulling my hair back, pulling it savagely so it hurts. But it hurts so very sweetly it makes me cry out; it makes me yell and shudder, and then I come, again, and again, and *again*, convulsive, and panting, and consumed, and *slumping* onto the pillows, sheened with postcoital sweat, dazzled by the orgasm, listening to the endless drumbeat of my own heart, listening to the vaporetti steaming up and down the Grand Canal.

One final, hot Venetian day, Marc directs our sleek wooden water taxi out of Venice, right across the torpid gray lagoon, to the island of Torcello. This green and lonely island was where, Marc says, the first Venetians settled at the beginning of the Dark Ages.

There isn't much to see: a lot of halfhearted rubble, a lonely brace of churches, and one or two costly restaurants. Why has he brought me here? I am rather hot and a tiny bit irritable at being bitten by enormous mosquitoes. But then we step into the cool and sacred interior of Torcello's ancient cathedral, and he shows me the startling mosaics, especially the tenth-century *Madonna Teotoca*—the Madonna God-bearer—on the opposite wall.

One large silvery tear slides forever down the Madonna's infinitely sorrowful face. It is unbearably affecting. The weeping woman. It reminds me of the Mysteries. Everything reminds me of the Mysteries. The truth, the dark, frightening truth, is approaching. I can sense it. The katabasis. The final revelation. I am scared and I am compelled. I cannot go on, but I must, and I will.

There isn't much else to do on this little islet of Torcello. We wander among the scattered ruins of the deserted city; I look at the old stone chair—the Throne of Attila—parked in the piazza.

We drink a desultory and overpriced martini in one of the little cafe-restaurants. Then we just sit on the grass and drink chilled prosecco, bought by the bottle from the bar. Sipping from our fluted glasses, we watch the stately white yachts pass down the thousand-year-old Torcello canal, and we fall asleep in the afternoon shade from the lemon trees, lying in one another's arms. *Perfetto.*

That night Marc and I are having drinks at a table outside Florian's. It is very touristy, but Marc assures me that everyone in Venice is a tourist, even the Venetians: he says everyone who lives in Venice or visits Venice is perpetually self-conscious of being in Venice. So it's all okay.

Therefore we act the part of rich tourists in Venice: we sit in Florian's as the warm evening descends over the most beautiful drawing room in Europe; the expanses of St. Mark's Square with its pigeons and campanile and the glorious palace of the doges, and the horses rearing above the cathedral.

Marc drinks his drink and looks at me. We are talking about the Fifth Mystery. He is not sure he wants me to do it.

"X, I have never seen the Fifth, not the female Fifth. But I have heard things . . . It is meant to be quite troubling, and difficult. Are you convinced you want to do it?"

"Not doing the Fifth means losing you. At the end of the summer. In about a month."

He nods. Gravely. I shake my head. Almost angrily.

"Marc, it is absurd. I cannot lose you."

"Are you sure? There is no law that says you have to continue."

"There may not be a law, but . . ." I look at him, at his effortlessly handsome features framed by the famous view of the Venetian piazza. Should I tell him the truth? That I am now, like

Françoise, quite addicted to the Mysteries? That they are changing me, liberating me, freeing me spiritually as well as sexually, in a way I cannot explain, yet cannot resist? That even if there was no threat of losing him, I would probably continue anyway?

"Marc," I say. "I'm doing the Fifth. That's the end of it."

He leans back and laughs, very quietly. "You know, if I was vulgar, I could call you a stubborn cow."

I look at him.

"*Tua vacca*, Celenza."

Your cow, Excellency.

He laughs again, and shakes his head. Then he leans forward, picks up my hand, and kisses it.

"Alexandra, I consider myself instructed. And I am very, very flattered."

We drink some more; we get quite drunk; we talk about art and sex and Venetian life. And then, as I sip my third Bellini, I gaze at Marc and say, because I have to say, because the time has come to say: "Marc . . ." I hesitate. Then press on. "Can you tell me about your wife?"

A pause. And then, there it is. That wince of pain. A glimpse of that concealed anguish, a passing symptom of Marc's inner sadness. But I have diagnosed these symptoms, now I need to know the cause.

"X . . ."

"I want to *know*, Marc. You keep alluding to her. I know she died. Tell me the truth."

He drinks, quite deeply, from his Bellini. He sighs, but also nods. And then he tells me the story.

"Her name was Serena. She was very young and very smart and very damaged and very beautiful." He gazes into my eyes. "She was the second loveliest woman I have ever met."

The pigeons rise and applaud next to our table, frightened by some child chasing them into the air. The campanile glitters in the descending sun.

"I should perhaps have been wary," Marc adds, toying with his Bellini, rather than drinking it.

"Why?"

"I knew she was from a Camorra family. Serious, serious *Camorristi*, from the Forcella. They'd made a lot of money, but they still had *all* the necessary connections. Her father claimed to be a marble exporter." Marc laughs, mirthlessly and bitterly. "You don't make hundreds of millions from exporting marble."

"He was a real gangster?"

"Clearly."

"So . . ."

"But it wasn't just the father. Serena's mother was also from a Camorra family. She had died young, perhaps in some vendetta, and when she died she'd left Serena lots of money, a legacy of her own." He looks at me again, then looks down at his drink. "So that was Serena's inheritance: crime, death, and money, too much money, and too much guilt. Taken together, her background— the death of her mother, the villainy of her father—all of it, some combination of it—I don't know—that is what made her so messed up, I imagine."

"But how, Marc? How exactly was she screwed up? What did she do?"

His shrug is contemptuous and melancholy at the same time. "Oh, the usual, *carissima*, the usual. Sex and drugs. She did quite a lot of heroin, cocaine, crack cocaine, she liked dangerous sex. She had been inducted into the Mysteries before me, at the age of seventeen."

"Too young."

"Far too young." A truth dawns. I gaze at Marc.

"She introduced *you* to the Mysteries, didn't she?"

"Yes."

"How old were you?"

He shrugs.

"Twenty at most. Barely more than a boy. She was eighteen, just a girl. I met her at a party in Posillipo, and immediately we fell in love; she was so sweet and fragile and cultured and broken. I wanted to protect her and save her. She was lovely, so lovely. And yes, I did the Mysteries for her, and they were as amazing as she said. Life-changing."

He turns from me, staring at the domes and ogees of the Doge's Palace, the pinkening sky above, the beauty of doomed and suicidal Venice. "And so we decided to get married—but almost everyone disapproved, everyone loathed the idea of our match. Serena's family were wildly antagonistic. They wanted her to marry into another Camorra clan, not an Anglo-Italian dynasty from the Chiaia. They also thought that, because the Roscarricks had no money, we were after *their* money." Again his blue eyes meet my eyes. Unblinking. "We weren't. I didn't want her money, any of it, I just wanted her. But the drugs and the drink . . ."

"And your family?"

"My mother was dead against it, too, because Serena was—well, because Serena was from Forcella. Very much the wrong side of the tracks. She wanted her only son—*the son and heir of the Roscarricks*—to marry some blue blood. Preferably someone posh from England or France, or America even, someone with money not derived from assassination and contraband, and the smuggling of China white heroin."

"And your father?"

"Strangely, he was okay with it. He was English, somehow more relaxed, paradoxically. He saw what I saw in Serena, the sweetness inside, the brokenness, the charm. But he was a weak man—my mother was much stronger. But anyway . . ."

"You married."

"Yes, we married, in a furtive and sad little ceremony, and we were still very much in love. But within months, ah . . ." He tails off, and drinks from his Bellini, then sets the glass down.

"Within months *what*?"

"Serena went even more off the rails; she thought I was having affairs, she went on drinking binges, doing heroin and other drugs. She would come home at six in the morning disheveled, drunk, stoned, in a terrible state, raving about her father the gangster, the absolutely terrible man, telling everyone, telling the world what her father did and how murderous he was, all the people he had killed. She got a very bad reputation, was in the papers, she would not shut up, and then one day I got the call . . ."

"A car accident."

He looks my way. His eyes are narrowed. Blue and narrowed—fierce and skeptical.

"A car *crash*, in the hills above Capua. She had been off to score from some dealer. God knows why."

"What do you mean?"

"There is enough heroin in Scampia for all the world—there is more than enough smack in Naples—but anyway she went all the way to Capua, I don't know why, and she scored. And on one of those hills, above Capua, at midnight, the brakes *failed*. They just stopped working, for some reason no one has fathomed. Serena was coming down a hill and then she—she went over the edge . . ."

A small orchestra has started up outside the cafe across St.

Mark's Square. The music is jaunty and jubilant, light opera, precisely the wrong music for this somber moment.

I can see where this is going. I drink from my own Bellini, and think, and then I ask *the* question.

"You don't think it was an accident?"

He does not react, not visibly. But in the depths of his blue eyes I can see the glitter of pain.

"I am pretty sure it was *murder*. I got the wreck of the car analyzed again and again, by the best people in Turin, and they all said the same: they couldn't find any reason why the brakes had suddenly failed. The brakes were fine. The car was new, an Alfa, her family had bought it for her. She wasn't even going that fast, thirty kilometers an hour. She wasn't stoned, either; her drugs were untouched. She was sober, for once. The postmortem showed it."

"So who killed her?"

"Probably her father, which is why the Naples police wouldn't investigate properly. He was too powerful. *Untouchable.*"

The music stops, horribly.

My words are faltering.

"But why? Why would her own father do that?"

"Because she was shooting her mouth off. Denouncing him in public. Stoned and drunk and telling the world what he did."

"But . . . his own daughter!"

"He had six kids. He could afford to lose a daughter." Marc sighs and runs his fingers through his dark, dark hair. He downs the last of his drink. "X, look, I don't know for sure. Maybe I am totally wrong, maybe it was another *Camorrista*, maybe it really was an accident, but this is what I strongly suspect. Someone from her family did it. Certainly her father was a malevolent influence. And a serious killer. He *is* the Camorra."

"That's why you hate them?"

"It's one of the reasons. So when I inherited Serena's money, I decided to put it to good use, start a business in Campania and Calabria, something that would be honest and yet profitable, show it could be done, something to defeat the mafias, something to *beat* the Camorra and the 'Ndrangheta."

I begin to see. I begin to understand. I put my hand on Marc's.

"Marc . . ."

"The death of Serena killed my father, too," Marc adds, almost casually. "He loved Serena; she was funny and lovable, even if she was flawed. A few months after she died, he had a heart attack." Marc withdraws his hand from mine abruptly. "And there we are; now you know it all."

"Why didn't you tell me this before?"

"It's not a story I wish to dwell on, X. And also, crucially, I have no proof. No proof that the Camorra killed her, let alone her own *Camorrista* father. It is all supposition, it is all games and masks, games and masks. And here we are, in the city of masks."

He sits back, his expression grave. And I want to kiss him. And the horses rear on their podium above St. Mark's Cathedral, forever trampling over some unseen foe.

I am at peace. I know it all now, however troubling. The final wound is healed.

The next day we fly to Naples, because Marc has business at home. All the regular flights are booked, so he has chartered a private jet. Jessica and I walk across the concrete to the waiting plane. I am childishly excited: I have never been on a private jet before. Jess is, however, strangely subdued. All our time in Venice she has been giggly and happy, obviously smitten by Giuseppe. Now she is mute.

Why?

Finally, when we get on board, when Giuseppe and Marc are at the front of the plane and talking business, Jessica touches me on the arm and nods significantly—without speaking—like she wants to talk in private. We sit in the back as the plane takes off.

The engines are noisy. No one can hear us. Giuseppe and Marc are conversing up front.

"What is it?" I say.

"Giuseppe got drunk last night. And he said something."

"What?"

"He was really out if it, X, totally banjaxed. He doesn't normally drink much—I think I am a bad influence."

"Okay . . ."

"And then he just let it slip, he was barely conscious. I bet he's forgotten he said it."

Her face is uncharacteristically somber, this is something serious.

"And . . . ? What is it?"

She turns my way.

"You know there is a Sixth Mystery?"

"What?"

Jessica nods, and looks at the front of the plane, where Giuseppe and Marc are laughing and joking.

"There is a *Sixth* Mystery. It is frightening and scary and very dangerous, and a big, big secret. That's all I know. At least that is what Giuseppe *implied*."

I am nonplussed. From the moment of revelation and final certainty at Florian's, I am all at sea again. Why wouldn't Marc tell me about this? Is he still lying? Why is he lying?

Why?

Thirty

"He really denies there is a Sixth Mystery? Still?"

"Yes."

"Hmm . . ."

Jess is standing before me in my Santa Lucia apartment in *Napoli*, assessing me in my new McQueen minidress. It is short, rose and black, and very pricey. And I am wearing no panties. Under orders.

I am getting used to couture, and a lack of underwear; I am not getting used to all the Mystery of the Mysteries.

Tonight is the Fifth. I thought it was the Fifth and Final, but Jessica has sowed that germ of doubt.

I have twice confronted Marc with this question: I first asked him when we landed back in Naples, two weeks ago. Marc dismissed it at once emphatically: "There is no Sixth Mystery." I asked him again two days later and he was even more adamant. And yet, ever since, I have noticed a definite frostiness between him and Giuseppe, a stiffness and a distance. Before they had been positively fraternal, joshing and amicable; now I sense a tiny wince of disapproval whenever Giuseppe is mentioned, or simply present.

Jess and I discuss this now as she makes me take a final turn in my dress.

"What can we do, X?" she says at last. "You'll find out soon enough. But be careful, sweetheart, be bloody careful." She steps back, nodding like the approving mother of a bride in her wedding gown.

"You look lovely. Knockout! You're gonna give that old goat Dionysus a heart attack."

I laugh. Uncertainly. Then I stop laughing and I feel a surge of passionate anxiety. The Fifth Mystery. The katabasis. I am properly scared.

Jessica reaches out to take my hand and holds it and says, "Are you sure you want to do this, X? You can stop. You can stop right now." Her friendly brown eyes meet mine. And mine are wet with near tears. "We can go to Benito's and drink Peroni and argue over pizza margherita and pretend none of this ever happened."

The idea is momentarily seductive. Just wipe it all away. Pretend the entire summer was a dream, from that moment months ago when I first saw Marc at the Caffè Gambrinus. But if I do that, I extract Marc from my life, and that concept is monstrous. An abomination. He is part of me, woven into my soul: Plati and all. And if I erase the summer I erase the Mysteries, and I adore the way they have changed me. I prefer the person I am becoming: more open and confident, more adventurous, more playful.

I squeeze Jessica's hand and shake my head.

"Thought not," she says.

Outside I can hear a car honking. It is Giuseppe with the silver Mercedes that was nearly mine; when I reach the sidewalk he wordlessly opens the door and drives me the short distance to the narrow street at the heart of Old Naples, Via dei Tribunali.

He parks outside a church. The Chiesa de Santa Maria delle Anime del Purgatorio ad Arco. St. Mary of the Souls in Purgatory. I know of this notorious Baroque church: I've gazed at it many times as I walked the narrow pavements of Tribunali. But I have never quite had the stomach to go inside before, thanks to its macabre reputation.

The exterior is off-putting enough: as Giuseppe opens the car door, I climb out—my high heels slipping a little on the rough piperno cobbles—and look at the three polished bronze skulls that sit on stone pillars. Repressing an inner shudder, I say, "*Grazie*, Giuseppe."

He nods graciously, but there is a slender trace of contrition in his demeanor. Is this because he is ashamed of having let slip the truth?

I'm not going to find out yet. Giuseppe turns and climbs back in the car, and the Mercedes rumbles away, watched by the local kids hanging languidly on their Vespas and the man in the newsstand selling *Oggi* and *Gente*.

I have to go inside the Church of the Souls in Purgatory. Guarding my fears, I ascend the shallow steps and press open the door. A small crowd is waiting inside; Marc is there in his usual dinner-jacketed finery. He is frowning. Even *he* looks a little grim and on edge. This doesn't help.

"*Buona sera*, X."

He kisses me on the forehead. I turn, and see that Françoise, accompanied by Daniel, her boyfriend—her *amant*—is also in the small gathering. So she is doing the Fifth in Naples. This reassures me a little. Françoise and I nod and smile encouragingly at each other. Traces of anxiety are visible in her eyes.

But there is no time to talk: already we are being led to some stairs at the side of the church. I know from my research where these stairs lead. Now I have to repress even deeper fears.

Downstairs is the hypogeum, the terrible and frightening crypt of Santa Maria della Anime del Purgatorio—the crypt where the ancient Neapolitan cult of skull worship can still be seen in all its macabre and enduring glory.

The steps are steep, and I sigh with slight relief when we reach the stones of the basement floor. Then I look around. And shudder.

The entire chamber is stacked with shrines, glass boxes and open chests containing human skulls and bones. There are skulls with necklaces dangling, and skulls with candles flickering before their hollow eyes.

The cult of skull worship was abolished in the sixties by the local Catholic hierarchy, but here it continues, as forcefully and heathenly as ever: many local people—young and old women, mainly—come here to pray to their own special and favored skulls, to make offerings to skeletons, to light candles in front of the sightless dead, to plead for luck or fertility or cancer cures or just because this place is so hideously compelling and intense.

"Are you okay, X?"

Marc places a gentle hand on my shoulder. I lie and say, "Yes."

"We go down from here."

I follow his gaze and see that our guide, a short, oldish man in spectacles, is lifting up a trapdoor.

Evidently we are descending from the crypt of Santa Maria of the Souls into deeper Naples, the great and famous labyrinth that is Naples Underground, *Napoli Sotterraneo.*

The city is built on tuffaceous and easily excavated rock. So people have been digging holes and wells and tunnels and cellars in these environs for thousands of years; add in the many millennia of dense settlements that have simply been *piled* on top of each other and it means there is probably as much Naples belowground as there is above it: the city sits on a mirror image of itself, an identical and opposite undercity, like a church poised above its own reflection in a Venetian canal.

As the guide flaps open the trapdoor, he turns to us and says, "*E 'piuttosto un lungo cammino. Potrebbe essere necessario eseguire la scansione . . .*"

It's a long way. We might have to crawl. I take a deep breath of foul air and let Marc assist me down the steps into the darkness.

"*Grazie.*"

Then we walk, crawling and squeezing, following the torch of the guide, scrambling our way through *Napoli Sotterraneo*, with its hundreds of miles of damp cisterns and secret chapels and old charnel houses and entombed Roman theaters and musty Bourbon dungeons. We pass shrines of the Mystery Religions—turned into warehouses used by Camorra smugglers, for storing drugs, liquor, tobacco, and guns. Many of the Mystery Religions did their rites in secretive underground places around here, just as the mafias do their business in the same sequestered places now.

The parallels are apt.

And as the air gets mustier and damper, older and nastier, I start to think. *To connect it all up.* I see the lineage, like spotting the resemblance to a distant and famous ancestor in a modern descendant.

"*Ci siamo quasi . . .*"

It seems we don't have far to go. Another narrow tunnel zigzags into a huge echoing cistern, built, Marc tells me, by the ancient Greeks. Marc is carrying his own flashlight in his phone—he flicks it this way and that and I stare. The cistern, now empty of water, is enormous. I gaze, in nervous wonder, at the mighty arches; the high, rocky ceiling; the grandiose and beautifully carved walls, a hundred meters tall or more. It is like the achievement of a long-dead race from a more advanced planet.

"*Avanti.*"

We walk on. The air is hot and somehow thin. I am feeling light-headed and have yet to drink the kykeon. Will there be kykeon? I hope yes, I hope no.

The journey continues down an even narrower corridor of Greek bricks and bare rocks. Damp, fusty, dismal, and dubious.

"Just a few more minutes, *carissima.*"

Marc's arm is comforting around my shoulder; I am not feeling especially solaced. I am truly scared now. We are so deep underground, so deep in the forgotten tunnels of *Napoli Sotterraneo*, undertaking the *way beneath the Earth.*

"Here," says the guide ahead of us, in English. I can see lights, albeit subdued. The tunnel opens out into a series of large vaults, lit by bare torches and blue lanterns. There are many people here, already assembled, drinking wine and talking. But the mood is entirely different from anything in the other Mysteries. The music is very simple and churchy: plainsong or Gregorian chants, or something even more archaic and Greek. And sad. And insistent.

Marc looks troubled. He is frowning very profoundly. I squeeze his hand to comfort *him.* He forces a smile.

We are guided into one of the low vaults. It has a curved, arched ceiling, like the inside of a large airliner, but made of damp stone. Narrow shelves of rock line the side, where people are standing and looking down.

Flaming torches illuminate the half cylinder of vaulting. They flicker and gutter, showing macabre reliefs on the inwardly curved walls, presumably dating back to the time of the earliest Mysteries in southern Italy, maybe the third or fourth century B.C. The stone friezes are delicate yet primitive, and they show men being tortured. A man having his throat slit. Another man being sodomized. A third man is being crudely stabbed in the back with a knife. The man grimaces and blood spurts from his wound.

I remember the strange scar on Marc's shoulder. So that is, probably, one mystery *solved*. The curved scar—a knife wound—must be his symbol of initiation into the Mysteries, like the tattoo on my inner thigh.

Reaching down I squeeze Marc's hand again. It is moist with perspiration. He is obviously worried: I have not seen him like this before. My own anxieties are tightening. What is going to happen to me?

The music rises to a singular intensity, a chorus of plain and unadorned voices, lamenting and maudlin, even discordant. But it is very distinct: I wonder if there is a choir somewhere in the neighboring vault—there are so many cellars and dungeons, and vaults, so many Dionysian temples interred by time.

"Drink," says a girl, thrusting a cup into my hands. She is not wearing a white tunic; this time it is plain and unredeemed black. But she seems to play the same role as the girls in all the other rites: the handmaidens of the Mysteries.

I look at Marc for support, or advice, but he has already grabbed his metal cup and drained the liquid to nothing. He wipes his mouth with the back of his hand and disdainfully gives it back. There is something odd again in his demeanor—this is not the gracious, smart, aristocratic Marc I know and love. It is a different man. The inner anger is more obvious.

"Marc, are you all right?"

He waves my question away with a gesture.

"Just watch, *cara mia*. I think you just have to watch. For now."

I turn and watch. A woman is being selected from the crowds. It is Françoise. There are three or four other girls that I recognize: my sisters of the Fifth, my fellow initiates. But Françoise has been chosen first.

We are all standing on the raised stone terraces at either side of the large barrel-vaulted chamber. Françoise nods and walks, slowly and dutifully, in her black dress, down some stone steps and then along the sunken, central, navelike space, to the end of the chamber—where I now see, on the terminating wall, that there is a large, primitive mural of a Greek or Roman soldier slaughtering a bull. But the soldier isn't just killing the bull; he is brutally raking a knife across its throat, so the blood spurts from the terrified animal's neck. The triumph of man over beast? Or the triumph of cruelty over kindness?

A middle-aged man is standing beneath this horrible wall painting. He is holding a silver bell, which he now rings, and he says, in English, "Do you agree to submit to the Fifth Mystery?"

Françoise replies hesitantly. "I agree."

"Then the first ritual can begin. Kneel."

She kneels.

"Pray to Mithras," he commands.

She puts her hands together uncertainly. And bows her head in the direction of the mural, of the man slaughtering the bull.

The master of the Mysteries rings the bell again. Françoise turns to face him as he instructs her.

"Now turn around and lie on your back."

The liquor from the metal cups is beginning to affect me. But it is not like the wines of Capri or Rhoguda, or the kykeon of the Fourth, it is a bludgeon of intoxication by comparison. I feel drunk, in a heavy, yet aggressive way; as if I would like to fight someone. It is not good.

I turn to Marc. I can see, even in the flame-lit shadows of the Mithraic vault, that he is experiencing similar sensations: he is grinding his teeth, like a man suppressing violence.

"You must be shared with Mithras and Dionysus," says the man with the silver bell. "Lift up your dress."

Françoise is lying on a beautifully patterned Ottoman rug. She closes her eyes and I can see the confusion and tension in her expression, but she obediently lifts up her dress, exposing her thighs and her sex, and the girls—the black-dressed handmaidens—step forward. They kneel before Françoise and begin to stimulate her with those warm crystal dildos. I can see that Françoise is responding, even as she resists. Her eyes are tightly closed. Standing on the stone terrace above her is Daniel. I cannot decipher his expression.

The music attains a somber intensity. This is the most religious of the Mysteries so far. I can hear the Latin and the Greek swirling in the smoky, incensed air.

Dionysian, Bakkheia, Skiereia, Apaturia.

I hold Marc's hand, just for support. I feel like I am about to faint. To fall from this stone terrace. This is too much.

Astydromia, Theoinia, Lênaia, Dionysian.

The drumming is intense. Some kind of lyre or stringed instrument is rousing itself to a climax. The voices join together. The air in the vaulted chamber is thick with incense and smoke from the burning torches. Now a man steps forward. He is maybe thirty. Tall. Stubbled. And his eyes are masked. *Camorrista*?

The man unzips himself. He is erect. One of the handmaidens slips a condom on his erection and he approaches Françoise, and then he kneels and enters her. He couples with her. That is the only word. *Couples*. If the Mysteries have been sexual in the past, even sublime in their eroticism—and they have—then this is utterly different. Serious, frightening, brutal, but bloodily symbolic. The woman is being shared with the god. The partner must submit. All must submit. I am quite terrified.

The masked man is finished. He extracts himself, and the handmaidens dart forward to lift Françoise to her feet. But I can see the bewilderment in her expression, she is turning her head away, her hands are clenched into fists, she is unnerved. And this is just the first ritual of katabasis?

Françoise is flushed and trembling. Daniel steps down from the stone terracing and puts a comforting arm around her, leading her away into the shadows.

"You."

The man with the silver bell is pointing at me.

I am not going to do this. Yet I *have* to do this to be with Marc. I cannot do this. I gaze Marc's way and he looks down and shakes his head, staring at his shoes, and then he gazes briefly into my eyes and says, "You can still stop. This is the last moment when you can stop."

Then he looks away again.

"I cannot stop," I reply. "I cannot lose you. I love you."

Dazed, bewildered, and determined, I obey the master of the Mysteries. I step down the stone stairs, and walk the length of the vaulted chamber. The bell rings. I am asked if I agree to submit. I say, "Yes, I agree."

"Kneel," the man says, and I kneel before the wall painting. I stare at the ancient soldier slaughtering the ancient bull. The ejaculation of ancient red blood is now faded to a sad and dusty magenta. The bell rings.

"Turn around, and lie down."

I clench my fists. Every shred of my soul is screaming: *No, no. No. Don't obey. Don't do this. Run away. This is WRONG.*

But the Mysteries have their grip on me so I turn and lie back. The bell rings.

"Lift up your dress."

I am lying down. I lift up my dress. I am wearing no panties, of course. The handmaidens are gathered at my knees, arousing me. As best they can. I look up into the smoke and the darkness seeking Marc, but he is turned away. *His face is turned away.*

A different, younger man approaches from the flame-shadowed darkness. He is about twenty. He has a small, disfiguring scar on his chin, but that is all I can see of him. He is also masked.

This young man is erect. He is going to enter me. I close my eyes and wait to be taken. That is the only word: taken, enslaved, abused. This is against my will, even as I submit.

"Cornuti!"

I open my eyes.

Marc.

It's Marc.

What?

Marc is standing on the floor of the vault and he is flourishing a knife—from where?—a small, sparkling, nasty steel knife. He grabs the scarred man by the neck—and presses the blade to the man's pulsing throat.

"*Estopa!*" The leader of the ritual, with the silver bell, is protesting in garrulous Italian. *No! You cannot stop the Mysteries. You have to share the woman now. You know the code and you know the price of disobeying.*

"Fuck you," says Marc, in plain English. Then he yells at me, "X, get up! Come here."

I jump to my feet and force my dress down to cover myself and run to his side. Marc still has the man by the throat; he has the scarred young man at his mercy and the kid looks terrified. As if he genuinely believes Marc will simply kill him in cold blood, the way he killed the pig butcher in Plati.

The leader of the rite is still protesting in Italian. But he is speaking very slowly and threateningly—and I can understand every word.

"Roscarrick. The *capos* will come after you. This is what happens in the Fifth Mystery. Just because you have brought your own woman makes no difference. If you do this, you will be committing suicide."

"So be it," says Marc. Then he lets the man go, and the scarred youth staggers to the side, clutching his unbleeding throat.

Then Marc grabs me by the hand and says, "Run."

Thirty-one

We run. Marc pulls me out of the Mithraic chambers, out into the narrow corridors, and this time we go left, taking a different route. For a second I look behind. There is shouting behind us, figures framed by the blue, sad lights—epitomized by the dwindling, haunting, chanting music.

"This way!"

The corridor zigzags, then it narrows to a slenderness so constricting I can feel the rocks pressing on my ribs, stifling and frightening—but we squeeze through and the brick and rock corridor widens once more. And now we sprint, and the tunnel opens out into another of those enormous Greek cisterns.

Marc turns and flashes his phone-light at the rocky wall. A steel ladder is screwed into stone.

"Probably installed during the war—these were used as bomb shelters. That means the ladder goes somewhere, it *has* to lead to the surface."

"We go up that ladder?"

"Yes."

I look up at the rusting metal ladder. I am in a minidress and heels.

"Give me the shoes," Marc says.

Slipping off the shoes, I hand them to him and he hurls them into the bottom of the cistern. Then we run to the bottom of the ladder and he goes first, climbing adroitly, and I follow, grabbing at the rungs—and slowly we ascend. The shards of black rust from the metal rungs are painful on my bare feet; the metal ladder is decaying and it creaks in eerie complaint as we climb. I simply daren't look down—twenty meters, thirty meters, fifty. If the ladder gives way, we will fall and we will die, smashed to pieces on the ancient Greek paving stones.

"Here."

Marc reaches down a hand to help.

I wave him away.

"I'm okay!"

Marc turns and climbs. A few painful minutes later he reaches the top, where there is a kind of ledge. He sets down the phone with its flashlight and reaches for me in the dark. This time I accept his help, taking his hand, and he hauls me up onto the ledge. I am panting, quite exhausted.

Picking up his cell phone Marc urgently redirects the flashlight beam. Another tunnel extends into the gloom, leading from the cistern into farther tunnels—but there are prickles of light as well. We are much nearer the surface, nearer the streets of the city above. The piercing lights must be from drains or manholes.

I hear more noises, echoing below.

"Is that them?"

"Hurry, *carissima*."

Marc walks a few meters and points up. Light shines through

holes in a wooden trapdoor. Steps cut into the rock lead to the door; Marc climbs and thrusts his shoulder at it. The trapdoor does not budge. The noises below are louder. Marc tries again.

"Quick."

There are voices echoing below, angry Italian voices. Marc crouches and breathes deep. He shunts again and the trapdoor slams open. Bright light dazzles us, as he hoists himself up.

"Marc!"

His hand reaches down and, with a mighty effort, pulls me up into the light. I gaze around as Marc briskly closes the trapdoor. He shifts a crate of wine on top of it, then another, and another.

A crate of wine?

We are in the back of a shop. A *salumeria*, a delicatessen in Old Napoli. Of course. Why not? So many of these tunnels and vaults surface in the most unlikely places: under washing machines in the *bassi*, in laundries and bakeries. So we are in a store and the store is open and busy with chattering people doing their evening shop and no one has heard us emerging. We can see people at the counter; we are hidden by shelves and surrounded by hanging salamis, hams, and wheels of cheese.

"Let's just walk out," Marc says.

We are grimy and dusty; he is in a tux covered with dirt and cobwebs. I am ragged and barefoot, my minidress is torn and I am obviously bleeding—where my ankle scraped the cutting rustiness of the ladder—but we have no choice. We just have to walk out, like ordinary shoppers browsing *salsiccia*.

An old lady is buying a paper cone of chopped-up bits of ox tripe; she turns and looks at us, but she doesn't even blink— the old woman simply tuts and shrugs, like she sees this sort of thing all the time, and then she goes back to haggling over the price of her tripe.

We have made it outside. Marc barks into his phone.

"Giuseppe!"

Now we are standing in a narrow street near the Duomo, I think; I am still barefoot. As Marc makes his call, frantically directing his manservant, we run left and right until we reach a busier street corner. And then we wait, hearts pounding, wordless and anxious. One and a half minutes later, Giuseppe roars into view. We jump into the car and it races away, away from Old Napoli, out into the broader boulevards. We jerk a vicious right, then another, straight into the Chiaia, and at last we are at the rear door of The Palazzo Roscarrick.

Marc pulls me from the car. He carries me barefoot indoors, shouting at his servants.

Lock the doors. Lock all the doors. Lock and bar the windows.

Lockdown.

We go up to his bedroom and I run into the bathroom to wash the blood from my bleeding ankles and the black rust from my feet. I feel like crying, but I don't. I brace myself, taking deep breaths. I rinse the dirt from my hands and face. Then I look in the closet for my clothes, and change into jeans, a cotton shirt, and sneakers. When I step back into the bedroom, Marc is buttoning the cuff of a blue shirt and speaking into his cell at the same time, the phone cradled under his neck: "*Sì, sì*, Giuseppe. *Sì!*"

His words are frantic.

I sit on the bed. Half listening to his rapid-fire Neapolitan, half distracted by the bewildering sequence of the night.

Marc finishes the call. And sits on the bed next to me.

"You need to get out of here."

"Why?"

"Because the Camorra will be after me now."

"The Camorra?"

He shakes his head.

"They have been looking for an excuse to kill me. Now they will have everyone on their side so they can kill me with impunity."

"Why?"

"Because I did the *worst* possible thing, X, the one thing you must never do. I broke the code of the Mysteries. I broke my vows as an initiate and interfered with the sacred ritual, the Fifth ritual. I stopped them completing the initiation."

"I don't understand."

He runs his fingers through his hair. And sighs. And rubs his face. Tired yet wired. And gazing at me.

"X, once you begin a ritual of the Mystery, a level of the initiation, then you have to complete it, otherwise you could be . . . a mere voyeur, someone seeking a cheap thrill, or worse, someone using the Mysteries to spy on others—you know there are many famous people who attend—commitment and secrecy are essential."

I nod. "Yes, I've seen them: politicians, billionaires. I saw them in Venice . . ."

The words dry in my mouth, and the logic takes over.

Politicians . . . Billionaires.

Enzo Paselli.

Of course. *Of course!* It is all revealing itself to me, all making sense. It is like the trapdoor has been opened to the tunnels below: and thus the secret labyrinth is exposed.

I have solved the Mystery of the Mysteries.

"Marc," I say, "the mafias run the Mysteries, don't they?"

"Yes," he answers. "I think so."

"The 'Ndrangheta. And the Camorra. They organize them and pay for the Mysteries. Yes?"

"Very probably."

He looks a little defeated. But I am not. The logic of it all is dazzling. I stand up and I pace Marc's silent and elegant bedroom. Working it through, talking aloud.

"I get it, Marc. *The Mysteries never died out—they became the mafias.*"

"Sorry?" For once Marc seems uncertain. He says again: "Sorry? What?"

"Don't you see, this is where the Mafia and the Camorra and the 'Ndrangheta *come from!*" I go across to him and hold his handsome face in my hands and kiss him on the mouth, then I turn back and pace the room—left and right, left and right, walking, thinking, unraveling and talking.

"Think about it, all that Spanish stuff is nonsense. The secret *criminal societies* of southern Italy descend from the secret *religious cults* of southern Italy. It has to be! They have the same codes of silence, the same oaths and vows of loyalty, the same emphasis— for the men—on blood and honor and violence. The same code of honor for men who want to stray once they are inducted."

"But . . . I don't see why . . . I don't get it."

"It's obvious. We know the Mysteries survived, the same way Ancient Greek survived in Calabria, the same way the recipe of the kykeon was handed down in Greece for twenty centuries, but this is *how* they survived!"

I stare at the darkness of the window. Still talking. "The historical evolution is obvious. The cults of the Mystery Religions, in their homeland of southern Italy, were driven into the shadows by the Christian faith in the fourth century A.D. *But they weren't entirely eradicated.*" My eyes are wide. "They endured, became even more occult, even more secret, a glorious and heathen freemasonry of wild, violent, and compelling sexual ritual, laced with hypnotic drugs." I am staring at the Andreas Gursky photos, I am bursting with mental energy. "And over time, these secretive sects, meeting in their secret places, became criminal and rebellious and organized. It would be a natural progression; they were already antagonistic to the Church, and the authorities, they needed money to finance the rituals, so they turned to crime, to robbery, extortion, kidnapping."

"It's a splendid theory, X," Marc says, shaking his head. "You're probably right." He stands and walks closer to me. "But it doesn't matter this minute. What matters this evening is what the Camorra and the 'Ndrangheta do *now*."

"I know what they do now!" I am almost shouting. "They get the rich and famous hooked on their sexy parties, they invite them to join, they initiate the powerful and the privileged—I've seen them, Marc, the ex-presidents, the great industrialists, the celebrities. And thus the Camorra and the 'Ndrangheta gain influence and leverage over the elite; that is why the mafias are *ineradicable*, they are protected at the very top by the people addicted to the Mystery rites."

"But we are *not* protected, X." Marc is standing close, and he is holding me by the shoulders, very, very hard. So hard it hurts. "Do you understand what I am saying? *They are going to kill me.* I have broken the code. They needed an excuse. Now they have it, and there is nothing I can do."

I gaze at him. Abruptly my intellectual euphoria dispels, it disappears to nothing—and I am left here in this bedroom with the man I love, who is telling me he is going to die.

"But we can run away?"

"Where?" He sighs, and sneers at the idea. "The Camorra will chase me down. You must have heard of Roberto Saviano?"

"The journalist who wrote *Gomorrah*?"

"Which was all about the Camorra. *And he is still in hiding now*, ten years later; the Camorra are chasing him across Europe. I don't want to be like that, X, moving from safe house to safe house, little apartments in Milan, in Hamburg, in Madrid—running away all my life. Running from everything I love." He looks at me, fiercely, and says, "I'd rather die. They will kill me. That is the end of it."

The room is silent. Marc walks a few paces, then stands there, in the middle of the bedroom, doing up his last cuff button.

I protest. "Marc. Marc. We have to run, or do something, we must!"

"There is nothing to do."

"You're just gonna let them kill us?"

"Not you. Me."

"Marc!"

He sighs. Profoundly.

"I had to stop the ritual. I couldn't let them do that to you. You didn't want that—you didn't want that, in the vault, did you? What was about to happen?"

"But I was prepared to do it. I agreed. And I don't want you to die for me!"

He shakes his handsome head again, and gives me that sad, sad, blue-eyed smile. He tucks his shirt into his jeans, leans, and does up his shoelaces. There is something awful and deliberate in the casual way he is doing all this. A man distractedly preparing for his own execution.

Then he comes close to me and takes me in his arms and he kisses me deeply on the lips and says, for the first time, "X, the truth is, I also couldn't bear to share you. I couldn't watch that happening, watch you with another man. I have gone too deep. Too deep with *you*." He kisses me again. "*I love you*, X. I love you more than I have ever loved any woman in my time on this earth. So if you die, my life is worthless. But if I die and you *survive*, I can die in some peace—knowing that you live. Which is why you have to go."

"No!"

"Go. You will never see me again."

"Marc!"

I am screaming. But someone is holding me. It is Giuseppe and another manservant, and someone else. Three men. They are lifting me. And I am screaming out, screaming at the man I love, as they pull me—as they carry me, fighting, struggling.

"X, they will help you get away. So you will be safe." He sighs, and goes on. "X. *Per favore, ricordate di mi.*"

And his eyes are wet even as his expression is deathly calm. This is the last time I will ever see him. I know it. This is it. The men are carrying me out of the room.

"No, no no no—Marc!"

But the bedroom door is closed, and he is gone. And all I can hear are his final words. *Remember me.*

Thirty-two

If it is possible to be very gently ejected from a building, then that is what is done to me. Giuseppe and friends—with infinite care and tenderness—carry me to the front door of the palazzo and place me in the street, red-eyed, distraught, angry, and inconsolable.

They offer to drive me, but I shake my head. And I stand there. Mute. Defiant. Simply refusing to move. Weeping.

The door shuts in my face but I go right up to it and knock with the big ancient door knocker—no one answers, so I knock once more; again, no one responds. The fourth or fifth time I lift and drop the great brass handle, polished by centuries of visitors, rich and poor, noble and ignoble, Giuseppe finally and reluctantly opens the door. He sighs, and looks at me with real compassion, but he shakes his head.

"I am sorry, X. I am *very* sorry. But you can never see the Signor again. It is his orders."

"But, Giuseppe, no, Giuseppe . . . please . . . *please.*" The tears are coming fast again. There are evening shoppers, passersby in the Chiaia, and they are staring, inquisitively, at the blond American woman crying and yelling at the door of The Palazzo Roscarrick. Let them stare. What does it matter now?

Nothing matters now.

"Giuseppe, you have to do something! Tell Marc to change his mind; I want to be with him. Whatever . . . whatever happens. I want to be with him."

"*Per favore.* This is from Signor Roscarrick, so you can go away and be safe." Giuseppe is trying to give me a big wad of money. I take the fold of notes and gaze at it in contempt, and then I literally throw it back at him: through the door, so there are fluttering fifty-euro notes everywhere, like orange confetti. Giuseppe does not flinch at my anger; he stoops and picks up one fifty-euro note. He presses it into my hand, folding my shaking fingers around the bill.

"At least take a taxi home, *signorina*," he says.

Then he shuts the door and I know, somehow, it will not open again. Not ever. And certainly not to me. Despite this, I bang on it, fruitlessly, several times.

After thirty minutes, the tears stop and the shock ebbs away. Deeper and darker feelings take over. So I hail a passing taxi and climb in. I ask for Santa Lucia, and look at the new, dark, empty space inside me, examine it, scrutinize it. Like a surgeon looking at a scan of a frightful tumor, like a jeweler looking at a terrible flaw in a gemstone.

This new, searing heartbroken sadness, I know, is going to be with me for a long time. It may be here for *keeps;* it is moving into the apartment, it will be sharing my home, my life, my conscious hours, it will be there when I wake up, it will be there when I go to sleep: because this is the terrible and abiding sadness of losing someone you love, someone who was so much more than any friend could ever be.

And then, one day, when I wake up, the sadness will actually *speak*, and it will say: *Today is the day.* And then I will turn on the TV or buy the *Corriere della Sera* and I will learn the inevitable news: Marc Roscarrick, the *molto bello e scapolo* Lord Roscarrick, is dead.

Killed by an assassin. Shot on the Via Toledo by some seventeen-year-old junkie from Secondigliano on a sky blue Vespa; shot for a bounty of one hundred bucks. And then the sadness will develop, then it will seep into my bones, it will grow into my soul.

"*Grazie.*"

I pay the cabbie, but as I do he looks at my tear-blotched face and, in that gentle, kind, very Italian way he says, "*Signorina? S'è persa? Sta bene? Posso aiutarla?*"

He wants to help. He is concerned. I just shove the entire fifty-euro note in his hand and turn and run into the apartment. Climbing the stairs, I slam the door shut and start crying again. Maybe I will cry myself to death; literally dehydrate.

My tears and sobs are obviously loud, because pretty soon I hear a quiet knock on my door and Jessica's tentative voice.

"X? What's up?"

"Nothing."

"X? You're crying—what's wrong? You sound terrible. Open the door."

I am sitting—practically slumping—on the floor of my stupid apartment in stupid Santa Lucia in stupid Naples and I am numb with grief. I don't know what to do or say or think. I look at my balcony and I wonder, for a moment, how easy it might be to just walk across the room and climb on that balcony railing and then gaze at Capri in the moonlight and then—it would be so easy—I might just accidentally slip and fall and then the sadness would be banished.

I come to alertness with a startling sense of shock. This is dangerous. I have to calm down; I need to talk to someone. Jess is outside.

Standing and wiping the tears from my face, I open the door and Jess is there, wearing white jeans with a blue top and a big, sad, patient and forgiving smile—but when she sees my face she says, "Oh bloody hell, X. Bloody, bloody hell."

"Jess . . ."

I stand back wordlessly and Jess comes into the room. She turns to me and we hug for half a minute and then she makes tea—a British cup of tea—in my stupid little kitchen where Marc kissed me and stripped me that night, that first glorious night.

No, I have to stop these thoughts. They are soldiers trying to breach the castle, aiming to force their way in. If I let one through, I will be overrun and conquered. Then I am lost.

Jess hands me a mug of tea, and sits on the floor beside me. The mug shows a picture of the Amalfi coast. It reminds me of my mom: where she went on her holiday all those decades ago. My mom. Maybe I could call her. I want my mommy. My heartbreak is so engulfing, *I want my mother.*

"Come on," Jess says, sipping from her own hot tea and staring me deep in the eyes. "Time to fess up, X. Tell me everything."

I take a big gulp of the tea even though it is scalding. I force the tears back down my throat, and then I put the mug on the floor and look at Jess—and I tell her everything, or at least, everything she needs to know. I tell her Marc broke the code of the Mysteries. I tell her the Camorra and the 'Ndrangheta *run* the

Mysteries. I tell her that the Camorra are now coming after him. And then, gulping some more of the tea and trying very hard not to cry again, enough crying, *enough* crying, I tell her that he has banished me, exiled me, forsworn me, because he believes he is a marked man, destined for assassination, listed to die one day soon. And therefore he wants me away, safe, and out of the picture, forever.

I stop talking.

Jessica shakes her pretty head and I can see anguish in her eyes, too.

"Oh God, poor you," she says, without a hint of her usual sarcasm. "Poor Marc."

She goes quiet and stares at the night sky outside the window. The faint crackle of fireworks can be heard, like gunshots in the distance; probably some Camorra gang in the Spanish Quarters celebrating the release from jail of one of their own.

"You know," she says, wistfully and quietly, "I heard a story the other day about the Spanish Quarters. How they got their name."

I say nothing.

She goes on. "You remember that street in the middle of the Quartieri, Vico Lungo del Gelso? *Gelso* meaning mulberries . . ."

I say nothing.

She goes on: "It got its name from the Spanish soldiers, who stained their uniforms by lying with local girls on the grass, making love." She looks at me. "The grass was strewn with mulberries . . . That's what stained their clothes. That's where the name comes from."

Jessica looks down at her tea. I can see tears on her face, too.

"This means Giuseppe and I are finished, too, of course." She lifts and sips the tea and shakes her head and says, "Brruh.

Enough, enough, enough." Then she leans and pats me on the knee. "We have to be strong."

"Strong?"

A helpless shrug.

"Well, stronger. It's horrible, X, I know, it's totally bloody horrible, but if it is as bad as Marc says, if he really is . . . If they really are . . . Well, I mean . . . You know how relentless the Camorra can be."

I nod. Desolately.

"If he really has broken some terrible law," she goes on, "then they will . . . they really will . . ."

"Shoot him."

"You are better off out of it. You really are. He is doing the right thing, a good thing, the noble thing. Because you are also in danger, X, serious danger." She sighs heavily. "However depressing it is, however heartbreaking, Marc is doing you a favor: he is trying to save you from, well . . . from God knows what."

"But, Jess," I say, looking deep into her soft brown eyes. "Jessica . . . *I love him.*"

The next weeks are weeks of total bleakness. Every morning I wake and there it is: the sadness. There is sadness in my cappuccino, sadness in my macchiato, sadness in my espresso; there is the taste of sadness in every cake I eat, the sfogliàta, the bigne, the baba; there is sadness in the cheap shellfish I have for supper, the fasolari, the maruzielle, the telline.

And the taste of this sadness is the taste of pure bitterness. It ruins everything. It sours the world. It is a black sun shining down on all Campania.

Sometimes I try to see Marc, despite it all. I walk in my lonely way down the Chiaia and up to the great big door of The Palazzo

Roscarrick, the door I first knocked on when I came here months ago, when he smiled and joked, and I saw the staircase for the cavaliers; but this time when I knock either no one answers or a servant I haven't seen before briefly opens the door, stares at me, then shuts the door again without a word.

Other times I call his cell phone. Maybe thirty times in two hours. Then the cell phone number dies for good and a brisk, automated female voice tells me in Italian, *The number you are calling is no longer available.* I write e-mails that go unanswered. Eventually these e-mails are pinged back, telling me that this e-mail address is now defunct.

So then I write letters, long letters in freehand, on tear-stained paper, and these letters, just like the e-mails, elicit no reply, and eventually they are returned unopened. He won't even open a letter? Not even a *letter*?

Even worse than this rejection is the tension I experience every morning when I walk to the newsstand on Via Partenope and I say "*Buongiorno*" to the newspaper guy and he looks at me and says "*Buongiorno*" and he hands me my daily copy of *Il Mattino.*

I don't want to read this paper. I hate this paper, but it is the best paper for reporting on Neapolitan crime: it is brave and remorseless in the way it covers the endless victims of petty turf wars in Scampia, drug slayings in the Forcella, and if I want to know if anything has *happened* to Marc, then this is where I will first see it recorded. And confirmed. And photographed.

So every day I walk back to the apartment, flicking feverishly through the inky pages, staring at pictures of men sprawled outside dingy cafes in Miano, with blood running from their bodies like they are leaking black oil; or sitting in cars in Marigliano with uncannily neat black gunshot wounds in their foreheads; or simply discovered as stiff and lifeless bodies in the endless piles of Neapolitan garbage in the Centro Storico. And as I scan these images I think, *Is that him, is that Marc, is that how it ended, is it all over?*

And each time my heart breaks open just a little more, and each time I realize, no, that cannot be Marc—but each time I also know that one day soon, I will make this penitential morning walk to Via Partenope and I will say *"Buongiorno"* to the news guy and I will hand over my coins and I will open the terrible pages of *Il Mattino* and then I will see Marc.

Dead.

Finally, one soft evening at the beginning of September when I am on the verge of dissolution, of turning into somebody I don't want to be, when it is all too much, I walk the sunny and shady pavements of the Chiaia to The Palazzo Roscarrick. I am going to have one last attempt, and then—then what? Then what can I do? I don't know.

I turn the last corner, and as I do my heart breaks just a little bit more. The Palazzo Roscarrick is different: the door is *padlocked*. The windows have been closed and firmly shuttered. There is no sign of life. There is a big FOR SALE sign plastered on the wall.

I don't know what this means, precisely. Perhaps Marc is already dead, and it has been kept quiet. This happens quite a lot. Alternatively, it is possible he has fled somewhere, the South Tyrol, London, New York, Brazil, and he is selling the house, so he can hide away. But the sight of this lovely house boarded up and emphatically FOR SALE makes me want to weep, all over again, but the emotion in me is more terminal this time. I am despairing and desolate, but I am also resigned.

I have accepted that he is gone from my life forever. Dead or departed. Does it matter? Now I suppose I have to save myself. Jessica was probably right: I am in danger, too. I have seen too much.

I trudge back to my apartment and pick up my phone to call my mom in San Jose. She has been ringing me and e-mailing me for weeks, wondering if I am okay. Her maternal telepathy has obviously sensed that something is seriously awry, but she cannot quite ascertain what it is—for the good reason that I don't want to tell her. I *can't* tell her. Without her knowing about the Mysteries she would be utterly nonplussed, and there is no way I can reveal any of that, not because I am ashamed or embarrassed—quite the opposite—but because it is too complex, it is too much—and because I can't bear to think about any of it, anyway.

The phone rings in distant California. It picks up.

"Hello?"

"Hi, Mom."

"Sweetheart!" There is a forced cheeriness in her voice. "Alexandra, darling, how lovely! How are you? The boys have been here asking all about you, and your father was just saying, just this morning, the—"

I stop her in midsentence.

"Mom, I'm coming home."

She pauses. Politely, and lovingly. She knows there is more to this than I am saying, but she is too kind to pry if I don't want to tell.

"Okay, sweetheart, Okay. Have you . . . finished your thesis?"

"Yes, I've finished it. I want to come home now."

I am forcing back the sobs.

"Okay, darling. Just let me know the flight number. We'll pick you up at the airport! Your father will be so happy; we've missed you so, so much."

She chatters on for a while, then I say I have to book my flight and so I have to go, which I do. The phone call finished, I go online and book my ticket. For tomorrow afternoon. In less than twenty-four hours I am flying home and not coming back.

The next morning, I pack up all my stuff. This doesn't take long because I am leaving behind all the lovely clothes *he* bought me. When Jessica comes to my apartment to help me pack, I offer the clothes to her, but she shakes her head and I totally understand why, and then I feel guilty and somehow squalid and I say *sorry*.

"Don't be an idiot, X," she says. "Let me come with you to the airport, let me help. Gonna miss you."

Her face is etched with sadness. Everything is inscribed with sadness. We get in the taxi and we duck and curve through the fuming Naples traffic. We pull up at the terminal and I check in for my flight. Jess hugs me so tight at the check-in desk, it is like she thinks she will never see me again, and then we wave good-bye. I walk through passport control and show my boarding card. *This is it*, I think. Good-bye, Naples. Not *arrivederci*, Naples. Good-bye. Farewell. *Adieu*. It is a cheap, cheap song that evokes the most powerful emotion.

My flight leaves in two hours. I sit on an uncomfortable steel bench, sipping my macchiato from a plastic cup, and stare into the nothingness of the future, reading a desultory advertisement for Taurasi wine on a wall. I think about all the wines I have drunk. All the food I have eaten. I think bitterly about this sometimes violent, sometimes ugly place, with its beauty and wine and its history and its glory, its *dolce vita*. Amazing food and terrible cruelty.

And then I think about the little snails they sell. The baba-lucci. I never ate *them*. It was a little too much.

The babalucci. *The babalucci!*

I stand up. Electrified.

What am I doing? Why am I sitting here? Why am I staring at the wall?

There is something I can do.

I run back through passport control, almost screaming with impatience, and the security guards shrug and sigh, letting me back into the bustle of the airport proper; then I dash to the check-in desk and demand that they unload my bags. I am not going to America, I am *not* flying to California.

I am staying. Because if Marc is still alive, somewhere out there, maybe there *is* some way I can save him.

My fingers are trembling as I dial my cell phone. Gabbling the words, I ask for the number of a restaurant in Plati, Calabria.

The languid woman at the end of the line gives me the number.

"Due, due, sei, cinque . . ."

I scribble this down on my boarding pass, then hang up and call the number. It is lunchtime. He will be there, he *must* be there.

A wary voice answers. A young man's voice.

"Si?"

I stammer my words, as fast as I can. I tell him my name is X. Alexandra Beckmann. The girlfriend of Marc Roscarrick.

Then I ask him if I can speak to Enzo Paselli.

Thirty-three

The other end of the line goes much quieter. I can just about hear the noises of a restaurant: some waiters talking, the clatter of plates, someone gathering cutlery.

Then a quavery, old man's voice speaks to me from three hundred miles away.

"Hello, Alexandra."

It is Enzo Paselli. I stutter a question, but he does not wait for me to get halfway there. He silences me with a terse little laugh, and then he says, "I know why you are calling me."

"You *do*?"

"Yes."

I pause, for several seconds. Because now I have to ask the terrible question.

"Enzo, please tell me. Is Marc Roscarrick alive?"

Enzo does not answer. He just breathes. So I stare helplessly through the plate-glass window of the airport at the gaggles of cabdrivers. Two of them are arguing, arms folded, heads tilted back, chins jerked upward and away—like Mussolini in a newsreel.

Finally Enzo answers, "Yes, I believe he is alive."

The relief floods me like adrenaline.

"How do you *know*?"

He gives no answer. I persist.

"Enzo, how do you know he is alive?"

"Miss Beckmann, *please*. It is, as I have told you, my job to know *everything*." His voice dwindles, I hear him speaking Calabrian to someone in the background. Ordering someone killed, or ordering more *ricotta calabrese*. Then he says, "What do you want me to do, Alexandra? You want me to save your boyfriend?"

"Yes! Yes I do. Please, Signor Paselli. I know you *run* the Mysteries. I worked it out—you, the Camorra, the 'Ndrangheta, you control everything: the initiations, the kykeon, the rituals. That's why you were at Rhoguda; it wasn't just the truce with Marc."

I expect this speech to unsettle Enzo Paselli, to give me some purchase, but his reply is as lucid and calm as ever.

"But you are aware, Alexandra, what Roscarrick did in the Fifth—he has broken the code. The Camorra are going to kill him soon; he knows this, we know this. Because this is the way of all things—it is written, and it is inevitable. I am sorry."

"I will do the Fifth again! Let me do it! They can do whatever they want to me, Enzo, they can—" I am trying to control my words, my emotions are riotous. "I will do whatever the Camorra want. You can do this, you are the *capo di tutti capi* of the 'Ndrangheta—the Camorra are scared of you, as they are scared of no one else."

That's it. That is my last bid. My terminal hope. My final

gambit. Another silence. The taxi drivers are still arguing out-side in the endless early September sun, the summer that never ends. Enzo Paselli clears his throat, and calmly says, "It is too late."

"Please!"

"The sin is not really yours, Alexandra. You were, I am told, prepared to submit to the Fifth Mystery. Roscarrick broke the code. It is too late."

"But—"

He interrupts me.

"But what, Alexandra?"

"I will do anything! Anything anything anything. *Please* . . . help me . . . help me."

He breathes in and out. I hear him speak in Italian to some minion, his tone is commanding. Then he sighs and coughs and speaks to me.

"You would really do *anything*?"

"Yes! *Yes. Anything.*"

"But . . ." He hesitates. Painfully. And then he goes on.

"Okay, Alexandra. *Va bene, va bene* . . . There is perhaps *one* thing you can do, which *might* alter things. There is one thing that might change the situation, perhaps to your advantage. But you will have to be very brave."

"What is it?"

"The Sixth Mystery. *You must do the Sixth.*"

Twenty-nine hours later I am sitting in my apartment once again. My mom has been told I have delayed my return by a few days, because of "things." She has complained and inquired, with self-evident anxiety, but I have bluntly ignored her questions. Jessica is equally perplexed—but I have fobbed her off with fibs. She knows these are fibs but she is a good enough friend to let me lie openly to her, and to ask nothing.

In return for my lies, she makes me a meal and gives me red wine. I love Jess. I love my mother.

But how much do I love *Marc*?

This is *the* question, because Enzo Paselli's words, his warning words about the Sixth, are now on some repeating loop in my head. *The Sixth is like no other Mystery. The Sixth is not erotic, it is dangerous. The Sixth can kill you. Very few initiates go on to do the Sixth, once they are informed of the dangers. But only the Sixth can provide true katabasis. The true release.*

What does this all mean? Am I going to die? Am I prepared to risk death if it means I can save Marc?

Yes.

I check my watch. It is seven P.M. I stand and walk out onto my balcony, the apartment I was meant to have vacated. My landlord will be here tomorrow, to make sure I am gone, and tomorrow I *will* be gone. Enzo's people are coming for me tonight.

I stare. Twilight falls rapidly over Naples, turning everything hazy and opaque, like the *sfumato* of a Renaissance painting. Capri looks like the dream of an island on the mild and milky blue horizon. It is a suitably stirring and wistful sight.

The doorbell buzzes. I go back into my apartment and press the intercom bell, then three good-looking and anxious young men are in my room. They say almost nothing. The youngest of them gazes at me with a tiny trace of pity—or something worse—and he graciously leads me downstairs. I am dressed in simple jeans and T-shirt and a black denim jacket; I am carrying an overnight bag. It feels totally ridiculous in my hand. Toiletries. Toothbrush. Lipstick. What am I thinking? I am not going for a weekend in some lakeside hotel.

I am going to do the Sixth and Final Mystery of Dionysus and Eleusis. I am proceeding unto the *real* katabasis. Whatever happens in the next twenty-four hours will change me forever; it may kill me. But it might save Marc.

Parked outside my block, on Via Santa Lucia, is a big dark blue van. I am assisted into the back of the van, which is furnished with blankets and pillows. One of the young men invites me to take a pill.

"What is it?"

He knows very little English. He answers, awkwardly.

"For sleep. It make sleep."

I take the pill and the proffered bottle of mineral water. I swallow the tablet and liquid together and recap the bottle.

"Now," the young man says, lifting a black hood, which looks like a hangman's hood.

They are going to put this hood on me, of course. I yield to the blackness as the hood is slipped over my head. I am not uncomfortable; I can still breathe easily. Indeed, the sheathing and enclosing blackness is somehow comforting.

The van pulls away; I can sense it moving. Here in the darkness inside my hood, I can also hear lots of traffic, evening Naples traffic, rush-hour horns and big trucks braking, taxis and radios and rasping scooters, and then I hear faster traffic—seething and roaring. I guess we are on a freeway? And then the noises fade slowly away as the pill kicks in and I lean to the side on a big, soft pillow; I sleep and dream of Marc trapped under ice, knocking at the ice, gesturing desperately to me.

I am on a frozen lake and Marc is in the deadly water, trapped, and I am hysterically trying to save him. I ask a passing man, a Spanish man, to help me, but the Spanish man is bleeding from the mouth. He grimaces and shrugs, pointing at his mouth, and he walks away. I can do nothing. Therefore Marc is dying under the ice—dropping, twirling into the sapphire deepness—falling away into starlit freezing space.

I wake up. How many hours have we been driving? Three? Five? Six? Ten? We could be anywhere in Italy: from the Alps to Sicily. We could be in France or Switzerland. The hood is still over my head. I lift myself into an upright position and I say, through the cloth of the hood, "I am thirsty. I need the bathroom."

I don't know who I am talking to. I sense there are other people in the back of the van with me, but I don't know who.

A disembodied voice replies. "Ten minutes, you must wait just ten minutes."

This is not the young man of before. It is an older voice; the English is more confident.

The man is also right. Ten minutes later the van stops and I hear the rear door being opened. I am bundled out, still in my hooded darkness, and hurried across some road, and then I sense that I am in a big, echoey building. But where?

The hands guide me down several flights of stairs; I stumble in my blinded state but the hands hold me firm, steering me left and right and left again. I sense old corridors. This is a stone building; it has the aroma of an ancient place—a castle? A monastery? What is this?

Then I am pushed into a room and a door slams shut, and the hood is removed. Enzo Paselli is standing in front of me, accompanied by a young woman.

He looks into my eyes and shakes his bald head, making his jowls droop and shiver. His skin is so deeply lined. He seems incomparably old; like Italy herself. Then he turns to the woman at his side, and says, in English, "Give her food and drink, then get her ready."

Enzo disappears before I can ask any questions.

Only the young woman remains; she is dressed in white. Of course. She hands me some mineral water in a bottle and I drink. Her gentle smile is compassionate and patient as she watches me quench my thirst. But maybe not *that* compassionate: when I ask her what is going to happen to me, she says nothing.

I gaze around.

Only now do I realize what a remarkable room this is: an enormous vaulted ballroom, or medieval hall, entirely decorated with frescoes on every surface. Yet there are no windows.

The frescoes look early Renaissance, or even late medieval: crowded with allegorical and religious scenes in vivid and tumbling colors, Christ and his angels. Saints and Madonnas. I am too confused to work it out. The floor is patterned with cold black-and-white mosaics. There is one item of furniture in the room. Behind me. A big wooden bed with red quilts of silk and cotton.

"*Sì*," says the girl. She evidently speaks no English. With a brisk gesture she mutely hands me some new clothes to wear—a very plain, sleeveless black cotton dress and no underwear at all—and points at the distant wall, where I notice a small door.

I have no choice. I must obey; I must complete the Sixth. So I cross the enormous vaulted room and I step into a large, clean, modern bathroom and change my clothes: removing my jeans and sneakers and showering quickly. Before I put the dress on, I stare at myself in the mirror of the bathroom: at my twenty-one-year-old face, less round and innocent than it was. How very much older I feel than that young woman who came to Italy in the spring. I maybe have a few gray hairs.

Marc Roscarrick, where are you? Are you alive?

Gathering my courage, I don the dress, brush my teeth, and

step back into the grandness of the great hall. The girl is still there, waiting in silence in the middle of this absurdly huge space. She is dwarfed by the immensity. And she has a metal cup in her hand.

"Kykeon?" I ask, walking toward her.

She half shrugs, half nods, and thrusts the cold metal cup into my hands.

I take the cup and drain it to the end. The taste is much more bitter than before, much less pleasant. But I drink it and wonder. Now what? What are they going to do to me? I know this intoxicant works very quickly. So I sit down on the bed and wait as the girl departs, crossing to the only other door. Shutting it behind her.

Two or three hours pass, or so I imagine: I have no way of really telling the time. No clock, no watch. No cell phone. Is it morning yet? How long were we driving? The thoughts in my head meld with the dreams and the drug and the sadness and the whirling images of the frescoes on the ceiling. The Holy Ghost descending. A dove and a saint. The resurrection of Christ. Penitent sinners weeping.

I, too, shed one or two tears. Then I lie back on the bed and fall asleep. I dream of a man coming into my room and having sex with me, forcing my legs apart, taking me.

But then I realize: a man really *is* fucking me. He is young and handsome. He is not naked but I am naked, and we are on the big wooden bed covered with soft, rich quilts. He is on top of me and inside me. I am being raped, and yet I am not: I agreed to all this. I agreed to the Sixth. The man spends himself. I am naked and he has finished. He buttons himself. He turns away and leaves the great room. His footsteps echo in the vastness of the vaulted hall.

And that is it. The kykeon spirals in my head.

Did that really happen?

It really happened. I might be half delirious, but it happened. In desperation I look around for the simple black dress but then the handmaiden returns, opening the door and crossing to the bed. She gives me more kykeon.

Then she puts her fingers inside me. Checking me? For what? Then two girls follow her, crossing the mosaic floor, and they make me lie down while they put lubricant inside me. Then another pointlessly handsome young man comes in and fucks me silently. And I just lie there, staring at the ceiling and weeping. I weep for it all. For the sex. For the girl I was. But mostly I weep for Marc.

I don't know what is happening or why. I have lost any sense of myself. The hours turn into a day, or two days, or three. I am consistently drugged—again and again: to the point of stupor. The boundaries between me and the world have gone. This is it. I am dying. I see now why people *die* in the Sixth. Part of me wants to die. I have been kidnapped, and it doesn't matter. I eat fruit and bread and then I fall asleep. I am quite exhausted.

I do not know if it is morning, but hours later I am woken by the girls and they put me in a tight blindfold and give me more kykeon and I am taken from the bed and bathed. Thereafter I am led back to the bed and I lie there, mumbling and crying, then not crying anymore. Now I sense some women touching me?

I sense soft women in the room, smell their perfume. They are licking me. Touching me. Licking me persistently. Then they give me more kykeon and the drug mixes with the sex, and I surrender. I cannot go on, they have defeated me. The caresses are endless, and tender, and pointless.

At one point I orgasm, convulsively, but it is reflexive, not emotional, I come only because my body is told to come, my mind is elsewhere, my soul has fled, my soul is not here, it is not me being fucked and massaged and kissed, it is someone else, some silly American girl. Alexandra Beckmann. I dimly remember her.

The hours. The many, many hours. I am given food that I have to eat blindfolded. Another girl massages me, rubbing calming oils on my skin. I lie there, blindfolded and naked. A man comes in and I am forced to suck him. So I suck. Robotically. My sight has gone. I suck him some more. Then the girls assist me across the hall into the bathroom, where they bathe me, sluicing me with warm water and caressing me with sweet foam.

I can smell the lovely soap, it reminds me of the soap Marc gave me, from Florence, and I cry again. I cry hard, and the girls lead me in my blindfold back to the bed. They wrap me in a soft bathrobe and then—for the first time in what feels like days—they remove the blindfold.

After so long I can see, once again.

Enzo Paselli is standing there. But after all this time, in the darkness of the blindfold, the soft light of the great room is too dazzling. As my eyes adjust, Enzo is little more than a black silhouette, yet I can recognize the shape. Small and old and powerful, and malign.

He gazes my way.

"Marc Roscarrick is dead." He shakes his head, and sighs. "You must have known that. You must have known that this was a real possibility. I am sorry."

I stare at him. I have no anger left, I am completed, I am drained. I shake my head. Maybe I did know. Maybe somehow in the last seventy-two hours—or however long it was—I learned that it was all a game, a theater of deceit, and that Marc was already gone.

Enzo squints at me.

"You knew he might be dead, you knew you were taking a terrible risk for the merest chance—yet the tiny chance that you could save him, for that slender chance, you were prepared to risk your own life?"

I nod. Dumb. And mute. *Defeated.* Marc is dead. Of course he is dead. It was all a lie, but I wanted the lie. And now I am feeling something like relief. I don't mind if I die now. It is over. I gaze around. There are other people in this room. Older men and older women. Like witnesses. Like members of a jury, dressed like a jury. They are condemning me. Let them do it. Everything is smoke.

"You have almost completed the Sixth. This is close to katabasis." He clicks his fingers and a handmaiden approaches. "There is one more ritual. And then you will be released. And you will be a true initiate. Very few complete the Sixth and survive. This is why Marc never told you of the Sixth; he wanted to protect you. To save you from this hollowness. This terror."

I can't even cry anymore. I watch as the people file out of the room, followed by Paselli and the handmaiden. I am on my own. So very alone. What have they done to me? They have, finally, made me careless of death. What is death? What was it? Just a passing change. I know that I loved Marc, I loved him truly. I was prepared to risk my life for him, my beloved, and they cannot take that away, they cannot deprive me of this one last shining fact, which is all that is left of Alexandra Beckmann: *I loved and I was loved.*

Everything passes, everything must die, just as everything

must be born, but these are just the symptoms of an illusion: the passing of time. The moment itself is timeless. If for one moment you loved, you truly loved, and you were truly loved, then you are in love forever. And death is defeated.

I remember the Sansevero Chapel. And the rising Christ. I remember Marc and me in Venice, happy in the Ca' D'Oro, gazing at the Mantegna painting. *Nothing but God endures, the rest is smoke.*

And now I remember that Pindar quote, and I understand it. I *wholly* understand it.

Blessed is he who, having seen these rites, undertakes the way beneath the Earth. He knows the end of life, as well as its divinely granted beginning.

I have undertaken the way beneath the Earth, and now I know the end of life. And I am not scared. Not anymore.

Sometime later, the door opens, and the girl in the white dress crosses the patterned floor. She is carrying some clothes. She hands them wordlessly to me: they are my own jeans, T-shirt, and sneakers. My old clothes, now washed. I put the clothes on. The girl waits, and nods, then shows me the blindfold once again.

The blindfold.

Obedient and submissive, I sit on the end of the bed, allowing the girl to tie the blindfold around my head. It now feels like the blindfold that precedes an execution. Perhaps they are just going to shoot me. So be it.

I allow myself to be pulled out of the great echoing room and guided along more corridors. I have stopped crying, the last tears have been shed. Marc is dead and little else remains. Nothing but God endures; the rest is smoke.

We climb some steps. I am pushed into another room. The door closes behind me, the girl is gone. Yet I sense I am not alone.

Someone else is in this room.

I hear a voice, a deep, soft, firm, male voice.

"Chi e? Chi e qui dentro? Who is it?"

A deep, soft, firm male voice.

I rip away my blindfold.

Marc Roscarrick is sitting in a metal chair, handcuffed to the steel armrests. There is a trace of dried blood on his face; he is faintly bruised around the eyes. He is firmly blindfolded. He is shouting now, he is sitting over there. And he is alive.

I run to the chair. I reach around to release his blindfold, fumbling with the tight silken knots. He breathes in sharply, scenting me; suddenly his face is amazed, unbelieving.

"X? Is that you? *X?* It can't be? X? X? X?"

I release the blindfold and he stares at me.

"But, X—*they said you were dead.*"

He is very close to tears, I can see it in the trembling of his mouth.

Thirty-four

We barely have time to talk before Enzo Paselli walks in. He is with two younger men.

Enzo stares at me.

"Marc Roscarrick came to us, he wanted to ensure you were protected from the Camorra and the 'Ndrangheta. We said we would not harm you if *he* agreed to do the Sixth. We told him the Sixth could be fatal. As we all know. Because in the Sixth you accept death in exchange for love."

I gaze at Marc; he is shaking his head, in shock perhaps. I look back at Paselli.

"I don't . . ."

"Understand? These are the Mysteries." Paselli shrugs. "But you should know this. As I have ascended to the top of the 'Ndrangheta, I have begun to detest the way the mafias have corrupted the Mysteries, used them for their own greed, to enrich themselves, to enslave our politics, in Italy and elsewhere.

The Mysteries are a great and noble gift from the ancients. And the Mysteries are being abused."

He crosses the room and he leans over Marc and turns a key in the handcuffs. Unshackling him. Marc, in jeans and grimy white shirt, rubs his wrists. They are red raw.

Paselli continues speaking.

"I am now the *Celenza* of the Sixth: that gives *me* great power. The *capos* walk in fear of me, of what I know, because I know everything. We film everything. And, therefore, sometimes I try to use the enormous power of the Sixth for good, as it was meant to be used. *But the Sixth is a daunting thing. It can easily go wrong.* Marc's wife insisted on completing the Sixth, despite my warnings. She went through what you both went through." He sighs. "But I was right. She was too fragile, it unbalanced her, it made her fearless of death—or careless of life. She committed suicide on that hill, near Capua; she was not murdered."

Paselli pockets the key. He walks to the door, then turns and looks at me. And then at Marc.

"Ever since that day, I have observed you from afar, Roscarrick, the way you assisted victims of the Camorra. I saw good there, true bravery. But I also saw danger, in this theater of masks." Paselli gestures to his young male assistant, who turns and leaves. Paselli himself walks closer to the door. "And now you are saved. Both of you. The Camorra will not touch you; I will let it be known you are both initiates of the Sixth. They will respect that; even better, they will fear you—so you have power. I hope you use it well."

He stands in the frame of the door.

"You will be kept here for just a few more hours, then you will be free to leave." He stares directly at me. "Perhaps one day we will meet again, Alexandra of the Sixth."

He is gone. The door is shut. We are alone. Marc pulls me to him but we don't kiss—we hug, tight, then tighter. I brush the dark hair from his bruised face.

"Marc, what did they do to you?"

"Nothing," he says. "What does it matter? What did they do to you? The same as me?"

I nod. And I kiss his forehead. And he manages to smile. For the first time since I entered the room, I see his glittering, happy, sad, lovely smile. And he speaks. "Oh God, X, I really thought you were dead; I thought it was all a trick. I didn't care what they did to me."

He stands. He walks into the bathroom. I go with him, and he stoops over the sink. I dip a towel in warm water and wash the dried blood from his face. The wounds are not deep; the bruising is not so bad. He is unharmed, brutalized but unharmed. He is still handsome, still Marc Roscarrick; most of all he is still *alive*.

For a few more minutes we wait, patiently, sitting on the bed, side by side. Then he says, "Let's see if we can get out. I don't care where we are, Palermo, London, Buenos Aires, I want to get out now. I want to breathe fresh air—come on."

Decisive, now, he takes my hand and we go to the door. It is unlocked. A dark stone corridor stretches into the distance. We walk along it, we find some stairs, then we find more stairs, and a wider corridor, barely lit by dim electric bulbs.

"It's empty," says Marc. "They've all gone."

The building is indeed empty; it is also very old. I have worked out that we must be deep in basements, deep in ancient cellars. But we keep climbing stairs, until at last I see a small stone window, and through it maybe the distant ripples of moonlit waves—are we somewhere on the coast? And, with growing expectation, we climb two more flights of steps. At last we emerge onto a kind of terrace, washed by night and darkness, and we run to the edge and lean over an elegant stone balustrade.

"Naples," says Marc, and he is quietly laughing. "We're in *Naples*."

He is right. I stare at the wide horizon in astonishment. It is the most beautiful view on earth: the noble sweep of the Bay of Naples, from the heights of Vomero to the Centro Storico, to the cliffs of Sorrento and Amalfi, and the dim and holy silhouette of Capri, glimmering under the stars.

"I know this place," I say. "This is the Villa Donn'Anna. In Posillipo. I came here once, to the beach."

Marc takes my hand in his. And we stare, still amazed, at the view. I look up at the trillionaire glitter of the stars, at Orion and the Pleiades; I look at the Constellation of Marc and Alex on Capri. The Constellation of Us.

Quietly, I say, "What will we do now?"

He does not answer. Instead he turns and, looking in my eyes, lifts my face to his and kisses me deeply, sexually, fiercely. And I run my white fingers through his dark and curling hair, because now I know the truth: nothing but Love endures; the rest is smoke.